Hope you enjoy it!

Yours aye,

Lexie Conyngham.

Service of the Heir

Lexie Conyngham

The Third in the Murray of Letho Series

DEDICATION

To M and E with love: it takes a special kind of stamina to have lived with Murray and me for that long!

Dramatis Personae

Charles Murray of Letho, a significant character
Charles Murray, younger of Letho, his elder and anxious son

Edinburgh Society:
Mr. and Lady Sarah Dundas and sons, he a lawyer who really doesn't need to practise
Mr. and Mrs. Thomson and family, he a lawyer of upper income
Mr. and Mrs. Armstrong and family, he a lawyer of middle income, she a sister to Mrs. Thomson
Mr. and Mrs. Balneavis and vast family, he a lawyer of very little income at all
John Douglas, a lawyer with no apparent dependents
Alester Blair, gentleman
Ebenezer Hammond, the greatest advocate in Edinburgh
Miss Christian Gordon of Balkiskan, a remarkable relic

Household:
Mrs. Chambers, a perfect housekeeper
Mrs. Mutch, a charming cook
Mr. Robbins, surprisingly a senior manservant
Mary and Jennet, upper maids but otherwise unalike
William and Daniel, junior menservants of limited promise
Iffy and Effy, kitchenmaids of no promise
Dunnet, the coachman
Jamie, the stableboy

Other inhabitants of Edinburgh, including:
Dandy Muir, smith
Matthew Muir, notary
Sundry members of the Town Guard, of little efficacy
Henry and Robert Scoggie, troublesome students
Two unnamed mammals of the genus *mustela putorius fero*

CHAPTER ONE

It would have been better if the ferrets had not disappeared at the same time.

Well, not better, exactly, but not quite as bad.

Well, not disappeared exactly, but they certainly made themselves difficult to catch. They were both silvery grey, and they slid, like drops of living mercury, through the bars of their cage and off amongst the assembled chair-bearers, causing chaos, confusion and minor blood-letting wherever they went.

Charles Murray would have sunk his head into his hands had he not known it was vital to have at least two eyes on the whole situation. His landlady was shrieking, and most of the chairmen were shouting or swearing or both, which did not aid the concentration and had the additional effect of rousing most of the neighbourhood from their beds. The ferrets scented fresh blood, and rampaged on, doing more damage than one would have thought two small mammals could. A charitable person would have said that they were frightened and upset: Charles had known them far too long to be charitable.

Henry Scoggie, on the other hand, the person nearest to being legally responsible for the ferrets, was frightened and upset, and was trying to chase them. He headed off into the crowd, collar up against the snow, calling them with tones of affection Charles could certainly not have managed. Instead, with a practised move he pinpointed Robert Scoggie, Henry's younger brother, attached finger and thumb to his ear, and relocated him abruptly to the parlour, closing the door firmly. Then, ignoring the ferret-induced panic (and privately hoping the damned rodents would escape and vanish for good), he began systematically to identify, pay off and dismiss the bearers of the fourteen sedan chairs, and associated link boys with their torches, currently parked outside his lodgings. It was not cheap.

It took the neighbours longer to disperse, though the way the darkness crept back as the link boys left helped. The neighbours were rewarded in their vigilance, however, when Murray's landlady, whose shrieking had subsided, suddenly let out a violent scream, and Henry, who had been rushing in her direction, stopped at once. Mrs. Fyfe began to batter her skirts with her hands, turning and twisting, while Henry stood frozen in the light from the hall door. Murray was at a loss, but then realised. He leaped forward, seized Mrs. Fyfe from behind and pinned her arms to her sides, then instructed her to stand absolutely still. Then,

'Henry,' he instructed, 'call your – your ferret.'

Henry made the kissing sound required, and with a sudden ripple of fabric a ferret shot out at the bottom hem of Mrs. Fyfe's gown. Henry, who had the first ferret in one hand, managed all the same to field this one, and for a moment there was only the sound of deep breathing and the occasional angry cheep of the ferrets. Then Mrs. Fyfe drew breath.

'Mr. Murray,' she said, very solemnly, and he released her arms with a little bow. 'Mr. Murray, this is the very last time. You and your charges will leave my house tomorrow. And that is final.'

'Mrs. Fyfe, please ...'

'Final, Mr. Murray. You and the boys have caused enough grief, believe me.'

The little cheer from the remaining neighbours did nothing to lighten Murray's mood. When a figure broke free from the crowd and came towards him, he braced himself, half-expecting a sympathetic punch in the face, but instead the stocky figure was faintly familiar.

'Mr. Charles, sir?'

He blinked. He had not been called Mr. Charles for some time – four years, he thought.

'Yes – wait – Dunnet, is it not?'

'That's right, sir. Mr. Charles, you must come at once. Your father, sir: there's been a terrible accident. You're to go at once – he's asking for you.'

'Where is he?' Charles asked quickly. 'Here or Fife?'

'Here, sir, Queen Street. Hurry, sir.'

Murray thought fast.

'Henry, fetch the ferrets' cage and put them in it. Bring them with us. Tell Robert to come at once. Bring your coats. Mrs. Fyfe, we'll send for our things in the morning.' He turned back to the man who was his father's groom. 'Is it serious?'

'Aye, sir. Very serious indeed.'

Charles shifted in his seat, and tried to flex his leg muscles without obviously moving them. As long as he did his duty, everything would be all right.

The heavy face of the – the corpse - was as pale as the candles that dangled from their still, bright flames in the cold air. On the other side of the coffin, Mr. Blair appeared to be asleep, his lower lip flapping regularly with a tiny clicking sound. At the foot of the bed, where his father's deerhound sat alert and miserable, the minister from Greyfriars was openly snoring, head back on the hard carved wood of his chair. Henry Scoggie was less easy in his rest, hands tucked hard beneath his elbows, shoulders hunched forward, knees pressed together. Charles could see he was feeling the cold. The fire was dying down. He wanted to rise and see to it, or rise and walk to the window to see if there was any sign of the dawn – pointless at this hour, at this time of the year – but somehow he had lost the ability to

5

move.

The coffin looked well, anyway, he decided, his eyes straying back to it. The black cloth was smoothed over the wood with not a crease, and the braid caught a little of the candlelight reflected in its dark silk threads. Beneath it, the bed was enveloped in white sheets that the housekeeper had produced, with a meaningful look, from a chest in her own room, and handed to the chambermaids as a sacred duty. With them had been stored the shroud with its neat ruffles, all smelling of lavender, a strange, summer scent in the depths of winter. Charles' eyes dwelt on the ruffles for a moment, and then slid back inevitably to his father's face, eyes closed, lips a little loose, cheeks sunken. A decent linen cap covered his head, covered, too, the strange dent that drew from high behind his right ear to the top of his forehead, and the rainbow of bruising that had surrounded it. Charles had not seen it. By the time he had arrived, it was smothered in bandages and salves, and the face beneath it was already settling, even while the breath was still in him, into this yellowy, waxy mask. If they had walked a little faster – but what good would that have done? And he had walked them as fast as he could.

He breathed in deeply, but all he smelled was lavender and the faint, woody smoke of the dying fire. Henry shivered in his sleep. There was no shame: it had been good of him to offer to sit up, and he was young. The minister snored. There was a polite scuffle and a clank at the door, and a maid entered, a black mob cap making her face startling white and her face in turn making the smudge of ash on her chin the more striking. She had a bandage on one finger, and looked tired.

She crossed the room, pausing to bob a little half-frightened curtsey in the direction of the corpse, and quickly revived the fire. The minister, roused by the sudden noise, jerked his head upright in a way too fast to be comfortable and exclaimed 'Aye!'. Henry jumped slightly, then woke and stretched his legs. The deerhound flinched, but did not move. Charles looked across the coffin at Mr. Blair. He had not moved either, but as Charles watched, he opened his eyes, gazed solemnly at Charles from amongst a network of wrinkles, then gave him a reassuring wink. He had, Charles noticed, done his oldest friend the honour of finding a relatively subdued waistcoat for the occasion, in pearl and grey silk. He smiled at Blair, knowing him for a kind of ally, then roused himself to open the door for the maid. He closed the door gently behind her, and asked,

'More brandy, Dr. Inglis?'

'Thank you, Mr. Murray, I will,' said the minister, fumbling for his glass and his glasses. Mr. Blair accepted a small one and a slice of cheese, which he began to nibble minutely, and Henry took a large helping of both, gulping the cheese then holding both hands against the brandy glass as if it would warm him. The minister and Henry both glanced over at the coffin, Henry probably to see that his tutor's late father had really not moved, Dr. Inglis possibly to reassure himself that no one had purloined the fine velvet mortcloth that the minister had brought along himself from the kirk. It lay, still folded, at the foot of the bed, ready for use. The Murray family's own mortcloth, Charles had discovered in the midst of the familiar, unfamiliar, frightening, comforting preparations, was kept at Letho, on the assumption, presumably, that most family members had the decency to go home to their country estate to die. Charles did not mind hiring the kirk's cloth: the money went to the poors' fund, he had discovered, and he had selected the finest there was – his father would have approved.

His father had been lying in this bed – coffinless, then – when Charles had thrown himself in at the front door and run through the hall. The housekeeper had followed, explaining again something about building works and a fall which she had to repeat, in hushed tones, before Charles could grasp anything beyond his father's awful appearance. His father, late on Friday evening, had unaccountably gone with Dunnet the groom to view the building work going on at the new feus some distance north of the far end of Queen Street. Although he quite frequently walked in the evening, and sometimes took the groom with him for a purpose somewhere between protection and company, he had never previously shown much interest in the new terraces. At some point in the walk Dunnet had been asked to return home to fetch, he had told the housekeeper, a particular walking cane, and by the time Dunnet had found it a link-boy had arrived to say that Mr. Murray was on his way home on a board, as the new coping on a wall had fallen and landed on him and another man. The other man was killed outright, but Mr. Murray was still alive and was asking for his son.

Now that his son had arrived, Mr. Murray, hearing himself addressed as father, had struggled to open his eyes. He found Charles leaning over his bed.

'You came,' he observed, and Mrs. Chambers hurried forward with a cup of water to moisten his lips.

'Of course, father.' He wanted to say he was sorry they had quarrelled, but could not find the words. He took his father's hand, possibly the first time he had ever done so except in a hearty shake.

'A shame George could not be here.' His father's eyelids slipped down, then with an effort lifted again. 'I had intended to die in better order for you, Charles, but then I'm sure you have the talents to arrange my papers.' The barb almost gave Charles hope: surely his father would not taunt him if he were really dying? 'My will is in the bookcase in the study here. I know you will see to it that George is always secure.'

'Father ...'

'You're thinner, boy. I hope you've been exercising properly.' He swallowed, with difficulty. 'I should say, you know, that none of this was Dunnet's fault at all. Not at all,' he finished firmly, and his eyes sagged closed again. A few moments later, Dr. Harker and Dr. Falconer, a pair of solemn angels guarding the gates of the living, pronounced Mr. Charles Murray senior to be dead.

The clunk of glass on table brought Charles' attention back to the present, and he looked up to see that the minister was once more asleep, his head held upright this time only by the angle of his collar and looking as if his powdered wig was pressing him down into his neck cloth. Charles drew out his watch and turned it to the light. It was eight o'clock, and in the distance he could hear the faint stirrings of the household. They would not have slept, but the minister had gone down to say a prayer with them after the kisting, when the undertaker's men had slipped the heavy corpse into the coffin, and now, bleary-eyed, they would be preparing food for the funeral. The housekeeper had given him, for his approval, a lengthy list of the funeral meats. He had glanced down it with a rising feeling of nausea, remembering funerals at which he had eaten well and drunk a little too well. Mrs. Chambers was distracting herself with business: she had been part of the household for years, since before Charles' mother had died, an exemplar of devotion and propriety. Charles was relieved to rely on her familiar confidence, and to be guided through all the endless duties of the bereaved. Under her direction, he had signed his name to elegant, swiftly-printed letters informing the recipient between the neat black borders of the death of Charles Murray, Esquire, of Letho, funeral to be held on the eighth of January, friends to attend at eleven at the Queen Street house. He had pressed his father's signet ring into the black wax and let it fall at last after a hundred letters, to dangle solidly on his watch chain, for his own long fingers were nothing to his father's strong, stout, muscular ones. He wondered what else he had to do, as his father's tailor came to measure him for mourning which was delivered so promptly he suspected it had been made up already. He wrote letters, all much the same, to neighbours in Fife, to the factor at Letho, to aunts in London who could not be expected to come to the funeral. He wrote to Lord Scoggie, his employer and the father of Robert and Henry, to explain (on one level at least) their sudden change of address. He tried to write to his brother George, found that no words would come to mind, and put off the task until after the funeral.

When dawn, only distinguishable from the night to those with a keen eye and an eagerness to look for it, finally paled the grey of the eastern sky, Dr. Inglis stretched his legs, loosened his collar round his mighty chins, and arose. Henry leapt up, too, and Blair dragged his elderly powdered wig from his head and shook it out, fortunately not in the direction of the corpse, as a heavy cloud of particles of dubious origin flew out and plummeted on to the carpet. One or two specks adhered to the black wall hangings, and Charles had a sudden urge to laugh.

A polite knock came at the door, and the same maid who had earlier stoked the fire bobbed her curtsey to the corpse again and announced,

'Mr. Charles, sir, there's hot water ready in the bedrooms upstairs, sir, and Robbins is ready standing by.'

'Thank you. Will you tell Robbins to go to the blue room first? And show Dr. Inglis there, please, first.'

Was that right? Was that the right thing to do? Maybe it should have been Blair first. But if he kept looking assured, maybe no one would question him. But the deerhound looked at him dubiously.

Charles followed his guests upstairs and waited in what had been his old room for Robbins to come and shave him. The room had been redecorated since he had last been in Edinburgh, and there was nothing of his left in it – he made a mental note to find out where his books had gone. He hoped not to the salerooms.

The room was cold, the fire only recently lit, but he made himself strip off coat, waistcoat and shirt before pouring the steaming water into the broad basin in his closet, and splashing it, light with soap bubbles, all over his face, arms and neck. He rubbed at his skin with the soap, wishing it were rougher, and then with the thin towels, watching the flesh redden, alive with blood moving under the pale skin and the fine black hairs, growing, vivid, vital. He thought of the waxy flesh of the corpse downstairs, all his father's fine flesh already turning to ruin, and shuddered.

Henry, stiff with cold, had no intention of removing the least article of clothing before he absolutely had to. He returned to the room he was sharing with his brother Robert, filled for the moment with all their belongings from Mrs. Fyfe's lodgings in Kirk o'Field. Robert groaned and sat up in bed, knowing he was there but not ready to open his eyes.

'Did you sit in that wretched room all cursed night?' he asked.

'I did.'

Robert blinked and stared at his brother.

'Who'd have thought our poor old tutor owns this?' He waved a hand around.

'I suppose.' Henry wondered if he could go to visit his ferrets. They had been removed to the stables after an incident with a maid.

'Do you think it'll be good food today? I'm starving,' Robert added, but Henry did not reply.

Mr. Blair was torture to shave. Robbins was used to the broad, smooth face of old Mr. Murray, who sat perfectly still and silent, rigorous with physical discipline. Mr. Blair jiggled endlessly, and the folds of untidy flesh that plumped out Mr. Blair's jawline were tricky. He also sighed, talked and occasionally whistled, but despite all this, Robbins decided he quite like the old piece of buckram. Mr. Blair asked interested questions, and found out more about Robbins' work and how he felt about it in twenty minutes than Mr. Murray would have done or cared to do in years. And while they talked, Charles stared from his window above at the dawn touching the cold, grey waters of the Forth.

People began to arrive, summoned by the letters, around eleven. Charles left the dead room again soon after, and went to the drawing room to see who had answered his letters. The room was already crowded, knotted with subdued groups. He almost fled at the door, but he was too slow and those who saw him drew him into the room, growing more solemn at the sight of him. Some muttered a sympathetic remark when he approached, others simply shook his hand, or some of the older women gave him a little squeeze on the upper arms, careful not to dislodge their shawls and wraps before the room warmed up.

Charles tried to find faces he was particularly expecting, not so easy when he had not seen any of them for at least four years. Most of the guests were friends of his father's from his days as an advocate, notably the Armstrongs, the Thomsons, the Balneavises and John Douglas, a close circle with whom he had stayed friendly even after he had inherited Letho and a fortune. Some of his acquaintance had not been so lucky.

Andrew Balneavis was there, with his plump, cheerful wife and one or two of their everlasting brood of children, released for the day from a close set of tiny chambers in the Old Town that served as office and home alike. Their clothes were not the most elegant, and Balneavis' elbows were shining a little in the lamplight. Mrs. Balneavis had not the figure to be flattered by the girlish, high-waisted fashion, particularly when her dress had been economically cut. Nevertheless they and their children were relentlessly smiling, clustered together, looking as out of place at a January funeral as a starving undertaker would look at a July wedding.

John Douglas still lived in the Old Town, too, but had elected, not without some considerable temptation to the contrary, to remain unmarried. Narrow and swarthy, he sat silent with David Thomson and Alistair Blair's widowed sister, Mrs. Freeman, conveniently, for the lady, close to a dish of sugar biscuits. There had been some gossip, Charles remembered, many years ago, that Andrew Balneavis had tried to make a match between Douglas and Mrs. Freeman, from which David Thomson had managed to extract a reluctant groom. All the interested parties had ended in laughter except for John Douglas himself, who had seemed to take it as a sign that any connexion with the fair sex was bound to lead him into the receipt of favours he could never fully repay.

David Thomson was clever, witty and comfortably handsome, but in all these he was outshone by his wife. Kitty Fleming, slender in fine black with seed pearls on her matching slippers, was posing with her sister and their daughters by one of the long windows, as if expecting to be sketched for *The Muses Bereft*, or *Naiads in Sorrow*. Her sister Elizabeth Fleming was married to Archibald Armstrong, and the families were close. Miss Catherine Armstrong, seventeen years old and just recently out, was particularly well-polished this morning, perfectly aware that black flattered her complexion immensely, and utterly conscious of every angle of her throat and cheekbones in the winter light of the window. She was at no disadvantage, therefore, when there was a movement at the door and the Dundases entered. Never mind whether or not Charles was in the room: now the social event could begin.

The Dundases made a grand procession, parents and sons, and walked as if they knew it. Touched by some of the fine appearance of his distinguished cousin, Lord Melville, William Dundas had built his career on his looks, his name, and his wife's money. Lady Sarah Dundas, daughter of an earl, had been the greatest beauty in Scotland in her day, toasted even in London and Bath, but Dundas had proved the perfect complement to her and the pair were never found wanting in any elegance. Their sons, Harry, Gavin and William James, were as yet bachelors, and there were not many young ladies in the room or in any other part of Edinburgh who would not be prepared to take on the name of Dundas for any of these three. Charles knew the youngest a little, having sometimes played with him as a child, but he saw the elder two still with the respect that one associates with the glory of those so far as three or six years older than you when you are young. In the same way, he knew Miss Balneavis and her older siblings, but as mere infants of nine and ten when he was already a man of fourteen. Patrick Armstrong he knew, and knew that he, like Henry and Robert, was missing lectures at the University today to be standing sombre in the drawing room. For Robert, this was little sacrifice, but for scholarly Henry, and for Patrick, driven by a passion for mathematics, it was akin to withholding a pipe from a dedicated smoker, and he fidgeted with his spectacles and played with his watch chain as though carrying out complex calculations on the abacus of its links.

Charles, feeling like a storm cloud on the horizon, wondered when to start. He badly needed his father to come up behind him and take his rightful place as host. Everyone seemed so beautiful, so elegant, so sophisticated: he felt his four years in the country like mud on his breeches. After a moment, he heard the door creak behind him and Dr. Inglis, who had had pressing duties at home, returned.

'Should we – that is, would you do us the honour of saying grace, sir?' Charles asked. The room, already quiet, hushed still further, and gentlemen who had been seated rose, folding their hands before them. The clock on the mantelpiece gave a muffled musical clink for the quarter hour, and Dr. Inglis cleared his throat.

The clock had clinked, pointedly, twice more when the Amen was finally said: Dr. Inglis, his status, style and indeed stature precluding any attempt to encourage brevity, had toured a wide range of subjects with a loose association with Charles Murray of Letho and mortality in general, and by twenty minutes to twelve Gavin Dundas, who had had a small bet with his brother William James concerning the number of times foreign missions might be mentioned, had won eight shillings. There was a responding Amen, not quite in unison, across the drawing room; shoulders relaxed, devoutly lowered heads rose, and Archibald Armstrong was nudged discreetly into wakefulness by his wife. Her sister caught her eye and raised her eyebrows sympathetically.

The servants began to produce the first of the onslaught of traditional funeral dishes that every prosperous household was expected to serve, cheese, cold meat, and porter. Charles took one look, and felt sick.

Out of the corner of his eye Henry saw the tall, dark shadow of his tutor Mr. Murray slip out of the room, and knew he was going back to his watch downstairs. He was standing with Robert near the Dundas gentlemen, and he heard the middle one, Gavin, muttering the words 'Eight shillings, I think,' at Willie Jack, the youngest. Willie Jack, porter at his lips, sputtered slightly and looked as if he would dispute Gavin's calculations, but saw his father's eye on him and swallowed, with difficulty. Henry and Robert had been introduced to the Dundases and made much of – their father was a lord, after all – but they had already recognised Willie Jack from the university, and knew that they had to be respectful to this family or suffer the consequences.

In conspiracy with the good fire blazing at each end of the room, the porter was having its effect even on those who had judiciously broken their fast before arriving at the Murrays' house. A few sporadic remarks, mostly concerning Charles Murray, Dr. Inglis' grace or the weather, broke the silence like a swimmer slipping cautiously into a cold river. Conversation, hushed, tested the water, backed off, tried again a little more bravely, failed again. Henry and Robert went to talk to Patrick Armstrong, whom they knew a little. The waters rose gradually around them.

CHAPTER TWO

After a suitable interval, Robbins nodded at the other servants and they cleared the table of the meat, cheese and porter, leaning back against the weight of the stacked dishes. Another wave of conversation in the room rose a little, still solemn, but ebbed again when the servants returned with trays of shortbread and glasses of rum, the next service in the relentless waves of funeral meats. The warm scent of the spirit mixed with the sweetness of the shortbread fought briefly with the aftermath of porter and cheese, struggled, and overcame. Robbins directed the two manservants and two maids, crisp in fresh mourning livery, with the air of a man who wants it to be thought his job is difficult, however easily he does it.

Once the second service was distributed, Robbins and the others had a moment or two to return to the kitchen and have their own funeral meats. Robbins led the way back down to the basement, aware as he went of how the four behind him relaxed by degrees the further they were from the drawing room. William gave a little skip to land flat-footed as hard as possible on the stone-flagged hall, and once past the solemnifying door of the dead room and safely on to the back stairs, Daniel ran his buttoned cuff loudly along the stair rods. Robbins turned and scowled at him past the maids, which stopped the noise, at least, though the gesture was felt rather than seen in the dim passage. Ahead, the kitchen's candles and fire put out feelers of light towards them through the open doorway. Robbins, the girls and the manservants were drawn into it, each silhouetted briefly against it as they passed into the room whose heat, on a day like today, was a brutal shock. The cook, acclimatised, was at the table, pulling brown paper and string from a series of dark fruity cakes and occasionally slapping the hands of the two kitchen maids who, while ostensibly helping her, picked stray currants from the paper and conveyed them almost absently to their mouths. The cook looked up at Robbins, alarm in her little eyes.

'They're no ready for the fourth service yet, are they?'

'No, no,' said Robbins, 'it's our turn for a wee bit.' He fetched himself some of the cheese and ale laid out at the other end of the bleached table, and ate the cheese as he stood. William and Daniel seized their share – Daniel perhaps slightly more than his share – and they retreated to a couple of creepie stools in a quiet corner like dogs with a bone, wary of being disturbed. Jennet pecked at a morsel of cheese while Mary, tall and dark, took her draught of ale like a man, then offered the jug again to Robbins and to the groom Dunnet as he sat by the fire.

'Any well-kent faces?' Dunnet leaned forward, staring oddly at Robbins. Robbins swallowed his cheese and reflected.

'I think they're all well-kent, in this house, anyway. The Thomsons and the Armstrongs and the Dundases – who were late, of course – the Balneavises, Mr. Douglas, about seven parts of the Faculty of Advocates and their ladies, a few merchants. Mr. Scott is here, which would do us some honour were he not so generally kind. Mr. Hammond has stooped to attend. Oh, and Mr. George, who was in town from Fife anyway. He was good enough to pass on his regards to all who know him in the servants' apartments.'

The cook sniffed.

'And well he might,' she snapped. 'From all I hear, there are a few servants' apartments around the East Neuk he kens better than most masters.' She began slicing cake forcibly, using her left hand to press the end of the blade firmly downwards. 'Take heed, Effy,' she said in parenthesis to one of the kitchen maids, 'cut the cake straight down to the table. It's no a loaf of bread to be sawed up like a piece of firewood.' Effy tried, but omitted to extract her fingers from below the descending blade, and there was a moment's diversion as a cloth was found to stop the blood and Mrs. Mutch, tutting, trimmed the edges of the cake where she felt it might be stained.

'Aye, he was a good master, our one,' she continued, following her own train of thought.

'Aye, I suppose,' Robbins responded, his mind on calculating the number of port wine bottles to be opened.

'You suppose?' growled Dunnet from his chair, his face reddened in the firelight. 'You suppose? You're an awful young man to be in your position of responsibility in a household, with many an older man still cleaning boots, and just *supposing* you had a good master!' Robbins raised his eyebrows, but said nothing. Dunnet stared into the fire, and took a long draught of ale. 'I mind when his old horse Juniper was having her first foal, and no doing so well out of it. All night we sat with her, and when the foal came it was back end foremost.' He ignored Jennet's genteel little gasp and Mrs. Mutch's tutting at such stableyard details. 'He was there with her and as clarty as me and the farrier when we brought that foal out, and to see his face when mare and foal were seen to be living and breathing was pure joy. And I'll tell you, Henry Robbins,' he turned and waved his ale jug at Robbins, 'I made a friend that night, where I looked only to find a master, and that's why, *that's* why it was me he chose to walk with him of an evening, and I'm proud to say it.' His dark face contorted into a ferocious scowl. Jennet gave another little squeak. Iffy and Effy were transfixed, clinging on to each other's apron fronts, blood still dripping from Effy's finger. William and Daniel, mouths open, waited eagerly for a fight. Mary, thoughtful, chewed on her cheese and watched Robbins. The clean, hard planes of his face were cut sharp in the unevenly lit room, his gaze on the floor, standing very still.

There was a scuffle at the door and the moment passed. Jamie, the stable boy, smelling strongly of horse, scuffed his boots across the flag floor and reported to Dunnet that all the guests' horses were watered and warm. Oblivious to the tension that his arrival had deflated, he went on,

'And Patie next door says that Mr. George's groom is going back up to Fife tomorrow and could take any horses back up to Letho, if you were to ask him.'

With Dunnet safely distracted, Mrs. Mutch nodded and tried the conversation again.

'Aye, a good man. And a good church man, too.'

Iffy nudged Effy, who giggled.

'He gave us our names, too,' said Iffy unexpectedly.

'Oh, aye?' said Daniel, managing to invest it with a certain indecent inflexion. Iffy, innocently, was encouraged.

'When our Ma was expecting us, our Da was thinking about enlisting because he wanted to before when the land was so bad but then the land was better and then Ma didn't want him to go but he thought he would and then she was expecting us and all the others weren't old enough anyway.'

'Well, they weren't,' whispered Effy, as though someone had objected.

'And then when we were born, well before, because he thought there'd be only one of us –'

'He could only live in hope,' muttered Mrs. Mutch.

'Mr. Murray said he was like A – ga – memnon,' she said carefully, 'and if we were a girl we should be called Iphigenia, so I am. But then there was two of us, so he said we should be Iffy and Effy, so we are.'

'Oh, aye,' said William, inspired by Daniel. Daniel jiggled his stool forward.

'I always had my doubts about that story. I mean, he was taking a bit of an interest, wasn't he?'

Iffy looked puzzled. Mrs. Mutch slammed her ale jug on the table and snapped,

'We'll have no talk like that here, young man!'

'Like what?' Daniel was all wide eyes, glinting in the shadows. 'Well, I'll give Mr. Murray this: he always remembered your name. I've heard tell of masters who call all their servants John or Jean, because they couldn't fash themselves to remember.'

'Mr. Charles remembers, too. Or Mr. Murray now, we should say.' Robbins drew open another port wine bottle, and drove William and Daniel to the door with a jerk of his head. Mary and Jennet took up the plates of fruit cake and preceded them into the dim passage, accustomed feet finding the dark steps with no call for a candle.

'Aye, I wonder what kind of master he'll make?' Mrs. Mutch asked of no one in particular as she handed the folded brown papers from the cakes to Effy to put away. 'Now, what next? Where did you put the currant bread, girl? It's nearly the half hour already.' Iffy flapped a hand to her mouth and scuttled into the pantry.

'So will he stay in town or go and live in Letho?' Mr. Dundas asked generally, taking a large piece of fruitcake between fine fingers. The conversation was definitely thriving now.

'He'll stay in town,' said David Thomson, as if it were obvious. 'He's a young man, and he's been off in the country for four years – of course he'll want to stay in town.'

'He might have acquired a taste for the country way of life,' suggested Archibald Armstrong, with just the least hint of wistfulness.

'What was he doing there, anyway?' asked Dundas, unable to fathom why anyone might acquire such a taste. Thomson stared into the fire for a moment.

'Well, he won't have much putting in order to do, here or at Letho,' he remarked, knowing Murray's affairs better than Dundas. 'I was talking about this very thing with Lord Braeburn yesterday. Old Murray never let much slip by him, and it isn't as if he was ill for long.'

'No, it was very sudden,' agreed Armstrong.

'Thank the Lord,' said Dundas absently. 'He didn't suffer long.'

'It's a fine estate, right enough,' said Thomson, after a respectful pause. 'He's done well out of it.'

'And by it,' added Armstrong. 'From what I hear, when his grandfather had it first, he chose his tenants himself, and like the farmstock they almost all bred true. And Murray's father rebuilt the steading and half the house himself.'

'Fancied himself a farmer, did he?' asked Dundas. Thomson looked at him expressionlessly, his globular eyes wide.

'So if young Charles follows the same pattern, what will they do with this place? Let it?' asked Armstrong, oblivious.

'George might use it when he leaves the army,' Thomson suggested. 'Though who knows when that might be. But I don't think George is a country man.'

'Or he could let it to Balneavis as a charity, give the poor man some idea of how the New Town half of society lives. At least if he moved out of the Old Town, my dear wife might condescend to visit Mrs. Balneavis.'

'Young Charles is bright, though,' said Armstrong, moving the subject gently sideways.

'I hear he's bookish,' said Dundas. 'And why he had to go all the way to St. Andrews to study is beyond me, when there's a perfectly good university here. Your son's happy enough at it, isn't he, Armstrong?'

'Oh, aye, happy enough,' Armstrong responded, frowning.

'Aye, well, Fifers,' added Thomson, smiling with resignation. 'You can't expect them to think like normal people.' He raised his glass to Charles Murray's portrait above the fireplace, and winked into the painted eyes.

'So will he stay in town or go and live at Letho?' asked Mrs. Armstrong. Through the lace at the side of her bonnet she observed, briefly, her daughter Catherine. Catherine's porcelain complexion seemed immune to the reddening effects of port wine closely following rum. Mrs. Armstrong felt that this lack of a warning sign was somehow cheating.

'Letho is charming,' admitted her sister Kitty. 'Where Mr. Murray found that gem of a housekeeper is beyond me.'

'I don't think –' began Mrs. Balneavis, uncertainly. Her fair face had no deceit about it and her cheeks were already rosy.

'Mrs. Chambers,' Elizabeth Armstrong explained rather over-kindly. 'She's been the Murrays' housekeeper since before Charles was born, nursed poor dear Annabel in her last illness. You'll have seen her from time to time, I daresay, here or at Letho.'

'I've never been to Letho,' said Mrs. Balneavis quietly. The wine she had drunk was beginning to have its effect in more ways than one, but she was reluctant to leave an interesting conversation.

'Never been to Letho!' cried Mrs. Thomson, who had been fairly sure of it. 'Oh, my dear Mrs. Balneavis, you have missed such a treat! The woods, the streams – a positive wilderness in the summer just off the drive, such a delightful house with everything as you would wish it. But I wonder,' she went on, 'if Mrs. Chambers might not find it a little too much, now. With the two houses and a much younger master ...'

'Oh, I doubt you'll steal her away, Kitty,' said Mrs. Armstrong, showing that at least part of her very active mind had been on the conversation, however much her gaze had been quartering the room. 'Mr. Dundas tried it once, I believe, and failed. She has always been devoted to the Murrays, and she is very well settled here. Besides, who else would keep house for young Charles, whether here or at Letho?'

'Young Charles,' said Kitty Thomson pointedly, voicing all their thoughts, 'might marry.' And three pairs of eyes moved contemplatively and respectively to Miss Thomson, Miss Armstrong, and Miss Balneavis, and Mrs. Balneavis, whose need for a prosperous attachment for her daughters was undoubtedly the greatest, gave a little sigh as she made for the water closet between the drawing room and the first floor bedchamber, and allowed herself, sweetly, to dream of a summer wedding beneath the leafy boughs of an Eden-like vision called Letho, under the wide Fife sky.

'Do you think Mr. Charles will want to stay here?' asked Jennet suddenly, as the maids followed Robbins back again into the kitchen.

'What do you mean, girl?' asked Mrs. Mutch irritably, replenishing the platters of sugar biscuits which had been brought down from the drawing room after grace. Effy had dropped one of the tins in which they had been stored in the larder, and Mrs. Mutch tutted as she sorted out the broken pieces from the rest. Daniel and William watched the growing heap of fragments with calculating interest. 'He'll no be going back to work for Lord Scoggie now.'

Jennet gave an unconscious curtsey in the direction of Mrs. Mutch.

'I mean, will we go to Letho?'

'Oh!' squeaked Effy, who had not thought of this possibility. Iffy came back in from the scullery, where she had been washing and breaking glasses, at the sound of her sister's voice.

'Back to Letho? But we've only just come here!' The twins stood desolate, like two damp dishcloths pegged by the corner on a line. Mrs. Mutch carried on sorting biscuits deftly.

'Just come? You've been here over a year – though a man would be hard put to know it from the little you've learned in that time. And you'll go back to Letho if the master goes back – that's Mr. Murray, now, Jennet, not Mr. Charles any more.'

Jennet blushed, and mouthed 'Mr. Murray' several times for practice.

'I dinna ken that I want to go somewhere strange,' she said. Mary said thoughtfully,

'I don't suppose we'd be better or worse off than we are now. I've never seen Fife, myself.'

'Oh, Letho's a grand place, isn't it, Daniel?' asked William, nudging his friend soundly with one bony shoulder. They had returned to their creepie stools, not too far from the possibility of stray fragments of sugar biscuit. 'You're always on about Letho. Or is it the girls you're fond of, more than the place?'

Daniel was pensive.

'Aye, maybe so. There was one, now, I mind. Nan, they called her.' He allowed his eyes to widen and pursed his lips, as if he could see her charms materialising in the firelight. 'Now, she was a fine girl. And very fond of me.'

Robbins rolled his eyes in despair, and sat in the fireside chair. Dunnet, going out to see to the horses, had left his mark in the form of a greasy spot on the high chair back. Robbins sat forward fastidiously.

William was more easily impressed.

'Was she fond of you? Aye, but will she wait for you? Will she wait for you even if we stay here?'

Iffy clutched Effy's hand and they giggled in harmony. Iffy controlled herself enough to ask,

'Is that Nan Watson you mean, Daniel Hossack? Nan Watson that's – that's –' The giggles began again, with a look of mild panic in her eyes.

'Aye, Nan Watson. She'll wait for me right enough, William. She's too damn' ugly to find anyone else.' He sat back with a superior smile. Jennet squeaked at the expletive. Mary looked unimpressed. Jamie, the stable boy, who had been listening bright-eyed at the door, asked,

'But if she's ugly, Daniel, why do you walk out with her?'

'Because,' said Daniel, grinning wickedly, 'she's willing.'

'Daniel! We'll have none of that in here!' said Mrs. Mutch severely.

'What's she willing for?' asked Jamie. The boy knew his horses well, but had yet to convert his knowledge to human terms.

'She's willing –' began Daniel with relish. William held his breath.

'That's enough, Daniel,' said a new voice from the door, and Mrs.

Chambers entered. Robbins rose and pulled Daniel and William up as well with a single-fingered gesture, discreet but ferocious. 'Today of all days, Daniel, you may wish to show a proper demeanour.' She moved to a branderback chair and sat carefully. Mary found a clean lidded goblet and poured her some porter. Mrs. Chambers thanked her, and told Robbins he could sit.

'Well, Mr. Robbins, how does it go upstairs?' she asked.

'Not badly, Mrs. Chambers. There are one or two points we might discuss later, and they drank more rum than we reckoned, but besides that ...' The conversation turned to the funeral guests and their behaviour. Dunnet returned, sent Jamie back to the stables and helped himself to more ale. Daniel and William, still standing, began to fidget. Robbins was conscious of it but reckoned they deserved to wait. The talk came full circle with Robbins asking,

'Do you know if Mr. Murray has any plans yet? About this house and Letho, I mean.'

Mrs. Chambers looked down at her black lace cuffs, and up again.

'He may close this and take a smaller house, with fewer servants. Would you be concerned if we returned to Letho?'

Robbins knotted his hands and pressed his thumbs under his chin before answering.

'I think I should sooner stay here, if I was given the choice,' he said at last.

'Ach!' spat Dunnet, 'I ken your problem. You're feared that if we go back to Letho you'll have your nose knocked out of joint. No call for two butlers, and when one's older and wiser no doubt but that he'll have the job, not a young lad wet behind the ears like you!'

Robbins' fingers tightened together, his knuckles yellow-white in the firelight like the legs of chickens, but he said nothing. Mrs. Chambers looked at Dunnet and after a moment succeeded in catching his slightly bleary eye.

'Dunnet, you know that Mr. Murray – the late Mr. Murray – brought Mr. Robbins here to be butler in Queen Street because old Mr. Fenwick is, regrettably, feeling the weight of his advanced years. There is no reason why Mr. Fenwick should feel obliged to resume duties that were, as he himself gladly admitted, becoming too onerous for him, and no reason why Mr. Robbins should fear that Mr. Fenwick might leave his comfortable retirement.'

'Aye, he won't come to Edinburgh, right enough, and leave his daughter and her bairns.' Dunnet managed to growl even in agreement. 'But he might well feel he could carry out his job at Letho well enough, and sooner do it than see a laddie blunder in his place.'

'Dunnet,' began Mrs. Chambers firmly, but Robbins interrupted.

'Leave it.' He looked over at her. 'Forgive me, Mrs. Chambers, but I feel that – that nothing can be gained from carrying this conversation further. You will excuse me now, please.' He turned to William and Daniel. 'Brandy, lads. The glasses are ready in the scullery.' He left the kitchen without looking at anyone. Dunnet muttered something that from its very tone was obscene, and threw himself back into the fireside chair. Mrs. Chambers contemplated him, then rose.

'Dunnet, Mr. Robbins has requested me to be more lenient than I should prefer. However, I think it would be wise if you had no more ale today.' She drew the cup from his hand and tipped the contents into the fire, then handed the cup to Iffy. 'Mrs. Mutch, I know you have worked extremely hard today, but please make sure that you all eat well this evening when the guests have left. If you need me,' her eyes travelled sideways to Dunnet, 'I shall be in my room until we are called to see Mr. Murray depart.' She left in a rustle of black and Jamie, sunshine to her rain, appeared again at the back door.

'I don't want to go to Letho either!' he announced, dancing to warm himself.

'You're a wise boy,' said Mrs. Mutch in the absence of other response. 'You stay here where you can visit your mother and father. You're a grand son to them, and don't let anyone teach you to be otherwise.'

'Well,' said Jamie, caught between pride in himself and not wanting to appear too dependent on his parents at his advanced age, 'they need me, ye ken. And besides, from all that Daniel says, I think the girls are better looking in the town.' He skipped again. 'Mary, what do you think?'

'Well, I'm not the judge of girls that you are, Jamie,' said Mary solemnly, 'and as to Letho, I'll go where I'm sent and make the most of it.'

Mrs. Mutch sat heavily in another chair, so short that she could swing her feet amidst her black skirts. Jennet fetched her a cup of porter, but before she could finish it, the drawing room bell and the bell of the street bedchamber, the dead room, rang almost simultaneously.

'That'll be us, then,' said Mrs. Mutch, widening her little eyes and jumping to the floor. She undid her apron strings and glanced at Iffy and Effy. 'We're to say farewell.'

She led the way upstairs and they passed the dead room door to file along the side of the hall. Mrs. Chambers took her place beside Robbins, and the girls, thin in black, lined up with Daniel and William, shuffled a little and stood, hands clasped and heads bowed. From the drawing room above, the guests descended in silence and filled the hallway, leaving a passage to the front door. Outside, dusk was gathering already, the street lamp above the steps glowing where William had been despatched hurriedly to light it. The male guests had coats and gloves on already, and held their hats in leathery fingers. The hall was cold, and outside would be colder: one or two of them surreptitiously tested the soles of their shoes on the flags, mindful of icy streets.

The door of the dead room opened. Only those on the right side of the hall could see, and they glanced up and down again as the clothed and caped coffin emerged, slowly, at hip height, mortcloth stiffly swaying. Charles followed, eyes down on the coffin, crape streamers on his shoulders and hat that fluttered a little as he walked. Mr. Blair came next, and Dr. Inglis, who moved to the stairs and added himself to the guests. Blair's eyes looked damp, but it may have been fatigue.

The undertaker's men paused, and in a smooth movement the coffin was raised to shoulder height. Mrs. Chambers lowered her head suddenly and frowned, pressing her lips together hard. Her hand was firmly on the collar of the deerhound, which looked as desolate as a dog could look. Then there was a silent signal, the coffin moved again, and borne on a river of black-clad gentlemen following, Mr. Charles Murray, late of Letho, became buoyant, and glided out into the dusk.

It was an hour's walk at a slow pace through the New Town, down to the foot of the North Bridge, then up its long straight ramp to the High Street, the dip of the South Bridge to Adam Square, and sharp right up the street that passed the new College. The College was dark and roofless, its windows eyeless sockets in the dusk, the spider's web of scaffolding that broke and rewove about the town clinging to its unfinished walls. The gentle incline led them solemnly through Argyle Square and Brown Square to finish at the top of Candlemaker Row, down which, on tentative soles, the undertaker's men edged with the coffin. People on the sides of street paused perfunctorily and men removed their hats. Avoiding the more dubious tenements at the bottom of the hill, they turned up left between high walls and into the kirkyard of Greyfriars.

The graveside ceremony was brief: the diggers had done their job and although they had, apparently, disposed of most of the contents of their traditional bottle, they remained quiet and respectful – Gavin Dundas, with a practised eye, reckoned they were nearer to stupor than to riotous behaviour. The earth was filled in over the coffin, the mortcloth folded in deft pleats, the heavy mortsafe cage was locked, and the key presented to Charles, who thought briefly that he would rather the Resurrectionists took him than be locked, however dead, in such a device.

Robbins and the manservants had brought the brandy and all the funeral-goers, freed at last from formality, gathered around and partook against the chill of the evening. Then they went their separate ways, the closer friends to meet again later at Fortune's Tontine Hotel for the funeral supper. Charles pocketed the cold key of the mortsafe and dismissed the servants to hurry back to home and warmth. The boys had stayed at Queen Street, too young, he felt, for this duty when they were not relatives. He was alone. He stood at the graveside for a moment, the fresh air a shock after so long indoors.

'Father, I'm sorry we argued,' he mumbled. He should have been a more dutiful son. If he had not quarrelled with his father, perhaps his father would not have felt the need to take a groom with him for company on his evening walks. Perhaps he would have been with his father, even if he had taken the groom and sent him home for his cane. If only he had not quarrelled, like a boy.

But on the other hand, even if they had not quarrelled, would he and his father ever have found each other congenial enough company to walk together of an evening?

His father had sent the servant home, and he had died.

He turned on the slippery grass and strode back down to the street, black weepers fluttering, back to the lights and the life of the town.

The brisk walk cleared his head, and the exercise set his blood running again in his veins. He had begun to think himself as stiff as his father's corpse over the last few days. He reflected back to his last real exercise, the mad run from Kirk o'Field, and wished he could instead go for a serious ride. He decided, as he had over an hour to dress for supper, that he would call in to the mews behind his father's house and see what horses he had in town with him.

The stable was lit by a good wall lamp, and the straw glowed a warm, light yellow on the beaten earth floor. Beside the corn bing by the stone wall, a boy was lying, hair the colour of the straw itself. His head was at a strange angle. There was a bruise on his cheekbone, and blood on the clean side of the corn bing. Beside him, crouched, and staring up at Charles with bloodshot eyes, was Dunnet, the groom.

CHAPTER THREE

As if he had negotiated his own personal exemption from gravity, the stable cat sprang to the top of the corn bing and arranged his paws along the edge, the better to survey the scene.

Murray's shouts had brought several of the servants running from the house, Robbins first, followed by William and Daniel. Almost before they could take in what had happened, William had been sent at a gallop for a police officer and Daniel for the family physician, Dr. Harker in Prince's Street. The moment's whirl of activity had passed and left four of them stranded on its shore. Murray, half his mind still numbed with grief and fatigue, found the other half beginning to observe the details of the scene as though he were parsing a difficult sentence in Latin: he noted cases and tenses but could not yet see how they fitted into the whole. He saw Henry's ferrets eager in their cage, paws against the bars, trying to see what was going on. He saw the horses, eyeing the scene from over their stalls, ears back, uneasy, edgy. He saw Robbins study the body and its setting in a manner almost calculating, and Dunnet, crouched like an incubus, staring at the broken corpse as if the sheer concentration of his gaze could somehow pierce the boy's heart and fill it again with life. Murray touched Robbins' arm and nodded, taking off his own coat and as Robbins moved to draw Dunnet back and away from his fixed vigil, Murray draped the good black cloth over the body, and the black crape weepers slithered amongst the straw, like roots finding a hold around the corpse.

Even in the hard-beaten earth you could see signs of a struggle, the marks of a shoe well-made and sharp about the heel as if new. Murray, rising, set his own foot contemplatively beside the footprint: it was smaller than his own shoe. He glanced around. Dunnet and Robbins both wore boots, Dunnet's old and as far as he could see under the groom's coat tails, needing building up around the heel. In the print on the floor, the toe was well pushed in, the pressure on the heel lighter. Murray manoeuvred his own feet quietly into the same position, and thought that it would give him purchase to shove hard, or to keep his balance against being pushed back.

Who would come to a well-lit stable in good shoes to struggle with a stable boy? If it had been a thief, he had apparently killed in vain, for of the five stalls, the farthest two held his father's carriage horses, a fine, almost matching pair of very dark bays, and the next held a saddle horse suitable for town use, calm and steady. The fourth and fifth were empty, swept and clean, and Murray knew of few horse thieves who cleaned up after themselves.

Perhaps it was an opportunist horse thief interrupted in his work by Dunnet. But having already killed the boy, it would seem an easy task to knock over a man who was not large and who, by the smell of ale about him, would not have been too steady on his feet.

The horses were growing peaceful enough now, though, made a little nervous by the fuss and so many people, and perhaps by a warning scent of death that only they could smell. Evidently the thief, if thief it had been, had not disturbed them. The lock on the press housing the expensive harness was also as it should be. Yet what reason could there be for Jamie's death but that he had attempted, however unintentionally, to stop a thief?

'What was his surname?' he asked suddenly. The cat looked up, affronted at the unexpected noise. Robbins blinked, but remembered that Jamie had not been with the family long.

'Paterson, sir. His parents live off the Grassmarket.' Robbins had pulled Dunnet back on to a heap of straw and stood beside him, mindful of the presence of his master. Dunnet seemed oblivious to everything but

Jamie.

'I'll send for them when one of the men comes back.' A father dies and then a son, he thought, involuntarily.

Footsteps he had barely registered as distant sounds on the cobbled street grew abruptly immediate, and William led the police officer into the warm pool of oil lamplight.

'Aye,' was the police officer's first reaction. 'Well.' He appeared to be addressing the black heap of the corpse on the floor, as he had no eyes for anything else. William, too, stood wide-eyed in the doorway, cheeks cold-pinched as he had run straight off on his errand with no overcoat.

'William,' said Murray, 'do you know where Jamie's parents live?'

'Aye, sir, off the Grassmarket.'

'Then bring them here, please. Tell them only that there has been an accident and that Jamie is dead. There is no need to distress them with further details at the moment.' He could hear his father's voice in his own, and did not know whether to be proud of it or irritated by it. 'And fetch a coat for yourself first.' William tore himself reluctantly away from the doorway, deprived once more of legitimate access to the scene of the action. As he left, there was a further sound at the door and Daniel arrived with Dr. Harker, still in black from the funeral.

'Good evening, Mr. Murray,' said the physician. He was a gentle man, and appeared somewhat embarrassed by the situation: perhaps he felt it to be indelicate to be summoned to a second death in a household where the bills had not yet been paid on the first one. 'This is the unfortunate lad, then?' He knelt in the straw with courageous disregard for the knees of his breeches, and gently pulled back the shoulders of Murray's overcoat from the base of the corn bing and Jamie's unnaturally laid head. In doing so, he obscured Dunnet's view, but the groom stared still as if he had not noticed.

'Right, then,' said the policeman, whose concentration on the corpse was, by contrast, broken by the arrival of the doctor. 'What happened here?' He addressed the question generally, but Robbins naturally allowed Murray to answer.

'I came into the stables and found Jamie Paterson here dead, and Dunnet, this man here, crouched over the body.'

'Seems a simple case, then, sir,' said the police officer, confidently. 'And who are you, sir?'

'Charles Murray. Of Letho,' he added. 'This is my stable, and Jamie was my stable boy.' He felt as if he were making false claims to his father's estate, and the police officer evidently heard the note of doubt in his voice for he was directing a dubious eye at him when a shout came from the open stable door.

'Rigg!' the voice exclaimed richly, every consonant furred with disgust. 'I might have guessed.'

A thin, shadowy figure, oddly shaped about the head, made its way forward into the light, and was revealed as a member of the Town Guard, cold and meagre under an over-sized cocked hat, in an old red uniform coat, faced with blue, of little more substance than the barrel of the worn musket in his matching blue-knuckled hand.

'Och, Bain, you're the plague of my life,' said Police Officer Rigg, with a fine disregard for the others around him. 'Can you no see I'm busy? There's been a murder, or would you no ken what one of them was?'

'I ken well enough, for I've considered it in connexion with yourself many a time,' replied Bain, propping his musket against the wall and folding his bony arms across his chest. Daniel looked questions at Robbins, who glanced at Mr. Murray, but Mr. Murray did not seem anxious to have either officer removed. He was scowling, in truth, but Robbins, who had the instincts of a good servant, suspected that Mr. Murray was having difficulty in stopping himself from laughing out loud. The element of complete unreality, coming at the end of such a dark day, was too much for him.

Rigg was allowing Bain's last remark to percolate through his cosy thatch of black hair. He turned in plumply assumed dignity.

'Are you threatening me, Davie Bain? Because a threat issued in front of another or third party is damned —'

Daniel's eyes widened in delight.

'Deemed, ye gowk, not damned!' Rigg gave a high cackle. 'No, the only reason, you ken, why I would think of murder in connexion with yourself – never, you would understand, meaning to wish you any *permanent* damage – is how the number of murders in the town has strangely increased, by my reckoning, since your police force started last summer. Would you agree, Police Officer Rigg?'

'So you've learned the counting in this last year, have you?' asked Rigg, pleased with this taunt. Daniel grinned openly, and was frowned at by Robbins, as aware as the gentlemen of the gross inappropriateness of this contest.

'It's time you did, Police Officer Rigg, so you could add up the number of murders and other dire crimes, and then take away – oh, aye, a wee tiny number indeed! – the ones where you've caught the man that did it, and that would leave you,' he grew solemn, 'that would leave you with the great number of restless souls, wrested from their bodies early and unavenged by the might of the law, that you'll have to answer to on the Day of Judgement!'

Rigg, who had lost the thread of this calculation somewhere about the mention of the second number, fell back on his knowledge of the law.

'You're in this stable without the permission of the owner. Do you ken who this is?' He threw a chubby but dramatic hand towards Murray.

'Oh, aye, I ken fine Mr. Murray,' said Bain coolly. 'Though I haven't seen you for a while, sir. I was sorry to hear about your faither, Mr. Murray, sir. He was a fine gentleman.'

Murray managed to nod his thanks.

'I should maybe explain, sir,' Bain continued confidentially, 'that this person is my brother-in-law – my sister, the Lord save her, is soft in the head and married him for the company – and he requires a kind of constant watch in case he does himself some damage. The police office took him in for kindness.' His voice was bitter enough for Murray to doubt at least the surface meaning of his words. 'Now,' said Bain, turning back towards Rigg and warming to his mathematical task, 'Do you want to hear a few more numbers, Police Officer Rigg? Now that you have the idea, right? If you take away four hundred and thirteen from four hundred and fifty, what do you imagine you might have left? You look a wee thing bumbazed, so I'll help you out.' He drew breath, and then shouted at the top of his thin voice. 'Thirty-seven! That's what you have left. That's all the Town Guard has left now that your new, valiant police force is set up! Thirty-seven men who served this town well – and four hundred and thirteen left with no uniform to their backs or axes to their hands, to defend this town from the works of the Devil! And left with no coin in their pocket or bread in their bairns' mouths!'

In the ensuing silence, the doctor rose with a rustle from the straw and gave a polite cough.

'Mr. Murray,' he began, 'the boy's neck is broken, and there is bruising about his face and arms, and on the back of his head where he struck the corn bing. In addition, his nails are broken back as if he scratched at something, perhaps in his own defence, but all I can see beneath the nails is embedded dirt, there for quite a while, I'm afraid.' He smiled slightly and apologetically at the floor. 'It does not seem possible that he died an accidental or natural death.'

Murray took in this information slowly, noting each point on the body before Dr. Harker once more covered it over, finding it astonishing that a man who had not even known Jamie could tell in so short a time so much about the way of his death. Robbins glanced at Dunnet, then at the floor, eyes pale in his skull-white face.

Rigg also digested the information, then stepped determinedly across and seized Dunnet by the arm.

'I'm arresting you for the murder of Jamie Paterson.'

'He was found with the boy's body, wasn't he?' asked Dr. Harker diffidently, moving to look into Dunnet's empty face.

'He was,' Murray agreed.

'How long ago?' asked the physician. He picked Dunnet's hands one by one from his side, and examined the nails and knuckles carefully. Charles, resisting the urge to tell him that Dunnet was not also a corpse, took out his pocket watch.

'A matter of less than half an hour.' It was four o'clock, and nearly time for him to leave to receive his guests at Fortune's.

'Where was this man two hours ago?' asked Dr. Harker, holding Dunnet still by one wrist. Securely held on the other side by Rigg, Dunnet might have been a newly-stuffed scarecrow, the straw adhering still to his coat and breeches.

'Why two hours?' asked Murray, puzzled.

'The lad's body is cold,' explained the doctor. 'I'd say he died rather more than half an hour ago, and two hours is more likely. Where was this man then?'

Murray and Robbins looked at one another.

'Where we all were,' replied Murray slowly. 'We were on the way to the kirkyard.'

'No, sir,' Robbins replied stony-faced, 'not Dunnet. He was the worse for ale, and Mrs. Chambers made him stay in the kitchen with Jamie and the women. He took Mr. Murray's death very badly, sir,' he added as an excuse.

'I see,' said Murray, after a moment. 'Daniel, will you be so good as to ask Mrs. Chambers and Mrs. Mutch to come here?'

Daniel darted away, and they waited in silent tableau. A horse shifted, and Murray could hear the ferrets scuffling in their bedding. William had evidently broken the news before he had left for the Grassmarket: the women, when they arrived, were already pale and tearful and avoided looking at the black bundle by the corn bing.

'Two hours ago,' said Murray, 'at two o'clock the funeral procession set out, and you were left here. When my father's coffin left the house, what did you do?'

35

Mrs. Chambers frowned, but answered,

'We – that is, the maids and I – saw the ladies back up to the drawing room and settled. Mrs. Mutch here and Iphigenia and Euphemia returned to the kitchen.'

'And Dunnet?'

'He did not leave the kitchen, Mr. Murray. He was – unwell.' She tried not to emphasise the word, and ended up half-swallowing it instead.

'What about Jamie?'

'He also remained in the kitchen, sir.' She coughed and despite herself, glanced down at Murray's coat in the straw. 'He smelled rather strongly of the stables, Mr. Murray.'

'And you, Mrs. Mutch.' Murray had known her, too, all of his life, and felt as though he was hiding behind his new authority like a mask. 'When you returned to the kitchen, who was there?'

'Dunnet and Jamie, sir. Dunnet was asleep by the fire, and Jamie complained that the stable was cold and he wanted to stay in the kitchen.' She pressed a sodden handkerchief to her nose and went on, indistinctly, through it. 'And the Lord help me, I told him he was a lazy wee boy and sent him back here!' Tears squeezed out of her currant eyes and meandered in channels across plump cheeks. Murray gave her a moment to sob before asking, to make sure,

'And have you been in the kitchen ever since?'

'Kitchen or pantry, sir, making the evening meal for us, sir.'

'And Dunnet?'

'Asleep by the fire until half an hour ago, sir, when he rose and said he'd have to see about the horses.'

'You'd swear to that, would you?' asked Murray. Mrs. Mutch, half his height, looked up at him, shocked.

'Of course, sir! The kitchen clock is my constant companion, you ken that yourself, Mr. Charles!'

Murray felt abashed. The thin Town Guard chuckled hollowly, scratching his fingers across his ribs.

'Well, Police Officer Rigg, what might you do now?'

Rigg looked as if the entire conversation with the women had bypassed him completely.

'Dunnet, I am arresting you for the murder of Jamie Paterson,' he repeated, shaking the oblivious groom by the arm. Dr. Harker held tightly to the other wrist and shook his head gently.

'He cannot understand you, Rigg. He is quite deeply shocked.'

'Besides, we have just proved that he is innocent,' added Murray. 'You cannot arrest him.'

Bain tutted, grinning.

'You'll have to excuse my friend here, Mr. Murray, sir. You ken, he's assured that the reformed police force can do no wrong, so he believes that some kind of divine judgement is granted him with his office. It's no his fault he wouldna ken divine judgement if he saw it this instant with St. Peter joogling his keys.'

Rigg turned angrily on the Town Guard, letting Dunnet go. The groom would have sagged back on to the straw but that Robbins caught his free arm and flung it over his own shoulders, holding Dunnet by the waist. Suddenly Murray remembered the tricks of tutoring small boys, and took control.

'Understand this,' he said firmly, breaking into Rigg's tirade at Bain. 'You have no grounds for arresting my groom, and you will not do so. If you wish to carry this further you may tell your superior officer to wait upon me at my house, tomorrow morning at eleven. Now, Daniel, when you have removed these persons from the stable, please assist Robbins to carry Dunnet to his room. You'll do your best for him, won't you, Dr.

Harker?' he asked, and as the physician nodded, he added, 'Although I think perhaps you have already saved his life this evening.'

The police officer, properly subdued, and the Town Guard, reunited with his musket, were propelled into the street. The doctor and the men departed towards the house, and Murray was left with Mrs. Chambers, Mrs. Mutch and the bundle that had been Jamie. The cat, who had regarded the foregoing events with dispassionate interest, began to wash. Murray looked up at the hayloft.

'He slept in here, did he?' he asked. Mrs. Chambers nodded her black lace cap. Murray turned and bolted the stable door, saw the two women through to the yard with their candle, and turned back to see that the horses were sufficiently provisioned. He glanced again at the hayloft, and a thought struck him. He climbed quickly up the ladder and peered around, but there was nowhere for a man to hide: all was neat and straight. In the corner nearest the little window a heap of straw covered with a couple of grey English blankets formed what had been Jamie's bed. Murray clambered into the loft and approached it, stooping, but could see little beyond a chamber pot, very correct and New Town in a stable, and an old tin mug, empty. A series of misshapen objects along the windowsill were unidentifiable by sight in the darkness: Murray felt them cautiously, found them to be inanimate and apparently harmless, and gathered them into his pocket for future investigation in better light. If they were Jamie's, they should be returned to his family.

Back on the ground, he paused, then crouched down to lift the collar of his coat back from the face of the stable boy he had not known. Fair hair, pale skin, dark lashes, still only a boy. This would have been his first post, his first steps into a man's world.

Even in Murray's own short life, he had seen other bodies, blameless and broken like this. When evil walked, the innocent were kicked aside like so many dead leaves. He knew that he would try his best to solve the puzzle of this boy's death, that he would not be able to resist, but not tonight. Not tonight.

He extinguished the lamp, then in the darkness lifted the body of the stable boy who had kept the place so well, and carried it in his arms through the yard to the kitchen, his black coat hanging in folds about the body like the mortcloth on his father's coffin.

CHAPTER FOUR

Robbins had given his coat a vigorous brushing while Murray washed carefully and pulled on a fresh linen shirt, clamping the high collar around his throat with a clean black neckcloth. Robbins thought his master looked older, and did not wonder at it.

Robert and Henry had waited for him, so all three were late at the Tontine Hotel. Murray felt ashamed at the kindly reproachful looks of his father's friends, all there before their host. David Thomson was the first to ask, avuncular hand on arm, if anything had happened to detain him.

'An accident,' Murray said briefly. 'An accident at home, to one of the servants.' He was looking about him as he spoke, checking to see that all were there who had been asked, finding himself shouldering small and unlooked-for responsibilities. A huge pool in his mind was completely empty, had been since the moment his father's doctors had declared him dead. It was as if he was busy trying to fill it, but all he was succeeding in doing was cluttering the shoreline.

'Nothing serious, I hope?' asked Dundas, smoothly. Charles gave him a brief, bright, smile, and found Mrs. Freeman to lead in to supper.

The meal was passable, the wine good, and the party, although still dressed in black, was beginning to take on the air of a normal supper engagement. While Murray felt disinclined to talk, his neighbours were poles apart: Lady Sarah Dundas was her normal monosyllabic self on his left, and on his right Mrs. Freeman, Alester Blair's widowed sister, spoke about a hundred words to Lady Sarah's one but with slightly less useful content. Hers was not the kind of conversation to stimulate a weary head. Murray often wished he had known Blair's parents, to find out if he could how one family could produce two such disparate intellects. Blair was an intelligent man, though he could be called eccentric, and certainly Murray's grand tour, made several years previously under Blair's unique guidance, had not been entirely conventional. There had been the back streets of Seville, for instance, and the Señora's flowerpots and the two gentlewomen from Bath whose good opinion of Scotsmen had undoubtedly been shattered forever. There was the incident of the geese in St. Mark's Square, when Charles, helpless with laughter and crippled by embarrassment, had followed Blair's fleeing coat tails, picking up the scattered contents of his pockets which had included, he remembered with sudden clarity, an egg (fortunately hard boiled), two withered rosebuds, and a well-thumbed pamphlet on the advantages of planting Swedish turnips.

Mrs. Freeman was eager to be up to date.

'Now, your two young charges – the Scoggies?'

'That's right.' Murray wondered what he was going to do with them.

'They are the boys you've been tutoring in Fife?'

'Yes, ma'am.' A familiar defensive feeling came over him. He could almost feel his lips forming the usual apology. 'Yes, my charges – yes, yes, so sorry. Of course – any reparation you might feel to be appropriate ...'

'The elder – Henry, is it? – seems most promising ...' Mrs. Freeman's eyes lingered on poor Henry. Apart from the ferrets he was much less trouble than Robert. He would have gone to the funeral if Murray had asked him, and had sat up all night with the body: Robert had taken the first opportunity to head for bed.

'Yes, Henry is a fine boy,' he agreed. 'They are both, ah – talented in their different ways.'

'Oh, yes: the younger is also ...' Mrs. Freeman tailed off, staring at Robert. Blair leaned across the table quietly, opening his watery eyes wide.

'The younger is also very young, my dear. And quite challenging, in his way, I believe?'

Murray blinked: Blair always seemed to know everything about everyone before anyone else. Mrs. Freeman clutched at the lace at her throat and looked dismayed. She was silent for a moment. Dr. Inglis, seeing a rare opportunity, drew her attention in his direction with a wave of his fork.

'Now, Mrs. Freeman, did you read that pamphlet I sent you about the missions to India, ma'am?'

Murray smiled inwardly. Robert had told him about Gavin Dundas' successful bet earlier, and wondered if he had repeated the experiment. Willie Jack would have been foolish to take him up on it again, anyway.

Robert Scoggie was near the far end of the table, between Willie Jack's older brother, Harry, and the eldest Miss Balneavis. Mrs. Balneavis had cried off sick, apparently, but the daughters were out in force, probably with full instructions. The next Miss Balneavis, Miss Helen, sat across the table. She was possessed of a rounded fairness that promised a middle age running to fat, and a perplexed innocence that seemed constantly overwhelmed by the world. At present, surrounded by the two younger Mr. Dundases, Helen, new to society, was so muddled by the sophistication of the Dundases, their reputed importance, and their proximity, in addition to her awareness of the impoverished status of her own prospects, that she could scarcely eat, and when one of the gentlemen directed at her any simple remark or question she could venture a reply only in the form of a nod or shake of the head.

For Mr. Gavin Dundas in particular, the contrast between Helen on his right and Davina, Miss Thomson, on his left, could not have been more pointed. Gavin saw himself as a wit and probably the most eligible bachelor at the table: John Douglas was his father's age and therefore past all thoughts of women, and his own brother Harry, who might have been considered fit competition, was himself nearing thirty and was besides as dull as a Sunday evening in Wamphray. Davina Thomson had inherited her mother's sharp good looks, fine eyes, and dark brown hair, and possessed, moreover, a wicked wit that licked like wildfire at the tinder of anyone else's stupidity, plainness or other social inadequacy. She possessed the ability to draw those around her into a conspiracy of venom that was all the more contagious for being funny. Gavin Dundas thought her splendid, a fit foil for his own clever remarks, and he performed with her a duet of delighted vitriol for the benefit of those he reckoned privileged to hear. Henry Scoggie on her left was silent, and Miss Balneavis, the eldest, smiled occasionally when she thought one remark to be kinder than the rest: both of them seemed intensely uncomfortable. Robert found Miss Balneavis on his left, who agreed with everything he said, pleasant but dull, and he had the impression that her mind was elsewhere. Instead, he talked to Harry Dundas on his right, feeling rather grand at fourteen to be holding his own here. Harry turned out to have an interest in horses, and Robert was interested in having an interest, when he could eventually afford it, so they found that, at least, in common.

Horses were also the subject under discussion further up the table.

'Out of Miss Whip,' David Thomson was saying with enthusiasm, 'by Scorpion. A lovely ride. I got her at Wordsworth's repository last February. Twenty-eight pounds and seventeen shillings. She's been worth every penny.'

'That was the Pencaitland sale, was it?' asked Dundas.

'That's right. And one of the fillies is up again. Two year old, now, went for twenty pounds as a one year old. You should buy her, Armstrong. And there are some grand little spaniels up at the same sale.'

'Oh, I don't know,' said Armstrong anxiously into his boiled chicken. When his friend Thomson's powers of persuasion were at their strongest, his freckled face grew pale and powdery. Why could he not stand up to him? What was he – a rumble of dyspepsia held together with a half-decent coat?

'Why is the filly up for sale again so soon?' asked Dundas cannily.

'Oh, wouldn't a spaniel be lovely, Mr. Armstrong, dear?' cried his wife. She sat at David Thomson's elbow and did not miss a word of the conversation, while dissecting her fowl with sharp efficiency.

'The auction is next Wednesday,' added Thomson, plumply persuasive.

'Och, to be honest, Thomson,' said Armstrong with a sigh, 'I can't afford it, neither horse nor dog, not and everything else, too. I've been thinking of buying some land in the new development up at Newington. They're going to start selling the feus this year.'

'Newington?' Thomson was astonished. He glanced across at his own wife, Armstrong's sister-in-law, but she was deep in conversation with Dr. Harker.

'Yes, nice little estates, they seem. I thought it might do the family good, a breath of air, green fields, that kind of thing.'

'But I thought you were going to take one of the new houses in Charlotte Square?' Thomson, who lived in George Street himself, had been looking forward to having his friend move into the vicinity.

'Ah, well, now, Charlotte Square ...' Armstrong tailed off awkwardly. 'We can't really afford –'

'Nonsense, man. You can't afford not to,' said Thomson good-humouredly. Elizabeth Armstrong hid her embarrassment with skill and eyed her sister, who was still, thankfully, apparently engrossed in Dr. Harker's account of something medical. Elizabeth Armstrong considered her marriage to have been her one significant mistake. It had seemed like a good one, until her younger sister had trumped her with Thomson. Thomson was still speaking. 'Think of your daughters – you'll never get them married off from some farm yard building site.' He smiled the smile of a man with one daughter married and the other unlikely to give cause for concern in that direction. 'Invest in the New Town,' he went on. 'The air's better, and they could go on expanding at Newington forever, while here there's a limit to what they can do. The countryside will never be far away.'

'They're talking of building further north even than the new feus in Queen Street.' John Douglas made a brief contribution to the discussion and returned to his own brand of ominous silence.

'Oh, that,' said Thomson dismissively. 'They'll never get the land for it, not down there. Queen Street will have a clear view to the sea for as long as the sea is there. No,' he returned to Armstrong, 'invest in the New Town. It's solid, been around for years. You don't know what will happen at Newington. The whole scheme could fall through.' His heavy round eyes were half-lidded in relaxed self-assurance. Armstrong wiped his mouth diffidently on his napkin. The curry sauce was heading down towards his stomach in a faintly menacing fashion. He noticed that he had spilled a little on the knee of his passable black breeches, and worry creased his amiable face.

'Well, James Reid is involved, and he's in the Exchequer.'

'And the other man is Bell, isn't it? A surgeon, eh? Bone-sawing body snatcher, no doubt – saving your presence, ladies,' he added facetiously. His breeches were no doubt spotless, thought Armstrong, and his tailor would have charged a good deal more for them than for Armstrong's own.

'They've been planning it for years,' said Dundas, his own black just as crisp and dark. Armstrong sighed inwardly. 'Bell has bought up all the land himself, now. I might think of investing a little there myself. A feu, or maybe two. St. Andrew's Square is all very well for business time, but a little place in the country, without having to travel far, would be very charming.'

Lady Sarah Dundas, caught in a gentle flow of conversation from Blair, looked sick. She was a woman who had once been the toast of Edinburgh, her beauty the kind that even other women hardly envy but must instead wonder at and delight in, as anyone might delight in the beauty of a flower or a view without wishing in utter futility that one could also possess that beauty. Yet while Elizabeth and Catherine Fleming, now Mrs. Armstrong and Mrs. Thomson, had possessed only ordinary loveliness, they had defeated the onslaughts of middle age simply, it seemed, by the expedient of ignoring them. But Sarah Dundas' once bright eyes were now dull, her high cheekbones stark, her smooth, glowing complexion dry and tired, her hair, once reddish blonde, quite white and confused with the lace of her cap. Though his father had often commented on it with sadness, Murray could even mark the decline through his own memory. His father, he remembered, had spoken of some family tragedy, which had reduced Lady Sarah to the husk of what she had once been. Yet she still entertained, and went about in society, and Murray wondered with a shiver what it might be like to possess beauty and to watch it fade in the reflections of the eyes of others.

Blair, he noticed, was always at his kindliest with Lady Sarah, and drew from her occasional whole sentences, and the memory of a smile. Seeing Murray glance at them, Blair tugged him into the conversation.

'I was just remarking to Lady Sarah how well the building work is going at the other end of Queen Street. You have no notion, of course, but I am ancient, now, and can well remember when this was all farmland, and whole idea of building here was a midnight fantasy at a town council meeting.'

'Oh, come, Mr. Blair,' replied Lady Sarah, lightly for her, 'you are scarcely that old.'

'Aye, aye, I am, ma'am. I am the Old Man of George's Square, and I shall sit in splendour and wear a turban, and smoke my pipe and the giddy youth of Edinburgh will come to crave the favour of my advice and wisdom.' Blair beamed, and jiggled happily in his chair. He was the only man at the table wearing a wig, and it sat with an inevitable lopsidedness on his head as if it were a bag of ice he was using to draw off a hangover. A thought seemed to strike him as he mumbled his way through a mouthful of food.

'The notary – was it a notary? What was his name?'

Murray floundered.

'Who?'

'The notary who was found dead where your father had his accident.' Murray felt something almost physical hit his stomach. The rest of the table seemed to have fallen silent. Thomson, Armstrong and Dundas glanced at Blair then exchanged looks of despair and irritation. They had been trying to avoid the subject of old Murray's death: the funeral was done, after all, let the son mourn in peace. Blair, however, had not been party to this policy and Thomson knew they should have had a word with him beforehand. It was not as if he could be relied upon to behave in a normal manner.

Blair was oblivious, and mashed his food happily behind closed but alarmingly mobile lips, waiting for a response. Murray strove to find any memory at all of what had been said to him about the other victim of his father's accident, and through his dismay grew irritation, first at Blair for being so indelicate as to ask, to remind him – as if he needed reminding – that his father was dead, and then irritation at himself, a dissatisfaction that in his concern over the endless details of his own mourning, he had forgotten his duty to the man and the family of the man who had died where his father had begun his own dying.

'I believe it was a notary,' he said at last, remembering something Mrs. Chambers had told him on the morning he had arrived from Fife. 'I am afraid that I cannot recall ever having heard the name.'

'Not exactly Ebenezer Hammond, then,' Thomson remarked, naming the most prominent notary of the day.

'Matthew Muir,' came an absent voice from further down the table. Blair turned, and Dundas looked up, apologetic. 'I believe his name was Matthew Muir. There was an account of the accident in the newspapers,' he explained.

'Was there?' Murray was surprised. He had not seen the death of his father as something affecting more than the two dozen people here with him, and had not, himself, seen the newspapers since he had arrived. He wondered if he should try to obtain a copy, then felt slightly sick at the thought.

'It is a curious fate,' said Blair, contemplatively, 'that leaves one man dead and the other dying. Did it say where he lived?'

Dundas shrugged.

'Somewhere about the Grassmarket, I believe.'

'That sounds familiar,' agreed Murray, 'though I'm not sure why.' He could go there tomorrow, he thought, adding it to the long mental list of duties he had to perform now that he was released from his dead room watching. He was grateful for them, the litter on the shore, a framework in which to hang an empty day. An empty day could so easily be devoted to an intense contemplation of just how unready he felt to deal with Letho and the Queen Street house and his father's various interests and investments, while part of him cried out unexpectedly to be back in Fife, ideally a week ago before his father had died, with all his duties for Lord Scoggie but so few responsibilities, so few difficult, unfamiliar decisions. How could his father have taken this last petty revenge, dying before Charles felt anywhere near ready to deal with it?

The party broke up at a decorous hour as befitted a funeral supper. Prince's Street was still busy, but the dark hulk of the old town above it was distinguishable against the night sky only by the lights prickling the tall buildings. Murray bade farewell to his guests, seeing them into their carriages or into chairs from the rank further down the street, refusing or postponing several kind invitations to supper that evening. Blair's was the least pressing invitation, but, he felt, the most warmly meant, and the resentment that he had built up against Blair in the course of the dinner dissipated much of its energy in confusion. Blair and his sister left last, and Murray watched their shadowy carriage trundle towards the North Bridge, back to the old town. To avoid passing the Dundases as they alighted in St. Andrew's Square, Murray steered the boys around and up Hanover Street, over the brow of the hill and down to Queen Street. Robert was full of chat about horses: Henry was unusually silent, even for him. Murray noted both but his mind left the note somewhere in the heap of jetsam on the shore.

Mrs. Chambers met them at the door and herself helped to remove their overcoats. Jamie Paterson's parents had arrived downstairs in the kitchen, she explained, where she, helped by Mrs. Mutch and Mary, had begun to lay out Jamie's body. His parents had insisted on taking him home, despite pressing invitations to stay at least until daylight, and Mrs. Chambers had seen fit to lend them a spare blanket to cover the poor child on their long walk back to the Grassmarket. Murray nodded his approval, and sent the boys to bed.

A fire had been lit in the street parlour, and he made his way there. The hound, Squirrel, was near the fire but scuttled under the table when he entered, and refused to come out. He sighed, and threw himself into one of the comfortable armchairs by the fire, with a footstool set just near enough.

He pondered a little on the deaths of his father, his stable boy and the unknown notary, before he finally succumbed to the unutterable weariness that had held him in its fleecy grip for days.

The scrape of shovel on bucket woke him with a start. A maid was attending to the darkened fire, crouching in grey wool topped with a bulky mob cap. This was not Jennet, whom he knew and whom he had seen in the dead room. He moved slightly and she heard him, rose and curtsied, and made to go. He was surprised to see her almost as tall as he was, with a pale complexion in which her triangular eyebrows and the dark half-moon lashes of her downcast eyes stood out like penstrokes in Indian ink. He turned his automatic wave of dismissal into a signal to pause, astonished at his father's having employed such an extraordinary-looking creature.

'What is your name?' he asked her.

'Mary, sir.' She gave the first syllable the long, flat sound of the Islander.

'And where are you from, Mary?'

'I am from North Uist, sir.'

'North Uist?' He nodded at her, and struggled for some subject of conversation, some human contact. 'Do you speak Gaelic, then?'

'It is the language I learned as a child, sir. English I learned when I came to Edinburgh.' She seemed neither embarrassed nor flattered by his curiosity, nor did anything in her tone show that she thought him anything but an equal.

'What brought you to Edinburgh, then?'

'Oh, it is a common thing, sir. My young man followed the colours, and I followed my young man. The recruiting sergeant came to Uist with a fine drummer, and both of them in their red coats, and my Roderick he was taken with it. So off he went and me after him.' She glanced at him, bright eyes checking his face. He nodded slightly, and she continued. 'But they were sent to the Low Countries, the Ross-shire Buffs, with my Roderick, and I was not on the strength and could not go, and here I am.'

'I thought that the service companies of the Seventy-Eighth had returned?' He longed for her to go on speaking. Her accent, simmered with the liquid Gaelic, had all but broken down the hard fibres of Edinburgh Scots.

'Oh, aye, they have, sir. But not my Roderick. And there are some of his friends that say he died a hero's death, and some that he's living yet, on his way to the Cape with a Dutch wife to his children. Ah, but who would you believe?' She dropped a somewhat informal curtsey that passed for both shrug and farewell, took the coal bucket and left the room, which suddenly seemed larger and darker for her absence.

Although he waited for her to reappear, and nearly rang for her, it was Jennet who brought and served his supper, her eyes red with weeping over Jamie and her hands, when not occupied with dishes, clutching a handkerchief to her nose. Nor was Mary in evidence when Mrs. Chambers informed him that the master bedroom was made up and ready, and Murray, with no recognition of the effort to which she and the maids had gone to remove the black hangings and make up the bed in fresh sheets and drive out the stale air, insisted on returning to the room he had always slept in, where the cool green stripes of the bed hangings calmed him like summer pasture. Had Mary been a dream? If so, it had been an interesting dream. He fell asleep quickly, hoping that he could slip back into it.

CHAPTER FIVE

When Murray woke the next day, it was to the indefinable feeling that he had overslept. Someone had already drawn the green silk curtains and lit the fire, and a low sun angled its way through the north-facing window. He pulled his long legs from under the covers, dragged a dressing gown around his shoulders and walked towards the sunlight, tugging, on his way, on the bell pull to summon hot water to his closet. There was a jug of cold water there already, and he dipped his hands into its icy depths, feeling the hard pain in his fingers, before splashing it across his face. Once he had rubbed his eyes and cheeks, he approached the window and propped himself comfortably against its panelled surround.

It was one of those days that Scotland in January produces like a glittering prize, a reminder to winter-bound dwellers in darkness not to lose all hope of Spring. The sunlight fell like a beaten blade along the streets he could see below, startling ice sheets in the gutter puddles into burning life. Winter, the overhung, muddied byway of the year's passage, had its sudden consolations, and this was the best. All the way to the sparkling Forth, the land lay jewelled with bright greens and browns, encrusted with white, striped with long shadows where the merest bush or hillock took the opportunity to make its mighty mark far across the land. In the distance, the hills of Fife stood green and clear, and called to him.

A sound at the door heralded Robbins, bearing a large jug of hot water and several clean cloths. Murray wished him good morning, and asked him, as Robbins laid out the shaving accoutrements, how the servants were.

'Quite all right, sir. Everything is just as usual.'

'And Dunnet?' Murray asked cautiously.

'Dr. Harker gave him some laudanum to make him sleep last night, sir. He appears to be carrying out his duties normally this morning.'

'Yes,' said Murray slightly irritably, 'but is he all right?' At Scoggie Castle he could simply have gone down to the servants' hall and found out for himself, but here he was master, and therefore much more constrained. Robbins paused, and gazed down at the shaving brush in his hand, his lips pressed together.

'Yes, sir, I believe so.' He stopped again. 'I should say, sir, if you'll excuse the liberty, that with Dunnet to know whether or not he is all right is more a matter of observation than of direct information, sir. Dunnet is very quiet this morning. He often is.'

He worked up a quantity of foam and began, expertly, to spread it in little circles over Murray's chin. Murray sat back, tried to relax, and closed his eyes.

He saw Dunnet, crouching over Jamie Paterson's body, and heard the doctor clearing him from blame.

He saw Dunnet again, leaving his father at the building site, and seeing his father return home on a board, and heard his father, with his dying breath, clearing Dunnet from blame.

He opened his eyes, and watched Robbins sharpen the razor's blade.

'The man who died with my father,' he said quickly, before Robbins began to apply the blade to his face, 'What can you tell me about him?'

Robbins raised his eyebrows and began to shave his new master.

'A Mr. Muir, I believe, sir. The newspaper said that he was a notary and lived with his brother in the Grassmarket. He was a young man, as I recall, sir.' He cleared his throat. 'He was killed outright.'

'So I believe,' Murray responded, taking his chance as Robbins flicked soap from the blade. 'Was he there alone?'

'That I cannot say, sir. Although, if you'll excuse it, sir, and I have not, of course, said such a thing to the servants' hall, it seems a strange thing that a few stones, however poorly balanced, should wait until two people came along on a quiet street before they fell down.'

'Quite,' said Murray, out of the corner of his mouth.

The street parlour had been laid for breakfast for Murray and the boys, and a newspaper had been set by his plate. Beyond the front page intimations and advertisements, the main news item inside was the illness of William Pitt, which did not appear to be responding to treatment. Murray found himself assuming that the politician was going to die: it seemed the usual thing to do, just at present.

Robert and Henry appeared, Robert his usual unstoppable self, and Henry smelling faintly of the stables.

'I'll escort you to your classes after breakfast,' Murray informed them. Robert let out a cry of protest, but Henry looked relieved.

Mary surprised him – and slightly embarrassed him – by proving to be real, and cleared away the dishes. Unable to think of anything to say to her, Murray smiled as he chivvied the boys off to fetch their coats and books. He was not sure they could both be trusted to attend all their classes without supervision, but he had plenty to do and he did not want Robert leading either Daniel or William into more trouble than they could find on their own.

By the time his father's Edinburgh lawyer had arrived at ten, Murray had returned and found, as promised, his father's will in the bookcase. The lawyer, Mr. Simpson, was relieved.

'I know well Mr. Murray was versed in the law, and not like to cause trouble, but with his death being so sudden, I was afraid we'd have to present a testament dative and have executors appointed by the Commissary Court. It can take years, with an estate as large as Mr. Murray's.'

'And now that we have a will?' asked Murray, avoiding his mind's-eye magpie nest view of his father's large and complex estate. It could not, he told himself, be much worse than the Scoggie estates: he had been dealing with the papers there for some years.

'Well, for our heritable goods – the money, the furniture, and so on, all our moveables – I shall take our will with me and visit the Commissary Office in the morning. We shall need to employ a valuer to draw up an inventory here and one at Letho, and assess what is owed to our various tradesmen and others: I fear that even I myself must present my own modest bill.' He simpered, and pressed well-manicured fingers gently into the black silk of his neckcloth. Murray made a brief note. All this was new to him, and although he knew his father had trusted Mr. Simpson, the man made Charles' skin crawl and therefore, unfairly, made him wary of being cheated by him.

'That's the moveable goods. I shall write today to my father's man of affairs at Letho to arrange for a valuation there.'

'Now, then.' Mr. Simpson laced his hands over his knee. 'For our immoveables, it will be the Chancery. A retour, or service of the heir, will have to be formulated, establishing that you are indeed your father's nearest heir. As I understand it, you are the elder son?'

Murray nodded.

'I have one brother who is younger. There are no other brothers, and no sisters.'

'Oh, sisters do not count where immoveable goods are concerned, Mr. Murray.' Mr. Simpson gave a little chuckle. 'Not where there are sons. However, it is worth noting, as I see that Mr. Murray's will is therefore quite straightforward. No need to make provisions for dowries, a few simple legacies to servants and to one or two friends, and a substantial sum to Mr. George Murray, younger son. You will want an advance of the money to pay for household expenses, and so on, I have no doubt, and as there does not seem to be any difficulty with the inheritance, there will be no obstacle to your remaining here – or at Letho – until the estate is confirmed. Now, as a matter of interest,' he unlaced and rewove the long, clammy fingers, 'how do you see matters proceeding when that has occurred?'

'I shall have to quit my position in Fife, of course,' said Murray, 'but I have not yet decided whether to reside chiefly here or at Letho. I assume that you are willing, for the foreseeable future, at least, to attend to my affairs here? I may wish to set this house up for rent, for example.'

Mr. Simpson smiled, as though to encourage a slow pupil.

'Precisely, Mr. Murray, precisely. In our own time.'

'But,' said Charles, 'I cannot, of course, make any firm decision until I have seen all the papers involved in both properties and in my father's investments.' Mr. Simpson's smile faded, and his orange eyebrows flexed slightly. Murray remembered that as a little boy he had been fascinated by the close similarity between Mr. Simpson's hair and orange marmalade. He and George had always wanted to put out fingers and discover whether or not it was sticky. 'So I suggest, Mr. Simpson, that you employ your valuer and approach your Commissary Court and your Chancery, and I shall study my papers and make my decisions, and we shall meet again in a week.'

'Oh, very good, very good.' Mr. Simpson pressed his palms together and spread his finger tips wide, though there was a faint scowl on his face. 'And is there anything else just now, Mr. Murray?'

'Yes,' said Murray, after a moment's thought. 'Do you know of a notary called Muir? Possibly Matthew Muir?'

Mr. Simpson frowned, clearly worried about possible competition.

'Why do you ask?'

Murray pushed his chair back from the desk, and contemplated the lawyer. It would be nice to dismiss him, he thought, but perhaps not yet. He was not good at burning boats.

'He died in the same accident that caused my father's injuries. I wished to pay my respects to his family.'

Mr. Simpson looked relieved, then thoughtful.

'Matthew Muir,' he repeated. 'Matthew Muir. No, I cannot recollect any notary of that name. He is not in the Society, anyway. I could ask Ebenezer Hammond for you, if you wished it. As the head of the Signet – and by way of being the principal lawyer in the city - he would know, if anyone did.'

Odd, thought Murray. The Writers to the Signet controlled the business of notaries and lawyers in Scotland, as the Faculty of Advocates, the spiritual home of Dundas, Thomson and Armstrong and of his own father, controlled the advocates at the bar. Yet the papers had reported that Matthew Muir was a notary.

The lawyer was packing up his papers into a box, and laid old Mr. Murray's will on the top before tipping down the lid. He nodded at Murray and stretched out one pale hand. Murray rose and took it, feeling that even that was more commitment than he cared for towards Mr. Simpson just at present.

'May I congratulate you, Mr. Murray,' the lawyer added as he turned to go, 'on an excellent funeral yesterday. Everything just as it should be. Your father would have been proud.'

'Thank you.' Murray was embarrassed, and pleased when the man finally bowed and left.

The remainder of the morning was taken up with going through the immaculate order of his father's bureau, thin folds of paper in neat bundles, servants' wages, accounts paid to Dr. Harker, to Mr. Simpson – far too much, Murray felt – to wine merchants and grocers, ironmongers and carriage builders. Some were endorsed with Mrs. Chambers' signature, all had to do with Queen Street and Edinburgh, and Murray assumed that the Letho papers were kept at Letho itself. He glanced through the servants' wages. Mary Macdonald, he noted, had been employed since October – presumably when his father had moved back to Edinburgh for the winter season. According to a note made on her first wage receipt by Mrs.

Chambers, she could both read and write. Clearly her time in Edinburgh had been well employed since she came from Uist, unless she could only read and write Gaelic.

In the final drawer, he found gathered into heaps, neatly labelled in his father's black hand, all the letters his brother George had written from various parts of the world, and all the letters he himself had written, from Spain, from Italy, from Germany, and from St. Andrews. No letters from Lord Scoggie's castle: he had never been able to bring himself to put them in the post. Had his father missed them? By the look of this collection, maybe he had – maybe he, too, had regretted their quarrel.

'Well, my dear Catherine, is not Mr. Murray everything a woman desires? Dark eyes and hair, a fine figure, a romantic air of tragedy, and now his father's fortune on top?' Miss Davina Thomson arranged herself on one end of a chaise longue and patted the other end for Catherine Armstrong to be seated. Catherine, having spent the morning in perusal of a section of Cicero's *Pro Caelio*, had arrived for dinner, but clearly she would have shift her focus from scandalous Roman law courts to the gossip of the present before she was to be fed. Davina had picked up her embroidery, but was watching Catherine's face. Catherine sat, and adjusted her shawl.

'Mr. Murray? His air of tragedy must be a temporary thing, and his fortune may have enhanced his appearance, but you could not call him handsome, Davina dear.' Davina was her best friend, but it did not do to compliment anyone or anything in from of her. Catherine had come to the conclusion that for Davina, to admire was to show weakness. Besides, Davina might have been her best friend, but that was no reason to trust her.

'Not handsome?' Davina was all amazement. Catherine steadfastly kept her gaze on her own embroidery.

'His nose, I fear, is on rather too grandiose a scale for the rest of his face. And his mouth – well, his mouth is far from perfect.'

Davina laughed, and began to ply her needle.

'But what woman desires perfection in the looks of a man,

Catherine? Very few, which is just as well, as there are few enough perfect-looking men to go round.' She paused, but Catherine knew better than to interrupt. 'And a great number of the perfect-looking ones have too good an idea of their own perfection to suit me.'

'Oh, indeed!' Catherine responded. Long experience of both Cicero and Davina had taught her when response was expected. 'But,' she added, as if forcing herself to be charitable, 'it should be said that whatever the faults of his appearance, Mr. Murray appears to be a kindly, gentlemanly young man, of an open and generous disposition.' She finished firmly, snipping at a thread with her scissors.

'Catherine, my dear!' Davina laughed. 'You sound as if you would write his epitaph. Mr. Murray, I am sure, is quite handsome enough to please any but those most afraid of having their taste doubted – or those already too fond of one man to find any other remotely pleasing.' Davina was pleased to perceive a very slight blush on the perfect cheeks of her friend, who continued to concentrate her gaze on her embroidery.

'How many shall we be for dinner?' she asked, after a proper pause.

'Oh,' said Davina, 'we are waiting for Miss Balneavis. Mamma has a headache and says she will not join us.'

'Miss Balneavis?' Catherine was surprised.

'Oh, Mamma's idea, of course,' Davina replied. 'She sees it as a charity to the poor girl.'

'Well, I know the Balneavises are dreadfully poor, but surely they are not yet on the parish? Are we to take soup to the rest of the family?'

'No, but really, Catherine, the poor girl seems to think that a kind of pious amiability is as good as a dowry.' Davina had noted Margaret Balneavis' stiff reaction to her witty remarks at supper.

'I suppose in some cases it might be,' said Catherine, deliberately dubious.

'But not, my dear, when you have the looks of the milkmaid and the sense of the cow. And speaking of marriage, how does your sister Ella do?'

'Oh! much the same,' Catherine replied. 'She is not as distressed as Mamma feels she should be, that I am out before she is married. But there! I do not believe she cares to marry.'

'Oh, really?' asked Davina, sorting that scrap of information into a mental deedbox.

'She is too like Papa. It is from him that she has her quiet disposition, her wish not to be noticed, which is so irritating. And, of course, her regrettable freckles and her sandy hair.' Almost unconsciously, she tilted her pure creamy face towards the light. Davina had the same colouring, but her face was sharper, thought Catherine, and of course, that little bit older.

The street bell rang, and after a moment a smartly-dressed maid announced Miss Balneavis. Davina rolled her eyes at Catherine, and they stood to greet the innocent victim of their unwilling charity.

Miss Balneavis' father, visible through the crush of lawyers by his fire-red face and the bouncing wave of cheeriness surrounding him, was making his way across the coffee house to where Thomson and Armstrong were waiting for him. The corner table was their usual one, and whichever of them was free from duties in the Law Courts up the High Street was usually to be found there. The irrepressible Balneavis was in fact almost resident at the corner table, spinning out a pot of coffee the length of the day if need be: he had fewer and shorter cases than the others, and not much room in his overcrowded tenement to attract the business he needed. Armstrong and Thomson considered him more unfortunate than incompetent: unfortunate to have married for love where money did not follow; unfortunate to number four daughters among his seven children, unfortunate to lack influence in society, and unfortunate to be brought up to advocacy in a town where advocates ruled and standards were high. In Perth or Glasgow, he might have done well enough. Yet he seemed persistently happy, and today, when he had had work and had done it well, his face in the tallow light shone like the city illuminations for the Battle of

Trafalgar: Thomson reckoned you could charge a shilling a head for the spectacle.

'Well, well, a splendid funeral yesterday for Murray, eh?' Balneavis asked as he took his seat. 'Everything as it should be, and an excellent meal. I was telling Mrs. Balneavis again this morning, an excellent meal. We are so lucky in our review of past pleasures.'

'Oh, aye,' said Armstrong, for whom the dinner was still very much a present evil. 'Fortune's knows how to lay on the comestibles. But a sad day, too.'

'Oh, yes, oh, yes,' Balneavis' dismay was brief. 'No sign of our friend Dundas yet, then?'

'He's in the middle of conferring with Montgomery about the Campbell case. It could be a good thing for Dundas if he manages it well.' Thomson absently penned a note in the margin of a speech he was preparing. 'Not that Dundas needs much more success. He could retire nicely on what he has, to judge from his way of living.'

'Aye,' said Armstrong, managing not to sound bitter. 'Though using his well-kent surname might not be so good an idea soon, if what they're saying about Henry Dundas of Melville is true. Misappropriation of public funds while he was Lord of the Admiralty – how would the Lord Lyon represent that heraldically?'

'Oh, on a fess argent a pocket filled with filthy lucre proper, and a hand gules,' Thomson chuckled. Their friend Dundas had recently applied, with the appropriate fee, to the Lyon King of Arms for his own heraldry, just before the scandal concerning his cousin Viscount Melville had come to light. 'But Melville will not be charged,' he asserted. 'And if he is, he will not be convicted.'

'Not even if there is a Whig government?' asked Armstrong quietly.

'Aye, I hear Pitt is not like to recover,' added Balneavis, at the same volume.

'There will be no Whig government till Bonaparte is dead.' Thomson did not even bother to look up from his work. 'It is too much of a risk to bring in reform at home when the army is overseas. Sir Ilay said the same thing to me himself the other day.'

Armstrong looked dubious, Balneavis plumply reassured.

'Now,' said Balneavis, 'turning to more important issues than the governing of the country. How can I marry my pretty daughter Margaret to Charles Murray's heir? For he's the only young man I know rich enough to take her without a dowry, and you know how delightful that sounds to my poor old ears.'

'What about one of the Dundases? They're well to do.'

'Oh, Gavin and Willie Jack are still bairns – well, Willie Jack is, and Gavin acts like one. Harry, now, is the right age, and steady, though a dull boy. Not stupid, but dull.'

Armstrong, ever cautious, glanced around to see if any Dundas was about.

'Young Murray is five years her senior, surely?'

'Aye, true enough, true enough. But I think that is a good age difference. Or perhaps he would take one of the younger ones? and Harry Dundas could have Margaret?' He smiled dreamily. 'She'd be a good daughter to look after me in my old age, but I'd sooner move to her household than keep her in mine.'

'I take your meaning,' said Armstrong, thinking of his own daughter Ella. His wife constantly despaired of the girl, but there was a steadiness about her that he liked, a calmness and a kindness that he feared his younger daughter Catherine lacked. He felt in his heart that Ella would never marry, and it grieved him deeply.

'Oh, I have some news,' said Thomson suddenly, putting up his papers. 'You remember young Murray was late for supper yesterday evening? Well, here is the reason: his stable boy was found murdered in his very stable!'

'His stable boy?' repeated Balneavis. 'That's dreadful.' His kindly face was briefly distraught.

'Aye, I had it from one of my servants this morning.'

'And you've never mentioned it till now?' Armstrong was curious.

'Forgot,' stated Thomson, waving his speech. 'Mind on other things.'

'Och, poor Charles,' said Armstrong, taking a sip of wine and regretting it, as it burned a path down to his disturbed stomach. 'Tragedy on tragedy. Do they know who murdered him?'

'Well, apparently the groom was found with the body, but the doctor says he could not have done it. The wee lad was cold when they found him. The groom has been acting very strangely, they say.'

'Aye, well,' Armstrong swallowed, to try to dilute the fatefully settling wine. 'I daresay it'll come up before one of us before long. Horse thieves, most likely.'

'But it does make you wonder,' said Thomson, rising to go, 'it does shed an unfortunate light on the death of Murray himself. After all, murder is one of those unpleasant things that repeat on one. It is difficult to restrict oneself to the one incident.' He paused thoughtfully and buttoned his coat. 'So was Murray murdered, too?'

CHAPTER SIX

As Murray set out along Queen Street in the afternoon sunshine, he felt as if he were conducting some kind of experiment, a test to see how the world would react to the near replication of a set of circumstances. Of course, it was not evening, and he was not his father, but he was going to inspect the building work on the new feus at the far end of the street, and Dunnet was coming with him.

You could fit two St. Andrews streets into the sweeping breadth of Queen Street, he reckoned, and the whole village of St. Monance would be lost between the east end where his father's house stood and the west end where the country began, the Earl of Moray's undulating estates. People he met as he walked noted and nodded at him, acknowledging the black crape weepers and knowing for whom he wore them, though he did not know all of them.

He had not mentioned to Dunnet where they were going, as he had a series of duties in mind of which the visit to the building site was merely the first. The groom, however, who had set out with movements like a child's crude wooden doll nailed at the joints, was becoming increasingly shaky in his walk and, though he had not uttered so much as a syllable to Murray, could now be heard giving an occasional mutter under his breath, as though engaged in conversation with some invisible companion. He walked a pace behind Murray, who, though he had brought the man out for a change of scene as much as for his service, was beginning to find his groom's habits rather disturbing.

At the building site, however, Dunnet became inaudible again, although this was chiefly because the competition was stiff. The noise was astonishing: the shouts of the workmen, the grating of stone against stone as another block was set in place, the singing chisels of the stonemasons working decorative carvings on stones set on wooden runners on the ground, ready to be hoisted into place when they were needed, while their apprentices worked on the simpler tasks of adjustment and basic shaping with bulging wooden mallets. Men slapped horses that hurled themselves against their harness in response, hooves slipping on ground worked into mud, pulling ropes that creaked through tackle high on the wooden scaffolding to hoist stone blocks up to the waiting builders, shirt sleeves peeled back from wind-scoured forearms, who swung the stones into place. Further along the row carpenters worked with saws on floorboards, with hammers and nails on window frames, and blacksmiths, their apprentices dancing around the fires like the devil's own disciples, wrought the elaborate railings and balconies that were slotted in place along the houses like combs in a lady's hair.

'Where did you leave him?' Murray shouted to Dunnet. It did not seem appropriate to shout, but it was that or nothing. Dunnet pointed to the front of a house where the builders were at work on the second floor: there were as yet no window frames, and the top edge of stonework, obscured by scaffolding, was castellated like a ruin. Murray peered up at it, and then looked down about him at the mud where his dying father and the dead notary must have lain, surrounded by toppled stone.

A man in a coat, who had been talking with some of the workmen, saw them and approached, looking somewhere between apologetic and belligerent. When he spoke, his accent was Glaswegian.

'Now, look, gentlemen, I'm sorry to have to say this, but could you move back? Two gentlemen were killed here last week, and if anything happens to anyone else the people who have bought these feus are going to start asking questions.'

'It was the place where the two gentlemen died that we came to see,' said Murray, moving back from the building and waving Dunnet further away.

'Och, not more sightseers!' said the foreman in disbelief. 'Why in the name of Heaven – or are you not sightseers at all?' He was suddenly wary. 'Are you one of the purchasers?'

Murray said,

'How did the accident happen?'

The foreman's whole anxious face became part of his shrug.

'I cannot say, sir. It's very unlikely, but it must be that a stone was left unsecured at the top of the building that evening, and fell. The scaffolding was badly damaged, and most of it fell, too. It was particularly cold that night, and it may be that that unsettled the stones.' Murray felt he could have sounded more reassuring.

'I see,' he said, and smiled at the man, feeling suddenly sorry for him. 'Thank you for your help.' The man nodded, still somewhere between anxious and puzzled. Murray took a final survey of the site from where he stood. A pleasant one, he thought, although the houses would face away from the view of the Forth he cherished.

The cold air and bright sunlight combined made his eyes and nose water, and he reached into his overcoat, and failing that, into his coat pocket, for a handkerchief. His fingers met a series of curious objects, and when he had finished the urgent business with the handkerchief he drew them out and spread them flat on his hand in the sunshine.

The collection surprised him for a moment, until he recollected his climb to Jamie Paterson's lair in the hayloft the evening before. There were in his hand the treasures that Jamie had kept so safely on his windowsill, to see last thing at night and first in the morning. There were a couple of pieces of wood, one roughly painted with his name, the other a piece of bone-white jetsam; there was a large, smooth pebble, probably from the same beach as the driftwood, perhaps both souvenirs of a day at Leith; there was a button, in fancy enamelwork, old rose in colour with a flower cloisonnéed on it, lost from a gentleman's waistcoat and a little scuffed at the edges, where it had survived a life in the gutter before being gathered in by the eager fingers of a young lad. There were a few shells, and the last item was a small piece of leather, expertly worked and stamped with a neat geometric pattern, but the stamp had somehow shifted and spoiled the design, and the piece had been cut away and discarded. There was nothing here of any value, except perhaps the button, but Murray found his spare handkerchief and wrapped them solemnly in it, for they had been his stableboy's most treasured possessions, and he was to take them to him.

After one or two attempts, he caught Dunnet's eye and, turning, led him back to George Street and on to the Old Town.

Margaret Balneavis, privileged to dine with such society darlings as Catherine Armstrong and Davina Thomson, was quiet when she arrived home to the dark stair in the High Street, and the stone steps, worn almost to a continuous slope in two hundred years of use, gave away little of her presence as they met her thin-soled, flat-heeled boots. Her mother, however, had been keeping one ear constantly towards the stair, and the second the risp rattled she was there at the door to answer it, all anxious curiosity, and she bounced the little maid back into the kitchen with a nod of her head.

'Well, my dear girl, how was your meal?' Mrs. Balneavis bustled her out of her bonnet and cloak and into the parlour, a relatively quiet room at this time of day. The younger children and John were still at school, and Helen, released from her morning's sewing, had taken a walk with some friends. The man in the flat across the stair, who made his money by giving fiddle lessons, was out. Upstairs, in the top flat, an elderly and impoverished peer from Ayrshire was bedridden and quietly mad. Margaret went to the window where the sunlight continued to warp the thin panelling of the shutters, and looked down at the bustle of the High Street. One or two of the Dragoons' black horses from the Castle were being ridden cautiously down the hill through the crowds, and when a ray of sunlight caught their furnishings they glittered like creatures from legend. The subalterns on their backs, however, made uneasy trying to control the huge beasts in the crowds, looked more as if they had stepped from a fair, and not in the least worth their eight shillings a day. Margaret smiled and continued to scan the crowds, leaning against the glass to see as closely as possible to their own front door.

'Did you enjoy your visit, dear?' Mrs. Balneavis repeated, plumping an arm around her daughter's waist.

'It was perfectly pleasant, Mamma.' Margaret smiled at her, but met her eye only fleetingly. 'Miss Thomson and Miss Catherine were quite charming.'

'They are, aren't they?' Mrs. Balneavis heaved a deep, happy sigh, and settled in an armchair by the dark fireplace, taking up her mending. 'And both so pretty! But then both their mothers, always so lovely. I remember them, you know, when they were only your age. Oh, it won't be long now till we see fine marriages made in both families, I don't doubt!'

She eyed her daughter speculatively, and saw fair hair and rosy cheeks and a round figure, all just as pleasing to her as Miss Catherine Armstrong and Miss Thomson could ever be. Pleasing, too, to men, she had no doubt, for had not she herself looked just so when Mr. Balneavis had asked her to make him the happiest man in the world?

Margaret came away from the window and seated herself on the edge of one of the hard branderback chairs at the dining table. From habit borne of the self-imposed necessity of making the best of herself, she sat with a perfectly straight back and feet, rather too large for a girl's, neatly side by side, peeping from beneath her grey wool dress. She selected a piece from her own mending pile, a worn sheet from the bed shared by her and her sister Helen in the second bedroom. It would have to be patched, not simply darned. She would have liked to have continued with the pretty embroidery she had taken with her to the Thomsons', a little thing for her own trousseau, but such silks were for company, and here there was work to be done.

'And who else was there?' asked Mrs. Balneavis eventually, after waiting in vain for Margaret to volunteer information. There had been a time when she had despaired of Margaret ever ceasing from talking. Now, even this question seemed to require consideration.

'Oh, no one at the meal, Mamma. Mrs. Thomson sent down to say she was unwell, and I left word with Miss Thomson to say that you sent your best regards, and I was sure you would join me in wishing her a swift recovery. And Miss Armstrong had a prior engagement, so we were a small party altogether.' She glanced at the table as she spoke, remembering the satin-polished mahogany at Thomsons'. The cloth here, a soft green, showed signs of its continuous passage, spinning, like the earth itself, as her mother moved it around the table to let it fade evenly. It had been fading evenly for as long as Margaret could remember.

'That was an intimate arrangement! And lovely for you, my dear.' She took great pleasure in any signs of particular notice of her daughter, real or imagined. 'And after the meal?'

'Mr. Gavin and Mr. William James Dundas called, briefly,' Margaret said. Try as she might, her mother could detect little more than indifference in her daughter's voice.

'Mr. Gavin and Mr. William James! My.' William James was little young, she thought, but a Dundas would be wealthy and elegant, and better than some of the options. 'And Mr. Gavin.' More charming, perhaps, but a little less gravitas. He tended towards fat, but it could be that Margaret liked that in a man – as she herself did, and kept Mr. Balneavis as well fed as was possible. 'And how were they?' she asked.

Margaret cut a careful patch to fit the worn area on the sheet.

'They were in good health, and were both perfectly pleasant.' She glanced at her mother, but her eye was caught by the armchair in which her mother sat awkwardly by custom, on bumpy stuffing and uneven cushions, the cloth of the arms and back patched again and again.

'Perhaps there is a match there for one of the girls,' her mother speculated aloud, 'though Willie Jack is a whiles young to think of marriage yet. Though both are presentable young men,' she added hopefully.

'Yes, Mamma,' was Margaret's dutiful reply.

'And did you meet with anyone else on your travels?'

'I do not believe so. I left shortly after the gentlemen. Wait, though, I saw Mr. Charles Murray on George Street, as I was coming away, and he walked with me to the Tron Kirk.'

Mrs. Balneavis beamed. She thought again of the paradisiacal Letho, and spring weddings, with Mr. Murray mysteriously free of mourning.

'All that way?' she prompted.

'Yes, well, he said he was bound for the Grassmarket. An errand to do with an accident to his stable boy.'

'A very responsible young man,' Mrs. Balneavis decided, after a pause, 'and confiding towards you. And how was he?'

'Very pleasant and charming, Mamma,' Margaret replied obediently. The patch was pinned and she began to sew, in the neat, economical stitches that she had learned so young she could not remember learning them. She thought of Mr. Murray and the ready smile that even when it evaded his mouth was trapped in the sideways flicker of his eyes. She thought of their walk along Prince's Street and up the North Bridge, how he had shortened his stride discreetly to hers even though she felt sure he had business to be about. She thought of her passage up the High Street from the Tron, lingering at the forbidden luxuries of the flower stalls as Murray, bright black in fine mourning, vanished into the crowds of the South Bridge. She remembered delaying about the law courts and coffee houses to greet her father's friends and acquaintances, smiling at neighbours, feeling the cobbles through the soles of her boots. She looked down past her mending at the sensible dark grey cloth of her winter day dress, purchased not to show wear as warmer velvet would, and she felt like weeping, not for her own fate, but out of pity for the shabby, mended, cosseted and dearly loved family belongings around her that Miss Thomson and Miss Catherine, in their fashionable extravagance, in their brittle wit and their privileged beauty, would have gazed at in proud bewilderment. When her mother left the parlour to talk with the maid, she allowed herself another moment to stare out of the window and see, not the tenements opposite, but dark hair and dark eyes that she had seen in living truth only that afternoon, seen to adore forever – but that she had not, despite her mother's daydreams, seen on Mr. Charles Murray of Letho.

Murray almost immediately regretted leaving the amiable Miss Balneavis at the Tron: not, it must be said, for her fair company alone. If he had not had the strong impression that she was tiring of him, his route to the Grassmarket might more easily have gone via the West Bow at the top of the High Street, rather than along the Cowgate Strand, a street he had never liked, or past Greyfriars Kirkyard, the memory of which was a little too fresh in his mind so soon to be revived. He reluctantly selected the Cowgate in preference, and descended by Niddry Street to its cavernous gloom, glad at last to have Dunnet with him. A visit to an old uncle in the decaying gentility of a flat in the Cowgate was one of his earliest memories of Edinburgh, and it was accompanied by memories of the nightmares that followed it, in which his uncle's stuffed owl had featured significantly.

The central drain, fortunately, after so little recent rain, was not as deeply flooded as it could be, and the children of the troglodyte denizens played in it quite safely, where at other times they could have been lost in the flow. Murray kept his gaze on his feet and his hands on his pockets, and his passage meandered, moving to the left to avoid a woman seated with her infant in a doorway, right to dodge something fascinatingly putrid a child had just dragged from the drain, left again to circumambulate the curling tail of a staircase outside the ground floor of one of the older tenements, climbing to disappear into the building on the first floor. When he glanced up, sometimes he saw fine buildings with ancient carved lintels in pious Latin or bold Scots, ornamented gables and delicate finials, and sometimes he saw wrecks of tenements thrown together with little love or care, impossible to date to a century ago or last week. But all were tall, all filthy, cliffs that undercut the distant sunshine and barred it from entry. Once, pausing at the foot of the Parliament Stairs, Murray looked up and saw golden light on the fine south window of the Great Hall of the parliament buildings, but it was so far away that it seemed like an insubstantial vision. He was aware, as so often before, that the old town was not a place for which a map was sufficient: an elevation was also essential.

The same people that bustled around or lurked on corners or sprawled in doorways in the Cowgate spilled into the Grassmarket. Here

the street finally broadened, making the air easier to breathe and the heart
settle to a steady beat. The stern, iron-crossed buildings of the Temple
lands on the south side, built long ago on the property of the Templars and
Hospitallers, were as tall as any in the Cowgate, but here the cave-dwellers
saw the light of day, the brewers and the innkeepers, the faded gentry, the
soldiers with queues of hair they could grease their muskets with, the water
caddies with cloth bound about their hands against the rough straps of their
barrels, the small traders and the stall holders calling out their wares.
Dunnet moved through it all as though through a dream, almost tripping
on a protruding front step had not Murray caught his elbow, as they
approached the curious assortment of buildings west of the Temple lands.
Murray, who had thought that Dunnet knew where Jamie's parents lived,
found out at this point that the groom was as vague as he was himself, so
he stopped one of the busy old water caddies and asked her where the
Patersons lived. 'Their son has just died,' he added, knowing that that
would help. The caddie did not know, said that they were not her
customers, sir, but passed the question on to an even older woman who
pointed them without hesitation to a tenement on the corner of the Vennel,
a long stair climbing south from the Grassmarket, and intimated with the
aid of very few teeth that the family was on the ground floor. Murray
thanked both ladies appropriately and followed the directions.

The street door of the flat stood open, but Murray knocked and
waited for an acknowledging voice before stooping and entering, as
awkward here as no doubt Jamie would have been in his own drawing room
in Queen Street. The door opened directly into the living room. A woman
who sat in a chair by the fire glanced up and rose, alarmed, at the sight of
him, and reached across the small room to shake the shoulder of a man
crouched on a creepie stool. He looked about him in shock and stumbled
to his feet, nodding automatically. Murray bowed, and the woman made a
curtsey, both seeking refuge in custom.

'Mrs. Paterson?' Murray addressed the woman. 'My name is Murray.
My father was until lately your son's employer, and I have come in his
stead, with your permission, to pay my respects.'

There was no question but that this was the right house. Had he not
known it from the piece of black cloth hung over the fireplace, the faded,

shiny mourning of the two adults and the near silence of the three or four children about the place, he could not have failed to see in the recess bed the small, pale figure of Jamie, lying as if asleep in his hayloft, his blonde hair brushed and his grave clothes sitting new and crisp about him. There was no coffin yet: his mother, helped no doubt by the daughter only a little older than Jamie, and perhaps a neighbour, had laid him out and washed him and bought the white cloths to make him look his best. Murray, black weepers trailing from the hat in his hands, felt the echoes and the pathetic contrasts until it was almost too much for him to bear.

'Will you sit down, sir?' asked Mrs. Paterson, showing the seat she herself had vacated, and going to the fire. Murray paused for a second, then explained the shadowy figure behind him.

'May I present William Dunnet, my father's groom, for whom Jamie worked?'

Mrs. Paterson bobbed a smaller curtsey and a look of understanding passed across her face. Here was someone of whom she had heard, someone whose presence she could comprehend. Mr. Paterson, bereft of his creepie stool, hovered by the recess bed, staring down wide-eyed at the corpse of his son, disbelief blotting out all other expression from his face. Murray looked at him for a long moment, taking in the older man's blonde hair and reddened skin, the cheery blue quilt inadequately covered in cheap black cloth, and then he sat in Mrs. Paterson's fireside chair. She brought him ale and oatcake with cheese, and served Dunnet with the same before perching on the creepie stool. She was as pale as her husband, though her hair was darker, and her eyes were red-rimmed and dark-ringed from her enforced wakefulness.

'You find us at a quiet time, sir,' she began cautiously. 'Our neighbours have been good to us, watching with us last night, but they must needs do their work during the day. They will be back this evening.'

'I make no doubt your neighbours are good to you, when you have lost so fine a boy.' Murray thought of the neat hayloft, the well-swept stable. 'I did not know your son well myself, and I am sure that had this tragedy happened before his own death, my father would have raised a fine eulogy for your son. But I can say that he did his work in a manner any man would be proud of, and the other servants weep for him as a friend.'

Mr. Paterson's head sank on to his chest, and he pressed one hand to the wall for support. Mrs. Paterson nodded her acknowledgement of Murray's compliments, and signalled to her daughter to bring the gentlemen more cheese and oatcakes. The oatcakes were homemade, and very fine.

'We were sorry to hear of your own loss, sir, begging your pardon,' said Mrs. Paterson, with an effort. 'Jamie always spoke well of him.'

Murray waved a hand in acknowledgement, and then hoped it had not seemed condescending. He was not helped by the ensuing awkward pause.

'Paterson is a porter for the brewery at the far end of the Cowgate,' Mrs. Paterson tried again. Murray smiled and nodded, though as Jamie had evidently inherited his light frame from his father he found difficulty in imagining Paterson at one end of a barrel pole. 'But Jamie was always the one for the horses, ever since he was a bairn. He always said Mr. Murray's horses were the finest in the New Town.'

'If they were, he contributed to that himself,' said Murray, though he knew his father would have been eager to take the lion's share of the credit. 'He must have found it convenient to visit you, being situated not so far away?'

'He was a good boy. He came every week, and more if Mr. Dunnet here gave him a little time. You were kind to him, Mr. Dunnet, and I am glad to meet you.'

Dunnet grunted, and his shoulders slumped slightly. She waited for more, but when she saw it was not to come, she went on with arranging oatcakes on a blue and white plate. Murray watched Dunnet's gaze flicker to the recess bed, and then meet his own eyes, only to drop swiftly to the floor.

'How did he come here?' asked Murray suddenly.

'What do you mean, sir?' Mrs. Paterson looked up from the oatcakes, puzzled.

'Jamie. Did he come up the High Street, or down the South Bridge and to Candlemaker Row, or along the Cowgate Strand? Which was his favourite path?'

Mrs. Paterson sat on a hard chair and gripped its edges, frowning into the fire. Clearly here was one of those gentlemen that was a bit odd, but you had to put up with it because he was a gentleman and quite possibly harmless. And after all, losing his father as he had done, he was probably as distracted by grief as she. In any case, she was happy to talk of her fine son, happy to look over her memories of him and see what had to be refreshed before he was gone completely out of her reach. She, too, glanced at the fair head on the pillow of the recess bed.

'He generally came here along the Cowgate, but went home by the High Street, sir, for he kenned I was worried about him in the Cowgate when it was dark. Besides, he liked to see the lights on the stalls in the High Street and walk by the luckenbooths, taking his time to look about him. You ken what young lads are like, sir. As if he had all the time in the world.' There was a wretched sound from her husband, who still stood by the bed. He turned, and spread his hands wide.

'Who killed my son, Mr. Murray?' the man demanded. 'Why can nobody tell me who killed my son? Accidents happen, aye, and illness, and bairns die like the rest of us die, but what has a child done to get himself murdered? How could he ever have deserved it?' At this he began to sob, and Mrs. Paterson rose and went to him, taking his hand and holding it close within her own hands, pressing her forehead against his shoulder. Murray looked away. Dunnet was staring out of the small window with a look of white-lipped desperation, his knuckles bloodless around the handle of his ale mug. Murray looked away again, and stared at the fire.

The silence was made more tangible by the mobile contrast of the background noise from the street, and after a long minute Mrs. Paterson freed herself to pour tea from the fireplace kettle for her husband. He obediently sat to drink it and to take an oatcake.

'The burial is tomorrow,' said Mrs. Paterson at last, trying to sound normal. 'You or any of your household is most welcome, sir.'

Murray inclined his head, then rose and felt in his pocket for the handkerchief containing the objects he had found in the hayloft.

'These were Jamie's, I believe,' he explained, handing them over. 'You'll want to collect, too, everything else you know about – clothes, and so forth. I wasn't sure, in the dark.'

She stared at him as she took the warm linen package from his hand, and then looked down at it, confused.

'I think,' added Murray, 'that they were his treasures. He had laid them out very carefully along the window ledge.'

She undid the package then, carefully, and took the pieces out one by one, passing them each to her husband, the leather and the driftwood and the shells and pebbles. At some she gave a little smile and nod of recognition, and at others a shrug. But when she came to the button, she picked it out and held it up to the light.

'I do not know this. This is too fine, sir, he should not have kept it.'

'It seems to me that it was lost in the street, and had been there for some time when he spied it.' Murray thought the button of little consequence, but it was causing Mrs. Paterson some anxiety, and she turned to her husband for support.

'John, this was not something we knew he had, was it?' Paterson shook his head. She continued. 'It may be gold. It may be valuable. Perhaps it fell from a waistcoat of Mr. Murray's. I mean – your father, sir,' she qualified, looking up at him.

'I must say I do not recall it,' Murray replied. Rose pink was not one of his father's preferred colours, but who knew what he might have worn in the last four years? He had not been the good son, visiting his father once a week.

'Perhaps from one of his friends, then?' She was not to be swayed. 'Jamie should not have kept it. Please take it, sir, and you may find its owner grateful.' She held it out firmly, and he could not without discourtesy refuse it. He replaced the button in his pocket, but declined the return of his handkerchief.

'Jamie was in the habit of showing you his prizes, then, was he?' he asked, with an encouraging smile.

'Yes, oh, yes, sir. He was forever picking up other people's leavings! He would come with his breeches pockets full of all sorts of trifles, half of them still wet from the drain in the Cowgate.' The Patersons both smiled in recollection.

'When did he visit you last?'

'Tuesday evening, sir.' She gave the answer quickly, having gone over it in her head already, the last time they had seen their living son. 'He came with sad news, for Mr. Murray had died and Mr. Dunnet had told him he could run here and tell us, for he had an errand to Mr. Blair's stableman in George's Square, and he came here on the way back.'

Mrs. Paterson seemed still to find talking a release, and Murray decided to press on, gently.

'And how did he seem to be, then?' he asked.

'He was just his normal self, sir. Sad, you ken, about Mr. Murray, sad indeed, but apart from that he was just –' She stopped. 'I – I beg your pardon, sir, but you ken yourself – you can be fine the one minute and the next you remember – everything you have lost.' She bowed her head, and Murray realised his time was over. He set his ale mug on the table.

'I must leave you now, Mrs. Paterson. I shall pass on your kind invitation to my household. And thank you for your hospitality here.' He bowed, and the Patersons rose and responded. Even Dunnet managed a stiff nod, and gave a last lingering look towards the recess bed.

At the door, Murray was struck by a thought.

'Do you know the family of a Matthew Muir, a notary? I understand he lived near the Grassmarket.'

'So he did, till recently.' Mrs. Paterson tipped a thumb backwards. 'He and his brother Andrew lived just up the Vennel till last month. They flitted at the New Year to the Canongate, I believe, west of the Kirk. There's no other family with them, that I kent of.'

'The Canongate, very well. Thank you, Mrs. Paterson, and God be with you and your family.' He bowed again to her curtsey, and left, followed by Dunnet. His head was busy with thoughts, facts, beginning to piece one or two things together, though he still felt the great dark chasm in his mind trying to suck in his thoughts. He turned to walk back east along the Grassmarket to the West Bow and the steep curve of the ascent to the Lawnmarket and High Street. Their shadows walked far ahead of them: the sun, after its unaccustomed burst of energy, was already resting on its elbows on the horizon, and if he took the diversion he intended, by the time they reached the Canongate it would be dark.

It was not a logical diversion, but the matter had been preying on his mind. He led Dunnet back down the Lawnmarket but instead of crossing straight over to the Canongate, he crossed South Bridge and entered the familiar half-finished walls of the College. At this time, Henry and Robert should be sitting in a lecture on natural philosophy, and he just wanted to satisfy himself that that was indeed where they were.

He left Dunnet in the quadrangle and tiptoed up some steep wooden stairs to enter, silently, a door at the back of the lecture room. He glanced around quickly, doing his best to attract no attention, looking for two well-kent heads or, at best, one: he would not have been surprised to find Henry here on his own.

He was surprised, however, to find that Robert was there on his own, slumped in his seat and playing with his slate. Where was Henry? Murray was so taken aback that he almost called out to Robert to ask where his brother was, but shut his mouth and retreated just in time, closing the door softly.

Out in the quadrangle he paused, puzzled. Where on earth could Henry be? He loved natural philosophy, and never missed a lecture anyway. He frowned, and was about to leave, hoping to ask the boys later, when he heard a little sigh from behind one of the tall columns at the front of the building. Following some instinct, he leaned around the column, and found Henry, head pressed against the cold stone, propped over a pool of his own vomit. His face was white as a handkerchief.

'Henry! What's the matter?'

'It must have been something I ate,' said Henry, just as shocked to see his tutor peering round at him. 'Dinner ... something like that.'

'You'd better come home.'

'No, sir, I'll be fine now.' He did not look it, and Murray had severe misgivings as he watched Henry pull himself upright, wipe his lips with his handkerchief, and disappear back towards the college door. He would have to write to Lord Scoggie: he was far from sure that Edinburgh was agreeing with the boys, and anyway, was it right to be keeping them in a strange house full of death?

CHAPTER SEVEN

'Scoggie?'

Henry glanced round at the sound of his name, but the only person he could see of his acquaintance was Patrick Armstrong, the bespectacled mathematician. He was presumably on his way to a late afternoon lecture, although Patrick Armstrong was quite capable of turning up at this hour for a morning lecture and wondering where his classmates were. He was about to dismiss what he had heard as a mistake when Armstrong called him again, and came trotting towards him. Henry halted, happy to have a few more moments in the cool air, and spent the second or two it took Armstrong to reach him – Armstrong gave little time to exercise and was not, in any case, naturally designed for exertion – in pondering what on earth could have provoked the man to go out of his way to speak to him. Patrick Armstrong was two years above him, and Henry would ordinarily have been prepared to wager that as he himself was not a mathematical theorem Armstrong would have been hard pressed to remember he existed. However, here he was.

'Scoggie, good day.' They bowed. 'I hope I find you in good health.'

'Yes, I thank you, and you?'

Armstrong nodded dismissively, as though health were really not a consideration.

'Is the news true?'

Henry frowned, wondering what he could mean, and almost instantly decided that only one thing could possibly have had this extraordinary effect on Patrick's social aptitude.

'There's been an invasion? The French are at Dunbar?' he demanded, wondering if Robert would run off to fight them. His heart bucked with alarm.

'The French?' asked Armstrong, frowning in turn. 'Why on earth should they be at Dunbar?' Henry's heart settled, but his breath was temporarily abstracted by Patrick's general innocence. 'No, it's not the French. Was Mr. Murray's stable lad found dead last night?'

'Dead ...' said Henry, feeling his head reel now.

'Murdered!' Armstrong's eyes, behind his spectacles, grew glassed like a fish's. 'Is it true, then? What do you think it means?'

'Means?' asked Henry, now feeling rather stupid himself.

'Well, Mr. Murray your tutor's father died, and the circumstances were, shall we say, open to interpretation. And now this is a definite murder! Do you not think it a strange coincidence?'

'A very strange coincidence,' said Henry firmly. 'So strange I think it unlikely to have any significance at all.' If he said it firmly enough, it must be true. 'Where did you hear about this?'

'Oh, my mother told me when I went home to eat.' He seemed to break off, and Henry waited politely for him to continue. There was a prolonged pause, and he was eventually forced to carry on himself.

'The funeral went well yesterday, did it not? A fine turn out.'

'Yes, indeed.' Armstrong stopped again, drew breath to add something but again did not continue.

'I trust your family reached home safely after supper?'

'Oh, yes. Quite without mishap.'

Henry, who was not at his best, felt as if he were feeling around on the floor for something he might not have dropped in the first place.

'It was an honour to meet your family – we had had no idea that Mr. Murray was an acquaintance there.'

'Oh, yes – I had not recognised him when he brought you to classes. I had not seen him for some time.'

'Well,' Henry gathered his notebooks firmly in his hand and dabbed at his lips again. 'I must return to my lecture, if you will be so good as to excuse me. Good day to you, Armstrong.'

'Ah, yes, good day.' Henry left him standing in the college quadrangle, still with the air of being about to speak. Henry wondered if it would help if he were to go back and count at Armstrong for a while, until the soothing sounds of the numbers brought him back to himself. Then he went behind a column, and was sick again.

Although the Muirs had not lived long in the Canongate, the brief notoriety of Matthew Muir led to their flat being well known, and Murray obtained directions to it without difficulty. It was on the first floor of a clean, bright stair with few of the lingering odours that so often permeated an area without direct ventilation. As at the Patersons', the stair door was ajar, and Murray knocked, quite loudly, to be heard above the row from within.

For the third time in two days, Murray found himself in a dead room. In this case the corpse, that of an unexpectedly young man, was already kisted and the coffin lay open on a fir table at one side of the room. The coffin lid was propped beside it, and the screws lay handy on the table, ready to be slipped in by the joiner. He was squatting on the floor, tools at hand, and a tankard of ale at his mouth. The walls were hung in tatty black, some of which seemed to have had a past lift as a woman's skirts, and already parts of it had come away, giving the impression that someone had lurched against it and grabbed at it for support. Every available seat and most of the floor was taken up by bodies scarcely more lively than the corpse itself, except for the constant flow of unhushed conversation and one man sitting cross-legged by the hearth, showing very neatly the inadequacy of his breeches in several respects, and singing a dirge-like appreciation of an individual named 'Fair Footed Nellie', apparently addressed to the poker.

The one visible armchair in the room was taken up by a man with overlong hair and disjointedly sprawling legs, whose new black coat had already ripped under one outflung arm with the pressure of too little cloth or too hasty stitching. He clutched a whisky bottle in one hand at an angle that would have proved disastrous had there been more whisky in the bottle. He fixed Murray with the over-accurate stare of a man with only one unsteady finger on the reins of sobriety, and raised his voice above the din.

'Come in, come in! Help yourself, everyone else in Edinburgh's doing it!'

'Good evening, Mr. Muir?' asked Murray, hesitating before picking his way over the first few revellers by the doorway.

'Oh, aye. But there's two of us, ye ken. There's myself, Mr. Andrew Muir, and there's my brother, Mr. Matthew Muir, late lamented, over yonder in that fine box. Here, Matt,' he addressed the corpse from a distance, 'you've attracted some fine gentlemanly friends to drink their fill at my expense!' He turned his precarious focus back towards Murray. 'Who are you, then? Did you ken my brother well or did he owe you money?'

'I did not know him at all,' Murray replied honestly. Andrew Muir's eyes blurred and refocused.

'Man, you're the bold one. Have a glass on me.' He waved his bottle grandly.

'My name is Murray of Letho. My father was injured, I believe, in the same unfortunate accident in which your brother met his death. I came to offer my sympathies, though I must confess to being surprised that the funeral has not already taken place.'

'Come here, then, Murray of wherever, and I'll tell you. Where's your father, then?' he asked as Charles decided to obey the summons. The man was beyond half-drunk and incapable of standing, and although none of the other mourners seemed to have taken any notice of their conversation as yet, it was not comfortable continually to be shouting across the room.

'My father died of his injuries on Sunday,' he replied, once again making it real for himself. He worked his way into a half-space beside the armchair, folding his lengthy frame down towards the bereaved brother.

'And you've buried him?' Muir tried to look up at him, but could not succeed without squinting.

'Yesterday.'

'Yesterday. Aye. Well, we had to wait for him.' He jerked his precious bottle at a man in the opposite corner, whose face was whiskered and dimpled with fat. He seemed sound asleep.

'Your own father?' Murray hazarded, though there was no resemblance.

'Ach!' Muir spat. 'That's no our father, he's dead long since. That's John Pollock, Matt's master.'

'His master?' Light was beginning to dawn. 'Then your brother was still an apprentice lawyer?'

'Aye, he was. The newspapers picked him up as a notary, and I had no desire to correct them. What difference does it make now?'

Murray nodded in polite agreement.

'So how did Mr. Pollock delay the funeral?'

'Old bastard.' Muir offered this almost as an alternative name. 'He's been at death's door these past three years, and knocking to get in. He went up to Montrose one winter on business and came down with who kens what, and he's been there ever since. Now he chooses this week to be restored to the land of the living, which is as well for him as Matt was the only one seeing to his interests here, and with him away there'd be no one very much interested in his interests.' He began to chuckle at his own wit, and the chuckle turned into laughter verging on hysteria which rendered him even more useless for a number of minutes. He began to recover as a small, frightened-looking woman of indeterminate position in the household came up with a tray on which were ale and oatcakes for Dunnet and Murray, and a chunk each of heavy funeral cake. Muir scowled at her, all laughter gone, and went to slap her arm, but she dodged him.

'No, Dandy Muir, I'll no have you so unkindly to a guest as that – and a gentleman, too. For all you may say about poor Matt, he knew how to be polite to gentlefolk.' She turned her back defiantly and scrambled over the mourners the way she had come, to what seemed to be some kind of kitchen, where she vanished once more. Murray took a mouthful of indifferent oatcake and diluted it with ale.

'The woman will have me eaten out of all my money,' Muir muttered. 'So here we are, anyway, Mr. Murray of Wherever, sir,' he added loudly so as to be heard in the kitchen, 'on Thursday, and my brother's no keeping very well.' Murray had already observed the twists of half-burned brown paper that had been wafted against the smell of decay. The flowers by the coffin must not have come cheap either, in January.

'Do you know if your brother was acquainted with my father? Charles Murray of Letho, that is.'

'I never heard the name before,' Dandy admitted. 'But then I didn't always listen to what Matt had to say. He was always the one for the wild plans that would make his fortune – with the least effort on his own part, I should say – but who's paying for his funeral? I'm no saying he never had any money, but it never lasted long.'

Murray, perceiving a slight change in Muir's attitude, perhaps a play for sympathy, pressed on.

'Did he tell you where he was going on the night he died?' he asked.

'Oh, aye,' said Dandy, in tones of disgust. 'He was away to meet a gentleman, one he'd met before. He was his partner, or so he said, in something big, something that would make him all the money he'd ever dreamed of – and that would have been a fair bit, for Matt was good at the dreaming. But what gentleman would ever have taken Matt as a partner? A half-finished apprentice with a sick master? What could he have done for them? It wasna you, was it?' he asked, suddenly suspicious.

'No, no,' said Murray, 'I was in Kirk o'Field.'

'Aye, well.' Muir seemed reassured, and did not ask what Murray was asking himself – what about his father? 'Matt had ideas above himself. He was at me for months to move to a better flat. Well, the Vennel was good enough for me, but Matt says no, the Canongate has a nicer ring to it. So here we are, and there he is, and in no position to appreciate it. You can be kisted as well in the Vennel as you can in the Canongate.' He flung his arms about to emphasise his point. Murray leaned away from the increasingly mobile whisky bottle. 'Now me, I'm a tinsmith. A master tinsmith, mark you, my apprenticeship served and I'm in the Guild. But that was not good enough for our Matt. He had a fine clerk's hand, and a fine way with the gentry, and he said he was in business with one of the finest gentlemen in town. That's what he said, but I never met the gentleman, and ach, Matt was all talk.'

Having partaken of the funeral meats in the form of oatcake and funeral cake, that even now were stuck solidly between throat and stomach, Murray felt obliged to attend the interment itself, particularly as the assistant minister of the Canongate Kirk appeared warily at the open door as Murray himself was about to leave. Since Dunnet appeared not to care, Murray decided that a little burial would do him good – after all, he had been too drunk to attend Murray's father's interment. They stood, therefore, while others did little more than lounge, as the assistant minister said grace and the joiner screwed down the coffin lid, accompanied by a steady muttering of imprecations as his hand slipped again and again. The minister affected not to hear, but drew the grace to a hasty close. He stood back to remain in prayer with the few women in the room, while the men who could stand – around three quarters of them – rose and straightened their black coats and five came forward to carry the coffin. A sixth had evidently been selected previously but was now *hors de combat* with his knees tucked up cosily to his stomach under the fir table. Dandy, rapidly sobering, replaced him hurriedly with a man of around the same height, and the coffin was manoeuvred down the closely curled stair and out into the street.

Here, as the cold air hit the mourners, one or two fell by the wayside and sat heavily on the road, or slumped in defeat against walls. The rest mustered, propping each other up in comradely fashion, and led by the coffin, they began the short walk to the kirkyard. The body was swiftly interred, the earth filled in, and the whisky bottle brought out again, causing several of the mourners to lurch for the nearest discreet corner to relieve, one way or another, their overburdened stomachs. Murray replaced his hat and nodded to Dunnet, and began the walk back up the Canongate to North Bridge and across to the New Town and home.

'I can't stop thinking about that poor wee lad,' said Mrs. Mutch suddenly, slamming down her pastry cutter. 'I just can't get it out of my head.'

Mrs. Chambers, who had come into the kitchen ostensibly to return a teacup from her room, was lingering near the fire, looking as if she would love to fidget with something.

'I know exactly what you mean,' she agreed. 'We were all just starting to get used to the idea of Mr. Murray leaving us – although there'll never be another like him, God rest him, and I miss him at every turn – but the bairn dying like that is just too much, coming on top of the other.'

Mrs. Mutch pulled a handkerchief from behind her apron and applied it to her tiny eyes, then stuffed it quickly back and took up her cutter again. From the scullery, Iffy and Effy could be heard sobbing softly as they prepared vegetables. There was a clatter of buckets from the maids' room next door, followed by a step at the door and Mary returned from seeing to the study fire, settled herself near a tallow candle and took up her mending. After a moment she looked out from under her triangular eyebrows and surveyed the rest of the room, but when Mrs. Chambers glanced at her, Mary's eyes were only on her mending. Mrs. Mutch looked hard at her.

'Don't say it,' she said sharply. 'I ken what you're thinking, but don't say it.'

'I don't know what you mean,' said Mary innocently.

'You Islanders with your un-Christian-like ideas, that's what I mean. You gar my flesh grue.' She scooped the pastry shapes efficiently on to a baking sheet, and waddled round the table to slide them into the closed-in oven.

'All I said was where there are two deaths, there'll be a third,' said Mary, not looking up. 'That's not only an Island saying.'

'That's what I mean.' Mrs. Mutch restrained the urge to slam the oven door. She checked through the glass at the pastries, and wiped her hands on a cloth. 'Iffy and Effy have had their teeth yattering since you said that this morning, and everything they touch is sodden with tears. And you've me looking in dark corners and over my shoulder, too.' She shuddered expressively.

'It was quite an upsetting thing to say,' agreed Mrs. Chambers, 'but we ought perhaps not to take it too seriously, Mrs. Mutch. I'm sure Mary did not wish to cause you distress, did you, Mary?'

'Oh, no,' said Mary amiably. 'I'm sorry, Mrs. Mutch.'

'Huh,' said Mrs. Mutch.

Robbins appeared and at almost the same moment the bell rang for the front door.

'That'll be the master,' he remarked, and turned back to climb the stairs to the hall. Murray was already in, removing his hat and gloves, and Robbins, who was something below average height, reached up to help him off with his coat. Dunnet had vanished to the stables.

'Mr. Blair sent round a letter for you, sir.' Robbins went to the hall table and brought the letter on a tray. Murray took it and tore round the wax carefully.

'Oh, Robbins, I have called on Mr. and Mrs. Paterson.' Murray remembered his commission. 'The funeral is to be tomorrow. All of you who wish to go have leave, of course: if necessary I shall eat in town.'

'Thank you, sir, I shall relay the message to the rest of the household.' Robbins stood waiting to be dismissed, Murray's overcoat neatly folded over his arm. Murray ran his eyes down the note from Blair, and nodded.

'Please tell Mrs. Chambers that I shall be supping with Mr. Blair this evening.' He nodded dismissal, then added, 'and I shall require Dunnet to accompany me, and two horses. Oh, and when the boys come back from the college, could Mrs. Chambers see that Henry is all right? He says he had some dinner that disagreed with him.' Robbins bowed and left. Murray looked about the hall for a moment, then investigated the study, where a good fire had been lit. Squirrel, the deerhound, spared him a look of distrust before retreating as usual under a table. Sighing, Murray settled in one of the low-lying leather chairs by the fire, stretched his long legs to a footstool, and found a book to take him gently to supper.

Murray had not been in Blair's house in George's Square for several years. As Dunnet led the horses round to the stables, the front door opened and Blair himself bumbled out, catching his sleeve on the door knob and coming down the steps at a crabwise pace in consequence. He slewed around and seized Murray's hand in both his own, jiggling it up and down warmly while he smiled broadly at him, wide-eyed, then continued to smile as he jostled Murray up the steps and into the house.

'Come in, come in, come in! It is so good of you to come, very good indeed, yes, yes.' He hovered around the manservant removing Murray's overcoat, then drew him urgently into the street parlour.

To enter Blair's house was to step back fifteen years. Nothing had been changed in the décor, that Murray could see, since the house had first been arranged for Blair' marriage to the lovely Bessie Hope, whose fashionable friends had despaired at the attachment while envying her new husband's comfortable income. As she became almost immediately semi-retired from society like her husband, her erstwhile friends had less opportunity than they might have to despair so utterly over her complete happiness. When she died in the midst of that happiness, having had the first sight of her daughter, the despairing friends felt themselves vindicated and attended a triumphant funeral, then left Blair in peace, for which he was duly and annoyingly grateful. That he had not changed the house since was more indifference to his surroundings than an effort to placate the shade of his wife: he had loved her too well to have need of any material reminders. So it was a consequence of his indifference that the staircase beneath which one passed to the street parlour was an astonishing size yellow, the wooden Venetian blinds in the parlour were orange, as was the fine plasterwork of the fireplace, and the pilasters around the doorway were picked out and shaded in French grey.

'My sister is out, you'll be relieved to hear, and Isabel has gone back to school, so we shall be a bachelor party of two, if that suits you?'

'That sounds excellent, sir,' Murray agreed.

The eating part of the evening was dispatched quickly: Blair's table habits were a little random, and despite Mrs. Freeman's efforts the cook's talents were equally unreliable. Blair rescued the brandy decanter from the midst of a messy table, and ushered him into the study where they could be cosier.

'Now,' said Blair, bundling himself up in a chair whose original shape was entirely disguised by rugs, scarves and cushions, 'what have you been doing today?'

Murray outlined the morning meeting with his father's Edinburgh man of business, the marmalade-headed Mr. Simpson, and his afternoon visits to the building site, to Jamie's parents, and to Matthew Muir's brother.

'Dandy Muir said that his brother had an appointment to meet a gentleman, the night he died. Do you know if my father had any dealings with such a man?'

Blair pursed his lips, and as if operated by some mechanical device his eyebrows rose at the same time.

'I cannot imagine why he should have had. Your father's Edinburgh affairs, as no doubt you know, were all dealt with through Simpson, and even had he wished to use someone different, for whatever reason, he could hardly have had need to use an apprentice notary of no reputation.'

'I agree,' said Murray. 'Do you know of anyone of my father's acquaintance who might have seen fit to use Matthew Muir?'

'Again, no. Even the poorer among your father's immediate acquaintance are all involved in the law – apart, of course, from me – and would be able to find someone better than Muir to work for them.' He poured more brandy into Murray's glass, and made faces into the fire. For a moment, the fire made the only noise in the room, a soft rushing up the chimney.

'What do you believe happened to my father, sir?' asked Murray at last, staring into the quick flames. Blair jiggled a little in his chair, and took a slurp of brandy.

'Well, um. What do you think, then?' he asked, as if he had answered the question to everyone's satisfaction. Murray began to straighten out a few of his thoughts.

'I do not feel that what happened was the simple accident that it seems,' he began. 'If Muir was to meet a gentleman at the new feus, where was the gentleman, and why there? If he was not to meet the gentleman there, but elsewhere, where else, and why again did he go to the building site? And as someone pointed out, why does a stone on a lonely road wait for two separate men to be beneath it before it falls? My father was a fit and quick man, well able to avoid perhaps not the stone, but the tumble of scaffolding, so why did he not do so? Was he trying to save Muir?' He paused for breath, and glanced sideways to see if Blair was laughing at him. Blair, however, was staring at the ceiling, lips pouting again, finger tips pressed together. A silence slipped in and stood a long moment between them, and Murray found his breathing heavy.

'Have you considered,' said Blair at last, without looking down, 'that your father – this may be an upsetting thought, my friend – was knocked out of his senses before the stone fell?'

'By the scaffolding, you mean?' asked Murray stupidly.

'By a more human agent, perhaps.' Blair lowered his gaze and watched benevolently as Murray drew a large mouthful of brandy, wincing as it burned his mouth. He swallowed.

'A failed robbery?' he asked. 'But his watch and ring were still about him, and money in his pocket.'

'No, I fear it must be something more sinister than that, Charles.' Blair grew solemn. 'Either there was some reason why someone wanted your father dead, and Muir saw them and was killed for what he had seen, or some person wanted Muir to die and your father saw it, or Muir tried to kill your father and in an effort to disguise the deed brought the scaffolding – and by chance a stone - down on your father, miscarrying enough to kill himself in the attempt.' Murray thought about this in the light of what he had seen at the building site, and admitted to himself that someone could have pulled the scaffolding down deliberately to kill. 'Two further possibilities are that your father was the unfortunate murderer, which I hope we can discount –'

'Indeed!' said Murray forcefully.

'Quite.' Blair gave him an odd look. 'Or that someone wanted them both dead and lured them to that spot for that purpose.'

'There is one other matter that seems to indicate that my father was the intended victim,' Murray reflected. The idea that his father had been murdered was, strangely, appealing, more comforting than that he might have died in a pointless accident. Besides, it gave his bewildered, empty, cluttered mind a distinct problem on which to focus. 'Jamie was undoubtedly murdered, so perhaps it was for something that he and my father had both seen?'

Blair nodded a concession that it might be possible, and offered more brandy.

'No, no, I thank you, sir. I fear there are many matters at present for which I must keep a clear head.' He had had plenty of previous experience of drinking with Blair. 'A phrase keeps ringing in my head, one that Mr. Simpson used this morning. He said that he had to draw up a Service of the Heir. I keep thinking it means my service, as Father's heir, my duty to him.'

'You have not done your duty to him for a while, I think you mean?' said Blair gently. Murray felt his face redden.

'Not for far too long,' he agreed, his throat tight. 'It's about time I did it again.'

CHAPTER EIGHT

Murray was trying to eat his breakfast with slow deliberation. Outside, the dawn had scarcely happened, and the sky was heavy with clouds that more than hinted at snow. They lumbered over the horizon to the west, dragging loose, tattered edges where snow was already falling, probably over the smooth backs of the Pentland Hills. Murray pretended to himself that he could not make a decision about the course of his day until he saw what the weather was going to do – even now a rather ominous wind was beginning to spin odd bits of rubbish past the window of the street parlour – but really, he was at something of a loss. Perhaps he should go to the college with the boys. Henry was still pale, and fiddled with the ham on his plate with unaccustomed apathy. Robert eyed it with calculation.

Jennet, the smaller maid, entered the room at speed, stopped, stared at the breakfast table, curtseyed, and left.

He knew it was next to useless to expect the men at the police office to investigate the circumstances of his father's death. For one thing, there was their general reputation, which declined, along with their popularity, from the high point of their foundation last year to the pit where it currently lay, as people discovered that they were only marginally better than the old City Guard. Many old guardsmen had in fact gone straight into the police force. For another thing, he had seen himself how keen the man Rigg had been to arrest Dunnet full in the face of Dr. Harker's assertions of his innocence. He felt sure they would make an arrest, but he was equally sure it would be the wrong one. But if he himself were to try to find out what had happened, what was he to do? He thought again of the way he had reacted to Jamie's death, to other deaths he had seen, but for most of them he had been on the spot very quickly after the event, when there was still a good deal of use to observe and piece together. Here he had come in so late, and the building site was in such a state of flux, that he felt it was almost impossible to make any pattern from it.

Nevertheless, he thought, he should begin by writing down anything of significance that he could think of, facts he had come across in the last couple of days, and see what he already had.

As he came to this conclusion, Mary appeared briefly, curtseyed at the door with a grinning apology, and vanished again. Murray blinked, and finished his tea. As soon as the cup was heard to hit the saucer, the door opened again and Mrs. Chambers herself appeared, with her fingers knotted at the front of her black velvet dress.

'Mr. Murray, excuse me, sir, but have you finished your breakfast?'

'Just now, Mrs. Chambers.' She hovered, about to speak. 'You may clear the table,' he added, as she seemed to require something. As if summoned by magic, Jennet and Mary shot through the open door and cleared the table as though there were a fiend at their backs. The boys were open-mouthed. Murray, with the cloth and his napkin swept out from under his nose, felt rather dazed.

'Oh, I am sorry, Mr. Murray, sir. But it is Jamie's funeral today, and you did promise that we could all go.'

'Oh, of course! It is I who should apologise, Mrs. Chambers. I had quite forgotten.' He rose and moved the table back against the wall. 'You are all going?'

'We would all like to, sir. But of course it depends very much.' She wrung her fingers. 'There's a fire laid in the study, sir, and another in your bedroom, in case you have need of them, but neither is lit as yet. Now, I can stay at home and make your midday meal, if you would prefer, sir.'

'Not at all, Mrs. Chambers. You must go to the funeral.'

'Oh, sir, I cannot bear to think of you here abandoned!' Her fingers became impossibly tangled, and she freed them with a sudden gesture of despair.

'Mrs. Chambers, I believe I can light a fire all on my own!' Murray soothed her. 'As you know, I am bound to the Dundases for dinner, and I intend to meet the boys in town before that – to make sure you're eating properly, Henry,' he added, then turned back to Mrs. Chambers. 'You will likely all be back for supper, which need not be elaborate in any case, And even should I feel the need of a cup of tea in between, I believe I remember where my father's kitchen is.'

She smiled rather dubiously at this, but chose to be reassured.

'Please do not be late on my account, any of you,' Murray reiterated. 'And please give my best wishes to Mr. and Mrs. Paterson, and tell them that if they ever have need of anything, they have only to ask.'

It was an odd feeling, he thought, to be able to say that, and he savoured it for a moment or two after Mrs. Chambers had gone. He had not asked Mr. Simpson what his income might now be, although he felt sure that all he had to do to find out was to ask the mothers of a few of the young ladies of his acquaintance: mothers always had you placed on a neat table in order of your virtues, chiefly financial ones. He wondered idly how far up the local table he was and looked about the room, at the elegant, simple lines of the furniture and the cool, clean colours of the walls, light and airy after the hot yellows and oranges of Blair's parlour. The room was modern and expensive. The portraits of his father and mother, a three-quarter length pair above the fireplaces in the drawing room upstairs, were Raeburns. He had never seen more than a miniature of Blair. Certainly this was a house that spoke of an easy wealth, though Blair would have made it, in a moment, easy, comfortable and downright messy.

He saw the boys off, hoping he could trust them to go straight to the college and telling them where to meet him for their meal. Then he tamped down the fire in the street parlour and crossed the hall to the study, where, as promised, another fire was laid. He lit it, and from it the candles in the sconces around the room, for the north-facing window brought in very little light at this time of year. While his thoughts dwelled on the supposedly significant facts he was going to write down, he tried again to write a letter to his brother George. It was not easy. He wished this whole business had happened when George was at home, not off with the First Regiment of Foot. For one thing, it would have forced them to meet again, though the circumstances would certainly not have been auspicious. And if George had been at home, would his father even have thought of sending for Charles? And how had he known where to find him?

He pushed aside the letter paper, and drew across another sheet. After a moment's thought he wrote across the top 'Father' and 'Jamie'. Then in neat columns he wrote the date and time of the incidents that had caused their deaths and the way in which each had died. He added the details of Matthew Muir's death to his father's column, and wondered briefly if he should have made three columns, but decided against it. He added the details of what he had seen at the stable, and the footprints in the earth, to Jamie's column. Then came possible reasons why each of them should have been killed, at which point he decided that he did indeed need a column for Matthew Muir, turned the page over and began again, this time adding the addresses, and in Muir's case the former address, of the deceased. When he came again to the reason for their deaths, he became fanciful, imagining that Muir's gentleman had gone back on their deal and killed him, that his father had known the gentleman concerned – this, he argued to himself, was quite possible, as his father had at least been acquainted with almost every gentleman in town – and had seen the death and had therefore been killed before he could tell the police officers. Jamie did not fit in well with this scheme, and as far as Murray knew, Jamie had been safely in his hayloft when Mr. Murray had been injured. Perhaps, though, if his father had known Muir's mysterious gentleman, he too had gone to meet him and had mentioned this in Jamie's hearing beforehand? But he would hardly have been telling Jamie, and if he had been telling someone else and Jamie overheard, then why had not the someone else told anyone? And indeed, why would Mr. Murray of Letho have gone to meet even an acquaintance at night in such a place? Why not go to the gentleman's house, or invite the gentleman to his own house, or if neither were truly possible they could have met at a hotel or a coffee house. Meeting where they did made it look as if they had not wanted anyone to see them, and that did not sound like the kind of business in which his father would have been involved.

Murray took a deep breath and sat back, staring at the bookcases against the wall. The gulf in his mind was yawning again. He looked down at the paper in front of him, and underlined the word 'Grassmarket' in Jamie's parents' address and Matthew Muir's old one, and felt that that, at least, was a concrete connexion. Whether or not his father knew Matthew Muir, or knew a gentleman who knew Matthew Muir, Jamie would have known the apprentice lawyer both by sight and name.

Snow was beginning to fall, tentatively, as Thomson and John Douglas left the law courts to seek a mid-morning respite in a coffee house. They stared at the snowflakes from under the dark portico, not fooled by the snow's apparent reluctance. Thomson looked up, shielding his face with one finely gloved hand, and saw that the distinctive spire of St. Giles' across the courtyard was beginning to fade in the thickening flakes. He turned to Douglas.

'If we do not go now, we might not make it. Coming?' and he took the smaller man's elbow. But just as they were about to force an advance, they were hailed from within the law court building itself, and when they looked about, they saw Dundas strolling towards them.

'May I join you?' he asked as he approached. 'I take it you're going to Baird's?'

'The nearest seemed the best in this weather,' said Thomson affably. 'Of course you're welcome to join us.'

They slithered on slushy cobbles past the south flank of the High Kirk and down treacherously worn stone steps to the open door of Baird's warm parlour. Thomson pitched on a corner table as another party vacated it and threw his hat and gloves down, giving a general order of warm rum to a passing serving-man even before he was seated.

'Poor old Balneavis is probably waiting for us at Stone's,' he remarked, as he arranged his coat over the high back of the seat, 'but it's really a bit of a gallop there in this weather. Besides, Armstrong was heading that way before the snow started. They'll be quite snug.'

'I assume Balneavis is as constant as ever in failing to find profitable employment.' Dundas did not directly associate with Balneavis. From Thomson's grin, you would not have thought that Thomson often pushed some of his own work Balneavis' way. Dundas certainly did not know.

'But we who are successful should not look down on the less fortunate, my dear fellow,' Thomson said with mock generosity. 'And we are very successful, are we not? Douglas here has more cases than there are judges to examine them, my own time is tolerably occupied, and you, my dear Dundas, have the Campbell case, which should keep you busy for quite some time. How does it go, by the way?'

Dundas shrugged.

'The Lord Advocate has decided there was no case to answer.'

'Jamie Montgomery? Taking away your bread and butter just like that?'

'Oh, hardly my bread and butter, Thomson,' Dundas smiled swiftly. 'The Campbell case would merely have afforded a little extra jam.'

Thomson laughed. Douglas watched both of them carefully, his dark eyes burning as always in the narrow face, but he said nothing. A wise man would not have believed either of them, and Douglas was reasonably wise. The rum arrived.

'And how does your work go?' Dundas asked Douglas, when they had warmed both their hands and their stomachs with the rum. 'I have not seen you in court for some time.'

'Oh, I watched him this morning,' said Thomson with enthusiasm. 'The same as ever, or if anything more fiery with the onset of middle age, eh, Douglas? The defendant was a young lad up for theft and reset – he had taken three stockings from a lady's washing line in Brown Square, lost his nerve before he could take the fourth, and sold them to a lady of a different kind in the Cowgate. The lad gallantly refuses to name his elegant customer, who is, in any case, no doubt too busy about her work by night to be able to appear in court by day, and the lady victim, now half-stockingless on alternate days, is crying out for his transportation to the colonies, although he has no habit and repute. But Douglas here raises a fine storm of passion, points out the boy's otherwise untarnished reputation, his youth and innocent demeanour, the honour of his position regarding his customer – whatever her standing in society, it cannot and should not reflect on this young man's courtesy and discretion, he said – and finishes by remarking that the young lad, finding himself by chance – I liked that part – in the rear of a house in Brown Square, was so dazzled by the wealth of the lady victim's home, without thinking to dwell on the base inequality of a Christian society that had in it both the lady and himself, removed her stockings from the line in a moment of confusion and later embarrassed by the possession of such delicate feminine garments he made the best use of them he could, selling them, out of the generosity of his own poverty, for only half what they were worth. The judge was in tears, I tell you, and the lady victim, too, for as the lad emerged from the court, I swear to you that the lady victim herself was pressing on him the fourth stocking, with which to finance his liberty.'

Dundas laughed heartily, and Thomson, out of breath, took a draught of rum.

'You have such strange ideas, Douglas,' Dundas said when he had recovered, 'that I believe you simply shock the jury into freeing your clients. But no one else can draw on such passion as you. It is fortunate for all concerned that you have never been in love, for I do not believe that you are the kind to love easily.' He contemplated Douglas, who avoided his eye and drank a little rum. 'Anyway,' said Dundas, sitting up and changing the subject, 'remember that you are both promised to dine with me later today. We shall be quite a large party, in fact: my cousin Lady Warwick is staying, with her daughters. Widow of one of the newer English baronets.' He made a face of mock disgust. 'Then there are you two, your family, Thomson, Armstrong and his, and young Charles Murray. My wife thought it would do him good to be out, and it is not as if it were going to be a ball.'

'Quite,' said Thomson. 'My own wife has said much the same. You'll have heard, of course, about his stable boy?'

'Oh, yes,' said Dundas. 'A shocking business, and on the very day of his father's funeral, too. Very bad.'

When they emerged from the depths of the coffee house, the snow had pronounced an adjournment, and it was nearing midday. They walked back down towards the law courts in coats with damp shoulders, and in the distance saw Charles Murray, sharply defined in new black, buying an apple from a stall further down the hill.

'It seems that young Charles is getting out after all,' Dundas remarked. Thomson was surprised at the slight resentment in his tone.

'It is not forbidden, I suppose. He's young. And besides,' he added, guiding the other two gently back to their place of work, 'just because he can buy an apple from a market stall does not mean that he cannot benefit from an evening or two in good society.' He nodded briskly at them, then looked back, but Murray had once more vanished from sight..

CHAPTER NINE

Murray was not quite sure why he had felt the impulse to buy the apple: there would be plenty at the house brought from Letho and well-stored to survive the winter. Perhaps it simply felt ordinary.

He reached the coffee house in which he had arranged to meet Henry and Robert for their midday meal, and went in, stooping below the low door lintel. Robert waved at him at once from a table at the back, where he was sitting with his brother and also, surprisingly, with Willie Jack Dundas. Murray was not entirely pleased to see that they had taken up with him, though Gavin Dundas would have been worse. He hoped that Robert had not added gambling to his list of new achievements.

The boys had waited for his arrival before ordering anything, so Murray now called for four bowls of broth. A serving maid brought them, smiled becomingly at the boys, saw Murray noting this and departed with a giggle. Murray found himself comparing her with Mary and her serene amusement. The broth arrived, steaming even in the muggy room, and glazed with bubbles of fat that twinkled on the surface.

'Have some bread, sir,' said Robert, passing him a pewter plate armed with hard brown wedges. 'It's better than it looks, honestly.' The maid overheard and grinned. Murray tasted the soup and the bread, and had to agree. After living in Scoggie Castle for four years, one grew to appreciate all kinds of things that did not start off well.

'You are well?' asked Willie Jack, giving Murray an odd look, though it may just have been that his stuffy nose stopped him swallowing easily.

'Yes, I thank you. And you? and your family?'

'Oh, indeed, as you see.'

'Have you been at the college today?' Willie Jack was not a student, as far as Murray knew.

'No, I was just passing and met these two – knew them from your father's funeral, of course.'

'Willie Jack said he'd heard a rumour – and people will keep asking us,' said Robert, plaintively, 'about your stable boy.'

'Well, there are all kinds of rumours going around,' said Willie Jack reasonably. 'I wanted to make sure I had the right one - er, to be able to contradict any errors I might come across,' he finished, unconvincingly.

'What kind of all kinds of rumours?'

'Oh! Everything from an accident to hanging himself in remorse for killing Mr. Murray with the lid of the corn bing.'

'Well, my stable boy is dead,' Murray said. This town was full of gossip, worse than a country village. 'Jamie was murdered, and there is no question of an accident or suicide. There seems to have been a struggle, and his head was struck against the corn bing, so that element, at least, of your story appears in the true account. The groom, Dunnet, found him and was very deeply shocked. A police officer tried to arrest him, but Dr. Harker – you know him, do you not, Willie Jack?'

'The physician, yes, of course.'

'Dr. Harker said that Jamie had been dead before Dunnett had gone into the stable, so with a certain amount of persuasion the police officer let him go.'

'Shocking,' muttered Willie Jack, nasally. He seemed perpetually afflicted with troubles of the nose and ears, an inelegant complaint in an elegant family.

'The funeral is today, and my entire household is gone to it, so we are reduced to eating in coffee houses,' Murray joked. 'It is distressing my housekeeper very much.' It still felt odd to say 'my housekeeper'. In what way was she his? His responsibility? His gaze rested for a moment on Henry, who still looked very pale, and was only running the spoon back and forth through his broth. Another responsibility – and one he intended to pass back to Fife as soon as possible.

Willie Jack cleared his throat noisily.

'The rumour also says – but it may be wrong – that the stable boy was murdered on the day of Mr. Murray's funeral. Was it after supper that all this happened?'

'No, before. I found Dunnet and Jamie in the stables on my way back from the burial itself. If you remember, Dr. Harker and we were a little late for supper at Fortune's.'

'I remember,' said Willie Jack. 'But you told no one? Not a word of this passed your lips the whole evening?'

'To be honest, it seemed easier that way,' Murray confessed. 'I was weary to my bones, and to begin to explain and describe – in front of the ladies, too – was more than I could bear to contemplate. In the end I believe I said too little in any case: I have no recollection of much of the conversation or my part in it that evening.'

'But to have said nothing of it at all!' Willie Jack seemed more shocked by Murray's discretion than by the murder. 'I can hardly see how that is possible!'

'But everyone there was grieving quite enough at the death of my father,' explained Murray. 'To expect them to face a further upset would have been too much. Of all of them there, Mr. Blair and I were probably the only ones who had even met Jamie. And I, too, was still very much distressed at my father's death, and had no immediate wish to reflect on another.'

Willie Jack sniffed again and finished his soup, then broke the short silence.

'Yes, we were all much distressed at Mr. Murray's death. The whole business was most tragic.' Henry gave him a wary look but Murray was interested, wondering what qualified as 'the whole business'. 'The night that the accident happened was quite dreadful. My father and my brother Harry had both gone out, and one of the servants came into the parlour to say that the servant from a house at the west end of Queen Street had just brought the news that there had been a terrible accident, and two gentlemen had been killed. My mother was beside herself, quite frantic, and even though Harry came in for supper, my father did not return until after midnight. We had to sit up with my mother, for she would not rest until she had seen my father safely home.'

'Had your father or your brother gone out that way, that Lady Sarah was so concerned for them?' Murray asked, as casually as he could.

'That I do not know,' said Willie Jack, picking at the last piece of the bread. In fairness it should have been Henry's, but he was taking no interest in it. 'My father said that he had been discussing business with some friends, but Harry did not say where he had been. It is not like Harry to be out so late alone,' he added innocently.

For thinking time, Murray felt in his pocket and brought out the apple and his pocket knife. He offered pieces to Willie Jack and the boys, but they politely declined. Regarding the mottled flesh, Murray did not blame them.

'So why would anyone murder Jamie?' asked Robert. 'He was nice. He liked horses, too,' he added, as if that were reason enough to preserve anyone's life.

'Was it robbery?' asked Willie Jack.

'There was nothing missing in the stable or coach house,' said Murray, 'and it seems unlikely that he had much of his own that was of value.' Except perhaps the enamel button, something at the back of his mind reminded him.

'Perhaps Jamie disturbed the thieves, and when they realised they had killed him they fled without taking anything.'

'Perhaps.' The thing at the back of his mind rebelled at the thought. It was too much of a coincidence, the three deaths. 'Though they were taking a risk in any case, attempting to steal from a stable during the day, with plenty of people about.'

'So why do you think he was murdered?' Robert asked again.

Why indeed?

Murray gave the easy answer.

'I haven't the least idea,' he said.

It was almost eleven o'clock when Mrs. Armstrong and her daughters finally descended into the narrow hall to greet their expected guests. Mrs. Thomson and Miss Thomson, the witty Davina, arrived shivering, and soon the stone-flagged hall was dotted with snowflakes flicked from bonnets, cloaks, muffs and pelisses, all in the most modish colours. Outside in the slightly faded elegance of St. Patrick's Square the coachman pulled blankets over the steaming horses and looked about for his usual howff in which to spend his allotted hour. Beyond the square, the snow fell hard over the bleak Newington farmland, divided, in Archibald Armstrong's mind, at least, into neat feus eligible for purchase.

'We had thought you might not come, sister, in this dreadful weather. We expected a message from you at any minute.' Elizabeth Armstrong led her sister Kitty to the fire and rang the bell for tea.

'The snow had all but ceased as we came out,' Kitty Thomson said, making herself comfortable. 'But the drive up the Bridges was very hazardous. They have put straw down, but the snow begins to cover it again. Of course, if you moved to the New Town, we should not have to undergo such dangers to see you, dear sister.'

Elizabeth Armstrong and her elder daughter, Ella, smiled politely at what was too old a remark to be either amusing or irritating: it had, indeed, become almost a tradition. Catherine Armstrong hurried her cousin Davina over to the window where a little easel was set up, on which stood a half-finished watercolour of Miss Davina Thomson. Catherine was eager to complete it, although the light was not ideal, and had her colours all ready to begin. Miss Thomson sat with easy grace, and assumed a three-quarter pose which made the most of the light on hair and skin.

'We had that dreadful Balneavis girl to dine yesterday,' Mrs. Thomson was saying. 'Poor unfortunate thing. I was so overcome by pity for her that I was forced to retire to my room with a sick headache, and sadly never saw her.'

'The eldest?' asked Mrs. Armstrong. 'She is a pretty thing now, but she would do well to get herself a husband before her looks fade. One has only to look at the mother to see how she will end.'

'But Mamma, she is a sweet-natured girl, which may count for much,' put in Ella Armstrong, who had a certain fellow feeling for any girl being propelled too hastily toward the married state.

'But alas,' remarked Miss Thomson from the window, head poised self-consciously, 'her nature is so sweet that all one tastes is sugar. There is no character, no flavour to it at all.'

Miss Armstrong smiled faintly at her cousin, and was inwardly amused to see that the very indifference of her own smile discomfited Davina more that criticism ever did. Davina liked an appreciative audience.

'As for the younger Balneavises,' Davina added, slightly defiantly, 'I find it almost impossible to tell them apart.'

'There! Finished,' said Catherine, who had not been listening. 'I knew there was only a little still to do.' Her mother, aunt and sister obediently rose to look at the painting, while the subject waited graciously for comparison.

'That's lovely, dear,' said Mrs. Armstrong, fondly. 'You have brought out the softness of her face very well.'

Miss Armstrong felt privately that her sister had brought out a good deal of softness in the face that was not there in the original.

'The cloth of her dress is very good,' she said with perfect truth: Catherine was better at drawing objects than people.

'Come and see, Davina. She has made you much more charming than you are, you should thank her,' said Mrs. Thomson, who was, after all, Davina's mother. Davina rose and examined the portrait, and was sufficiently flattered to be sustained until the tea arrived.

Once seated around the tea table, on which a fine selection of tea breads and cakes was laid to challenge the natural slenderness of the Fleming frame, Mrs. Thomson returned to her subject.

'At least the Balneavises will not be at the Dundases for dinner this afternoon.'

Elizabeth Armstrong felt it was time to divert her sister.

'Oh? Who will be there, then?'

'Well, the Dundases, of course, you five, if Patrick is to attend, and the three of us, and John Douglas, I believe.'

'John Douglas, eh?' said Mrs. Armstrong, meeting her sister's eye.

'No, my dear, I don't think so,' replied Mrs. Thomson. 'I've said so before – not for any of them.'

Miss Armstrong kept her eyes on her tea cup, knowing very well what they were talking about but having no wish whatsoever to encourage them. She could feel her mother's contemplative gaze on her, the gaze of a mother who has not quite given up hope, is still looking for points to improve. But Mr. Douglas, aside from being her father's age, never laughed, rarely smiled - and never then at anything obvious - and hardly ever spoke. Ella did not agree with those who said that the devil looked out of his eyes: these were mostly men, in any case, who had seen him at work in the law courts. Women, for the most part, saw him as a lonely figure, in need of comfort and attention: watching how he reacted to this comfort and attention when it was offered had rendered Ella certain that far from seeking this consolation, John Douglas had many years ago made his decision about how to lead his life, and his plan did not include a wife. In the face of such a decision, which she could only regard with respect, even the strongest affection would not have drawn her to try to break down his reserve.

'You will be courteous to Mr. Douglas this evening, dear Ella, won't you?' asked her mother, innocently. 'You know he is a good friend of your father's, and of your uncle Thomson's.'

'Yes, Mamma,' said Ella politely.

Mrs. Armstrong sighed. She had heard that particular politeness before.

'And who else is to be there?' she asked.

'Some female cousins of Mr. Dundas' mother, I believe, from Harrogate. A mother and two daughters.'

'Hum. Here in search of husbands, no doubt!' said Mrs. Armstrong, somewhat hypocritically.

'And I believe that Mr. Murray has been invited.' Another significant look passed between the sisters, but this time, Catherine Armstrong did look slightly interested. After all, whatever she and Davina might say in private, Mr. Murray was quite a catch, and had the additional merit of being, as it were, new on the market. She would not have rejected him as a brother-in-law, and even as a suitor for herself he bore contemplation.

'We shall see,' said her mother, as if she had read her thoughts. Knowing the Fleming sisters, she probably had.

Oblivious to this important discussion, Murray arrived home to the recollection that there was no point in ringing the doorbell. However, having brought out his key, he found that the door had been left unlocked for him. He set his hat and gloves on the hall table and unbuttoned his coat, shaking the snow off it, and wondered where Robbins usually put it. In the end he settled for draping it over a hall chair, since, after all, he would have to put it on again in about an hour.

He felt that a bath would be in order after his rather muddy return from seeing the boys back into the college, and assessing the situation he decided that preparing a bath for himself was not something that should be beyond the capabilities of a healthy man of two and twenty. Hot water was the principal requirement – and deliciously plentiful here compared with Scoggie Castle – and for hot water in bathlike quantities the descent to the kitchen, with which he had threatened Mrs. Chambers, had to be faced.

He could not remember having used the back stairs since he was thirteen or fourteen until the night before last, when he had carried Jamie's body into the kitchen and used the back stairs to return to his part of the house. Then, their darkness had seemed appropriate and somehow inevitable: now he wished he had brought a candle. He stumbled twice between top and bottom, but by the end the glow from the kitchen fire, seen around the cracks of the door, guided him past Mrs. Chambers' room and Robbins' pantry and the maids' room where they kept their buckets and shovels and aprons, and into the bright, blue-green walled kitchen. The rancid smell of homemade grease candles slithered through the air.

There was a squeal and a sudden scuttling noise from the pantry, and Murray, taken by surprise, crossed the room in four long strides and pulled open the pantry door. At the far end was a small scullery maid, a biscuit in her trembling hand, hiding her mouth behind the other fist and her eyes open nearly to popping. Beside her, wearing an equally long, terrified face, was Squirrel, the deerhound. Murray tried hard not to laugh.

'Hello,' he started kindly. 'What's your name?'

'Effy, sir,' came indistinctly from behind the tight fist. Euphemia, presumably: he had seen her name in his father's papers.

'Why are you not gone to Jamie's funeral, Effy? And try and take your hand away from your mouth, I can hardly hear you behind it.' He spoke as though to a nervous horse, and almost felt himself putting a cautious hand out for her bridle. She was stringy and wispy, perpetually unravelling at the ends. Still, she made an effort to pull her hand away from her mouth, whence it descended to the waist of her apron and seemed to become attached there. The other hand gripped the biscuit hard.

'Mrs. Chambers said you weren't to be left without anyone, sir, and as I'm the youngest I was to stay.'

'Have you had anything to eat? Besides the biscuits, I mean.' He smiled, but she took it badly.

'Oh, no, sir! Not a thing, honestly! I'm no like that!' She was almost hysterical.

'My dear Effy, please calm down. You must eat properly or you'll be cold and hungry.' She seemed to suspect a trick, but was prepared to listen to him. 'Is there any hot water?'

'A little, sir.'

'Then put on some for a bath for me – do not worry,' he added, glancing at her waif-like arms, 'I shall carry it upstairs. In the mean time, give Squirrel some meat – too many biscuits aren't good for her - make some tea and bring it to the study – do you know where that is?'

'Yes, sir, Mrs. Chambers showed us when we came here.'

'And use some of the hot water to warm some ale for yourself, and I'd recommend a couple of the larger biscuits with it. Can you manage all that? Feed Squirrel, bring me the tea, have some warm ale yourself, and then come and tell me when the bath water is hot.'

Feeling like a trespasser in his own house, he left her in the pantry and went slowly back through the kitchen, noting the well-kept copper, the scrubbed tables, the neatly stored crockery for the servants. He hoped that none of the neatness had been occasioned by the threat of his visit, but there was something about it that made it look habitual, and knowing Mrs. Chambers he was sure it was.

The tea arrived with an example of the servants' crockery, which would have shaken Mrs. Chambers to the core, but it was good, and was accompanied not only by a plateful of sugar biscuits but also by a curtsey which Effy had clearly been practising downstairs. Squirrel, too, had followed her upstairs and vanished under the sofa. He waited politely until she had closed the door, when silent laughter overtook him and made him no good for anything for five whole minutes.

The bath was more successful: Murray did as he had promised and carried the water up to the second floor himself, to the dressing room he shared with the other front bed chamber. The bath tub was there, and towels, and the steam rose gloriously as he soaped away the mud and sweat of the Bridges. He was used, at Scoggie Castle, to bathing without an attendant, and he had even thought to light his bedroom fire before he had started bathing so that his bed chamber was warm when he returned to it. He felt very capable.

Once dry, he returned to the dressing room to shave and to find appropriate dinner dress, complete, again, with a black neckcloth. He noted that one or two new ones had arrived as ordered from his tailor and had been put away by Robbins, and hoped that the second suit of mourning day clothes for which he had been measured was also on its way. He knotted the neckcloth, buttoned his high-collared, double-breasted black waistcoat, eased his coat over his shoulders, and examined himself critically in the mirror. No, he felt, he would not let Robbins down too badly like this.

CHAPTER TEN

Guests began arriving at the charming home of Mr. and Lady Sarah Dundas at the appetite-whetting, fashionable hour of a quarter to three, and shivered as they mounted the shallow steps to the open front door. St. Andrew's Square had seen some of the earliest building work in the New Town, and it was here that Sir Lawrence Dundas, distant cousin of this evening's host, had played a sleight of hand with the planning committees and built his town house, with its star-pierced dome, on the very spine of the New Town where the town planner, James Craig, had intended a church. The building was now the Excise House, but that did not stop the envious glances cast at it by the neighbours.

The guests in their fine evening footwear pretended to defy the snow that was now quite thick on the ground as well as in the air. Dundas had had the servants put down straw and earth on his steps and on the street outside. The ladies tried to keep to the straw and avoid the earth, which was now stiff mud, even in the cold. There was no wind, and apart from them the Square was oddly silent, the light from the flickering lamps falling in soft pools freckled by snowflakes.

Murray arrived on foot, among the first to appear. Inside, the Dundases were arranged in force, husband, wife and trio of sons, waiting in the drawing room to welcome their guests into the warmth. The Thomsons had arrived just before him, and were in the midst of being introduced to William Dundas' cousin from Harrogate, Lady Warwick, and her two unmarried daughters, all at present visiting Edinburgh. Mrs. Thomson and Lady Warwick eyed each other like the masters of two adjacent hunts, after the same fox. Murray greeted the Dundases and was snatched into conversation by Gavin, who was already tired of his lady relations. Murray was happy to let him talk for a little, while his fingers thawed around a glass of negus and the pain in his face diminished, skin tingling in the heat.

The room was very attractive, he decided, only half-listening to Gavin's account of his recent card games. The three tall windows overlooking the Square would have a pleasant prospect in the daylight, but now were well wrapped in thick damask curtains in warm coral, a nice compromise between Blair's hot colours and his father's cool ones. Above the large fireplace, well stocked to heat the room's ample proportions, was a Raeburn of earlier date than his father's portrait. This one showed a younger Dundas standing and a Lady Sarah, while she was still the reputed beauty, holding an infant in her lap that had to be Willie Jack. You could almost see the runny nose. Gavin and Harry, their hair curling past their wide ruffled collars, stood in self-consciously adult poses, Harry solemn, Gavin bored, on either side of their mother, and their father's hands rested lightly on the shoulders of his wife and eldest son. Behind them were a sturdy tree and a vague landscape: no one paid Raeburn for landscapes. But it was Lady Sarah that drew the eye, with an exquisite, compelling beauty. Murray wanted very much to turn and look at the lady as she was now, but sternly resisted: he could only barely imagine what it must be like to have that kind of beauty, and then to lose it, to lose the power it held. But how infinitely worse it must be, he thought, to have that daily reminder, and always to have people look, look again, and compare.

'And he was so drunk he didn't even notice!' Gavin was saying. Murray grinned, not sure what the rest of the story had been. 'I laughed so hard I could hardly get home, but you know what it's like when you've had a bit much, and the road just flies past under your feet.'

'Ah, yes,' said Murray, who had indeed watched the streets of St. Andrews fly past more than once in his student days. 'The Warwicks, are they to stay long with you?'

'Why, fancy one of them, do you?' asked Gavin, basely. The two Misses Warwick were pale blonde and dressed in white, looking, Murray thought, like rather chilly angels.

'Hard to tell,' he said, non-committally.

'Well, you're welcome to both as far as I'm concerned,' said Gavin, with uncousinly decision. 'According to them, the Scots are all savages. I'll swear they were surprised we had plates and did not simply eat roast mutton straight from the fire with our hunting knives. In their book, Harrogate is the centre of the civilised world, with London in the season a near second. I don't know why they bothered coming here, unless they were short of men down south. Even the journey was just one long whinge.'

Murray looked at the family with renewed interest, to see how they were taking their first dinner engagement in the land beyond civilisation.

'And when we reached Berwick, well! The weather!' the mother was saying, as if to prove Gavin's point.

'I'll introduce you,' said Gavin, cruelly, and drew Murray over to the circle. There, he completed the introductions and then adroitly cut Davina Thomson out and made conversation of his own with her.

'Well, Mr. Murray, and are you also an Edinburgh man?' asked Lady Warwick. Murray felt himself being tabulated.

'No, ma'am.' She began to smile. 'I am from Fife.' The smile vanished.

'And have you a profession?'

Murray could see, from the corner of his eye, Mrs. Thomson raising a gracious eyebrow at this direct approach.

'No, ma'am.'

'Then perhaps you should find yourself one.'

Murray, choosing to be amused by her rudeness, decided to tease.

'I am a little occupied at present, my lady, with my late father's estate and his house on Queen Street. He died there last Sunday.'

Lady Warwick, for whom Murray had risen several points on the mention of a house in the New Town, was shocked. Her voice rose to a slight shriek.

'And you are keeping a dinner engagement with your father not yet in the grave?'

Even the Armstrongs, who had just entered the room, paused at that.

'In Scotland, we manage things a little differently, ma'am,' said Murray clearly. 'My father was buried on Wednesday.' He bowed stiffly, and left her. Mrs. Thomson nodded reassuringly at Lady Warwick, and told her,

'He has a large estate in Fife, and eight thousand a year.'

She smiled sweetly. Murray, who had heard her, nearly laughed out loud.

The Armstrongs had brought John Douglas with them, rather a crush in their carriage, but as everyone was now present the Dundases waited a few respectful moments before leading their guests downstairs to dinner. Murray found himself seated between Miss Armstrong and Miss Lily Warwick, and was reasonably satisfied with the arrangement: so were Mrs. Armstrong and Lady Warwick, who was rapidly and visibly retabulating Murray. Gavin considered himself wasted where he was: Mrs. Armstrong on his left, and Miss Armstrong, who was pretty enough but nothing to her younger sister, on his right. He would willingly have changed places with his brother Willie Jack, who had landed the great good fortune of being between Catherine Armstrong and Davina Thomson, and not sensible enough, Gavin reckoned, to appreciate either.

Davina was also feeling slightly frustrated, and amused herself by giving an impromptu and very quiet verbal laceration of Miss Warwick to Patrick Armstrong, who sat between Davina and Miss Warwick. Patrick was therefore unable to give either lady his full attention. Miss Warwick, fortunately, was more occupied with responding to Mr. Thomson's polite enquiry as to how she found Scotland.

'Mamma brought us as a distraction, really, and we have seen so little of the country or the town that it seems hardly fair to comment.' This at least was more diplomatic than her mother. 'You see, it is a year since our beloved brother Melville died, and naturally we are all quite upset.' She said it in a tone suggesting that questions would be received with favour, and Mr. Thomson obliged in a smoothly avuncular fashion.

'What a dreadful tragedy, my dear. How did your brother come to meet his untimely end?'

'Melville was in the Horse Guards, and rising very quickly in the estimation of all who knew him in that connexion,' Miss Warwick was pleased to recount. Murray thought he heard Gavin Dundas mutter:

'Rising from a very low base, I imagine,' but he might have been mistaken.

'But alas!' Miss Warwick continued, 'one day he was riding in Hyde Park – in London, you know –'

'Thank you,' said Mrs. Armstrong, tingling with irony.

'- when he observed a young lady who was having difficulty controlling her horse. As he watched, the horse bolted, leaving the lady's groom far behind. My brother spurred his charger to full gallop and made to rescue her. He was always most gallant, you know, quite the dashing young officer.'

'I can imagine,' remarked Mrs. Thomson.

'Indeed, ma'am, if you could but have met him! Then you would know what it was to meet a young gentleman of the first degree.'

Probably consideration of this tragically-missed opportunity caused the profound silence around the table at this point.

'So how did the sad tale end, my dear?' asked Mr. Thomson, first to recover from his disappointment.

'Oh! as he galloped so gallantly, his horse stepped in a rabbit hole and he was felled in an instant. The injury to his head was so great that he died in a fever only hours later. Attended, of course, by his loyal fellow officers.'

'So really,' Murray definitely heard Gavin this time, 'he just fell off his horse.'

'And what became of the unfortunate young lady?' asked Mrs. Armstrong, almost as if she were interested.

'Oh, she was quite safe, as it happens. But devastated, of course, on hearing what had happened to her intending rescuer.'

'Oh, indeed.'

'But death often seems so senseless,' Mr. Thomson remarked. 'And so random. Poor young Murray, down the table there,' he gestured, and lowered his voice. 'Lost his father this week, scaffolding fell on him on Friday night at the far end of Queen Street, and he died on the Sunday. Now, I was walking along that very street myself that night – had to see a client in St. James' Square, you know the one, Armstrong – and I even met the party bringing my dear old friend back to his home. It could have been me under that scaffolding, but instead it was poor Murray. A tragedy.'

'Hardly for my sister Mrs. Thomson and your children, my dear Mr. Thomson,' said Mrs. Armstrong drily. She noticed that Lady Sarah, silent in the midst of this conversation, looked even more unwell than usual.

Mr. Thomson might well have lowered his voice, but at the mention of his name Murray, who was not at that moment engaged in conversation, could not help but listen. At the finish, to prevent his mind from dwelling on it, he turned to Miss Armstrong and asked her how she did. Her mother had chosen for her the shade of pale blue-green she wore, which brought out the depth of her sandy hair, and though such things were not a priority for her she was not above knowing that she looked her best this evening.

'Tolerably well, I thank you,' she replied with a friendly smile. 'I hope you are not too overwhelmed by your responsibilities at this busy time.'

'They can appear a little daunting,' Murray acknowledged with a short laugh. 'Only today I worried the housekeeper and frightened a scullery maid out of her wits, by the simple expedient of descending to the kitchens.'

The conversation continued pleasantly on both sides, and carried on until the ladies withdrew at the end of the meal. The gentlemen did not long delay, and went upstairs to the drawing room to find Miss Catherine Armstrong already engaged at the grand piano. Thomson, not always noted for his own carefulness with money, considered the possession of a grand piano typical of Dundas: it was an extravagant affectation in a town where every sensible person was perfectly content with a high quality – and Edinburgh-made – box piano. Still, his niece made a pretty picture behind Dundas' grand in her white gown, and his own daughter stood turning the pages as Catherine sang.

The gentlemen disposed themselves about the room, ready to applaud at an appropriate moment. Murray found himself once more beside Ella Armstrong.

'Do you intend to give us the pleasure of hearing you play this evening?' he asked.

'Not at all,' Ella replied decisively. 'My playing was never more than adequate, and now that I have a much more accomplished younger sister to uphold the family honour any comparisons are harmful to my vanity, and I am better placed in an appreciative audience.'

'Then what do you see as your accomplishments, without which any young lady is unarmed in the world's battles?' Catherine's song ended, and Ella waited until the applause had died down. Davina Thomson was next pressed to play, and as Catherine retired in temporary triumph, Gavin Dundas moved swiftly to turn the pages for Davina. The speed was noted by every mother in the room, and Miss Thomson began to play.

'What use are accomplishments, except to decorate a life which has enough decoration of its own? Why should any woman of passable looks and a reasonable dowry be expected also to play, sing, paint, embroider and make lace? It cannot be simply to ward off boredom, for after marriage so many women forget everything they have learned. I keep a sensible head on my shoulders, and can run a household economically and well, and that should be accomplishment enough.' She spoke with a hint of bitterness, then smiled it away. 'For my own vanity, I should say that I read Latin and read and speak French and German quite fluently. But many young ladies speak French without any intention of ever going to France, and if the French do invade our shores, we are unlikely to find such a poetic, drawing room version of their language of much practical value.'

Murray laughed, picturing the Napoleonic army confronted at Dunbar by a mass of pastel-clad young ladies commenting lyrically on the beauty of their gardens.

Accomplishments were also the topic of conversation between the now lauded Miss Thomson, Miss Catherine Armstrong and the Misses Warwick. Miss Lily Warwick was to play next, although there was a slight delay while Lady Sarah fetched a particular piece of music.

'And do you paint or draw, Miss Thomson?' asked Miss Warwick.

'I? A very little. Catherine here is the artist in our circle. Only today she completed a painting of my unworthy self which seemed to me like my own reflection.' Catherine blushed slightly and gave a modestly satisfied smile. 'If you had an interest in the subject, I am sure we can show you some excellent views around the town, considered picturesque by the most artistic in our society.'

'How kind. Perhaps we should wait, however, until the weather improves.' Miss Warwick's look said 'Savage.' Miss Thomson's smile said 'Weakling.'

'And perhaps you have an aptitude for languages?' Miss Catherine asked politely. 'French, for example?'

'We have chosen not to learn French,' replied Miss Warwick, haughtily.

'*Ça alors*,' remarked Davina. '*Qu'elles soient bêtes.*' Catherine smiled sweetly.

'The French are fiends,' Miss Warwick continued, as if Davina had not spoken. 'No civilised person could wish to learn such a language.'

At that point, mercifully, Lady Sarah returned with the music, and Miss Lily advanced to the piano. Gavin was trapped into turning the pages for her, though he endeared himself to Davina by making discreetly bored faces at her above Miss Lily's head. Miss Warwick was led away by Harry Dundas, who wished to show her a painting at the other end of the room. Mrs. Armstrong and Mrs. Thomson, observing the meeting of their respective daughters with the Misses Warwick, sat back like a couple of generals well satisfied with their infantry: Mrs. Armstrong, seeing that her troublesome elder daughter was still deep in conversation with young Murray, felt a certain glow of contentment. Several of the older people, Lady Warwick and the silent John Douglas included, formed a table for cards, and Mr. Armstrong exchanged a number of words with his son Patrick, which resulted in their spending the rest of the evening at opposite ends of the room, although both parties seemed less angry than anxious. Mr. Armstrong ate several peppermints, and asked a servant for a glass of water. Murray watched, and talked with Ella Armstrong. Inspired by Harry and Miss Warwick he walked with her to admire the paintings and sketches about the room, and when she pointed out a curious small picture by the fireplace he went with her to examine it more closely. It was a chalk drawing of an infant, less than a year old, a pretty child, and beneath it were the words, 'Catherine Gordon Dundas, 1787'.

The snow had stopped falling when Murray reached home, his final footprints on the broad steps of his own house framed crisply by a hard top layer of frost. He checked to see that the boys had returned and been fed: Henry was not quite as bad a colour as he had been, he thought. When he went to bed, the fire, refreshed by the newly-returned servants, was fighting a losing battle with the advancing walls of cold, and he tugged the extra eiderdown over the counterpane and huddled beneath it, warmed by his supper and the oblong patches where the bedwarmers had been. He fell asleep easily enough, but when that warmth had diminished, he found himself chilled again to wakefulness. He shook his head, clearing it of a dream where he and his father had both died in the tumbling scaffolding. Determined to break away from this image in his mind, he rose and pulled on a thick wool robe, as the cold slapped his bare legs and shuddered up his spine. He quickly tucked the bedclothes back around the warmed sheets and bundled them to keep in what heat they had, and padded across the carpet barefoot to the window. The cold air fell on him as he drew back one side of the heavy striped curtains and stepped behind it, opening a shutter and settling himself on the frozen cushions of the window seat. He reckoned it must be between two and three in the morning.

Outside, the moon was full and high in the sky, with no warming blanket of cloud between earth and heaven. It drew a trail of white metal sparkle on grass and stones, and the silver tracery of trees in the moonlit gardens mesmerised him. The Forth and the shadowy hills of Fife were only a memory in the distance. No one was about on a night like this, and the street was a silent platform from which he, sole watcher, surveyed the landscape like a primaeval god, like a king above his kingdom, like an architect or a builder or a rat in a riverbank hole, watching a world too full for perception.

He breathed on the glass, blotting out the steel-sharp lines, watching each tiny bubble of water begin to slide and merge with its fellows, drawing the moonlight with it down the glass, and then used the back of his forefinger to smear the mist across the pane in bright stripes of light and dark. The curtains were so thick behind him that they soaked up any sound from the room, and he would not have noticed the door opening except that the cloth moved in a tiny convulsion. He drew breath sharply, wondering if Robert was up to a prank, or if one amongst the servants could possibly be entering his bedchamber, unbidden, at this hour of the night. He caught a glimpse of a chink of light between the curtains, but it was not the light of a candle: it was brighter, and seemed to dance. He tried to press his eye to the chink without moving the curtains, and was just in time to see a figure, apparently in white, hurling something bright at the bed. The bed burst into flames.

CHAPTER ELEVEN

The figure turned and ran to the open door, snatching it shut behind him. The bed, once a cool green, began to blossom red, orange, yellow at its centre, a burning bush of flickering light. Murray, beating the entangling curtains from his legs, ran to the door, opened it, found breath to bellow, 'Fire! Fire!' in the direction of the servants' stairs. The fleeing figure was nowhere to be seen.

He turned back to the bed, grabbed the bell pull and jangled it furiously, then spun to the cupboard where a pitcher of cold water stood for the morning. He snatched it up and tipped it towards the abundant flames. No water came out. He shook it stupidly, then peered inside to see a thick plate of ice covering the surface. A moment's work with the poker freed the water, but also let the fire grow, sending out branches towards the striped bed curtains. He flung the water at the curtains and heard an angry hiss from the injured flames.

Robert stopped agape at the door and, grabbing Henry, ran back to their room for more water. Murray gave a brief thanksgiving for the boy's quick thinking. By now, sleep-dazed servants were gathering at the door, clutching their own jugs. The sight of the fire roused some of them: Dunnet, more awake than the others, hurled his jug on to the bed and seized Mrs. Chambers' jug to follow it, though his haste made him less than accurate. Robbins ran forward with his jug, and after throwing the contents into the blaze began to bundle up the edges of the counterpane over the flames. Murray did likewise on his side of the bed. Robert returned with both jugs, Henry jogging behind, and sloshed them into the smoke. Bustling at the door resulted in Mary, thick hair braided, carrying two buckets of water bobbing with chunks of ice. She was followed by Daniel who with a certain sense of enthusiasm emptied the contents of his chamber pot over what was by now a smouldering heap. There was an interesting moment of silence as they all stood about, realising that the fire was overcome, and inhaling with disgust a mixture of burned wool and second-hand ale.

Murray drew breath and looked about at them. Robbins' face was black with the smoke that had enveloped him as he tried to smother the flames, and under the soot his eyebrows looked suspiciously absent. Mary was solemnly gathering her buckets together, the long ends of her shawl swinging as she bent to them. Mrs. Chambers, holding the only candle, was white in its light, staring at the bed, as was Dunnet, who wiped the back of his hand against his brow and mouth. The sleeve of his nightshirt was torn in the rush: Murray could see the threads caught on the edge of the doorframe. One of the buckets clanked and Mrs. Chambers shook her head slightly, and gave a little pat to her night cap.

'Mary, Jennet, go and put pans in the bed downstairs. Leave the buckets here.' Jennet bobbed and Mary curtseyed, and they became white shadows in the dark hall. 'Iffy, take these buckets back to the chambermaids' room, and you and Effy fetch the tin bath from the outhouse. Well, find a candle, then, girl! Now, Mr. Murray, you come along with me and we'll make you a hot drink. Effy, when you bring the tin bath up here, put the bedclothes into it and leave them just now: we don't want them soaking through and spoiling the mattress.'

There was no time, then, for thinking, nor for the cold shivers that ran through him when he looked at the ruins of the bed and wondered what would have happened had he been sleeping there. Mrs. Chambers whisked him away to her own room in the basement, where she set up a kettle on the fire, quickly lit, and heated milk for chocolate. She sat him in an old armchair made comfortable with cushions, laid a rug over his knees, and generally treated him like an invalid. He allowed it all with a faint smile but saw little of it, and only sensed what was happening when she pressed a large cup into his hands and told him to drink.

CHAPTER TWELVE

'"Whereas",' Robbins began solemnly, '"fires often happen by the negligence and carelessness of servants" – William, put it down and stand at peace.' Robbins had seen William's fidgeting with the sugar cutters in reflection in the scullery window, but William did not realise this and was alarmed enough by Robbins' mystical powers of seeing through the back of his head to replace the cutters quietly on the dresser. '"Be it therefore enacted, by the authority aforesaid",' Robbins continued, '"That if any Menial or other servant or servants, through negligence or carelessness",' he paused, and gave a meaningful stare to the gathered servants, '"shall fire, or cause to be fired, any dwelling-house or outhouse, or houses or other buildings" – and I think we could safely say that covers the master's bedchamber – "within the Kingdom of Great Britain, such servant or servants, being therefore lawfully convicted by the Oath of one or more credible witnesses, made before two of His Majesty's Justices of the Peace, shall forfeit and pay the sum of one hundred pounds unto the Churchwardens or overseers of such parish where such fire shall happen, to be distributed amongst the sufferers by such fire, in such proportions as to the said Churchwardens shall seem just:" now, a hundred pounds is more than any of you is likely to see in your lifetime, so you should listen carefully to what happens if you can't pay. "And in case of Default or Refusal to pay the same immediately after such conviction, the same being lawfully demanded by the Churchwardens" – or the elders, you ken, this is an English insurance company that wrote this - "that then, and in such case, such servant or servants shall, by Warrant under the Hands and Seals of

Two of His Majesty's Justices of the Peace, be committed to the Common Good, or House of Correction'"; here there was a small shocked squeal from Jennet, and the twins, although they had heard this notice read when they arrived at the household, stood with wide eyes and clutched one another's arms, "'for the space of eighteen months, there to be kept to hard labour." And you needn't think,' added Robbins, turning from the notice again to address the servants directly, 'that there would be a position for you in this household at the end of the eighteen months, either. Now, about your duties.'

The lower servants dispersed slowly, quietened by Robbins' severity and the awful import of the notice. It was affixed to the wall of the kitchen, beside the dresser, and was read to the staff each time a new servant was appointed, but inevitably its significance paled between each public airing. This time, though, when the maids were already on their way to deal with the ruined bedding upstairs, the impact of the notice was rather greater, and the servants found themselves glancing at one another, wondering if any of them had, through negligence or carelessness, set fire to the master's bed, and worse, had through negligence or carelessness been seen doing so by one or more credible witnesses.

Murray woke up in confusion, behind bed curtains of the wrong colour with light of the wrong kind coming in from the wrong direction. Then he remembered the events of the early morning and came to rather fuller consciousness, leaping on to the Turkish carpet in his father's ground floor room, from the bed last occupied by his father's corpse. He went to the nearer window but it presented no long view of Fife, but a short, snow-covered garden, terminating abruptly in the rear wall of the stable block. He remembered that he needed to hire a new stable boy, and at the rate matters were progressing, perhaps a new groom.

Robbins arrived with the wherewithal for shaving, and Murray preceded him obediently into the dressing room, where he noted with astonishment that his clothes were already arranged. He sat and closed his eyes as Robbins spread soap across his chin, and tried not to think about staring at his valet's bare forehead.

'So what is the extent of the damage upstairs, Robbins?' he asked when an opportunity arose.

'I believe Mrs. Chambers wishes to report to you more fully on it in person, sir, but I understand that it could have been much worse.'

'Partly thanks to you, Robbins. All of you acted very promptly, and please convey my thanks to the staff for that, but your own expedition to suffocate the fire was the saving of us all, I think, and it was not done without danger to yourself.'

'I shall take your message to the others, sir,' Robbins said. He cleared his throat diffidently. 'Did you have it in mind to go out this morning, sir?'

'I don't believe so. The boys seem able to take themselves to college now.' Murray thought about his plans for the day, which included only a vague intention of calling again on Dandy Muir, to see if he had any information when sober that he had forgotten when drunk. He reflected on Robbins' tone of voice. 'I sense, Robbins, that there is some difficulty with any plans I might have to leave the house before, say, dinner?'

Robbins looked down at his own hands thoughtfully, then went on with courtesy.

'A small difficulty, sir, yes. You have, you see, sir, at present, only the one black hat with a crape bow, and it would of course be most improper for you to be seen without such a thing at this time.'

'Quite. And?'

'And the said hat, sir, is in a sorry state. I can only assume from the damage to the crape, sir, that although the servants at the Dundas household brushed it free of the snow they could see, they did not shake out the weepers and the loops of the bow, which therefore sat damp all evening. They have spoiled it very considerably, sir: I wonder that you did not notice it yourself as you came home,' he added, somewhat reproachfully.

'Well, it was dark.' Murray was defensive, and at the same time rather pleased that his servants were superior to those in the wealthy Dundas household.

'You may wish to order a new bow, sir, but if you wish to go out today it will take me to spend the morning on it.' He had little irons he kept for such purposes, and though the job was fiddly he took some pride in it. 'And in any case, sir, there is your new suit of black.'

'Oh, has it arrived at last?' asked Murray, happily.

'Yes and no, sir. That is to say,' Robbins had finished shaving by this stage and was keeping his hands busy ensuring that the razor was singularly free of soap. It allowed him not to look Murray in the eyes. 'That is to say, it has arrived, and appears to have been very good, but it will not be fit to wear until this afternoon, either, sir.'

Murray stared at him.

'Well, the Dundas servants can't have got their hands on that. What happened to it?'

'The messenger lad brought the package this morning, sir, but when I took it in I found that was soaked all down one side. The messenger lad claimed that he had fallen in the snow, and indeed he looked more than a little damp himself, but then Daniel reported that he had seen the boy set down the parcel in the snow, the better to defend himself against a snowball attack.'

'In which Daniel was involved?' Murray had few illusions as to Daniel and William.

'Curiously not, this time, sir.' Robbins continued to concentrate on the razor. 'The attacking snowball came, it appears, from an upper floor of this house.'

'Robert,' said Murray instantly. Robbins nodded.

'I'm afraid so, sir. On investigation, it appeared he had collected snow from the garden and taken it upstairs in two buckets. The grocer's boy had also suffered. Your clothes are now drying, as are the coffee beans and the sugar.'

'Dear Lord,' commented Murray, and wiped his face with a towel.

When Robbins had departed, leaving him again dressed in his old black, Murray wandered back into the bedchamber, wondering how shocked Mrs. Chambers would be if he refused point blank to go on sleeping here. The bedhangings here were a cool cream, embroidered by his mother before her marriage with pale blue cornflowers and pale yellow daisies, summer flowers in winter colours. There was a drawing of his mother as a young girl over the mantel, and Murray knew that a secret compartment at the back of one of the night tables contained his mother's jewellery, put aside for his wife or for George's. He crossed the room to the bed and felt in the hanging cloth watch pocket for his watch, but the pocket was empty. He looked about the bed stupidly for a moment, and then remembered that his watch had been placed in the watch pocket of his own bed upstairs. Since in any case he felt an urge to inspect the damage in person in the cold light of day, he left the bedchamber and turned the corner to go up to his own room.

Mrs. Chambers, watched from a safe distance by Iffy and Effy, was cautiously poking the contents of the tin bath with a pair of wooden laundry tongs as Murray entered the room. The bed looked curiously bare: the end curtain had gone, along with the counterpane and the quilt, and there was a singed stain on the topmost blanket. The smell was not at all pleasant, and Mrs. Chambers' mouth was slightly open as if she were trying very hard not to breathe through her nose. She heard his step on the pine boards and hurriedly straightened. Iffy and Effy, nudging each other, curtsied carefully.

'What is the extent of the damage, Mrs. Chambers?' Murray asked, advancing and peering into the bath.

'I fear,' she replied, pulling out the end of a piece of green silk in her tongs like a piece of pond weed from a dubious source, 'that the curtain from the foot of the bed is quite ruined. The flames went up it very quickly, it appears, and we are indebted to Mr. Robbins and to the grace of our heavenly Lord that the canopy did not catch.'

'Mr. Dunnet, too, moved very quickly to pour water on the flames.'

'True, very true, sir,' Mrs. Chambers agreed, 'and I believe it is thanks to him that much of the counterpane can be saved. We can use some of it to patch the damage on the quilt cover, and the rest can be saved to cover cushions. The window seats, for example, could do with new covers. I shall visit Jackson & Niven today to see if there is any silk to match for a new counterpane and curtain. One blanket is lost, though with some patching it could be used as a rough blanket elsewhere.' She straightened again, and contemplated the damp heap.

'I am sure that Daniel was very well-intentioned,' she sighed, 'but I do not think that he should be allowed to drink quite so much ale, even at a funeral.'

Murray nodded.

'Well, I fear it will mean a good deal of work for you and the maids, Mrs. Chambers. But there is no urgency to it.' He tried not to grit his teeth. 'I am quite happily settled downstairs.' But he could not resist crossing to the window and taking in, like his first breath, the view of the snow-covered carpet to the Forth.

'Right, then, girls, take this downstairs.' Mrs. Chambers dismissed the twins who between them struggled out on to the landing with the tin bath. Mrs. Chambers waited until they could be heard closing the door to the back stairs, then spoke.

'Please excuse me asking, Mr. Charles, but how did the fire start?'

At first she thought he had not heard, for he remained at the window, gazing out at the Forth.

'I am not sure,' he said at last. 'I had woken, and had come here to look out at the moonlight, when I heard a noise within the room and looked back to see the bed on fire.' He paused again, wondering how much more to say, wondering indeed if he had dreamed it, though as he himself had not lit any candle he could not see how else the fire could have started. He crossed back over to the bed, felt in the watch pocket and drew out his watch, tucking it into his waistcoat pocket to arrange properly later. 'It seems to be a mystery,' he finished, not looking at his housekeeper but fingering the singed blanket.

'Your breakfast is ready in the street parlour, sir.' Mrs. Chambers seemed to acknowledge his silence on the subject with something like relief, and he held the door open for her to precede him on to the landing. Yet as he was about to close the bedroom door behind them, he noticed again the tuft of white thread on the lock housing in the door frame, where Dunnet in his rush to put the fire out had caught and torn his nightshirt. Something, however, did not seem quite right, and as he paused to think about it, it dawned on him that the sharp edge of a nail holding in the lock plate had caught the threads on the bedroom side, not the landing side. At some point, it seemed, Dunnet had run not into the room, but out of it, and as the tear on his nightshirt had been on his right sleeve, the sleeve next to the lock plate as he would have left the room, that would seem to confirm it. Murray tried to think what Dunnet had done after he had tossed the two jugs of water on the fire, and beside the thought, like a companion piece, he saw a glimpse of the white-robed figure fleeing from the room as the fire caught in the middle of the bed.

Breakfast as usual had been laid in the street parlour, and as was indeed not uncommon, it was accompanied by an intensive interrogation and reprimanding of Robert Scoggie. Robert wore a look of bored contrition on his face along with some boiled egg, but his excuse was a novel one.

'I thought it might cheer Henry up,' he claimed, and indeed Henry was as wan as ever, pushing his food around his plate without enthusiasm.

'Henry, would you rather remain at home today? Here, I mean? You could go back to bed if you wanted to.'

'I'm not feeling well, either, Mr. Murray,' Robert claimed at once. 'My head's very bad, and I could just go back to bed this minute.'

'The only thing wrong with your head, Robert,' said Murray, eyeing him, 'is that it devotes its time to divilment when it could be doing something more useful. Henry, what do you think?'

'I'd rather go to college. I feel fine.'

'You're sure? You look very pale.'

'It's the winter. I always look pale in the winter.'

Murray had taught them for four years, and did not remember having noticed this as a particular phenomenon before. But he sighed, and left the subject.

There was a note by his plate from Andrew Balneavis, asking if Murray would be so kind as to dine with him at Stone's. Murray had no other engagement, and was assured by Robbins that hat and clothes would be approximately presentable by then, so William was sent up to the Old Town to say that Mr. Murray was pleased to accept Mr. Balneavis' invitation, and would see him at two. William was also therefore able to escort the boys to the College, and Murray retired to the study.

He drew out a piece of paper intending, once again, to write to his brother George, but again, no words would come, and he found himself writing instead:

To Lord Scoggie of Scoggie:

'My Lord,

'Thank you for your kind condolences on the death of my father. I do indeed feel the loss most acutely.

'As I informed you in my previous note, I have brought Henry and Robert here to my father's house in Queen Street and they have since the funeral continued with their studies at the College. Henry derives great benefit from these and I believe that Robert, too, is' - he paused, and considered for some time - 'acquainting himself to some degree with the subjects taught.' He grimaced, and then drew a deep breath as though he were about to put the next point to Lord Scoggie face to face. 'However, since the boys have been brought up gently and for the most part peaceably in the country,' – barring the odd spate of violent deaths, he thought – 'I am anxious that the pace of life in the city is rather upsetting for Henry and a little too distracting for Robert. They are each in their own way not quite ready for Edinburgh,' – nor Edinburgh for them, he reflected, thinking of the ferrets and the chairs. 'Henry is not enjoying particularly good health at present, though he insists on continuing with his studies. I feel that a period in the country would be beneficial to him and might restore some calm to Robert.'

He continued the letter with a more detailed account of what the boys had studied so far, for Lord Scoggie valued learning above all else, and finished with the usual civilities. He was not quite sure where he stood, and struggled for a little to find a delicate way of asking Lord Scoggie if his services were still required: on one level he longed to hand Henry and Robert over to someone else, but on another he found that he still had a profound sense of responsibility for the boys – in moments of deep emotion he could almost find it in himself to say that he was quite fond of them.

Ignoring the beginning of the letter to George, he turned once again to his father's papers, to mark, if he could, any possible connexion between Charles Murray senior and the late Matthew Muir. However, no legal papers appeared that did not seem to have gone through the hands of the gingery Mr. Simpson. Murray wondered then if perhaps his father had purchased, or intended to purchase, one of the feus at the building site as an investment, although property speculation was not normally his preferred way of making good returns on his money. Again, there was no evidence of any intention or any transaction carried out, which proved nothing.

Murray sat back in his chair and pondered. Why would his father have gone to look at the building work? Whether his father intended to purchase a feu or not, it might be helpful to know who had bought them: one of the owners might know something, or might be the 'gentleman' partner of whom Matthew Muir had spoken to his brother. Or he might be the murderer. He wondered if the records would be with the Council, who sold the feus, and whether or not he might be allowed to look at them, but then he remembered that it was Saturday, and he could do nothing about it now until Monday at the earliest. He tapped on the desk and sighed impatiently, and rang the bell to find out how near Robbins was to finishing his hat.

Balneavis followed Old Town ways and tended, when left to his own devices, to dine quite early. Dining early meant that one could sup early and therefore retire early, with a consequent saving on tallow and firewood in the winter months. Such considerations were important when one had four daughters to marry and three sons to school.

He was already seated at the corner table at Stone's when Murray arrived, his usual pot of coffee at his elbow and a number of case papers before him, through which he worked his way slowly and methodically: there was rarely any rush with his work. He saw Murray almost immediately and the characteristic beam spread across his face as he rose and bowed with dangerous enthusiasm in the small coffeehouse.

'Please, come and sit down, Charles, my dear boy! It is a pleasure to see you looking so well and healthy. You have looked mightily strained this week past what with one thing and another.'

Murray felt the smile stiffen slightly on his face in mild confusion, wondering how to respond, but there was little chance.

'Come then! Two dinners here, please, Colin my man! Mrs. Stone is one of the finest cooks in Edinburgh, you ken, Charles.'

'Ah, yes, I believe my father used to mention the quality of the food here.'

'Indeed, my boy, he ate here with us long after he gave up advocacy and took to being a gentleman.' He paused as soup arrived, a finer quality than the broth in the Scoggie boys' favourite haunt. Murray tasted and admired it, and caused a flurry of wrinkles to pass over Balneavis' face. 'Do not cause yourself distress, Charles! This is my treat, no need to concern yourself with the depth of your pocket!' He beamed and seemed to expand on the bench seat, plump and happy. It was nearly impossible not to smile back.

'So, my boy, have you settled yet what you are to do with your time, now that, you know, you are *independent*?'

The question seemed to obsess all his father's friends, though whether from concern or curiosity it was difficult to tell. He went through once more, with some speed, his reasoning and his lack of decision on the matter.

'So you have no absolute plans to quit Edinburgh, then, and live entirely in Fife?'

'Not at the moment – I am fond of both places.'

'And yet both are large properties, and I believe your good lady housekeeper is not as young as once she was. Have you no plans to marry, and ease both her burden and your own solitude?'

Murray laughed.

'I have scarcely been solitary this week! And after tutoring two boys for a number of years, solitude is often a precious state. And I think Mrs. Chambers would take it very much amiss if I married purely to relieve her of her duties!'

Balneavis chuckled and nodded agreement. He noted with satisfaction Murray's new black suit of clothes and the presentable black neckcloth about the collar of his bright white shirt. It did not make him ashamed of his own yellowing cuffs: he was comfortable with what he was, but eager to achieve better for his family.

'But should a young lady catch your eye?' he prompted. Murray was unsuspicious.

'Perhaps, if I were very taken with a young lady, I might consider marriage. But at present there is no one ...' His mind dwelled fleetingly on Ella Armstrong, and even more briefly, as if running down a list, on the other ladies at the Dundases' dinner. He smiled faintly at the memory of Mrs. Armstrong, Mrs. Thomson and Lady Warwick, seen from the corner of his eye, studying and analysing his every moment in Ella's company.

'You are wise to take your time,' agreed Balneavis, 'although I myself married young and have dwelt in perfect happiness with my dear Mrs. Balneavis, and we had not, if I may make mention of it, the financial advantages which you have.' Murray felt embarrassed, and wondered if he ought to pay for dinner. 'No sense, though, of course, in pushing your own children into the same thing simply because it worked for you.' He scraped his soup plate clean and pushed the wine jug towards Murray. Balneavis himself adhered to ale out of impecunious habit, which did not make Murray feel very comfortable about pouring himself another glass of burgundy.

'Take my girl Margaret, for instance, my eldest,' Balneavis went on, folding his arms and leaning back. 'She's a lovely girl, beautiful complexion as if she's spent her days in the countryside, and such an agreeable nature as you never came across –' Murray began, unaccountably, to feel slightly nervous, and took a rather larger sip of wine than he had intended. 'And only a few years younger than you. Your good father and I used to draw parallels, you know.' Murray deeply doubted it. His father had had no intention, as far as Murray knew, of his son marrying anyone who would not bring a very good dowry to the occasion. 'It's such a good balance of ages, a good combination, yours and hers. It's the ages my dear Mrs. Balneavis and I were when we were wed. Now, Mrs. Balneavis,' he went on hurriedly, evidently sensing that he had stepped a little too far, 'Mrs. Balneavis is eager to have her married off, Margaret, that is. I think it is perhaps something too soon. What do you think?'

Murray was cautiously relieved.

'Oh, certainly, there is no rush, I should have thought.' He managed to sound quite composed, he thought, but greeted the interruption of the arrival of the next course with the delight of a doting parent seeing a favoured child return home safely.

'No, no need to rush her,' Balneavis continued, when the taciturn Colin had once more retreated. 'And truth to tell, we should all miss her very much at home, she is such a dear girl. But there! it would be good to have her settled, to see her happy. Daughters are such a trial, as I am sure you will one day be lucky enough to discover, Charles, but they are a joyful trial, all the same. I do not know, as I said, what we should do without her, for her mother has her so well trained and her own in-born skills – well, such needlework as you never saw, as in my handkerchief, for example.' He showed Murray some discreet white threadwork which made the cheap linen a little more luxurious. 'And so practical in the household, she could run it herself if my dear Mrs. Balneavis chose to become more leisurely! She is such a help, but then eldest girls often are, I believe: Mrs. Balneavis was the eldest of nine, you see, and it always tells. Well-trained from the start, and then eager for a household of their own.' He sighed, and wove his plump fingers over his plate, his worn elbows propped on either side. He peered at Murray over the tops of his knuckles.

'It is undoubtedly a great virtue in a young woman to be able to run a household well,' Murray responded dutifully, remembering his conversation with Ella Armstrong. The faint sounds of the street were suddenly dominated by the noise of a company of soldiers marching by to a solitary drum and a few flutes, accompanied by the shouts of the crowd that had increased over the months in friendliness and encouragement in direct proportion to the threat from France. For a wild moment, Murray considered running out to join the soldiers.

'And it is good to see an eldest daughter married,' Balneavis continued, as the flutes faded and Murray's fantasy with them, 'for it encourages the others, as often as not, and allows them a little more into society. But there! Mrs. Balneavis has the whole thing planned, for she is so fiercely protective of them, of their interests and their prospects! For money may be one thing, and one path to attracting a husband, but a good character is a surer one, and will attract a better husband, however wealthy he may be, and all the money and finery in the world cannot buy a reputation. And Mrs. Balneavis is keen, you may imagine, to see her established in the very best of households.'

Murray, who was reflecting belatedly on the risks of accepting unexpected dinner invitations from impecunious fathers, wondered briefly if he were being offered a wife or a domestic servant.

'Oh, she is so like her mother at the same age!' Balneavis enthused. *Either he is ignoring me completely, or I'm better at hiding my feelings than I thought*, Murray noted. *Surely no man, however determined, could carry on with his efforts if Murray's reluctance had been clearly visible.* 'And you, my dear Charles, you remind me so much of myself at your age, poised on the threshold of life!'

But that was enough. Balneavis had to be disabused of this notion, before it went too far.

'Mr. Balneavis, I feel I ought perhaps to have made my position clearer at once, and yet to tell the truth I am not sure of it myself in some respects. Miss Balneavis is indeed a delightful girl, but for that very reason I should hate to see her forced to wait an indeterminate time for someone as yet not sure of his future, while she might well have the pleasant opportunity of offers far more worthy. It is not right,' he finished firmly, 'for such a charming girl, from such a fine family, to be the victim of any false hopes.'

'Oh, aye, aye,' agreed Balneavis cheerfully. 'As I say, I'm no so willing for her to be handfasted to anyone just yet. I was just airing my problems, you ken.' His speech, which had been becoming more refined as he envisaged his daughter becoming Mrs. Murray of Letho, relaxed again as he accepted that this round, at least, had gone to Charles – though it was, of course, not necessarily the end of the fight.

'Well, exactly,' said Murray, feeling his pulse slowing. 'And speaking of problems, Mr. Balneavis, have you ever heard of a man named Matthew Muir?'

'Matthew Muir ...' Balneavis pondered, happy to accept the change of subject. 'I seem to recollect that I have heard the name somewhere recently, but I just cannot mind where.'

Murray thought about it.

'Mr. Dundas mentioned him at my father's funeral supper. And the name was in the paper at the time of my father's accident.'

'Oh?' said Balneavis vaguely, a brief frown of confusion twitching his eyes and vanishing as quickly as it had come.

'He was the notary killed when my father had his accident. An apprentice notary, as it turns out. Do you know of any reason why he would have had dealings with my father?'

Balneavis was tipping more wine into Murray's glass and at that moment his hand slipped, knocking the glass with the jug and sending the wine in a pink arc into his own lap. There was a moment's confusion, as Murray snatched the glass and Balneavis tried to save the jug and dodge the wine. The attempts were moderately successful: the wine spilled mostly on the table and on the bench beside Balneavis, and the glass was secured without breaking. Murray reached for his napkin to soak up the puddles and found it had slipped off his lap. He leaned under the table and retrieved it from its perch on Balneavis' well-worn shoes.

'Now, John Douglas might ken him,' said Balneavis. 'He knows every notary from Ebenezer Hammond down. Are you well acquainted with Douglas?' Murray shook his head, privately doubting that many were well acquainted with the gentleman at all. His own father had always spoken of him with respect, but rarely with intimacy. 'He's a fine man to know well,' Balneavis asserted. 'Perhaps we could invite him to meet us for dinner next week, if you have no objections. Would Tuesday be suitable, for example?'

'Tuesday is, I believe, quite suitable,' Murray agreed, wondering if the dinner time blandishments of Balneavis were going to become a regular occurrence. If they were, he might just return to Scoggie Castle, whether or not Lord Scoggie wanted him.

'Then I shall ask Douglas this very day,' said Balneavis happily. 'He is good company, and besides, if you ever chose to enter the law he has great influence among the powerful here.' He beamed at Murray, who again, despite himself, found it impossible to do anything but smile in reply.

CHAPTER THIRTEEN

The wine had been strong and, apart from what had gone on the table and off it, had been generously poured. Murray found himself a little light-headed as he emerged from Stone's and began a slithering descent of the High Street in over-trodden snow, to attempt his intended visit to Dandy Muir. There was still enough virgin snow at the sides of the road for the occasional snowball fight between gangs of boys, causing him to wonder obliquely if the coffee beans had yet been dried in the kitchen, and to feel a brief pang of guilt over the Scoggie boys. Should he offer to keep them here in Edinburgh with him? If he did, he would have to devote much more time both to overseeing their studies and to keeping them in check.

He ducked instinctively as a snowball whistled past his hat, then realised that it had been aimed with solemn concentration at a shop sign painted high on the wall of a tenement, showing a picture of a black hat on a red ground. It was now speckled with white where the snow adhered, and the hatter, who had come in for one of the wider shots full in the chest, shook his fist at the boys from his window as he wiped muddy snow from his coat. Murray smiled, and found himself thinking of Jamie, wondering what he might have played or what mischief he and his friends might have done on his way to and from his parents' home.

The stair to Dandy Muir's flat was still as fresh and clean as it had been the day of his brother's funeral. A well-dressed, elderly maid was leaving the building as Murray entered, and he drew back to let her past, then mounted the stairs again to the first floor, and knocked on Dandy's now closed door. After a moment Dandy, sober and tired-looking in a suit of better black than he had worn to the funeral, came to the door and treated Murray to a fairly hostile stare.

'Aye?' he said, non-committally.

'Dandy Muir,' said Murray, half to reassure himself that this was, in fact, the same man with whom he had spoken on Thursday.

'Aye?' repeated the man.

'My name is Murray. I attended your brother's funeral.'

'Oh, aye?'

Murray sighed shortly.

'Do you remember me? Do you remember why I came?'

Dandy shifted in the doorway, transferring his weight from one foot to the other and propping a shoulder against the doorpost. He folded his arms.

'Aye, I ken well who y'are and why ye came. I was no sae drunk as you thought, see.'

'I see,' said Murray, rather cross but trying not to show it. 'I wondered if perhaps you had remembered anything more about what Matthew said concerning his gentleman friend?'

'No,' said Dandy briefly.

'Well,' said Murray, mentally counting slowly to ten, 'would you be kind enough to reflect for a moment, and see if there is anything you can add to what you told me?'

'No,' said Dandy. The doorpost looked fractionally more moveable than he did. Murray contemplated him for a long moment. The man's eyes were definitely bloodshot, but his fingers, gripping the new black cloth of his coat, were tense. Murray glanced down at his feet. His stockings were thick wool, warm and still unworn. He wore no boots, though the stockings would never have fitted into shoes. Dandy watched him in return, and met his eyes again.

'You were eager enough to talk on Thursday,' Murray remarked, in a slightly lowered voice.

'Was I, then?' asked Dandy, quite loudly, then more quietly, 'Well, maybe I was towards the edges of being drunk, after all. So it was my only brother's funeral, and him the last family I have in the world.' It seemed to Murray that, just briefly, the defiance in his eyes turned to a kind of plea. Murray blinked, and tried to think quickly.

'And of course,' he said quite clearly, 'you could tell me nothing of your brother's business even then, for as you said, it was something of which he never spoke to you, and in which you took no interest.'

'Look,' said Dandy angrily, though his face was friendlier, 'I tellt you all that on Thursday. You're a mighty slow learner, for all you're a gentleman,' he finished loudly, then took Murray quickly by the sleeve and whisked him through the door, slamming it behind him.

'Now hear this,' he hissed, waving a finger at Murray, 'I dinna ken what you want, but you tellt me on Thursday your own faither was killed where Matt met his end, and I've taken you in good faith on that, aye, maybe more than I should have. But I made mention of things to you at Matt's funeral that I shouldna have said, and if the word gets out about them there's more than me will suffer. Matt wasna the only family I have left, you ken. I have a sister, Margit – you saw her at the funeral – and she has bairns that are as good as my own to me.' He took a shaky breath, and moved away from the door. Murray said nothing, but turned as he moved to keep facing him. He noticed, absently, that there was now a second armchair in the shabby room, and a decent enough bottle of whisky on the table beside it. Dandy nodded at him, seeing where he was looking.

'Aye, it seems Matt had the power to leave me some money after all.'

'But not, I should say,' said Murray quietly, 'through his will in the normal way?'

Dandy gave a smile that was closer to a grimace. He gave the new armchair a kick.

'It came under the door the night of the funeral,' he admitted at last, without looking at Murray. 'There was a wrapper, with money in it and a letter. Now, Matt might have been the one for the writing but I can read well enough, and that letter said if I talked to anyone about any of Matt's business, there would be trouble for me and for mine.' He scuffed his stocking soles along the leg of the armchair, hands in his breeches pockets.

'How much money?' asked Murray curiously.

'Fifty pounds.' He looked up. 'Oh, I'm no like Matt, you see. I bought this and that, but the rest of it is safely away. You never ken the minute, do you?'

'Very true,' Murray replied automatically. 'This letter, do you still have it?'

'No. It said to burn it, and I always do what I'm told by nameless strangers that threaten me.' He grinned again.

'Was it a good hand? An educated hand?' asked Murray. Dandy thought about it, picturing the letter, his foot still for a moment.

'Aye, I would say so. The paper was ordinary, like, but the hand was I suppose you'd call cultivated.'

Murray asked the obvious.

'And no name or address on it?'

'Not a thing. Just 'By hand' on the wrapper.'

'And fifty pounds in coins?'

'Aye, guineas and such, and small bits too. All good, ye ken.'

Murray nodded.

'I'd better go now,' he said. 'Thank you for your help, Mr. Muir.'

'Aye, well, I think I'm a better judge of a man than Matt was,' said Dandy, his foot on the move again. 'Do not prove me wrong.'

Murray went to the door and opened it.

'Well, since you have nothing of value to tell me, Mr. Muir,' he said loudly and crossly, 'I shall take myself elsewhere. Good day to you.' He left and pulled the door behind him. His last glimpse of the flat showed him Dandy's grinning face and a hand reaching for the whisky bottle.

Outside on the landing, he took a deep breath, which turned to a gasp when he heard a step behind him. He spun around, to find the elderly maid whom he had met downstairs, once more descending the stair. He found a smile and drew back to let her pass, but she shook her head and he noticed belatedly that she was wearing neither cloak nor bonnet, but had her apron on over a decent black gown.

'Excuse me, sir,' she began with a somewhat coy smile, 'my mistress would be happy if you would step upstairs to share a cup of tea with her.'

'Your mistress?' queried Murray. 'Am I acquainted with her?'

'Perhaps not, sir, but she would be happy to remedy that situation. She is Miss Gordon, sir, and as she is *elderly*,' she whispered the last word forcibly, 'she does not receive as many visitors as perhaps she once did.'

'Then I should be honoured to make her acquaintance,' said Murray politely, and waved the servant up the stair in front of him to show the way. Miss Gordon might, he reflected, have been a friend of his father's and have recognised him from the window, but in any case there could be no harm in visiting an old lady. She or the maid might even be able to tell him something of the Muirs and their dealings.

In accordance with the Old Town way of living, so curious now to the airy dwellers in the New Town, this tenement stair held people from different strata of life. Dandy, as a tradesman, occupied rooms on a lower floor, but Miss Gordon's elevated station in life was indicated by the fact that her rooms were at the very top of the building, where one emerged at last from the dark coils of the staircase on to a landing lit by a final high window. Here, herbs nursed through the winter's dark and cold grew in little pots and the doorstep was clean from the passage of few feet. The walls had been washed white to reflect all the available light, and the door was a surprising blue. It stood ajar, and the maid pushed it to lead the way inside.

If Blair's house was a relic of the 1780s, this place made it look as modern as Bath. The walls, where one could perceive them, were washed white, but covered in tapestries that shrank the size of the tiny hallway and enveloped all the other rooms that he could see. The curtains were rough and heavy, and had been designed for much larger windows than those in a Canongate tenement: great folds had been taken up with tacking thread and pinned back to let in some venturesome daylight. Murray had hardly walked two yards before he had rapped his shins on the ferocious studded corners of an oak chest and narrowly avoided a second one. The carpets seemed also to have been folded to fit the rooms and were several layers thick, irregularly shaped and lumpy. The maid, who moved amidst the obstacles easily, relieved him of his hat and top coat and led the way to a tapestry which she pushed back to reveal a door, through which she went. Stronger than she looked, she held the tapestry back on both sides for Murray to stoop beneath, and curtseyed to the occupant of a large chair, saying:

'Your visitor, ma'am.' She closed the door behind her, there was a faint sweep of falling tapestry, and Murray stood alone in the middle of the room.

A fine fire was blazing in the fireplace, above which a gap between tapestries allowed room for a slightly faded plaid. It framed like lambrequin an oval portrait of a young man of sixty years ago, fresh-faced and powder-wigged, with the pop-eyed, narrow-lipped smile so fashionable in portraits of the time. On the mantelpiece lay a sword, untarnished and without so much as a suspicion of dust on it. He had already drawn one or two conclusions when the figure in the chair spoke.

'Well, good day to you, my bonny lad, and what do they call you?' Her voice was high and clear; she was small and upright, with a face nearly as rosy as the one in the portrait, though soft with wrinkles.

Murray bowed.

'Charles Murray of Letho, ma'am. Have I the honour of addressing Miss Gordon?'

'You have. Christian Gordon of Balkiskan, and last of my line.'

'Ma'am.' Murray bowed again.

'You may sit, laddie,' she laughed. 'There is a stool behind you. Jessie will bring refreshments in a moment. You have time to stay for a cup?'

'Certainly, ma'am, if you wish it.' Murray busied himself finding the stool and arranging his hard-won new coat tails behind it as he sat.

'A well brought up young lad, and with a good name.' She gave him a satisfied smile. 'Charles was always my best-favoured name. Many a fine man has borne it before you, and not brought it shame. How came you by it?'

'It was my grandfather's name, ma'am, and my father's,' Murray explained.

'And is it for one of them that you now wear mourning?' He noticed as she spoke that she too wore black, though it was older by far than his.

'For my father, ma'am, but lately dead. His funeral was on Wednesday.'

'I am sorry to hear it,' she replied, and plucked irritably at the end of her shawl. 'There are too few good Charleses left.' She sighed, then caught his eye and nodded up at the wall above the fireplace. 'I make no doubt but that you can tell who one of them was, now long gone, can you not?'

Murray was embarrassed. He had been brought up not to talk much about the events of 1745, an episode that polite society preferred not to remember, when Scot had taken up arms against Scot. The few Jacobite supporters still left were treated by society with distant respect, and Murray had had little to do with them. He had, however, guessed from the plaid and the portrait that he might now be faced with a more direct encounter – he hoped that information about the Muirs might be his reward. He drew a breath.

'I should say, ma'am, that you were amongst the supporters of – of Charles Edward Stuart.' He had been about to say 'the Young Pretender', but decided that it would be less than tactful. She smiled wickedly, as though she sensed his dilemma.

'You are a laddie born long after such events, and consequently have had to rely on your elders for histories of them, so I hold no blame to your account that you look as though you would draw your coat tails up from my carpet.' She laughed as he made to shift on the stool and stopped himself again. 'Aye, it's no your fault. It's your loss, instead, to live through a time of fighting for the mad old man in London against the country as closely allied to the Kingdom of Scotland as any other, rather than to fight for the finest young charmer ever to take Edinburgh and lead his men to glory! And the man you see up there, above the fireplace, that was the lad that would have followed the Prince to the ends of the earth, and I would have walked beside him.'

Murray examined the face again. It was young, and serenely vacuous, like the faces in many portraits of the period: impossible to judge charm or character beneath the glaze of convention. The tapestries shifted behind him, and Jessie the maid entered, bearing a tray with two glasses and a plate of dense, rich tea bread, partly cut and with a heavy-handled silver knife laid on the plate. Murray saw no teacups. Jessie was waved by her mistress to a neat bow-fronted cellaret below a sideboard. She was given a key to unlock it, and brought forth a bottle of brandy from amongst a clutter that Murray could see there. His heart sank: his head was still mobile with the effects of his dinner time wine. Jessie poured two generous glasses full, and set the open bottle beside them on the tray, then placed the cellaret key in Miss Gordon's open hand, curtseyed and left.

'We are both partial,' said Miss Gordon confidentially, 'to a glass of brandy now and again. I, alas, am confined to the bounds of this chair, so if I keep the key, neither of us is able to partake of more than we should. Please help yourself, Mr. Charles.'

He took the nearer glass and a slice of the bread, hoping that it would soak up the liquor. It seemed, however, to have been soaked in the liquor already, and all but squelched as he bit into it. He had to clear his throat before asking,

'And what became of the young gentleman in the portrait, ma'am?'

'Oh, well, he never aged,' said Miss Gordon, 'which is a gift not generally bestowed. I was betrothed to him, on our own terms, but against the wishes of my family, who were firm in the service of the Government. But my young man was a romantic, and who would not be in the face of such an opportunity? We were nineteen, and we knew little, though we thought it was everything.' She gave Murray a stern look, warning him against such illusions.

'My parents disowned me, as near as makes little difference,' she went on, 'and I went to dwell with his family while he joined the Prince. They didna approve either, but felt sorry for me and responsible, I suppose, for their son's behaviour. But they and I did not see much eye to eye either, and after he died it was a hard place to live.'

'He died at Culloden?' asked Murray with kindness.

'No! Thank the Lord, he never lived to see that day of tragedy! He died at Prestonpans, in the midst of his army's most glorious victory, and the Prince himself sent me his plaid and his sword, and thanked me for his service. Oh, I wept then, more tears than ever you would think possible, and that plaid is stained with them and with his blood, though little worn else. And I believe then that my family would have taken me back and nothing more said on the matter, had not my own brother died in the service of Butcher Cumberland at Culloden before I could persuade myself to go.'

'A tragedy, indeed,' Murray agreed, and sipped some more brandy. It was old and strong.

'Aye, for like my sweetheart he died in the midst of his army's triumph, though it was a poor triumph indeed over starved and worn out men. I believe he must have tripped on his sword and fallen on someone else's, the poor fool, for he was never a fighter. I would have made the better soldier of the two of us!' She chuckled, and drained her glass. 'But he was my parents' only other bairn, and they could not bear that he had should have been killed by such people, so that was me out of favour again. My father died soon after from the disappointment, and the lands came to me, of course, and the furnishings between me and my mother. Balkiskan and other sundry plots are all mine, and no one to claim them after me,' she laughed again, 'except some simpering cousin of my father's. He'll spin in his grave,' she said with satisfaction. 'Have some more brandy.' She poured it with a steady hand despite his refusal, and leaned back in her chair to contemplate her own refilled glass.

'He was a kind man, our Prince,' she reminisced. 'Perhaps he was a thing too kind for a strong leader, a thing too thoughtful, but an honour to have met with. He would have kept Edinburgh for the Scots, you ken, not allowed this anglified expansion they cry the New Town. That's no a cosy place for folks to live. I'd knock it all down tomorrow and give it back to the country people, if they'd give me a big enough stick. There's land of mine over there, but they'll never build on it while I'm alive, I swear it!' She had made herself angry now, and scowled at Murray. 'I'll stop them, you know. Where do you live, then?'

'In Fife, ma'am,' said Murray diplomatically. She looked as if she did not believe him, but nodded at last.

'Aye, aye. And what kirk will you be at tomorrow?'

'Greyfriars in the morning, ma'am, I hope, and perhaps again in the afternoon.'

'Aye, aye. I shan't be seeing you, then. In the days when I could be moved they took me to the Episcopalian Chapel. And I didn't kneel to pray for that mad old man in London, though I suppose he needs our prayers as much as anyone.' She emptied her glass again. 'Here,' she offered him the cellaret key, 'lock that bottle away before you go or she'll be after it. Aye!' she said crossly. Murray did as he was told, and felt dismissed. He found Jessie in the over-furnished hall.

'Do you know much of the Muirs downstairs?' he asked her as she helped him with his coat. 'You met me at the door there.'

'They have come but recently, sir. There were two brothers, but one died and the other is now on his own.'

'Has either visited Miss Gordon?'

'One is a tradesman, sir. The other was a notary, and he paid a call once, sir, though my mistress did not take to him.'

'And have you seen any gentlemen call on them?'

'Gentlemen, sir!' She was shocked. 'None except yourself, sir.' She seemed to feel that this could be taken as some kind of criticism, for she blushed and bobbed stiffly. Murray nodded, disappointed, and picked up his hat to go home.

'Well, my dear, and what came of that?' asked Mrs. Balneavis.

'Nothing as yet, my dear.' They were in the dim hallway, and kept their voices lowered by habit in the small flat. 'He seemed quite determined not to choose a wife until he feels more settled.' He sighed. 'It is an honourable intention.'

'But not so convenient for us, though,' his wife pointed out.

'I would not pin my hopes altogether on that suitor, my dear Mary,' Balneavis said gently. 'Have a wider range of targets, and we are less likely to miss entirely.'

'I shall find her a husband before the year is out, the poor girl,' said Mrs. Balneavis with determination. 'She shall be wed and established, and keep you in your old age, you'll see.'

Balneavis beamed at her, but there was an uncharacteristic sorrow in his eyes.

CHAPTER FOURTEEN

The evening was in the process of being dull, and Murray was wondering if even an unconsidered marriage might be preferable to solitude. He had overseen the boys making a fair copy of their lecture dictata, and they were now seeing to the ferrets in the stables. He almost found himself wishing they would get up to some mischief to distract him. A ferret had bitten Squirrel on the nose, which was painful to contemplate but hardly exciting. The servants were still cowed by the thought of the fire and the loss of both their master and Jamie, and while they continued to work well, they did so in an atmosphere of something like awe. Murray was beginning to think he might brave the cold and go to call on someone of his acquaintance – almost anyone would do – when he heard the street door bell ring and Robbins go stalking across the flagged hall to answer it. In a moment, he appeared at the door of the parlour.

'Mr. Blair, sir,' he announced. Murray was delighted, and rose to bow as Blair bumbled around Robbins and patted the servant on the shoulder in a friendly manner. He wore a green coat and an extraordinary pair of apricot breeches, the pockets so full that his haunches looked like those of a well-pampered lap dog.

'Dear boy, how do you do?' he asked, shaking Murray warmly by the hand.

'You will stay to supper, sir, I hope?' asked Murray, catching Robbins' eye.

'Oh, well, if it's not – I'd be awfully happy to, if there's no – you know – may I?'

'Please inform Mrs. Mutch that we shall be four for supper,' Murray confirmed to Robbins, who nodded smartly and left. Blair perched on a footstool and jiggled his apricot legs happily in front of the fire.

'What a night out, what a night!' he said, rubbing his hands. 'A thaw coming upon the snow, everything mud and slush, the Bridges a hazard to every footstep! But there, my dear boy, my sister is off to spend the night with friends in Colinton, because she would not travel twice in one day in the snow, so she has the carriage and the house is empty, so I came to you in search of entertainment. Have you a board of backgammon anywhere? For I have played myself so many times today that I believe I can now predict my own next move, which makes it a very dull game indeed.'

Murray smiled and went to the cupboard to find the backgammon board, and pulled a small table out to accommodate it. Blair was prevailed upon to move to an armchair, as otherwise the board was at the level of his chin, and as Murray began to lay out the black pieces Blair chivvied the whites into place.

'And what have you been up to since I saw you last?' asked Blair.

'Oh! there have been great events!' Murray tried to make light of his days. 'I have been lured into the apartments of a Jacobite, I have arranged a bath for myself, I have dined at the Dundases and I have narrowly escaped being burned in my bed!' Blair's eyes widened in alarm, and Murray told him about the fire, then, after a pause, told him also about Dunnet and the ripped nightgown. Blair grew solemn.

'You must have him arrested immediately, Charles. There is no knowing what he will do next time.'

Murray handed the dice in their cup to Blair, and frowned.

'Yes, well, perhaps I should,' he said. 'But I'd like to know why he did it, and I don't think I'll find out if I have him arrested. I'd rather have him here where I can watch him.'

'And who is watching him while you are out all day? or while you are asleep? Remember, Charles, it is not just your life you are putting at hazard here: you have the other servants to think of, too.'

'You are right,' Murray admitted, slightly ashamed. 'I shall speak to Robbins about it tonight.'

'Good.' Blair grinned at him, and threw the dice. 'A double six. Now, where shall I begin?'

Throughout the game, which was regularly punctuated by Blair's double sixes, Murray told him in more detail how he had spent his time and what progress he had made concerning the mystery of his father's death. He left out, for discretion's sake, the bulk of his conversation with Andrew Balneavis, but finished with Dandy Muir's curious confession and a brief account of his unconventional tea with Miss Gordon.

'Bribed, was he?' asked Blair thoughtfully, skipping Miss Gordon in his mind. He ran the last of his counters off the board. Murray still had several left. He sighed, and started to slide them back into their starting places for another game.

'By someone with an educated hand and plenty of money about him, by the sound of it,' he agreed. 'I must add the information to my notes.'

'You have made notes?' Blair was always interested in things written down. Murray left him shuffling pieces on the board while he crossed with a candle to the study and retrieved his page of parallels between the three deaths.

'I see you have marked the connexions with the Grassmarket,' Blair commented, fidgeting with the paper.

'It seems the only connexion, however,' Murray sighed.

'Not at all,' said Blair. 'There is the connexion that Jamie and your father both lived here. There is the connexion that Dunnet your groom was close by, but not present at, both incidents. There is also the opportunistic nature of the assaults.'

'How opportunistic?' asked Murray, taking the paper back to add notes. Blair had already made the edges of it soft with fiddling.

'No weapon was brought to the scene in either case. Your father died because the scaffolding hit him, however ably assisted by human agents, and Jamie's head was knocked against the corn bing and his neck broken.'

Murray brought over a pen and ink and made a note on his paper.

'Interestingly,' he said, 'I have heard over the last few days that both Harry and Mr. Dundas were out at the time of the building site accident, and Mr. Thomson admits to being on Queen Street as my father was brought home.'

'Very interesting,' agreed Blair. 'However, all three of them were at your father's burial and could not, according to Dr. Harker's observations, have murdered Jamie.'

Murray was pleased with himself for being able to speak of all this so unemotionally. It felt very grown up, even if it required a kind of mental barrier in his mind. He remembered something then, and reached into his pocket.

'Do you recognise this at all?'

Blair picked Jamie's button out of his hand and turned it towards the lamplight, pursing his lips and scowling at it.

'It seems familiar,' he decided at last. 'There was a fashion for waistcoats in this colour not long ago ... I fancy Archibald Armstrong had one, though I may be mistaken. How did you come by it?'

'It was amongst Jamie's possessions,' Murray explained. 'Now, the other idea I had was that it might be useful to find out who has bought the feus at the building site. Who do you suppose could tell us?'

'Ah,' said Blair, rising from his chair and feeling in his left breeches pocket. 'Now, I know someone –' he felt in the other pocket, drew out a flat parcel wrapped in waxed cloth, frowned at it, tutted, replaced it and felt in the left pocket again, '- someone who knows a man –' he produced another package, smaller this time, and peered into it cautiously. 'No. A man who works at the Council offices, and he –' the second parcel went into the right hand pocket and the first parcel came back out again, '- might be able –' the first parcel was unwrapped and revealed itself as a thick memorandum book with a calf cover '- to tell us who has done what.' He flicked the book open, removed a short steel pen from its spine, and looked about him as if expecting ink to appear by magic.

Supper was hilarious and even Henry was seen to smile slightly. After Blair had left and the boys had been sent to bed, Murray did as he had promised and summoned Robbins to the parlour.

'Ah, this is a delicate matter, Robbins,' he began, and watched from the corner of his eye as Robbins' face passed from curious to rigid. 'It concerns last night's fire. It is not something with which I wish to burden Mrs. Chambers.' He wished he had thought to sit down and look relaxed, as if he dealt with such domestic crises as fireraising servants every day, but now he felt stuck at the fireplace, with his fingers slowly throttling one another behind his back.

'I have reason to believe that last night's fire was set deliberately, by one of the servants, whom I have identified. For my own reasons, I have no wish as yet to have this person arrested: I wish, for example, to know why it was attempted. However, keeping this servant in the household unchecked has of course its own dangers, and I feel that you should be aware of them.' He stopped, tangled up in his own pomposity. Robbins' eyes flickered towards him under their naked brow.

'Is it Mr. Dunnet, sir?' he asked quietly.

'Why do you ask?'

'He was awake and running very promptly when you called, sir, and it occurred to me to wonder at that at the time. That in addition to his other strange behaviour recently, of which you know, sir.'

Murray nodded.

'Well, it is Dunnet. I do not wish it generally known, however. I am quite sure that he is innocent of Jamie's murder, and therefore of my father's, so I cannot see the reason for his behaviour. You will of course be aware of his doings during the day. At night, you might perhaps wish to lock his door after he is asleep. He has his own room, I understand?'

'Yes, sir. It is some time since Mr. Murray brought two grooms to town.'

'I trust your judgement, Robbins. Be discreet, and do as you see fit.'

But left on his own in the empty parlour, watching the ferocity of the flames about a new piece of wood in the hearth, Murray began to think again of the fire, and of his father's death, and of Jamie's, and to wonder just how safe he was even here in his own house. The parlour seemed suddenly darker, the house suspiciously quiet, as though it were waiting for something.

He rang again for Robbins, if only to hear noise and speak to another human being, and announced that he was going to bed.

CHAPTER FIFTEEN

Sunday had been almost fatally dull. Murray had been filled with a nervous, edgy energy that made any activity tedious within seconds – the dark waves nibbled at the shore of the cluttered beach in his mind, agitating the various bits of rubbish on the sand – and he made himself a nuisance to servants wanting a quiet Sabbath by turning up where he was least expected, in the parlour where they were laying the table, in the study where they were laying the fire, and in the stables where William and Daniel, under Dunnet's lacklustre direction, were doing more to disturb the horses than to comfort them, partly through ignorance and partly through the excitement of novelty. There was a limit, in any case, to what could be achieved on a Sunday.

Murray took the boys to a rather underfilled Greyfriars Kirk for the morning service to hear Dr. Inglis preach on missions to India, and afterwards inspected his father's grave, pretending to himself that it was simply a patch of land he had to care for. Henry and Robert stared solemnly beside him.

'The frost-hardened soil will have deterred any grave-robbers, sir,' Henry offered, and Murray was grateful to him for he spoke so little at the moment. He checked the mortcage.

'And even though it's started to rain,' Robert followed helpfully, 'the body will have gone off a bit by now. They won't be so interested in it if it's reeking.'

'Thank you, Robert.'

They walked back through the drizzle to dinner.

The afternoon sermon was given by a visiting preacher from Ireland with a weaselly face and front teeth that seemed designed to prop up his thin whiskers. Murray knew many members of the congregation, but his mourning seemed to deter them from all but the most distant salutations. Halfway home he discovered that Henry had his ferrets with him, but he was too enervated to feel anything more than relief he had not discovered this during the church service. By the time they reached Queen Street he was depressed and rather grumpy, and the rain descended in a steady torrent that promised no end and permitted no visiting. Evening, almost indistinguishable from afternoon, drew in. Supper was served and cleared, and Murray could not have said ten minutes later what he had eaten. He made the boys read to him by the street parlour fire afterwards, but did not object when they lapsed into a backgammon game and the ferrets curled up on an armchair. He spent a little time trying to coax Squirrel out from under the table, but without success: Squirrel raised her bitten nose in reproach, as though the ferrets were his idea. He went to bed early, feeling the day had for the most part been wasted, and dreamed of endless sermons in rainy mission stations.

Monday morning, however, promised at least a rudimentary brightness, and after the boys had been sent off to college, Murray took two horses and Dunnet, with some caution, and rode out. He felt a desperate cramped closeness about the town, a slowing constriction, and he longed to shake off the streets and find somewhere where he could view the town from a distance, and put his various preoccupations into their respective bundles and stop seeing them as one vast complex problem. He followed the streets south through the Old Town, and Dunnet followed him, past the University (he resisted the impulse to check to see if Robert and Henry were at their lectures) out to the Meadows, where a morning mist made the leafless trees shadowy fence posts. The Council had men at work on a new central drain running the length of the low-lying park, and the thawing muck in the exposed old one gave off an odour all of its own which added a sharp edge to the morning air. The horses flared their nostrils in protest.

On the other side of the Meadows, they passed the dilapidated, dripping Cage where in the summer ladies would sit to rest during their walks, glad of the shade. Murray veered slightly east, and struck out into the wintry fields between Edinburgh and Nether Liberton. Already Murray felt the ride doing him good, the exercise of controlling the trotting horse on the rough road, the damp air with its promise of sunshine, the freshness of the light breeze beginning to lift the mist away from town and country. He led the way, slowing to a walk along Nether Liberton's street of low cottages, through the warm scent of the distillery and the muddy ruts scoured by distillery carts, and began the steep climb through fields once more, up the brae to Kirk Liberton. Here they paused at last, next to the kirkyard. The comfortable, angular old church was settled at one corner to their east, with the forestairs to its various galleries winding down the sides of the building like roots worming down firmly into the good earth of God's acre. To the west, towards the Braid Hill, lay the farmland of Tower Mains, while north of them, spread out now in the wet sunshine, lay Edinburgh town, decently shrunk by distance to a manageable size. Murray grinned and took off his black hat, holding it so that the weepers blew away from his horse's side, and felt the breeze on his brow. He drew a deep, relieved breath, knowing he had rushed here but feeling that the haste had been worthwhile: this was what he had needed.

Below, the flattish town was slashed by the jagged line of the Castle rock and stopped by the shadowy cliffs of Salisbury Crags, and in the distance was the green punctuation of Calton Hill, marking the east end of the New Town and the head of the road to Leith. Where Queen Street had once been the neatly hemmed northern border of the New Town, now the edge was becoming frayed and uncertain, the gardens on the north side of the street no longer the beginning of the countryside but a threatened bastion of green between two rows of building. As Murray looked, he began to see the Old Town with eyes more like those of Miss Gordon of Balkiskan, his Jacobite acquaintance. He saw the grid of the New Town as an uncompromising, iron siege engine, driving against the town from the north, while on the south the elegant villas beginning to appear like squadrons of cavalry harried the Old Town's retreat.

It was no good: his brief sensation of tranquillity was gone. Dismally Murray replaced his hat and began a slow descent back to the town, into the blue haze of winter smoke like the powdery air of the battlefield after the fighting, and as Dunnet, silent and grim, followed behind, Murray felt like a soldier who had tried to desert, but whose conscience had won him back before even his crime was discovered. His sense of urgency returned, as though he would lead a charge if anyone would give him a sword and direct him to the enemy. But no one did, and he returned home as frustrated as when he had gone out.

Andrew Balneavis climbed the last turn in the worn stairs and the maid, who was polishing the door handle, curtseyed in a careless fashion as he passed.

'Is everyone ready?' he called in the little dark hallway. There was a small panicky shriek from the bedchamber shared by the girls. Balneavis smiled happily, knowing he had roused one of his daughters from dreamland again. He went to his wife's chamber and found her struggling to button herself into her pink dinner gown.

'The maid's fingers were so groosie from the brasses that I said I'd manage by myself,' she explained, as her husband came to her rescue. She was quite breathless with the effort, and when he had secured the buttons she subsided on to a stool, hands on her knees, face reddened as she beamed her thanks up at him. He smiled back, and touched her chin with his fingertips.

In the next room, one of the younger Balneavises was frantically searching the limited storage space for her other slipper.

'Meg, will you not *help* me, instead of standing there with your two arms the one length! Oh, where *is* it?'

But Margaret stood by the window, gowned and groomed, her eyes far away and a little smile on her lips.

The Armstrong ladies, better provided with maids and space, were sitting ready and waiting in the street parlour. It was not in the nature of

Fleming females to be late. Catherine was reading to Ella and her mother from *Titus Andronicus*, a fact which she was comfortably sure would shock the dreadful Warwick girls. It served, too, to distract at least part of their minds from the fact that when Mr. Armstrong had appeared home to change for dinner, he had been met at the door by his elder son Patrick who had an unusually intense look on his freckled face, and father and son had been closeted in the study ever since. Mrs. Armstrong regretfully doubted that they were discussing mathematics.

Lady Sarah Dundas, arranged in careful satin and with her velvet pelisse conveniently by, at last drew a deep breath.

'My dear, I do not feel that I am well enough to go to dinner. Pray make my excuses to the Thomsons.'

William Dundas did not look up from his newspaper.

'Nonsense, Sarah,' he said with empty kindness. 'You simply need to go about a little more. Dr. Falconer said you required only distractions and changes of scene.'

Lady Sarah was silent. Dr. Falconer had indeed recommended distractions, and Dr. Harker had suggested a strict diet of white meat and raw vegetables, which was difficult when one had to be about in society. Dr. Lamb had insisted on purges and bleeding, Dr. Macdonald had recommended sea bathing, but only in the summer and when the wind was from the west, and Dr. Hope had rather alarmingly produced evidence that a treatment with electricity had worked well in such cases. Fortunately Mr. Dundas had drawn the line at that one. It had been altogether too expensive.

She sighed inwardly and waited for her sons to return home with the Warwicks, so that they could all go out again. Her gloves were a crumpled heap in her working hands.

Mrs. Thomson, resplendent in deep green velvet, paid her last visit to the kitchen before dinner and was assured by a selection of terrified servants that everything was in perfect order. She was suspicious, but chose not to investigate, and when the sound of her footsteps had died away the scullery maid under the table hurriedly continued to mop up the remains of what had been a full tureen of soup. The cook, cleverer than she was given credit for being, was improvising furiously over a saucepan.

Mr. Thomson was standing before the fire in the street parlour, snow-perfect hair capping his heavy head, warming his coat tails and contemplating his dinner with pleasure. A good selection of guests, he thought: rich and poor, fashionable and unfashionable, interesting and eager to be entertained. He had finished his newspaper, and would pass it on later discreetly to Andrew Balneavis.

CHAPTER SIXTEEN

Murray changed into dinner dress and walked fast to the far end of George Street, to the Thomsons' house where he had been invited to dine. Despite his speed, there were quite a number of people already there, he was pleased to see, and it was easy to slip into the crowd, and look about to see who was talking to whom. He nodded with a smile at Ella Armstrong across the room, but found himself beside her brother instead. Patrick had Ella's sandy colouring, with his father's pale blue eyes, too. He was the same age as Murray, and as children they had shared an interest in collecting rocks, he suddenly remembered. Mathematics had, however, taken over as Patrick's passion, and Murray wondered how he was going to reconcile it to the career in law that his father probably expected of him. Patrick blinked at him as he approached, and gave an uncertain smile as if out of practice.

'Hallo, Murray,' he said. His pale eyes looked weak and weary behind his spectacles. 'How do you?'

'Quite well, thank you. And you?'

'Ah. Indeed, yes.' His gaze wandered to another corner of the room, and Murray was about to move on when he remembered a reason to speak to Patrick. He felt in the pocket of his breeches and drew out the button that Blair had said he thought belonged to Archibald Armstrong, Patrick's father.

'I wonder,' he began, 'if you wouldn't mind looking at this?' He laid

163

it on his flat hand under Patrick's nose. Patrick refocused and fixed on the button, and his eyes opened wide with alarming speed. His mouth popped open but no sound came out.

'Have you seen it before?' Murray prompted. 'I think it is quite unusual.'

Patrick Armstrong breathed in sharply and out again.

'No,' he said, definitely. 'I have never seen it before.' His fingers, pale on his watch chain, carried out complex calculations on the abacus of its links. 'And anyway, he never goes out at night, never at all, he's always in.' His voice was urgent, tight. His gaze was back on the other corner of the room, eyes still wide.

'Who is?' asked Murray, a little puzzled at Patrick's reaction.

'My father,' said Patrick, over-loudly, '*never* goes out in the evening.'

Andrew Balneavis appeared suddenly at Patrick's elbow. He had left John Douglas in the middle of the room, it seemed, frowning at them, as if he had overheard Patrick's curious statement. Murray felt himself shiver at the expression on Douglas' face, but Andrew Balneavis merely looked interested. Patrick abruptly walked off, and Murray discreetly pocketed the button. Balneavis had brought Margaret with him, and Murray smiled brightly to stop himself sighing in despair.

'My boy, with all your long sojourn in Fife, you and my dear Margaret here have never really had the chance of a proper conversation. You really have so much in common, it seems a shame not to share it!' he finished brightly, leaving Murray to try to patch together some kind of a dialogue with a girl who, though pleasant enough, clearly had her mind on other things – or other people. He wondered how soon he could decently run howling from the room. Mrs. Thomson and Mrs. Armstrong noted them from the fireplace, Mrs. Thomson with an acid remark about milkmaids, Mrs. Armstrong with some anxiety. Charles Murray could be much better employed following up on that smile he had exchanged with her daughter Ella when he came in – Mrs. Armstrong had seen that. Ella instead was apparently tending to Lady Sarah Dundas, who had just arrived. That was not going to find her a husband.

Alester Blair, emerging into the room blinking like a mole from the earth, arrived with his sister Mrs. Freeman, and Mrs. Thomson had to leave her sister to greet her last guests. Blair beamed at her and let his watery eyes swim through the crowded room, and leaving his sister in the capable hands of David Thomson, he ambled, via Lady Sarah, across the carpet to Murray and Miss Balneavis.

'Excuse me, Charles.' He bowed, folding himself up untidily. 'Miss Balneavis, may I say how lovely you look this afternoon? It is undoubtedly an honour my young friend here does not deserve, to have your solitary conversation. Please allow me to intrude.'

Miss Balneavis laughed in surprise, and Murray grinned, observing with some pleasure what a difference the unaccustomed compliment made to her rather diffident bearing. She could indeed be very pretty. However, he recognised, too, Blair's intuitive rescue attempt, and was both glad and ashamed of being glad. He glanced around the room to find where Patrick Armstrong had gone, and could not see him. He saw Harry Dundas attending to the Warwicks, the girls just as colourless as ever while the mother surveyed the room with her bitter currant eyes, calculating and critical. Ella was still with Lady Sarah, her calm kindness seeming to envelop Lady Sarah protectively. The younger Dundases were flirting with Catherine Armstrong and Davina Thomson. When dinner was announced, he turned to find Blair escorting Margaret Balneavis safely away, and found himself instead paired off with a Warwick, without much interest on either side.

The soup had been served by modishly-clad servants, and the lids were replaced on the chunky blue and white tureens. Mrs. Thomson swooped a kestrel-like gaze around her guests, hovering and passing on, making certain that all were well provided for and comfortable in their places. She had been obliged to put the rather difficult Mr. Blair on her right, but was more than pleased to find that he was devoting his energies to Margaret Balneavis on his other side. It allowed Mrs. Thomson to indulge in conversation with Mr. Dundas, who was in his usual good humour, tempered of course with the aloof dignity becoming his position as the distant cousin of somebody very important indeed. The pleasures of such a conversation did not distract her, however, from the conversations of the rest of the table: she noted, for example, that her brother-in-law Mr. Armstrong was unusually quiet this evening, even for him; that her beautiful new broad mahogany dining table was effectively cutting the conversation in half as no one could be heard across it; that despite its width, Miss Warwick and Harry Dundas exchanged one or two meaningful smiles across the polished expanse; that her daughter Davina was not too pleased at being placed so far from Gavin Dundas; that young Charles Murray was by contrast quite happy to sit by her niece Ella; and that her husband was struggling, at the far end of the table, with a combination of Lady Sarah's silence and Mrs. Freeman's nonsense. His tactic appeared to be not to stop speaking himself.

'You may have met my cousin Thomas Thomson?' he was saying, his food mostly untouched. 'Always has his head in books. I believe he lives more in the sixteenth century than in the nineteenth. They're to make him Deputy Lord Clerk Register, you know, a new post. I said to Lord Frederick myself – he's the Lord Clerk Register, and the work he has had to organise the Register House is astonishing. My cousin, on whose behalf I take leave to boast, has been indispensible to him. Lord Frederick was just telling me how indispensable Thomas has been.'

Lady Sarah smiled weakly and tried to push away some of the preserved apricots from her chicken. One doctor, although she could no longer remember which, had told her that preserved fruit held too much lethargy. Mrs. Freeman eyed Lady Sarah's plate. She had already finished all her apricots and looked likely to offer to dispose of Lady Sarah's, too. Mr. Thomson, with a practised glance at each of them, moved smoothly on.

'Of course, Register House is the jewel in Edinburgh's crown of the New Town. Mrs. Armstrong,' he called down the table to his sister-in-law, 'have you managed yet to persuade Mr. Armstrong to take up a feu here? You see, as you always do, how prettily situated we are, in the best of society and the cleanest of air.'

'Indeed, sir, but I believe that between Adam's Square, Brown Square, George's Square and our own St. Patrick's Square we have society and titles enough to fill your New Town! And besides,' she added more kindly, for she was not at all averse to moving to the New Town herself, 'if we lived in the New Town, such close familiarity with it might lead us to disregard it as merely ordinary, while coming to it from the Old Town we can wonder afresh with each visit at its charms and society.'

Further up the table from his mother, Patrick Armstrong looked at her from behind his thick spectacles and seemed about to cry. Murray might not have noticed but that Ella suddenly broke off their conversation to stare at her brother. A moment of slightly awkward silence was not made any better by a heavy groan coming from Gavin Dundas – stuck between Lady Warwick and Mrs. Balneavis, he seemed to be the object of a tug-of-war for marriageable daughters. He reddened and sat back suddenly.

So many of the guests were dissatisfied to varying extents with their positions at the table that there was more relief than usual felt when the ladies rose and retired upstairs to the drawing room. There was much pushing back of chairs and undoing of waistcoat buttons, particularly around Blair and Balneavis stomachs. Archibald Armstrong felt in his pocket and slipped a peppermint into his mouth, praying that it would cool the fires of his dyspepsia.

'And are you in the end to buy anything at Wordsworth's auction on Wednesday, then?' David Thomson called up the table to him.

'No,' said Armstrong. 'Canna afford it, dinna need it.'

Andrew Balneavis grinned encouragingly. He had lived by that maxim for many years.

'I was thinking,' said Harry Dundas with deliberation, 'of buying a saddle horse. A quiet one, was what I had in mind.'

'Suitable for a lady, as they say, eh, Harry?' suggested his brother Gavin.

'Something of that nature,' Harry agreed calmly. His father smiled, and remarked,

'Murray used to have a good one. Charles, what happened to that keir black one your father had?'

'It was hardly quiet,' Murray remembered. 'It used to funk and yunk, as they say at Letho. The quiet one is the bay.'

'I didn't see it last week,' commented Dundas.

'Last week?' Murray asked curiously. Thomson and Balneavis looked slightly sheepish.

'When we were going, ah, to the funeral,' said Balneavis, grinning awkwardly.

'That's right,' said Thomson. Embarrassment was unfamiliar to him. 'We had each arranged to leave the Courts and meet our families at your house before going in, and we were early, so we walked round to the mews to see your horses. You know, sometimes with all the fuss in a household, the groom is forgotten about, and he can become a little lax, you know? And we wanted to make sure you weren't being taken in by him, for example. So we had a word with him and took a look at the horses, and came away. But the little bay wasn't there.'

'No, I gather she's up at Letho. She does not care for cobbles,' said Murray, automatically. On the one hand, he was rather annoyed at this invasion, however well-intentioned – or were they just seeing what horses might soon come up for sale? On the other, it was true that Dunnet could not be trusted. Why had the groom not mentioned this visit?

'So have you any plans for the beasts?' prompted Dundas.

'I shall keep them, for now,' Murray answered. Dundas looked disappointed. Murray glanced up the table at him, and was surprised to find John Douglas staring at him, with what looked suspiciously like sympathy.

Mrs. Armstrong had noticed Lady Sarah Dundas' velvet pelisse on her arrival, and wanted to know all about it.

'They really are the very latest thing, are they not? Quite the *ton*.'

'Are they?' asked Lady Sarah, looking as if she could not quite remember what she had been wearing. 'Mr. Dundas gave it to me.'

'How lovely,' said Mrs. Thomson, eyeing a portrait of her husband speculatively. 'And the best ones are those with the embossed velvet ribbon all around them, I believe.'

'I should love a purple one,' sighed Mrs. Armstrong, 'and Catherine would look pretty in blue, and Ella in brown. Ah, well, we can but dream!'

'It could be worse, dear sister,' said Mrs. Thomson quietly. 'I am sure Mrs. Balneavis has had that pink gown for five seasons at least.'

'Oh, no, dear; surely it is only four,' Mrs. Armstrong countered charitably.

'And last week I met her in the High Street, and I'd swear she was wearing tartan ribbon in her bonnet – you know, the kind that was popular two whole years ago!' Mrs. Thomson said in tones of delicious horror.

'Perhaps it is to come in again,' Lady Sarah suggested vaguely. 'Oh, here are the gentlemen.'

The gentlemen made themselves immediately useful by pulling the box pianoforte into a more prominent position and arranging some chairs to form a little auditorium, having fixed it that some of the young ladies at least would be expected to show off their accomplishments. Catherine Armstrong was the first to play and sing, setting the tone of jollity with 'Miss Fitzgibbon's Lament', a witty Irish song brought over early in the season and very much suited to her high voice. She played again for Gavin Dundas to sing, better than Murray had expected. Then the Misses Balneavis were ushered to the box piano, and Catherine retired on Gavin's arm to the applause of the house.

Miss Helen Balneavis, a younger sister, settled herself nervously at the piano, one far superior to what she was used to, and played a tentative scale on the keys, faintly surprised to find that none of them stuck. Margaret handed her a sheet of music, and she started to play, while Margaret drew breath and smiled, and began to sing.

As I went out from Duns one day,
I heard a lovely lassie say

> *'I'm waiting at the kirkyard lea –*
> *Ah Johnnie, will ye no wed me?'*

Murray grinned to himself: he had heard a particularly scurrilous version of this song at university. There appeared to be some kind of disturbance on his left, where the Balneavis parents were sitting: perhaps they, too, knew of the other version. Margaret sang on.

> *'You said you'd wed when May was come,*
> *When leaves were green and winter done,'*

There was a definite feeling of something in the room now, which Murray could best describe as concern. Margaret's gaze seemed very fixed, and Murray realised that it was focussed on someone or something just behind him. He could not remember who was sitting there.

> *'The blossom's fair on hill and tree –*
> *Ah Johnnie, will ye no wed me?'*

Ella beside him shifted uncomfortably in her chair and looked at the floor. Beyond her, Catherine Armstrong smiled but looked faintly guilty. Davina Thomson was grinning as wickedly as a proper young lady could, while nearer the piano her mother contrived to hide her amusement rather better. Only Helen Balneavis, concentrating at the piano, seemed oblivious.

> *'My gown is white sprigged all wi' green*
> *The tears flow from my mother's e'en,*
> *But not a sign of you's to see:*
> *Ah, Johnnie, will you no wed me?'*

Margaret sat down to relieved applause, looking very satisfied. Helen followed, blushing prettily. Mrs. Thomson, suddenly remembering her duty as a hostess, hurried the two Misses Warwick to the piano and bade them play something, quickly. Murray, still puzzled, was beckoned over by a scarlet-faced Balneavis. He excused himself from Miss Armstrong and went as he was bid.

'My dear boy, my dear boy,' Balneavis said quietly but urgently as he approached. 'You must not be dismayed, no indeed.'

'Dismayed?' asked Murray. Miss Warwick, accompanied by her sister on the piano, had begun to play a guitar. It seemed a likely source of dismay, but not one that Andrew Balneavis would necessarily comment upon.

'My daughter Margaret. She's very young, you know, and she doesn't understand such things – though such a sweet girl! so innocent! But she doesn't see. I mean to say, he's one of my dearest friends, but ...' He tailed off, glancing around him. Margaret was being talked at fiercely by her mother. Helen Balneavis was leaving the room in tears.

'But what, sir?' Murray asked. He still had no idea to whom Margaret had very pointedly addressed her song.

'But he has no money, and he looks like a fiend from hell,' finished Balneavis in frustration. He waved a hand towards John Douglas, who sat impassively watching the Misses Warwick. 'How could any father want that for his daughter? But she's been like this since she was fifteen, and the more he ignores her, the more she dotes on him. What am I to do, Charles? What can I do with her?'

The guitar music was actually quite bearable, and Miss Warwick courteously refrained from singing. Mrs. Thomson and Mrs. Armstrong sat and scowled at both Misses Warwick, under a veneer of polite interest. At the end of the piece, Miss Lily retired from the piano to be replaced by her sister, and Harry Dundas, to everyone's amused surprise, came out to sing a duet with her. No one could remember having heard him sing before, but he had his father's voice, deep and rich, and they sang well together. Miss Warwick's eyes shone. So did Ella's, Murray noticed, but not perhaps in quite the same way.

After the performances the chairs were moved back and dancing was hastily arranged for the young people. Murray watched in disgust. As he was still in deep mourning, it was inappropriate for him to dance, which he very much enjoyed: in particular, at this point he would have liked to have danced with Ella and to escape from Mr. Balneavis. Balneavis had indeed fallen silent, but it was a silence of near despair and it seemed unkind to leave him.

A Thomson brother took Ella to the floor instead, while Harry Dundas led out Miss Warwick, who had to be nudged through what was to her an entirely unknown dance. Harry, too, was not entirely confident. Davina Thomson derived great amusement from them and shared it with her partner Gavin Dundas: the pair danced with supercilious ease, aware of the elegant show they put up. Catherine and Willie Jack made up the set for a Strip the Willow, while the two Misses Balneavis sat out with their mother between them, a picture of anxiety.

Patrick Armstrong unwittingly helped by taking out Miss Helen Balneavis for the next dance. Patrick liked to dance, as he liked music, for the mathematics and the geometry of it. When Miss Lily Warwick, as unfamiliar with this dance as her sister had been with the first, made a mistake and set to the wrong person, he scowled horribly, leaving Miss Helen rather frightened. At the end of the set he left Helen rudely in the middle of the floor and seized Miss Lily by the arm.

'Look,' he said fiercely, 'it is a pattern. It followed a pattern of circles interlocked with triangles, and the outside edges of the triangles form curlicues, like – like this. Look.' He snatched his handkerchief from his pocket, walked her over to a table with a drawer, drew out pen and ink and in a few careful strokes produced for her a little diagram, perfectly drawn, like an ornament in plaster or parquetry, pretty as embroidery on the heavy linen. He returned the pen and ink to the drawer, handed her the handkerchief and strode off. Miss Lily took it almost reverently in her white fingers, and gazed at it and its author until she could see the pattern even when her eyes were fixed on him.

Dancing and more music kept the younger folk occupied until supper, while some of the older members of the party gossiped or played cards, commenting occasionally on the performances. The Dundases and Warwicks, promised elsewhere for supper, took their leave with Mrs. Armstrong going down with them particularly to torment herself with the loveliness of Lady Sarah's velvet pelisse. Murray finally managed to dislodge Balneavis without offence, and contrived to find Blair on his own for once, having just bid goodbye to Lady Sarah.

'My dear boy.' Blair shook his hand as if they had not met for months. 'How do matters go with you?'

'In an interesting fashion, sir, but not fast enough,' Murray replied. 'Your friend with friends who work for the Council, have you spoken to him?'

'Alas, I only found him this morning.' Blair's eyes widened and his pursed mouth drooped in a horrible mask of dismay. 'But the enquiry is in train, dear boy, progress will and must be made, you know.'

'I know,' said Murray, 'I know. And thank you for your help, sir.' But inside, he could still feel the need to fight, to run, could feel the waves agitating, a clock ticking, marking the time from his father's death to the capture of his murderer, ticking too fast for Murray to catch up with it.

He walked home along George Street, following a wretched link boy with a failing torch. The rain had begun again, an invisible soaking blanket in the darkness. He could hear its constant patter on his hard hat, feel the light pummelling on his shoulders. He strode quickly, passing other hurrying figures, huddled against the penetrating damp cold or bundled into sedan chairs. Even when the ice was thick on the ground, the cold was not like this, not this seeping chill in every limb.

Why had his father's three friends really visited the stable before his father's funeral? It seemed such a strange thing to do, but perhaps that was because he was looking at the event with eyes that had seen Jamie dead in the same stable. Perhaps at its most malevolent the visit really was a reconnaissance for a future sale. Had they often visited the stable? Did they know Dunnet by sight, and Jamie? Or was it, for one of them at least, perhaps the first time they had seen Jamie there and realised where he worked, so that later that gentleman came back and killed him?

But that would not work. All three gentlemen had come inside the house to the funeral meats with their families, and Jamie was still alive at that point. Later, all three had gone to the burial - he had seen them himself, there could be no doubt – and Jamie had been murdered while they were there. None of the three could have killed him.

Why had Dunnet not told him that they had called?

On the other hand, had Dunnet spoken to him at all since he came to fetch him to his father's death bed?

A lamp still burned outside his own front door, and he hurried up the steps, reaching at the same time for the doorbell. Robbins took a moment to answer it, and let his master into a somewhat duskish hallway.

'And now the lock as well,' he muttered. 'Something has happened to the candles, sir,' he explained. 'I just noticed it as I came up now. I looked in the hall table for a spill or flints, but they are not there.' He looked apologetic but efficient: there was a problem, but it was recognised and the solution in hand, and in a very short time it would have been dealt with. Murray nodded, and said,

'Well, don't worry about it now. I intend to go straight to bed in any case. Are the boys back safely? We shan't need much more light here tonight.'

'Mr. Henry and Mr. Robert have retired. At least, sir, I shall go and fetch fresh spills and flints, in case it is forgotten about.' He disappeared towards the back stairs.

Murray followed in the same general direction, taking his gloves off and laying them with his hat on the table under the stairs. He was pulling out the drawer in a half-hearted attempt to look for the missing spills when he heard a step behind him, and turned, expecting Robbins, to see Mary's pale face in the dull light, framed by the dark twists of hair loosed from her cap. She carried a tray with, as far as Murray could see, a glass and decanter on it.

'Sir,' she began with her curiously unrespectful curtsey, 'Mrs. Chambers asked that I bring you some brandy, against the damp of the night.'

'Very well, Mary, that was good of her to think of it.' He turned back to push the drawer of the hall table back in place, then realised that she was walking past him towards the street parlour door.

'Ah, Mary,' he said, intending to direct her to leave the brandy in the study. She turned carefully with the tray, looked back at him, then cried,

'Sir, look out!'

There was a crash. Her tray hit the stone floor. Murray lunged to save it as the long-stemmed glass seemed to bounce and hover in the air a single, long second, then burst into a thousand pieces. The crash echoed behind him, too, in the angle of the stair, and it came to him that there had been two crashes, not one. He spun round. On the floor was a heap of fragments which had been a Chinese vase on the first floor landing. It lay just where he had been standing when Mary had cried out to him. Above it, on the stairs, shivering in the half-light, stood the shadowy figure of Dunnet, the groom.

CHAPTER SEVENTEEN

The decanter lay in pieces on the hall floor in a pool of tawny brown brandy that was fast becoming a damp stain on the stone slabs. Robbins had, however, fetched another bottle in a prudent manner from the cellar, and had opened it without dusting it and poured a substantial quantity of the contents into three glasses, as he had been bidden, in the street parlour.

Murray took up the nearest glass and handed it to Mary, who was sitting, straight-backed and pale, in an armchair by the fire. The shawl which had covered the back of the chair was around her shoulders but she still looked cold. She took the glass in long fingers and sipped the liquid as if she knew it would do her good but otherwise could not sense it. Murray took up his own glass and gestured to Robbins to sit as well, at the table where he himself was. Robbins paused and then sat uneasily, knuckles white around the glass but not drinking.

Downstairs, Dr. Harker was still with Dunnet, escorted by Mrs. Chambers and both Daniel and William, in case of any further violent outbursts. It seemed unlikely that there would be any. When Murray had run up the stairs towards him, Dunnet had simply subsided to sit on the steps, and started to cry. It had been much more distressing than any violence could have been. Robbins, appearing from the basement with a handful of tapers, had been aghast at the sight of the crouching figure, Murray's white face, the smashed vase, glass and decanter and Mary, statue-still with her hands to her throat. Murray and he had virtually carried Dunnet down to his room, and Robbins had stayed with him when Murray

176

ran to the kitchen to send William for Dr. Harker. The doctor had been downstairs for some time now.

'I am – more than grateful to you, Mary.'

She shook her head sharply, but said nothing. Murray leaned forward towards her to emphasise the point.

'No, it is the truth. Had you not seen Dunnet on the stairs I fear I should not be here now.'

'I know, sir,' she said quietly, without immodesty. Her eyes were downcast, her lashes dark crescents under her triangular brows. The usual suggestion of a smile was missing for once. She looked angry.

Robbins rose from the table but went nowhere, standing rubbing the pad of his thumb along a line on the tablecloth. He was stunned by his own failings: Dunnet must have escaped from his room, he thought over and over, William or Daniel must have failed to lock the door. It was his responsibility, they were his staff. He had promised Mr. Murray to prevent Dunnet from endangering anyone, and it was Mr. Murray himself who had been put at terrible risk. Daniel had said Dunnet was asleep: he must have escaped from his room, fiddled the lock, Daniel must not have locked the door. He himself should have gone along to make sure. He should have been suspicious when he found the candles blown out in the hall, he should have known that something was wrong. When he knew that something was wrong he should not have left the hall, he should not have left Mr. Murray unguarded. His thumb rubbed up and down the line, starting to burn against the thick cloth. He had failed, failed, failed. He would be sent back to Letho.

Mrs. Chambers came through the door and frowned slightly when she saw Mary established by the fire, but said nothing except to announce Dr. Harker. She left again immediately: Jennet should be sent to clean the hall floor before the brandy made a permanent stain.

Murray rose and offered the doctor a seat, which he took wearily. There was a spare glass ready, and Murray himself poured him some brandy. The doctor acknowledged it and drew a leather-bound notebook from his bag. His spectacles, dangling on a chain, were replaced on his nose and he opened the notebook carefully, then looked directly at Murray for the first time.

'Your groom is deeply disturbed.' His eyes moved discreetly in the direction of Robbins and Mary, asking silently if Murray wanted him to go on in the present company. Murray nodded. He felt they had a right to know: they had become involved, now, too. Dr. Harker's eyebrows rose very slightly, merely a confirmation, and he went on. 'I have given him opium to make him sleep, but it took a large amount to render him at all peaceful. In the course of the drug taking effect, he talked at some length, although very slowly, and it took some time to establish the full meaning of his words. In effect, his concerns have been growing for some time and have several layers. They stem from the evening of your father's accident.'

Murray nodded again. The groom had previously been a quiet and sometimes surly man, but his recent behaviour had been extreme.

'Dunnet was genuinely attached to your father, who seems to have treated him as a friend. I knew your father well, Charles, and he did appreciate quiet company, so I can well imagine that this was true. Dunnet alluded to the saving of some mare in foal, which was not clear. He felt that he had deserted your father in his hour of need, and this was compounded when he found your stable boy dead. I should reiterate here that I am quite sure that Dunnet had no hand in that, if your servants' evidence as to his time spent in the kitchen is quite correct. Dunnet seems to be fiercely loyal, although this has been well hidden, I believe. Two such deaths of people he saw as being his charge, in such a short time, has affected him very adversely. He has been feeling very guilty, and this, because of his character, has become a feeling of defensiveness against what he perceives to be the criticism of others, real or imagined. This in turn has grown into a conviction that, despite my own efforts to exonerate him, and your defence of him in the face of the police officers, we all believe him to be guilty of both your father's death and your stable boy's murder. Apparently you took him to the site of your father's accident?'

'That's right,' said Murray cautiously.

'And to the home of your stable boy's parents? He thinks that you were trying to exact a confession. He has been living under some considerable strain now for over a week. In the end, it seems to me, he decided in his state of serious instability that the only way to save himself from a charge of murder was in fact to kill you. Mrs. Chambers mentioned a fire.'

'Ah, yes,' said Murray. Robbins, whose face was still only furnished with rudimentary eyebrows, frowned. Mary looked up slowly.

'The fire failed, so he tried the vase. He failed again, and was so obviously witnessed, that he has now broken down completely.' Dr. Harker closed his notebook, to which he had not referred, and watched Murray closely. 'I recommend his removal to Bedlam.'

'I cannot do that,' said Murray. 'He is part of this household.'

'Well, you cannot keep him on here as groom. And I can offer no guarantee that he will not prove dangerous again.'

'All the same,' said Murray, 'Bedlam is not the place for him, sir. Is there no hope of his recovery?'

Dr. Harker breathed out thoughtfully through his sharp nose.

'With rest and careful supervision, and a light diet, he might in time be well again. And it is possible that some work with horses will have a therapeutic effect.'

'Then I shall employ a man to take care of him and send them both to Letho for a while. He can work in the stables there: it is certainly more peaceful than the mews here.'

Dr. Harker sighed, finished his brandy and rose to leave.

'You are your father's son: I suppose I should have expected this. I know of a good man who has experience of cases like this: he is kind, careful and discreet – and strong. Shall I send him to you?'

Murray rose, too.

'I should be most grateful, sir. For the moment, what should we do with Dunnet?'

'I have asked William to stay with him. He will sleep now until late tomorrow morning, by which time my man should be with you, but I shall look in in any case and see that he has woken well. Now, let us see you.'

He drew Murray nearer the fire and examined his eyes, felt his forehead and the pulse in his wrist. At Murray's suggestion he did the same to Mary.

'Nothing to worry about: the brandy and the warm fire will chase away any chills from the shock of the evening. Good night, Charles: you really are leading a most exciting life at present. Do take care.'

Robbins, as if controlled by strings, saw Dr. Harker to the front door where his own carriage was waiting to take him home. Murray reflected that the doctor's accounts, which had not been submitted since his father's death, would this time make quite interesting reading. He waited for Robbins to return to the parlour, and drew a deep breath.

'I feel I owe you both an explanation.'

'And I feel I owe you an apology, sir,' Robbins interrupted, uncharacteristically. He stood to attention with his hands clenched at his sides, his head high, and his eyes fixed straight ahead. 'I have failed in my duty, sir. I failed to obey your instructions and to protect you and the household from further harm as you asked. I shall be seeking other employment, sir.' He finished smartly, and seemed almost about to salute. Murray remembered that he had spent some time in the Fife Volunteers during his employment at Letho.

'Don't be ridiculous, Robbins,' Murray retorted. 'If anything, it is I who owe you an apology, for giving you a task which you could not possibly have had the time or the men to carry out properly. I have put everyone at risk, I have upset Mary and you, but I shall be bold enough to ask you to remain here in your post. Your service has always been valued, and will continue to be so.'

Robbins' gaze dropped, and his hands relaxed very slightly. He seemed to breathe for the first time in several minutes.

'Now, an explanation,' Murray continued, waving Robbins back into his seat. Robbins sat. 'You heard what Dr. Harker just said about poor Dunnet. Although we knew that he had not killed Jamie and felt we could safely assume that he had not killed my father, I was quite sure that he had set fire to my bed last week, and had been keeping him near me in order to watch him. I felt that whether he was guilty or not, he was in some way connected with the deaths and might be able to tell me something about them. I also,' he explained to Mary, 'asked Robbins to keep an eye on Dunnet when I could not, but in that I asked too much, I believe.'

Mary frowned.

'Why do you persist in linking the two deaths of Mr. Murray and Jamie, sir? Surely there is no connexion other than coincidence? Sir?' she added belatedly, as if the question were more important than any courtesy to her employer. Turned a little away from the firelight, her face was all angles of light and dark, but her eyes shone with intelligence. Murray gazed at her for a long moment, biting his lower lip. Mary and Robbins watched him, waiting. At last he made his decision.

'I believe,' he began, '- and I am not alone in this – I believe that it is possible that my father was also murdered. That being so, there is a strong link between his death and Jamie's that makes coincidence seem unlikely.'

'Indeed, sir.' Mary nodded thoughtfully. Robbins, too, seemed to accept the statement.

'Do you have any plans for what to do about it, sir?' he asked. 'If I may say so, the police officers did not seem very helpful.'

'Quite right, Robbins. I was not impressed by their response, and as they do not seem to have followed any line of investigation after Jamie's death, I am reluctant to involve them in the more delicate matter of my father. Besides, I have been afraid that they would arrest Dunnet and that I should prove powerless to stop them.' Both Robbins and Mary raised their eyebrows: Murray tended to forget that he was now a rich laird. He leaned back, happy to talk about his problems at last. 'Now that Dunnet is to be sent back to Letho, that matter is at least simpler. But before he goes, I must ask him one question: apparently Mr. Thomson, Mr. Dundas and Mr. Balneavis were in the stables on the morning of my father's funeral, and I should like to find out, if I can, all the details pertaining to their visit. None of them could possibly have killed Jamie, as they were all at the burial at the time. But there is reason to believe that a gentleman was involved at least in my father's death, so, shocking though it seems, even my father's friends are not above suspicion in this matter.' He drew a deep breath, and told them of all he had learned concerning the apprentice notary, Matthew Muir.

They were silent during the recitation, and almost motionless in the candlelight. When he had finished, the silence continued, thoughtful, waiting, and he looked away from them and at his father's ring on his watch chain, catching the light from the fire. Mary was the first to react.

'It seems to me, sir,' she said, leaning forward, 'that your best move now is to the Grassmarket.'

'Why there?' Murray asked.

'Because, sir, you have two possible paths to follow,' she said with earnest precision. 'You can follow the unknown gentleman, or you can follow the man that spoke of him. Now, you do not know the gentleman, or you do not know if you know him, and that makes it difficult. But what makes it harder still is that you yourself are a gentleman, and you are dealing with your friends and acquaintances. I have watched the way gentlemen and ladies talk, and they are so scared of what they might say that they talk and talk and say nothing. But if you talk to ordinary people, even though you are a gentleman, you will find out more from them. And because of that, it will be easier for you now to leave the unknown gentleman and follow this Matthew Muir.'

Robbins nodded slowly.

'It makes sense, sir. But it would work even better if you had someone – not a gentleman, sir – to ask your questions for you.'

Mary gave him an angular grin.

'Aye, that would work. You need to go to the Grassmarket and ask people who they saw Muir with. If he saw much of a gentleman down there, it will have been noted.' She nodded to emphasise her point, then added as an afterthought, 'And go at night. In the day people are working hard and aye, they like to stop for a yarn, but they always know well what they are saying and who might be listening. At night, even discounting the possible effects of drink,' she smiled, 'people will talk because they are not so afraid of who will see them. If Matthew Muir was about dark business, he may have been about it after dark, and the night people will have seen him.'

Murray considered all this, and looked at the clock on the mantelpiece. It was past midnight. The agitated waves irritated the shore in his mind.

'I feel the force of your arguments,' he said to them both, 'but I am eager to make progress with this matter, and I do not feel that it would be fair after this evening to ask any of you to accompany me, so I shall go alone. Robbins, I need some older clothes, before you retire.'

Robbins rose to leave, but stopped.

'No, sir, we cannot let you go alone. If harm came to you in your own house, how much worse can it be in the Grassmarket or Cowgate at night?'

Murray had not considered the possibility of trying the Cowgate, and the thought was not a welcome one. He did not want to go on his own, however urgent his thoughts.

'How soon do you wish to leave, sir?' asked Robbins, business-like as he pressed home his point. This was his chance to redeem himself, in his own eyes, at least.

Murray sighed.

'Very well, then, in half an hour. If you are sure you are not suffering still from the ill effects of this evening.'

'Quite sure, sir.'

Murray rose, and finished his brandy, but Mary remained firmly seated.

'Sir,' she said. 'There is a more fitting person to go than Mr. Robbins.'

Someone who knows the Grassmarket well, even at night, and knows the people and can guide you safely.'

Robbins looked rather sour.

'Who is that?' said Murray.

'I, sir,' Mary replied, then went on quickly. 'Do not discount me at once for being a woman, sir. When my man left for Holland I lived in the Grassmarket, and still attend the Gaelic Chapel there when I am permitted by Mrs. Chambers. I have friends there. Mr. Robbins has lived only in the New Town when in Edinburgh, and does not understand Old Town ways. Sir, I do not wish to do down Mr. Robbins, but I am the better man for this work, sir.'

CHAPTER EIGHTEEN

They strode up the North Bridge in silence. Mary showed outwardly at least little satisfaction at having won the rather prolonged argument that had followed her assertion. Robbins had been quite outspoken in his opinion that what Mary was proposing was not fit activity for any woman, certainly not for a respectable servant in a more than respectable household. He made quite a lengthy and unselfconscious sermon about propriety, a subject which in the end seemed to be equated in his mind with Mary's personal safety. Murray, who also found that the thought of including Mary in the expedition appalled him as much as it appealed to him, hardly had a chance to make his feelings heard. He had never seen Robbins quite so vociferous, and by the looks of things, nor had Mary. She sat quietly throughout, having said what she wanted to say and wisely seeing no sense in wearing herself out with trying to compete with Robbins' verbal outpourings.

In the end, the half of Murray that really quite wanted Mary's company found an excuse: Mrs. Chambers could not possibly be left on her own with Dunnet in his present state, and Robbins was, of course, as usual, in charge. Neither William nor Daniel was really reliable enough to take the place of Mary on the expedition and neither had Mary's specific knowledge of the area. Daniel was not even from Edinburgh, and would have no reason to be familiar with the Grassmarket – Murray tried to state this as convincingly as possible, in the face of his own deeply-held belief that a young man of Daniel's type had probably already more familiarity with the

Grassmarket and its surroundings than he ought to be encouraged to have. His reputation would live on for some time in Letho.

Robbins, he could see, was angry at being over-ruled: his face shut again, and he returned to his normal laconic self, but he could hardly argue with his master, however strong his feelings in the matter.

There remained, therefore, only one or two administrative problems: Mrs. Chambers had to be told directly of Mary's involvement, rather than to hear it later, perhaps from a third party. Mary, after all, shared a room with Jennet, who, partly through worry, perhaps, and mostly, certainly, through an anxiety to keep on the right side of her superiors, was bound to mention Mary's absence to Mrs. Chambers in the morning. Mrs. Chambers, summoned for this purpose, was not happy, and eyed Mr. Murray and Mary with what could only be described as distrust. She had known Mary from last September, and was convinced that she was much cleverer than she pretended to be. She had known Mr. Murray from birth, but considered him to be something of an innocent. Mrs. Chambers was not, however, told the whole story as Murray had told it to Robbins and Mary. She was led to believe that some facts had to be ascertained relating to little Jamie's death, but that was all. Murray felt that any suggestion that his father had died a deliberately violent death would come as a great shock to her. He had known her from birth, and considered her to be something of an innocent.

Further problems had arisen when it came to the subject of clothing for the outing. Robbins was allowed to salve his conscience by being represented on the expedition in the form of his oldest jacket and a hat which had, apparently in distant history, belonged to his own father. Murray wore his own shirt with no collar and a neckcloth recovered from use as a duster by Mrs. Chambers, who, in a spirit of co-operation, had decided that if the expedition were to go ahead it would fail through no fault of hers. Robbins' coat was several inches too short and significantly lacking in width, which certainly contributed to Murray's appearance as something less than gentlemanly: the hat, too, bounced on his hair and lacked a desirable snugness of fit. His breeches had been found in a chest of clothes not worn since his last visit to Queen Street, over four years ago, so in size at least they gave the impression of having belonged to the same person as the jacket. Finally, his boots had been borrowed, perforce without the owner's permission, from Dunnet, and had a fine aura of the stable about them. Mary reckoned privately that while under close inspection he would never pass muster as anyone other than a gentleman, at least he could walk down the street without exciting attention. Any suspicions she might have harboured that the proposed expedition was nothing more than a gentleman's whimsical play-act, to be humoured and praised, were dismissed by the serious expression in his eyes all through the farce of preparations.

She herself was cloaked and hooded, and almost as tall as Murray as he shambled slightly in the constricting clothing and down-at-heel boots, matching her stride. He could not see her face as they walked, except in brief flashes when the damp wind caught at her hood and flicked it backwards. In these moments, her eyelids were always lowered, though whether in concern, in modesty or against the weather he could not tell. His own feelings were considerably mixed. Laid against the promised pleasure of being in her company for the rest of the night was the old feeling of urgency, the need to run faster than his battered boots would allow and demand to be told all that he had to know about his father's death, and then there was the satisfaction of knowing that he was in fact doing something for once, instead of sitting around in drawing-rooms, well-fed and warm with wine, watching elegant people politely hiding their feelings. Mary's words about gentlefolk had struck him as an awful truth, and made the company of his own kind seem suddenly suffocating, smothering his search. It was refreshing, exciting, instead to be moving through the dark, his respectable mourning shrugged off with relief as much as with guilt, no longer marking him out, his eyes darting about as if he would see the murderer waiting for him on a street corner, his breath coming quickly in time with the beats of his heart.

The link boys now were few and far between, their distant guiding torches an unsteady blur in the light rain and black night. Once or twice, a chair hurried past, the bearers panting with the effort of carrying some comatose gentleman back from his drinking club to his New Town comforts. There were few other walkers, and the pair of them could hardly be seen on the Bridge, but as they moved up into the Old Town they could feel, rather than see, other shapes around them, brief outlines against lit windows, the scuff of cloth as they passed, the smell of wet wool, or of ale or tobacco or worse from damp bodies, mercifully invisible.

They had decided before leaving Queen Street to descend to the Grassmarket by way of the West Bow at the top of the Lawnmarket, under the final steep alley to Castle Hill. Murray had tried not to lay too much stress on his aversion to the Cowgate in front of Mary. It made him feel like a coward. The Lawnmarket, and the High Street from which it continued, could be seen quite clearly even tonight, misted with rain but outlined and glowing in the light from hundreds of windows, from below street level to points impossibly high above them. Here life went on at night even outdoors, unlike the sedate New Town: here the police officers, cloaks over their new uniforms, watched as the latecomers and late-leavers went to and from their dwelling places, as groups and couples met and parted, and each shadowy figure hurrying through the damp night was a fragment of the view from a thousand possible openings, lit and dark. Murray had looked finally at his watch before leaving it safely above his bed, and reckoned that by now it must be about two in the morning. There was no sign of the old town settling for the night.

They passed Balneavis' elderly stair on their right as they climbed the Lawnmarket, all lights economically out, as they were too in Douglas' flat which, Murray believed, was directly below Balneavis'. All good advocates were safely in their beds, he thought to himself, and grinned. Mary, glancing about at that precise point, saw the grin and gave an angular one of her own, her eyes suddenly full of mischief. A shiver ran down his spine and he drew breath to speak, found he had nothing to say and waved to indicate that they should proceed. His jacket creaked ominously about his shoulders as he turned to follow her.

The gallows at the crossroads was invisible, though as always it made its presence felt. They turned left and immediately began the steep descent of the West Bow, clutching the worn wooden posts that held up the wigmaker's on the corner. The Bow dog-legged between precipitous tenements, wider at their summit than their narrow bases could reasonably bear. The ground was slippery with the rain, and in Dunnet's boots he was more vulnerable underfoot than Mary, whom he would have liked to assist. She, however, carried on blithely as though walking on level ground, while he clung to the wall or the fronts of closed-up cloth stalls. He fingered his way gently down, stepping in one or two spots of discomfiting softness as he did so. Unseen in the dark, something had evidently been tidied against the wall, and gave off a peculiarly powerful smell when disturbed. When they finally reached the bottom and the spreading entry into the Grassmarket, Mary drew him to one side and stopped him.

'Now, sir, with your permission that is the last time I shall call you sir this evening,' she began. Murray nodded obediently. 'You are only moderately well disguised in these clothes, and there is no call for drawing attention to ourselves. Think about what you look like, now. Keep your hands hidden if you can, or make them dirty. They are far too white, unless you wish to claim that you work in flour or bleaching linen.'

Murray looked at his ungloved hands, which were now somewhat marked by the progress down the West Bow. One knuckle was gashed and filthy. He knew little of work in flour or linen. He turned, and rubbed the backs of his hands, too, against the wall's lichened dampness, and rubbed them again until they finally met with Mary's approval.

'Walk a little less proudly, too, loutch along. Stoop your shoulders, hang your head a little.' She stepped back and surveyed him, chin pointed at him critically. 'Aye, well, it's the best we can do without a surgeon and three years' diet of potatoes,' she remarked. He did not know whether to smile or not. This woman was, after all, one of his servants: on the other hand, until recently he had been a servant himself. 'The first place we shall go,' she announced, turning towards the lights of the wide-open Grassmarket, 'is to a howff.'

'A howff?' he repeated, concerned. To draw Mary down into this undesirable part of town was one thing: to take her into a drinking establishment was quite another. She, however, grinned again.

'Aye, an alehouse. A place where they serve the very milk of Auld Clootie himself, and the language and the doings of the inhabitants would make the hearts of all good Christian folk turn to stone at the very mention of them.' She raised her pointed eyebrows wickedly, and strode off into the dark heart of the Grassmarket, and Murray, not at all sure of himself, forced his ill-shod feet to follow at their best speed.

The howff was well hidden from any passersby who happened to be deaf and deficient in sense of smell. The entry was along an unlit passage at the bottom of a stair, and the premises were down a flight of steps at the rear of the building, below ground level. There were no windows, and the candles had evidently been made from the fat of some very elderly and unwell animals, to judge from the reek. The ale itself added a rich, heavy scent, which slid on the greasy tallow smoke and wound its way out of the rooms and into the passageway, and oozed out into the street like a river of treacle. Along with it, as if an integral part of it, came the noise of a large number of very happy people at varying levels of intoxication, striving to make themselves heard over each other and over the deafening effects of insobriety.

The candles were more efficient in producing smell than in producing light, to such an extent that Murray wondered which was their primary purpose. Had he been coming into the room from daylight rather than from darkness, he imagined that it would have taken him some time to see anything at all, but as it was dim shapes were perceivable, becoming slightly more defined the closer they were to the soggy light of the candles.

Not many people looked up as they entered, silent compared with the noise around them, but one round red face did turn their way, broke off in mid-laugh, scowled horribly as the mind behind it was put to work, then split into a wide smile.

'Mistress Macdonald!' the man cried. 'I thought you were a long away frae here?'

Mary made a serene progress through the throng towards the bench where the man and his cronies sat. Murray followed the path she drew, and was, like her, squeezed on to the bench amongst them. The strain on his breeches was considerable.

'Aye, well,' she said, her eyes modestly downcast, 'I'm just back on a visit. You're looking fair and fat, Eck Moffat.'

'All the better for seeing you, hen!' cried one of the other drinkers, with a generous nudge to Eck. A third drinker, squatting on the filthy floor next to the bench, sang 'All the better for seeing you, hen!' in a wavering tune that seemed to Murray faintly familiar. He was a thin man, but his breeches were thinner still and barely decent. They made Murray's own feel quite secure by comparison.

Mary and Eck Moffat began to talk of common acquaintances, ably supported by the Greek chorus around them. Murray, half-listening to them, took the opportunity to look about him as his eyes grew more accustomed to the light. The place was, he had to admit to himself, better than he had expected. There was considerable drunkenness, it was true, though tasting the decent mug of ale that was pressed into his hands from an unseen source he could understand why. But although he could see perhaps three women in the place besides Mary, and none of the three looked particularly savoury, there was none of the debauchery he had been led to believe characterised the alehouses of the Grassmarket. While part of him was relieved for Mary's sake, the rest was rather disappointed: when the risk was lessened, the adventure was lessened, although to whom he could possibly have told his story he was not sure. Blair was probably the only one in his circle who would appreciate it in the least. He remembered suddenly an inn in Naples which had been much, much worse than this one, and smiled at himself.

'And what about yourself, Mistress Macdonald?' Eck asked at last.

'I have a grand job in the New Town, now,' said Mary with mock pride.

'Oh, aye?' responded the chorus, gleefully.

'I'm in service to a very good family – well, to a young gentleman.' The chorus made appropriately scandalised noises. 'Oh, not like that!' said Mary, pretending to be shocked. 'It's very respectable. But I have been thinking of seeking a new place.'

'What?' said Murray, and received a sharp Macdonald elbow in his poorly protected ribs for his trouble. He shut his mouth abruptly. Mary had her audience captivated and no one even noticed him.

'It seems just lately to have been an unlucky household. First the master dies – not the young gentleman, but his father – and then at his very funeral his stable boy is found with his neck broken!'

'That would be John Paterson's eldest,' said someone, nodding solemnly.

'Young Jamie?' said Eck. 'His parents live just across the Grassmarket. And you work for the family, too? It's a gey small world here.'

'I know,' said Mary. 'I was here last week for the funeral. His poor mother is very brave. How she can bear it I cannot tell, and when not a soul can even tell her who throttled her son's life from his wee body, nor why.' Her audience were all wide-eyed and quiet now, in the face of the row from the rest of the room.

'Was it someone hoping to steal the horses?' asked the man on the other side of Murray.

'Well, the horses were left in their stalls,' said Mary, 'and it seems a strange thing to murder a lad to steal horses and then not to steal them.'

'There was some talk that the groom had killed him,' said Eck.

'No, the groom is innocent of all blame in that,' said Mary firmly. The chorus nodded, accepting the word of someone they knew.

'It's terrible,' said Eck at last. 'And them such a respectable, decent family and all. They work awful hard, the pair of them. You'd never see them in here, would you, boys?' Relieved by this, the chorus laughed, shaking their heads in agreement.

'Now, tell me,' said the man on the other side of Murray – he heard him referred to as Patie – 'Your master that died, was he no the one in the same thing as Mattie Muir that lived up the Vennel?'

'So I hear,' said Mary.

'Aye!' Patie laughed. 'It would have suited Matt just down to the ground to die in the New Town! For him it would be the next best thing to living there!'

'Oh, he was that big,' agreed Eck. 'He was muckle, the way he put on airs! Nothing would do him but he'd elevate himself out of the Grassmarket – nothing near good enough for the likes of him – and pross in the

Canongate. Just the next step now would have been the New Town. He had all the connexions, from all he said to me, all the gentlemen friends that would come calling. He'd have fitted in just fine. He'd have been having breakfast with Viscount Melville himself in a week!'

The chorus laughed, as much at Eck's assumed genteel accent as at anything he said. Then the man on the floor spoke up.

'Aye, but his brother's no bad. You canna say the same thing about Dandy, now.'

'That's true enough,' said Patie without hesitation. 'Dandy's a fine lad, and a hard-working one, though he has a temper on him that would show Bonaparte a thing or two if he ever landed on these shores and took his Imperial army a thing too near Dandy's whisky bottle.'

'He made a fine thing of Matt's funeral,' said the man on the floor, and Murray realised where he had seen and heard the man before, kneeling on the floor of Dandy Muir's flat playing troubadour to the poker. It seemed he had been wearing his best clothes for the funeral: these ones were truly dire. Fortunately he did not seem to recognise Murray.

'And did Matt bring any of his fine gentlemen friends in here?' asked Mary innocently. This caused another moment of laughter at the very thought.

'Gentlemen in here?' sputtered Eck. 'It was a rare thing for Matt himself to be seen in here, we were so far beneath the soles of his boots. No, it's few enough gentlemen that make their appearance in this establishment. Although sometimes a herd of they pluffy young gentlemen from the University will pay us a call, which is well-bred of them, and play their cards and drink our ale and avail themselves of other local pleasures' – that his gaze wandered at this point to a well-set-up young lady in an economically-cut dress on the other side of the room was, of course, coincidental – 'and return refreshed to their labours.'

Murray's attention was drawn to the young lady by this, and as he hoped that Robert and Henry had not been among the said pluffy gentlemen he studied her more closely. She was perhaps older than he had first thought, the impression of youth created by her red hair flowing loose down the low back of her green dress. As she turned in the middle of the small crowd of which she was a part Murray could see that the front of the green dress was even lower than the back, and would have benefitted better from a modest covering of hair, like Mary Magdalene. However, it was the front of her dress, however limited, and its contents that seemed to be the principal topic of conversation within her group, and two men in particular seemed intent on this subject of debate, on which they appeared, from their waving hands and scowling faces, to have two very different opinions. As he watched, the argument was becoming more and more heated, and the smaller man poked the larger with his finger – a simple action, but one designed to give as much offence as possible. The larger man's fist was clenched and on its way to the smaller man's face faster than thought, but even so the smaller man jerked to one side, and dodged the impact. At this, the crowd around them surged forwards and with a yelping like hounds on the scent, they bore the two men outside on to the street. The alehouse emptied behind them, and Murray found himself being rushed along with the crowd.

Outside, the two men had been granted a circle of space, outlined by their friends, including the lady whose charms had started the trouble. They stood opposite each other, the large man with his heavy jaw tight and his fists great newel posts on the half-flexed pillars of his arms. The smaller man looked more relaxed, ready, but unconcerned. They appeared to be waiting for a signal.

Murray never heard or saw it, but suddenly the fight began. The large man lunged, and the small one stepped back neatly, leaving his opponent unbalanced. Then he sauntered around behind him.

The crowd roared with laughter, and pressed forward collectively to see better. Murray felt the hot, living force pushing at his arms, his back, his legs, crushing him. They stank of ale and tallow. A hatless head of hair, thick with grease, was shoved backwards into his face, and he turned his head away as far as he could. His hands were too far away from his pockets. His heart began to thump.

Beside Murray, a man was taking bets with a professional air.

'Three to two on Archie,' he murmured to his customers. 'The man from Lithgae's bigger, but I've seen Archie at this before.'

The man from Linlithgow, thus identified, was circling again, staring hard at Archie as if to frighten him with a mere look. Archie circled too, watchful but still not tense. The Linlithgow man swiped with his right, and Archie ducked. He swiped again with his left, more to keep his balance than to attack, but Archie had seen it coming and was elsewhere.

And where was Mary? The crowd surged and swayed with every action in the ring, and despite his comparative height, Murray could not see her. He felt suddenly alone in this madness, where the crowd's movements dragged his feet from the ground, shoved his arms back and forth, punched out his breath. Where was she? They should never have come, not at night, it was an insane risk. He struggled to see the mass of people on the other side of the circle.

At last through the grinning faces he saw her, about a third of the way round the circle from him. She winked at him, and returned to a philosophical contemplation of the fight, on which Eck was commenting almost constantly. Murray could not hear him above the noise of the crowd, whose sympathy was with the big man but whose money was chiefly on Archie.

Archie had broken into a kind of leisurely, high-kneed trot around the ring, bowing politely to the green gowned lady as he passed like a knight at a tournament. Linlithgow, too slow to pursue him, stood in the centre of the circle aiming blows at his head as he turned. Archie kept jog-trotting until he was bored. He stopped to remove a well-placed handkerchief from the apparel of his lady and wiped his brow with it. Linlithgow, seizing the opportunity, raised his hands above his head and brought them down in a whistling, double-fisted hammer that had it connected with any part of Archie would have done him some permanent damage. But Archie was somehow already around the back of the large man, and hooked one foot casually around his opponent's leg. At the optimum second, he pulled, and Linlithgow crashed resoundingly on to the ground. To the cheering of the local supporters, Archie trotted another circuit of the ring, waving the handkerchief graciously to left and right, and the bookmaker near Murray began to collect his money. Murray noticed that most of his debtors had Linlithgow accents.

Mary joined him again with a faintly contrite look.

'And after that entertainment, time to move on, I think,' she said. 'There is a place down here where people meet to talk, even at night, and to watch what the world brings to them.'

The place was a well, where by day Murray remembered seeing the usual Old Town crowd of water caddies squabbling over their order of precedence. Even now one or two could be seen squatting on their kegs by the light of a little fire, faces in shadow under their big black hats. There were others about, too, stopping for a while on their way from one place to another to warm themselves at the fire and gossip. Mary, face bland, moved confidently into the group and bent to the fire. She nodded to the man who sat on the other side of its smoke. There was little wind in this soft rain.

'Good evening, Mr. Ramsay,' she said with a smile.

'My, it's Mistress Macdonald again. I hope it is a happier occasion that brings you to the Grassmarket this time?' asked the man. He was lame, Murray noticed, one leg twisted almost backwards, and his left arm hung undemonstratively by his side. His right hand, which appeared sound, wielded a clay pipe.

'Not much happier, I fear,' Mary responded, with a little sigh. 'It is to do with Jamie Paterson's death that I am here.' She saw that the man was staring at Murray. 'This is a fellow I work with,' she explained, gesturing to him casually. 'He's a man of few words, but he's as anxious about this as I am. Do you mind I told you at the funeral that no one had a notion why the lad was struck down?' Her voice, Murray marked, her whole attitude, was much more respectful than it had been in the alehouse, and it was something else, too: it was, he decided finally, more careful. He concentrated on saying nothing and listening well.

'I mind you told me that it was nothing obvious,' the man agreed.

'We fear,' said Mary, looking down at her hands, 'we fear that we may have some information. I told you the police officer wanted to arrest the groom but the doctor and the master stopped him. The police officer has shown no inclination to arrest anyone else, and we have an idea that that could be because it was a gentleman that killed Jamie. A gentleman perhaps with influence.'

This had not occurred to Murray. He had assumed that the black-thatched police officer Rigg had failed to arrest anyone for the murder through apathy or incompetence: he had not suspected corruption. And yet, given what he knew of the deaths of his father and Matthew Muir, it did make sense. He wondered if it was Mary's own idea, or whether it was common talk in the servants' hall. Out of the corner of his eye, he saw a youngish man watching him, a frown of mild confusion on his thin face. He ignored him.

'All gentlemen have influence,' said Ramsay scornfully.

'And we'd like to find out who this one is,' said Mary, as if agreeing with him. Her cloak and skirts beneath it trailed crumpled into the mud.

'What good will that do you?' asked the man. 'Do you imagine he'll go down on his knees and confess? Present himself to the Lord Advocate and plead to be hanged for his sins?'

'We need to know,' said Mary simply. 'Mrs. Paterson needs to know. She has to know why Jamie was killed.'

'Who can say if there was a reason, or just a whim?' asked the man. 'Go away, Mistress, back to your secure job, your gentlemanly household. It'll no be so secure if you go about asking questions that disturb fine gentlemen. Go on home.'

Mary crouched in silence for a long moment. Murray held his breath. She was perfectly balanced, so still her skirts did not shift on the ground.

'At least tell me what like of gentlemen you see passing down here,' she said at last, reasonably.

'What like?' Ramsay sneered. 'All like, single and married, alone or in crowds. They don't come down this way much, you ken, for there are cleaner places to find your amusement away from your stiff-backed parlours. Now go away, Mistress Macdonald.' He shuffled until he had turned sideways, facing away from her. He hid the effort well, but in the firelight Murray could see the damp on his brow that did not come from the rain.

Mary rose carefully, holding her cloak clear of the fire. She raised her eyebrows rather dismally at Murray, and picked her way back out of the circle again towards him. They turned to walk slowly back east towards the West Bow.

'I had hoped for more from him,' she confessed. 'He is a very clever man.'

The crowds were a little thinner now, the drunks less steady on their feet, the groups less noisy, the couples less inclined to linger.

'Did you notice his leg and arm?' she asked.

'I did,' said Murray, absently. He had the impression that one of the shadowy figures was following them, but when he turned to look around, he could see no movement in their direction.

'A carriage ran over him when he was a child. The gentleman that owned it sent his driver to give him a penny, as he lay helpless in the road. I think he would have preferred a whipping for getting in the way.'

'An insult indeed,' Murray agreed. They passed a dwindling fire with several sleeping forms around it and a bloodied fighting cock in a wooden cage. It was becoming harder to see their way. Behind them, he heard the sound of a slipping foot, and a little gasp of surprise, quickly suppressed. He could feel that they were being watched, and his back tensed. How would Mrs. Chambers explain this to poor George, if he died? Would George even care? His heart was off again, pattering like rain. His hands were ready to clench in an instant.

'So he is not fond of gentlemen,' Mary continued. 'He is often pleasanter during the day, but at night he suffers much pain, I believe, and cannot sleep, so he comes to sit by the well and find his own distractions. But he is, as I say –'

She stopped. Murray's hand was tight on her elbow. A cry shot from a passageway, a yelp of pain. They stood stock still. There was a thump, and a grunt. One light shone near the mouth of the passage, from a low window. The fight was beyond it, in the darkness, discreet and desperate. They should have moved on, but before they knew it, there was a harsh breath and a sudden sharp movement, and a man came flying into the patch of light. He fell on his back like a bale of cloth, and lay still, face white, eyes wide, blood at nose and mouth. They froze.

CHAPTER NINETEEN

As they stood, a man stepped forward into the light, and wiped blood from his fist. His hands were large and white against the dark of his clothing. He looked impassively down at the body, then seemed to sense them and glanced up, moving back into the shadow in the same motion.

'Run,' said Mary quietly, and they turned and ran, slipping and staggering over unseen obstacles, Murray's hand tight on Mary's wrist so that they should not lose one another in the dark. Only when they had put around three dozen people between themselves and the alleyway did they slow down, and Mary, panting, laughed. Murray stared at her.

'Laugh!' she whispered, and carried on herself. 'People won't wonder what you're running from if you laugh.' And she leaned on the wall and cackled. Murray, after a second's reasoning, joined her, and found it contagious, one part nerves and three parts relief.

But as they were recovering, wiping their faces with their filthy hands, Murray noticed a shadow standing near them. He tensed, and the shadow moved and came out into the dim light, and resolved itself into the young lad that had watched Murray so curiously by the well.

'Donald!' said Mary in surprise. 'What brought you after us?'

'Saw you at the well,' he said to Murray, 'Sir.'

'Oh, dear,' Mary remarked. Murray sighed.

'And you have seen me before, have you?' he asked, not bothering to modify his accent, although he kept his voice low.

'Aye, I have, sir. Don't fret, Mistress Mary,' he added, 'I shan't tell Mr. Ramsay you're going about with gentlefolk.'

'Well, it was good of you to come and tell us,' said Murray.

'Oh, it was not that which I came to tell you,' the boy answered. His accent was like Mary's, at the same time fluid and precise. 'You were looking for gentlemen that come down here. Well, I know of one of your acquaintance, sir, that is down here now and then.' He appeared about to go on, but Mary looked about her suddenly and said,

'We should be better indoors. Is Jeanie at the same place, still?'

'She is, Mistress Mary. And Angus is there tonight. I'll take you.'

Murray realised for the first time that they had run so far that they were well into the nightmarish Cowgate. The high, ancient walls had already closed about them, the dark sky invisible high above. He had no time to shudder, but followed Donald and Mary as they leapt the central drain by instinct rather than sight and negotiated the tricky path on the other side of the street. At last Donald selected an outside stair and ran up it, leading the way into a room partitioned by curtains into three or four separate chambers. A couple were arguing invisibly but vociferously in one of them, and snoring came like a protest from a second. Donald took them to another section, and called out,

'Angus? I have callers for you.' He found the gap in the curtain and ushered them inside.

Here, the sounds from the rest of the room were muffled by the cloth. Angus, a broad black-haired man in need of a shave, and Jeanie, thin and fair, were sitting on a narrow bed. The only other furniture in the chamber was a wooden trunk with a top polished from the seats of many breeches. On a hook on the wall, a red coat with yellow facings hung, in the rough serge of the ordinary soldier, and a white crossbelt with the oval regimental badge on it.

Jeanie and Angus greeted Mary a little too effusively. Murray wondered at this, until he realised that Jeanie and Angus were married but, since Jeanie lived here and Angus was only staying the night, Jeanie was not on the strength, not a sanctioned wife who would live with the regiment and help with laundry and nursing. She was in the same position, in fact, as Mary had been, but the difference, and the reason for their guilty effusiveness was clear: Angus had come home from campaign.

Mary took their greeting calmly and settled on the lid of the trunk, and with a wicked look said quietly, wary of the room's other inhabitants,

'And may I present Mr. Charles Murray of Letho, my master.'

Taken by surprise, Jeanie and Angus quite forgot any due civility, and remained seated on the bed staring. Then, slowly, Angus slid to the floor and bowed. Murray returned the bow, feeling slightly foolish, and Jeanie, spurred on by this, hopped down from the bed and made a curtsey. There was then a little confusion as they tried to offer Murray the bed to sit on, and he tried to decline as there was clearly only room for two, and in the end Jeanie solved the problem by going to fetch a kettle of water to warm some ale, while Angus and Murray demurely took their places on the hard straw mattress. Angus did not, markedly, ask what Murray was doing down the Cowgate well after midnight dressed the way he was: Angus had known, from a distance at least, quite a number of officers in his career, and they were without exception, though in different ways, quite mad. He had decided that it came from having too little to do with themselves.

Donald had taken up a position near the gap in the curtain, through which he occasionally peeped. It added to the impression he gave that something momentous was about to happen: his eyes were very wide, and he jiggled his feet inside over-large boots as he stood. It was making Murray nervous. Mary watched him for a moment.

'Well, Donald,' she said, 'you might as well tell us whatever it is.'

Donald fidgeted a little more, as he said to Murray,

'I have seen you before, sir, in the place where I work. And the gentleman you had dinner with there, I have seen him in the Grassmarket.'

'And where do you work?' asked Murray, trying to work out what the boy was trying to tell him.

'At Stone's coffee house, sir, in the High Street. The gentleman you were with I see there often, and have heard him called by the name of Balneavis. He is a fat man, with a face like the sunset, and he smiles a great deal and eats little.'

'That is the very gentleman,' Murray agreed, and looked at Mary. Her face was bland.

'So where did you see him in the Grassmarket, Donald?' she asked.

'In more than one place, Mistress Mary,' Donald replied, and a frown appeared on his face. 'But only ever in the street. I have never seen him go into a building or leave one.'

'And with whom does he keep company?' asked Murray.

'With no one, sir, but himself. It is strange behaviour, even for a gentleman, but I have noticed him several times, and it is always the same.'

Murray felt that there must be more.

'So what does he do, that it seems so strange?'

'He watches, sir.' Donald stopped, then expanded. 'He does not simply walk along the street from place to place, nor does he stop to talk to people nor to look for drink or women. He walks a little, then he stops and looks about him. Where he stops, it is usually a darker part of the street, or even in an alley.'

'And does he watch anything in particular?' asked Murray, feeling perplexed.

'I could not tell, sir. The times I have seen him, I have looked about me but have seen nothing out of the ordinary except for his own curious behaviour, sir.'

Jeanie had returned during this statement, and with Mary's help was pulling pewter cups from the wooden trunk. The ale with which she filled them was warm and tinny.

'What is all this for?' she asked, once she had squeezed in beside Mary on the trunk. Mary explained once again about the police officer's reluctance or inability to find the murderer of Mr. Murray's stable boy, the son of John Paterson in the Grassmarket.

'I heard about that,' said Jeanie. She had a sharp face and an accent from somewhere in the West. 'That was the lad with the fair hair, not much below Donald's age?'

'That's the one,' said Murray. 'Did you know him well?'

'Ah, no, but I saw him often enough. He wasn't as bad as some of them, who'll have your washing down and into the drain if the fancy takes them. Oh, aye, he was up to divilment like all of them, but he was never the one that started it, and betimes you'd see him just on his lonesome, happy as larry, picking up some wee bit of nonsense off the street to take home to show his ma. He'd be well mannered enough, then, too. Oh, I can think of some of them would have deserved being killed off quicker than him.' Her hands were thin and prim round her cup, red with the laundry work she had mentioned. She no longer seemed to find Murray's presence the least strange. Clearly if Mary felt at ease with the gentleman, as she seemed to be, then why should not they all?

'What do you know of Matthew Muir?' Murray asked. 'Or Dandy, his brother?'

Angus, less familiar with the neighbourhood than his wife, looked at her, and she shrugged.

'That's the man the scaffolding fell on. Up in the New Town somewhere. I scarce knew he had a brother.'

'They say he was great friends with a lot of powerful gentlemen,' said Donald. 'I never saw him in Stone's, and I never saw any gentlemen with him around here. I think if he saw them he must just have seen them in their own places.'

'If he saw them anywhere but in his own imagination,' added Mary sourly, 'from all I've heard.'

'Oh, he saw them,' said Jeanie suddenly. 'I've just minded. There was one night I had laundry to take to Fortune's in Prince's Street. The boy that works for us had hurt his leg, and I said I'd go instead. It was the middle of December, and already dark although it was only maybe three in the afternoon. People were dining at Fortune's when I went there.'

'And where did you see Matthew Muir?' asked Murray, leaning round to see her past the bulk of her husband.

'I'm not well acquainted with the New Town,' Jeanie replied obliquely. 'I found Fortune's quickly enough, but then I had to find the back, and I wandered up and down the alley at the back for ages. Then I thought if I looked up at the windows above me, I might see if they had a sign up or if I could see where it looked like a hotel and not like a private house. It was then I saw Matthew Muir at a window. He was on the second floor up, and the light was behind him – it was the back of Fortune's, as it happened – but it was certainly him. I heard him say, 'And it will all be over there,' but I don't know where or what he meant, because he turned back to the room then and someone else came to the window. I couldn't see his face, but I saw his arm and shoulder, pointing, and then pulling the sash down. His coat was well-cut, and his shirt was fine. It may have been two floors up,' she admitted, 'but I am a good laundrywoman, and I can tell these things.' She looked at Murray's jacket as if to prove her point. Her self-confidence certainly inspired trust. Murray thought for a moment.

'Could you tell,' he asked tentatively, 'if it was a big room or one of the small private ones?'

Jeanie considered, a frown sharp on her pale brow.

'A small one, I think. From the sound, and from the light. But I couldn't be sure.'

A private party, then, probably. With private business to discuss. What business could a gentleman have with an apprentice notary? And who, in Heaven's name, was the gentleman?

They finished their ale, and through the window in some invisible section of the shrouded building they heard a high clock striking four. Murray caught Mary's eye.

'Time, I believe, for us to return home, Mistress Macdonald.'

Mary nodded, and picked up her cloak which had lain across her lap. Jeanie and Angus rose politely.

'Thank you all for your help,' said Murray. 'I hope that the reward of all our efforts will be to find Jamie Paterson's murderer, and to bring him to justice.'

They nodded solemnly, and bows were exchanged. Mary received a sisterly embrace from both, and gave Donald a hand on his shoulder. They left through the gap in the curtain. Donald followed, gave them good night, and vanished proprietorially into the next closet. The argument had stopped, but the snoring was still as lively as ever.

Outside, the soft rain continued relentlessly and the air was sodden. Mary drew up her hood, and Murray balanced the hat on his hair. They descended the winding forestair carefully, and at Murray's instruction took their route home circuitously, back down the Cowgate to the Grassmarket. Most groups of drunkards had dispersed, and only individuals lurched across their path, or two men would hold each other up as one vomited in a corner, or was overcome by the sudden discovery of gravity. A couple stood ferociously embraced in a doorway, the man's ungloved hands pale roots feeling their way beneath the woman's loose, dark hair, light from the doorway behind her showing the ends of his neckcloth abandoned and tossed over his shoulder. Murray looked away from them, and deliberately watched his feet, as best he could. It was a relief now that there were no crowds to jostle, to brush against his arms or knock him from behind in haste or carelessness. In his society, people might very well lie politely to your face, but at least they left you some breathing space while they did it.

It struck him how aloof Mary seemed from it. She held herself serenely and sailed through the crowd in the alehouse, in the street, or by the well: it did not seem to touch her, not spiritually and almost, indeed, not physically. He need not have worried about any taint attaching to her here. She had apparently lived with these people or amongst them for many months, and they accepted her and trusted her, but she was not of them, any more than she was of those she lived with in the New Town, where maids dressed much more fashionably, and the servants were almost gentlemen themselves. She was apart, and it fascinated him.

He could not hide in the same way. He could borrow old clothes, stoop and slouch, keep his mouth shut and make his hands filthy with mud and blood. Given time he could even roughen them, and live on the diet of potatoes Mary had suggested. But nothing in all of that could hide what he was, because beside these people, beside the poor and the undernourished and the crippled, he could not hide the fact that generations of good food, warm clothes, and fresh air had made his bones strong, his hair thick, his skin and eyes clear. And however much he could give to the poor, however much he could contribute for the use of a mortcloth, he could never give an individual generations of health.

He stopped his wandering thoughts, and concentrated on their route home. They walked in steady silence to the Grassmarket, past the alleyway where they had seen the second, vicious fight. Murray allowed himself to look sideways without turning his head, but the light was out, now, and he had no wish to search for horrors in the darkness.

The West Bow was easier going uphill: although he slipped twice, he did not quite fall, and did not have to resort to the wall again with whatever hidden delights lay at its foot. He hoped William or Daniel would scrub his borrowed boots well before giving them back to poor Dunnet. That was something to be organised in the morning – this morning – for it was already Tuesday. Dunnet should be awake by dinner time, and in the afternoon Dr. Harker would send his useful man to nurse and guard, and on Wednesday – tomorrow, indeed – the pair could set off for Letho. He should tell his poor long-suffering steward by letter this morning to expect them.

They were up in the Lawnmarket now, where there were very few left outside, and those who were had the air of being up early for work, rather than out late for pleasure. A man hurried past them, head down, and by his trailing neckcloth Murray recognised the male half of the passionate embrace he had tried to ignore in the Cowgate. It had been a good night kiss, then: the man was alone. Before he vanished entirely out of their sight,

Murray realised with some curiosity that the man looked familiar to him, even in the dark. He peered after the flying neckcloth, and saw that the man had stopped and was entering the foot of a stair on the north side of the street, the left as they descended the hill. Murray looked up at the tenement as they passed, and recognised it as Balneavis'. In the Balneavis household, all was in darkness, as before. But on the floor below, as they passed, a candle was lit, and the man with the trailing neckcloth came to the window to close the shutters. It was the intense advocate, John Douglas.

CHAPTER TWENTY

Robbins woke him early, as he had requested. Murray's eyelids felt as if they had been sewn together, his head had been filled with glue in the early morning, and he scowled at the stinging pain in his knuckle where he had grazed it on the wall of the West Bow. Mrs. Chambers, who had waited up for their return like an anxious chaperone, had tutted over the injury, scalded it with the hot water she had ready for his bath, scraped invisible dirt from it and then bandaged it with one of her numerous salves, which had been known to treat everything from a blister to a broken heart.

Murray saw her off, and sank wearily on to his bed, about to blow out the candle on his bedside table. It was probably just as well he was not holding it, as he would have dropped it in shock at the sudden appearance of a nightshirted figure at his bedroom door. It was not Dunnet this time, though, but Robert.

'Robert!' Murray's heart tried to find its way back to the proper place. 'What are you doing out of bed?'

'I was wondering what was going on, sir. There's been lots of noise, and now here you are back really late, and I'd wager you haven't been at a ball.'

He nodded at Murray's odd clothes, tossed for now over a chair.

'So how long have you been sitting awake?'

'Hours and hours, sir.'

About twenty minutes, then, Murray guessed.

'You're not going to be fit for your studies tomorrow – er, today, are you?'

'Well, I'm not the only one, am I?'

'But I'm not going to college lectures, am I? Now you should be taking every opportunity your father gives you –'

'I didn't mean you, sir. I meant Henry.' He squirmed a little, arranging his face in an unaccustomed frown. 'Actually, I'm quite worried about him.'

Murray was, too, when he had time, and now guilt at the lack of attention he had been able to give the boys struck him again.

'What makes you worried?' he asked, trying to sound neutral.

'He's not sleeping very well – he keeps waking me with his wriggling.' That was more like Robert, concerned for his own comfort. 'And he sort of mutters in his sleep.'

'What does he say?'

'I don't know. When he starts I poke him and he wakes up.'

Murray bit his lips.

'Anything else?'

'He's not eating. I wouldn't mind, but even I can't finish all he leaves. And if he does eat anything, he bokes it back up later. Professor Chalmers says he's going to talk to you about it soon.'

A shame Professor Chalmers had not acted a little more swiftly, thought Murray, irritably – but then, he himself knew that Henry had been sick, and had done little about it.

'I've written to Lord Scoggie, Robert, concerning your possible return to Fife,' he said. Guilty as he felt, five in the morning was not the time to concentrate on what to do next.

'Oh, I don't need to go home, sir! I like Edinburgh! It's just Henry that can't take it. He's always been much more delicate than me, of course.'

'I'm just not sure that Edinburgh can take you, Robert. I do think that Henry needs country air, as soon as possible. But in any case, it will be for your father to decide. Now, I suggest you return to bed and try to get what sleep you can, however extraordinary your constitution.'

'The ferrets keep me awake, too, sir.'

'I thought the ferrets were in the stables?'

'Henry had to bring them up to our room. He said the stables weren't suitable.'

'He did, did he? Well, it's nice to know that the ferrets are being well treated, anyway. Now, go away and go to sleep.'

'Yes, sir ...' Robert drifted off through the door, though whether or not he would obey the second part of the instruction was not so clear. Murray waited, then pulled himself grumpily out of bed and slammed the door that Robert had left open. He was asleep almost before he had returned to the bed.

Robbins, because he had been left instructions by Murray to do so, made his preparations for Murray's shaving unnecessarily noisy, so that Murray would have no chance to fall asleep again. He disentangled himself from his bed, feeling that it had not had time to be properly appreciated, felt for his dressing gown and stumbled blindly over to the dressing room door. He was reminded of one of the most valuable lessons any student learns: no sleep at all is better, much better, than too little. He was sure he could still taste both the alehouse's ale and Jeanie's more metallic version, and he considerately tried to avoid breathing on his manservant. As he was shaved, he gave Robbins, as best he could, an edited account of the night's activities and the information they had obtained. Robbins seemed pleased not to be excluded, he thought. In turn, Robbins reported that Mary had apparently suffered no ill effect from her adventures.

'And what of Dunnet?' Murray asked finally.

'He appears to have passed a quiet night, sir. Mrs. Chambers sent William in to relieve Daniel an hour ago, and Daniel said he was starting to become a little restless, but was still asleep. Mrs. Chambers will go back in once she has given the others their orders for the day, so if he does wake the two of them will be there. We have cleaned his boots and put them back, sir, he will not know they have been gone.'

Murray joined the boys for breakfast, conscious of them watching him hold his knife awkwardly with the bandage on his hand. The first note arrived along with a pot of coffee. Henry ignored it, while Robert craned to see if it was anything interesting, like a letter from their professor excusing them all classes for the rest of the week. It was not: it was from Blair.

'My dear Charles,' it began. 'Forgive me the liberty of sending you this short message. I trust that this finds you quite well. On my return home from supper last night, I found a message waiting for me from my acquaintance with the connexions of which we spoke. He has endeavoured to discover the names of those involved in the enterprise in which we have some interest, but finds that contrary to our expectations we require to *begin* our search with names. In short, he cannot find the information without first having the information. Perhaps you will do us the honour of coming to supper this evening, and we can discuss how to proceed. Your friend, Alester Blair.'

Murray sipped his coffee, and thought. He assumed from Blair's discreet and somewhat convoluted construction that the feuars of the New Town properties were registered by name, rather than in order of the plots they had feued from the Council, and that the task of searching through the register for the plots of land north of the east end of Queen Street would be too onerous or too lengthy for Blair's acquaintance or his connexions in the City Chambers. He wondered how they could proceed, if that were the case: he could perhaps give the man a list of possible names to look for. This did not seem an entirely honourable thing to do. He pondered the problem.

The second note came with the porridge, but was rather less digestible.

'To Mr. Murray, Tutor to Lord Scoggie's Sons.

'I should be grateful if you could once more wait on me today at one in the afternoon, when it may please you once again to explain the behaviour of your charges. Patrick Chalmers, Professor of Divinity.'

'Have you been up to anything particularly unpopular at the college recently, Robert?' he asked, not expecting a helpful answer.

'I try not to do anything unpopular, sir,' Robert replied innocently. 'I believe my friends amongst the students find me quite amusing.'

'Oh, dear,' Murray remarked. 'You might wish to consider, for the moment, finding a way to amuse the professors as well.'

'Is that from old Chalmers?' Robert demanded. 'You needn't bother with him. He's just an old fool.'

'That's all right, then, I'll tell him that. Though I must say that when I met him previously on your account, he seemed pretty intelligent.'

Robert filled his mouth with porridge and gestured that he could not possibly reply.

The third note came just as the boys were about to go upstairs for their satchels, but the sight of the writing on the cover stopped Robert abruptly.

'That's from Father!' he cried, seizing Henry by the elbow and pulling him back. 'Don't tell me he's sent for us already!'

'Sit down again a moment and let me read it, and I'll tell you,' said Murray, his heart less calm than his words. He slid his long fingers under the seal, and tore the cover open.

'My dear Mr. Murray,' it began, 'I trust you are well, and swiftly coming to terms with the care of your estates.

'I thank you for your thoughtful letter concerning Henry and Robert, to which I have in turn given considerable thought. As you know, I had thought that at St. Andrews they would remain too much under my influence and protection, but I can well believe that Henry finds the capital a little daunting. I had hoped that in time he might become hardened to it, but alas, I fear he is in many ways his father's son. As for Robert, no doubt (reading between the lines of your letter) he would find mischief to make even in the most elevated seat of learning.

'I have therefore sent a letter to the Principal withdrawing the boys from Edinburgh, and with this letter to you have sent my coachman who will bring the boys back to Fife, setting out after a couple of hours' rest. Will you be so good as to see the boys' trunks packed, and if they owe any monies I shall reimburse you as soon as is convenient.

'My dear Mr. Murray, I imagine that you have too many other duties at present to be able to continue acting as my secretary and tutor. May I say what a pleasure it has been to have your assistance, and assure you that if ever you have need of a refuge from your worries, or advice, however old-fashioned, on the management of an estate, you will always be welcome at Scoggie Castle. Yours, etc., Scoggie.'

Murray had to swallow a couple of times before he gave the boys a summary of the parts of the letter affecting them. It was surprising how much he missed the old goat-faced peer and his eccentricities, surprising how much he wanted someone else to make the decisions, take the responsibility ... perhaps not that surprising, actually.

The boys spent the morning packing, under Murray's supervision. Henry seemed – unless it was Murray's imagination – to be a little more cheerful at the thought of going home. He saw to it that his precious ferrets were comfortably established in their cage with suitable provisions for the journey, and Murray tried not to count the minutes until the wretched animals left his house. Robert turned out to have a whole box of sketches he had made of various people around the town and college, which had to be found room: some of them were rather good. Squirrel came to watch them with anxious fascination: Murray wondered if the hound was concerned that the boys were leaving, or concerned that they were taking so long over it. She kept well clear of the ferrets.

The coachman had been told to collect them and their luggage at noon, so they had an hour to cross to the gardens and stretch their legs before their long journey. Squirrel bounded along adjacent to them but not absolutely with them. Murray made himself enjoy his last hour with the boys: he let them trail sticks and poke them into bushes, chatted with them about what they might find at Scoggie Castle and told them a bit about his time at St. Andrews, in answer to their questions about their next college. When they returned to the house, the coachman was already there and the luggage half-packed: it was a matter of minutes, then, before the boys tapped the mud off their boots, took the ferrets into the body of the coach from their prospective perch on the roof, said goodbye to the servants, and shook hands with their erstwhile tutor. Murray waved, the coach trundled off along the cobbles of Queen Street, and one of the bulkier pieces of jetsam floated off again from the cluttered beach of his mind, leaving an unaccountably mournful gap behind.

Murray set out for the college to meet Professor Chalmers just before one. The interview was significantly less painful than previous ones on the same subject: the fact that the boys had been withdrawn had made Professor Chalmers a very happy man, and Murray was more than willing to pay off the last debts caused by Robert's popular antics – this time he had pasted cartoons of all the professors, in large size, unexpectedly high up on the walls of their respective lecture rooms behind where the professors would be standing. Murray was most impressed by the quality of the drawings, but most disappointed that Robert had been unable to resist signing them. The paste had proved resistant to soap and water, and expensive methods of removal had had to be resorted to, meaning that certain humbler members of College staff had to be placated, as well. Murray was about to take his leave, when Professor Chalmers suddenly said,

'And as for Henry ...'

'Yes?' Murray had never had trouble at the college with Henry before, except when he had been unwillingly caught up in Robert's plots.

'Is he quite well?'

'I'm not sure, to be honest. He says he is.'

'He has missed several lectures, but he is to be found instead in the yard – he has often been sick.'

'Often?' Murray knew he should have given more time to this. What on earth was wrong with the boy? If he could have had Dr. Harker look him over before he left for Fife ... 'His father knows that Edinburgh has not suited him: I'm sure he will tend to him in the best way possible.'

'He has the makings of a scholar, you know, Mr. Murray.'

'I know. I think he knows it, too – and his father will support him in that.'

'Robert, however ...'

'Indeed.'

Murray headed back towards the Lawnmarket and Balneavis' flat, his mind spinning with his feelings of failure over Robert and Henry. What had he really done for either of them? Why would Henry not tell him what was wrong?

Then he remembered that he and Balneavis were to dine with John Douglas, and a new wave of concerns and questions began a whirlpool in his mind. How could he draw the conversation round to discover what each of them was doing in the Grassmarket and the Cowgate at night, and why? In Douglas' case, it had, on the surface, seemed obvious: he was an unmarried man, who chose to descend to the Cowgate to purchase some relief from his solitary state. Yet, Murray felt very strongly that the manner of the embrace in which Douglas and the young woman had been so firmly bound together did not suggest a passing fancy or a purely financial arrangement. The passion with which Douglas spoke in court, which Balneavis thought demonic, seemed to have other outlets, too. Was it, though, the kind of passion which could also lead to murder? Somehow, Murray found it simple to picture Douglas, friend of his father's though he might have been, throttling Jamie as he thrust him back against the corn bing. But Douglas had also been at the burial.

He arrived at Balneavis' flat before John Douglas, and little wonder, since those who live nearest are often the last to arrive. Balneavis himself met him in the hall, and hurried him enthusiastically into the little parlour. Murray bowed to Mrs. Balneavis, rosy and plump as ever, and to Miss Balneavis, Miss Helen, and the two youngest daughters, whose names he seemed to be expected to remember but could not. All of them were engaged in making a gown which had something essential to do with Miss Helen's especial friend from school, a Miss Lyall, who was expected at any time - again, Murray seemed to be expected to know her intimately. The smallest Miss Balneavis, aged about eight, was stitching expertly at the dark crimson velvet, the richest fabric in the room by a mile, and Murray was for a moment bustled round the room in an effort to find him a seat that was not covered in a fine layer of deep red fluff from the cloth. Pin cushions and needlecases prevailed, and Murray found himself rather nervous in his chair, afraid of touching the wrong thing. He had already discovered a nasty pair of scissors by the simple expedient of moving his leg in the wrong direction: Miss Helen, quite pink, relieved him of them. He hoped she was going to take them back to the battlefield where they belonged. Balneavis, by contrast, used to the inconvenient juxtapositions of his cramped accommodation, was quite composed.

'I have asked our friend to meet us here at two o'clock,' he said to Murray, with a cautious glance at his daughter Margaret. It was worrying for a father when his daughter's worst temptation lived so near by and had such a claim to be acknowledged socially. 'It wants but five minutes to the hour now, we should not find it necessary to encumber the ladies with our presence for much longer.' He beamed at his wife, who smiled broadly back at him.

'Not at all, my dear Mr. Balneavis, you must not give Mr. Murray the impression that he is not always welcome here! Mr. Murray, I pray you will call as often as you wish, but as you see we do not stand on ceremony. My girls are taught always to be as easy as anything in company, but with you

you may be sure such ease is not contrived.'

Murray bowed his head in acknowledgement.

'I am sure four such charming young ladies as the Misses Balneavis need not fear being uneasy in any company, for they will always be greeted with respect and delight.'

The girls blushed collectively as much as was proper (though it might have been the red velvet fluff), and Mrs. Balneavis received the compliment like a broad-bowed ship breasting a full wave.

However easy and charming the Balneavis sisters, Murray discovered that he was expected to provide the principal part of their entertainment during his brief wait. He passed some pretty if ignorant compliments on the cloth with which they were working, and was told by gradual degrees for whom it was being made up, and the occasion for which it was required, and how pretty Miss Lyall would look in it for it was just the colour to bring out the best in her complexion, which was something too pale for true beauty (this from Mrs. Balneavis, glancing proudly at her four rosy daughters). The subject drew to a close, and Murray found that he was again expected to begin with a new one. He could hardly discuss music, after the embarrassment of the previous evening – he remembered this just in time, for the previous evening seemed very long ago. Any other subject seemed suddenly to lead back to that, and he sat in awkward silence for a moment. He shot a look discreetly at the old clock on the mantelpiece, and saw that it was already twenty minutes past two. Balneavis seemed to notice at the same moment.

'Where in Heaven's name is that man? It's not like Douglas to be late!' he exclaimed, and instantly regretted his lack of caution as he saw Margaret's gaze become very fixed and her needle pause, a loop of red thread hanging motionless for a second before she skilfully drew it through to form the tiniest of stitches.

'Perhaps we should call on him and see if anything is – is delaying him,' Murray suggested hurriedly. Balneavis agreed with grateful speed. The gentlemen rose, Murray with some caution, looking about him for sharp objects. The ladies rose, too, in a dim cloud of red fluff, the fronts of their sober grey gowns faintly pink.

It was but three seconds' walk to descend the stair to the next landing, and go to the door directly beneath Balneavis'. The sound of a decidedly amateur violin fingered its way down after them from another flat. They paused to listen through it to any sounds coming from Douglas' flat but without success. Murray rattled at the risp, while Balneavis, suddenly impatient, thumped on the door with one plump fist. The violin staggered on. There was no response from Douglas' flat. Balneavis thumped the door again. Upstairs, the violin came to a halt, and then was evidently returned to its master. A toccata suddenly burst forth, the sound running and dancing up and down the stair, echoing on the stone walls, racing on worn steps and rusty railings, glittering, exciting, sharp as needles. Balneavis hammered at the door. He called out Douglas' name. His voice was urgent, anxious. The violin upstairs pattered, laughing, to the very top of a scale and stopped. The door opened, and Douglas appeared.

CHAPTER TWENTY-ONE

Douglas looked at them completely blankly for a long moment in the sudden silence of the stair, then appeared abruptly to recollect who they were, if not quite what they were doing there. He drew back and waved them into his flat.

The flat was constructed in exactly the same pattern as Balneavis' upstairs, and Balneavis led the way to the parlour with the assurance of a man who had been there before. They were through the small bare hall before Murray had a chance to notice it, their feet sounding on the carpetless boards. In the parlour the floor was also bare of carpets, or at least that was what Murray deduced from the little of it he could see. There were in the room a broad firwood table, of the kind one might find in a kitchen, and two hard upright chairs. A third chair, cushioned but worn, stood by the fireplace. The walls, plastered plain white, were mostly covered in shelves, and on these stood a proportion of the vast number of books and papers with which the room was filled. The table served as an over-sized desk, and was littered with open books, papers, notebooks and pens, and adorned with a huge silver penstand and inkwell which looked as if it had never been polished in its existence.

Douglas followed them into the room and sank on to one of the hard chairs, which was positioned in front of the table. He had not said a word since opening the door to them. Now that they had a chance to see him properly – the room had no curtains, Murray noticed, and the shutters were open, so what light there was outside had no impediment – they had quite a shock. Murray wondered if he himself looked as bad after his own night out: Douglas' eyes were sunk in dark circles of fatigue that made their demonic fire even less earthly by contrast. The lines from nose to mouth and across his brow appeared to have been burned in with a thin poker. His black hair was lank and dull, and he had not shaved that morning. Nor had he fully dressed. His waistcoat lay open, his neckcloth was not tied, papers were sticking out of his breeches pockets, and his boots lay beside his chair as if he had kicked them off there when he had returned home. Douglas rarely looked the fifty-odd years he must have lived, but today he looked all of them, and more besides.

Balneavis gently cleared some papers from the fireside chair, but did not sit down, and hovered anxiously beside it. Murray stood nearer the door. Douglas did not look as if dinner were the most immediate matter on his mind, and Murray felt they should simply leave. But it was not for him to say. Douglas gazed at them for a while, or not quite at them, perhaps collecting his thoughts, and at last cleared his throat roughly.

'I must beg both your pardons. I am not myself. Am I engaged to you today?'

'You are, my dear Douglas,' said Balneavis, with an encouraging smile. 'You are bound to dine with us at Stone's, half an hour since. But do not fear, they will always keep a table free for me.'

'If, that is, you are quite well enough, sir.' Murray felt he had to make some concession to the man's appearance.

'Oh,' Douglas drew himself up from his seat as if stiff in every limb, 'I am quite well, I thank you. Pray be seated, and allow me a few moments to complete my toilet. You must forgive my lateness: I had a restless night last night in contemplation of a new case, and overslept this morning. Please make yourselves quite comfortable.'

He had a low, quick way of talking when he did talk, that made him seem faintly conspiratorial as his dark, glowing eyes met those of his companions. He left the room, boots in hand, and could be heard distantly in the next room, chinking jug against basin with a somewhat unsteady hand.

'Look at this,' said Balneavis, in tones of mild distress. 'Small wonder the man looks ill. Outside the air is thick with damp, and yet in here there is no fire, no warm shawl, no coat, even, and in his stocking feet on bare wooden floors as if he were no better than a common beggar! He has no money, and anything he does make from his cases he spends on books and paper and ink. How any woman could live with it – and how any man could allow his daughter to marry it, even without the disparity of ages …' He tailed away, muttering to himself, placing a flat hand against one wall as if feeling for damp, tutting over the chaotic heaps on the table. 'This monstrosity!' he said, tapping the inkstand, 'gift from a grateful client. As usual, one who could not pay any other way, but still managed to pay more than most. A man with a talent like his should not waste it on the defence of hopeless people who will hang one day, if not another. He has no business to – ah, here we are, Douglas!' he beamed.

Douglas' face was red and raw in patches, since he had evidently shaved in cold water, but at least it indicated some life in him. He had completed his clothing and donned his boots, and apart from the dark circles around his eyes he looked quite normal and presentable. Murray reflected that he himself had at least the luxury of servants to organise him when he had had little sleep, and perhaps Douglas had had a more energetic night than he – besides being some thirty years older.

They trooped through the bare hall and down the stair. Out on the street they had to pause as a company of soldiers passed, their concerted movement raising a slight breeze on their faces that brushed away a little of the mist. There was growing talk of the French attempting a landing at Dunbar, and between there and Edinburgh, every garrison was doubled, with more soldiers camped in fields and billeted in towns. Murray thought about his brother George, and wondered if he, too, was keeping an eye on developments at home.

Stone's was busy, but Balneavis, as he had predicted, managed to secure them his usual corner table. Murray found that he was famished, having been too sleepy to eat much at breakfast, and he launched into his soup with great good will. The spoon was easily managed, but when it came to a knife and fork he found himself in the same difficulties as he had done at breakfast, the smooth bone handle slipping against the bandage over his knuckles. The length of his sleeves had kept it discreetly hidden until then, but now it was only a matter of time before the all-seeing, ever-noticing Andrew Balneavis commented on it.

'Whatever happened to your hand, my dear boy?' he asked solicitously. Douglas shot it a sharp glance.

'Merely a scratch,' said Murray, as smoothly as he could. 'My housekeeper fusses about these things, and wraps it as if to stop the fingers falling off.'

'Quite right,' said Balneavis. 'These things can so easily go bad, and then she would have much worse to deal with. But you should have told my dear Mrs. Balneavis about it. She would have made sure of its being properly seen to. She is so clever about that sort of thing, you know, and she has all the girls so well trained in every little thing. When the housemaid cut her finger, my Margaret bandaged it so neatly that it healed without the least scar.'

'Speaking of servants,' said Murray hurriedly, 'does either of you know of a good groom available?'

'I thought you had a good –' said Balneavis, but broke off.

'I do,' said Murray, 'but he has fallen ill, and is like to be so for some time. And without my stable boy as well, matters are becoming quite difficult. My manservants could perhaps manage, but I am unwilling to overwork them and besides, neither of them seems quite comfortable with the horses.'

Douglas shook his head. Balneavis pondered for a moment, but then also shook his head.

'One of my clients –' he began, 'but no, I am not sure. She is recently widowed, and was contemplating letting the stable go. I shall make enquiries for you, if you wish,' but he sounded unsure, as if he had just remembered something that made him doubt the arrangement. Murray thanked him, but did not allow himself to sound too enthusiastic.

The next course arrived, carried by Donald the pot boy. Murray was quite startled to see him: he had forgotten some points of the previous night. Donald was remarkably fresh and alert, particularly when compared with Douglas' appearance and Murray's own thickish head. He did nothing more than glance in Murray's direction, very properly showing him no signs of recognition. Murray contained a smile. Balneavis steered the conversation on to the matter of the legal profession and its benefits in young men, drawing Douglas into one or two laconic comments on his own experience. Murray found that he was expected to pay attention and learn, and was happy enough to do so, though he had no intention in the world of becoming an advocate. Douglas, however, tired of the subject before Balneavis did, and changed to a thoughtful account of a talk he had been to at Creech's several days before, where they had discussed the new *Lay of the Last Minstrel,* a popular book by an unknown author. Creech was growing very old, he reported, but still controlled the literary discussion with the air of an orchestral conductor. Murray wondered suddenly if Douglas were drawing comparisons between Creech and Balneavis,

Douglas' character was strong enough to keep the conversation easy till the end of the meal. It had not been an unpleasant couple of hours. Donald came with their coats and helped them on in turn, Balneavis first and Murray last, and while Murray waited, he felt in his pockets for money to pay for the meal. There seemed to be less than he had thought, and he emptied what he could find out in handfuls on to the bench he had shared with Douglas, to sort out the problem. Some of his pocket contents, including the enamel button found by Jamie, fell on the floor, and he had to crouch down to scrabble about for his belongings under the bench. His head reeled slightly, the effect of fatigue and dinner time wine. Eventually he was reorganised, quarrelled politely with Balneavis to pay for the dinner (Douglas did not interfere), and won, giving Donald a sizeable tip. They ascended the steps to find that the mist was thickening rather than thinning, and went their separate ways fading quickly out of each other's view, Balneavis back to his flat, Douglas to the courts, and Murray home. He wondered if the boys would be crossing the Firth in the fog.

He was already into the New Town when it occurred to him to check in his pockets again to make sure that he still had Jamie's button. He found it almost immediately, and with it a piece of paper that he remembered picking up from the floor, but could not immediately identify. He drew it out to look at it, and found that it was a note, quite fresh although the paper had been folded, with no cover and no address at its head. The writing was carefully printed. He had read it, thinking it his, almost before he realised that it was not.

'The next payment has now fallen due, and should on this occasion be placed in the Cage in the Meadows tonight about nine o'clock. Do not linger.' It was signed, 'One who wishes you no harm.' Murray stared at it for a few seconds, leaning one shoulder against the wall of the General Register House, then turned it over. On the reverse were the two simple letters, 'J.D.'.

He remembered seeing papers sticking untidily from Douglas' breeches pockets when they had first met him that afternoon. This paper had certainly not been under the dining table at Stone's for very long, for the floor was damp and grubby, as all these places were in wet weather, and the paper was clean. It seemed reasonable to form the conclusion that the note had in fact been dropped by Douglas at some point during dinner, and Murray had turned about and was going to walk back to the law courts to return it to him, when he considered. The note was short and simple, and Douglas had quite likely taken its contents by memory. In addition, it would be hard to pretend that he himself had not seen the contents, as the note was open. It might make things easier if Murray simply pretended he had never seen the note.

He turned back towards his home, and walked slowly, thinking. Perhaps he was influenced by his knowledge of some of Douglas' night time activities, but it occurred to him that the note was very much like a demand for blackmail, and blackmail that had been going on for some time, as the note showed that this was not the first payment.

If Douglas were to make the payment at the appointed time, he should leave his flat around a quarter to nine, or earlier if he chose to go by way of South Bridge, rather than cutting through the Grassmarket and up the Vennel in the dark. Murray was not promised to Blair's until ten, their supper hour, and it was near to the Meadows. Would a blackmailer be a murderer? Murray decided that if possible, he would follow Douglas to the Cage and wait to see who would collect the money.

He spent a tedious afternoon wondering how the boys were on their journey, thinking about writing a letter to George, trying to entice Squirrel out from the corner of the study to be stroked, and eager to hear what Blair might have to say to him that evening. He began to make a list of possible names to look for in the council records, Armstrong, Thomson, Balneavis, Dundas, and felt guilty. Around four, Dr. Harker arrived with the man Liddle, who was to look after Dunnet, and they were sent off by post carriage to Cupar where a man from Letho would meet them. Dunnet was dazed and quiet, easily managed, and Dr. Harker explained that Liddle was experienced in administering opium and managing violent outbursts. Murray liked the look of Liddle, who had the air of a retired pugilist with a decent if battered expression. When they had left, he found himself some old clothes and went to see to the horses, deciding that whatever the dignity of the situation the horses would benefit more from his slight skill than from Daniel's or William's careless ministration. He found, too, that the straightforward stable chores and the effort of remembering them took his mind off his other problems. Grooming the horses was soothing, and he deliberately turned his back on the corn bing, where the cat sat and watched him benevolently. When he had led the horses, one at a time, up Queen Street and down again, it was time for a bath and a change into evening clothes, before the hands crept round to eight o'clock and he allowed himself to leave, lest he should miss Douglas.

He wrapped up warmly and left. The fog was so thick you could taste it, like plunging your head into cold sea water. Murray's black weepers hung damp and limp down his back, and a dew settled dull almost immediately on his coat and gloves. Drawing air into his lungs felt unhealthy, as if it carried all the town's smoke and filth and disease. He coughed, and from all around him there came a chorus, it seemed, of disembodied coughs, half-smothered by the fog. His mouth tasted salty.

Navigating chiefly by the varying slope of the streets invisible under his feet, he found his way at last to the entrance of Douglas' stair, and discovered, by virtue of jarring his shins on it, a closed-up stall in the street that he could hide behind and still see anyone who came out through the door. There would be few people on a night like this able to see, let alone wonder at, a well-dressed gentleman in mourning lurking about the Lawnmarket. He propped himself against the worn stone wall, tried to ignore the general damp, and prepared to wait.

It was lucky that he had, as usual, left home too early. About a quarter of an hour before he had reckoned it would happen, a figure emerged from the doorway and walked briskly down the hill, past Murray's hiding place. Although the fog was still thick, the sharp lines of the advocate's angry face, outlined by the soot-black stroke of his short whiskers, stood out against the grey breath of the mist. Evidently Douglas had an equal horror of being late.

The darkness and fog were, Murray reflected, both his friends and his enemies. He stood but little chance of being seen by the man he was following, and sound echoed strangely in the fog and made the noise of his footsteps deceptive. On the other hand, on occasion only his knowledge of where Douglas was heading helped him to distinguish the advocate from other dark shapes in the icy air. Douglas moved at a slower rate than Murray usually did, being rather smaller in build, but Murray would have lost him altogether in Nicolson Street near the College but that Douglas stopped to cough, as Murray himself had earlier, when the fog caught in his throat. Murray took two long strides to bring himself closer to his quarry, and settled back into his former slower pace.

Soon Douglas cut through to George's Square, where there were fewer people on the street and it was easier for Murray to follow at a greater distance. Murray nodded in the direction of Blair's house, but Douglas took a route to the southern corner of the square, veering on to the road at one point to give a wide berth to a party climbing into a carriage, who were calling farewells to their hosts at a lit doorway. Murray, as cautious as Douglas, veered likewise. They reached the corner in neat sequence, and one by one turned right towards the north end of the Middle Walk.

In the Meadows, the fog was thinner, and lay lower. It came to shoulder height on Douglas, and his hat and head seemed almost to float across it, disembodied. Murray, protruding rather further from it, dropped back again to be unobtrusive. The avenue of trees, in any case, bare black pillars, lined the walk and would confuse Douglas should he chance to look back. Underfoot, gravel mixed haphazardly with mud gave off a dull crunch, muffled and soft. No one else was around.

About halfway along the Walk, they must have crossed the ditch where the Council were digging the central drain, but Murray could only detect its presence by the sharp smell of decay that rose from it. Ahead of them, at the end of the path, the dilapidated summer house known as the Cage loomed like a shipwreck, rafters showing clear black ribs where the lead was missing. About thirty yards away from him, Douglas waded through the mist to the steps, rose like a bather from the sea, and disappeared inside. He was only there a matter of moments: Murray hardly had time to choose where to place himself, when Douglas appeared again and plunged into the fog, walking quickly towards where Murray stood. Murray was beside a tree: he allowed himself to sink slowly down towards its roots, knees bent, face turned away from the approaching man, and stayed perfectly still in the depths of the fog. Incredibly, Douglas strode swiftly past, and did not seem to see him. Murray waited until Douglas had reached again the north end of Middle Walk, then rose and moved cautiously towards the Cage.

The steps were slippery with damp, and Murray moved carefully on them. A broken bone here and now could mean a deadly chill by morning. He looked around in the dim enclosure, wondering what Douglas could have found to do in such a short time, in semi-darkness. He did not know, either, how long he might have to find out, before the blackmailer arrived to claim his money.

A bench seat ran around the inner edge of the summer house, and a smaller one formed a concentric circle around the supporting central pillar. Murray paced around between them, looking from left to right for anything obvious, then decided he would have to descend to his knees and look underneath the benches. He sent a silent apology to Robbins for the state of his breeches, and knelt gently on the wet floor.

He had completed almost one circuit on his knees before he noticed, not a fold of paper under the bench, but wet footprints on it. He had automatically disregarded anywhere that Douglas with his small stature could not easily have reached, but these were clearly his prints, quite neat and small, and freshly made. Murray rose and straightened, looking up the wooden post which met a corner of the tattered roof. Above him, at the very top of the post, there must have been a small gap between post and roof beam, and tucked into it like a handkerchief into a waistcoat pocket was a thick paper wrapping, crisp enough not to have been there for long. He was about to remove it, when some instinct told him to look round. In the distance, advancing along Middle Walk, was a figure in a tall hat. Murray crouched down and left the summer house in an undignified rush on his hands and knees, and still keeping low he darted around the back of the building, out of Middle Walk and behind one of the large trees outlining the southern edge of the Meadows. Then he breathed again.

Murray waited. The fog, disturbed by his awkward passing, settled again around him, lapping its cold waters about his arms and legs, seeping into his bones. He dearly wanted to see the distant figure approaching, but even more dearly did not want the distant figure to see him. At last curiosity, abetted by a fear of his limbs becoming completely rigid, led him to remove his hat carefully and, holding it clear behind him, he peered very slowly round the edge of the tree trunk.

The man, for now he could see more definitely that it was a man, was just in the act of stepping off the bench directly below the point at which Murray had seen the paper wrapping. Through the open sides of the building he appeared as a stocky individual, not much above the middle height, but still too far away in the fog for Murray to tell more. In contrast to Douglas' grim, determined stride, this man scuttled back down the steps, looked about him nervously, and trotted off into the mist back the way he had come. Murray shot out of his hiding place, jammed his hat back on his head, and followed as quietly as the gravel would let him. Again, his height and length of stride would stand him in good stead.

They were almost halfway along the Walk, both cutting swiftly through the pools of mist, when it happened. Murray, in his urgency, was not even trying to see what was under his feet, and a smallish branch, broken from its tree in the recent snowfall, was quite invisible even to the cautious walker. He placed one foot on top of it, found his step unsteady, drew the other foot up quickly to help his balance, caught it on the rest of the branch, and fell solidly on to the path. There was a yelp, which for a moment he thought was his own voice. Then he realised it had come from the person ahead of him, who, alarmed by the sudden evidence of company in the fog, broke into a run. Murray cursed quietly. But suddenly there was a slithering noise, a shriek, and the unusual sound of a very heavy body being received into the various and welcoming contents of the Council's new drain.

There was a long moment of silence. It was followed by an unattractive sucking noise, and a slap as if of someone pulling their arm or leg free from the morass and letting it fall once more. There was a whimper, and Murray began to pull himself up from his prone position and make his way, with considerable wariness, towards the scene of the accident. Sounds of choking made him add an inch to his stride, but as he approached it became clear that the victim was not so much on the point of drowning as on the point of abandoning his supper to the drain. The smell up on the path was atrocious: in the drain itself it had to be diabolical.

Murray found the edge, made sure he had his balance, and called out,

'Hallo there! Are you injured at all?' He found that his pulse was racing, waiting for the reply.

'Murray? Charles, is that you, my dear boy?'

'It is.' Murray swallowed hard. 'Can I help you out of there? Are you all right?'

'I fear,' said the man, to the accompaniment of a tremendous slurp from the drain, 'that my clothing has suffered more injury than I have. I wonder, my dear Charles, if I could trouble you for a hand to guide me out?'

Murray edged nearer to the lip of the ditch, crouched, and took a generous hold around the trunk of a tree. With his left arm, he reached as far as he could towards the voice. After a moment, he felt a gloved hand fasten on to his, slippery but strong. He pulled. There was a scrabbling and a squelching, a few frantic steps on unsure ground, and up on the path, bulbous with indescribable filth, came Andrew Balneavis.

CHAPTER TWENTY-TWO

'My dear boy, what good fortune!' Balneavis exclaimed quickly, flicking particles of unnameable substances from his sodden sleeves. 'I was just returning from a client in the Boroughmuir – house over there, in fact –' he waved vaguely southwards, 'and he had just paid me, so I was feeling very nervous. He likes to pay all his bills at once, you know? And I heard a noise, and thought I was about to be robbed, so I fled – and fell.'

'Ah, yes,' said Murray. He felt very embarrassed. He was quite sure that he had not lost sight of the figure from the time he saw it step off the bench in the Cage to the moment he fell over the branch. The chances of his quarry vanishing and Balneavis independently falling into the ditch within a few yards of each other seemed to Murray a little slim. Not even Willie Jack Dundas would have put money on it. Besides, in the hand that had not seized his own, Balneavis was clutching a paper wrapper which looked familiar, and to which he clung as if his life depended upon it. Presumably, if Murray asked, Balneavis would say that it was the payment from his client. 'You must be very uncomfortable,' Murray suggested at last. 'And you are probably quite chilled. We should go on to Blair's house, I think, and see you warmed and changed. Unless you know anyone nearer by?'

Balneavis had indeed started to shiver. He nodded.

'No, dear boy, I fear we must impose upon my good friend Blair.'

They set off at a brisk pace, gradually easing the sharp bruise in Murray's knee and also, when they had reached a good speed, allowing the ripe scent from Balneavis' clothes to fall behind him, rather than linger around. It was a few minutes only before they arrived at Blair's doorstep, and the manservant's expression changed magically from welcome to alarm to distress. He brought them quickly into the narrow entrance hall and murmured something about finding Mr. Blair. As he vanished round the corner towards the street parlour, Murray noticed him snatch his handkerchief from his pocket and slap it over his nose.

A moment later, Blair appeared, his portly body enveloped in a banyan intended for a taller man, and an expression of kindly anxiety across his careless face.

'My dear Balneavis, my dear Charles, what has happened? Never mind, not now. Smith, take their coats.' The manservant reappeared, looking determined and with his mouth slightly open, and removed the coats to some distant part of the house. Murray could not see whether or not he was breathing. Balneavis was ushered rapidly into Blair's own chamber, where there was already a fire in the grate, and maids were instructed on the provision of bath and hot drink. Murray himself, refusing fresh clothes as his own were reasonably dry under his coat, was brought into the street parlour. A goggle-eyed maid brought brandy which Blair warmed at the fire, and Murray felt his first sip sending trickles of heat down into his cold limbs. Blair immediately topped up the glass from the jug, and settled back into his chair, eyes wide with curiosity.

'Well?' he prompted, jiggling with excitement.

'Mr. Balneavis fell into the new drain in the Meadows,' Murray said briefly.

Blair looked oddly at Murray, his head on one side, and Murray met his eye with meaning. Blair nodded, his wig bouncing perilously.

'How very fortunate that you came to be passing.'

'Yes, most fortunate. Although he would have found his way out eventually, the fog made his path very uncertain, and a voice calling to him from the bank may indeed have rendered him some assistance.'

There was a moment's silence, during which they could hear the distant clanking of servants bringing hot bath water to the bedchamber next door. Then Blair bounced in his seat.

'But Charles, what in Heaven's name were the two of you doing?'

'Well, Balneavis says he was visiting a client in the Boroughmuir, who had just paid him, which is why he was jumpy.'

'The day Andrew Balneavis contracts with a wealthy client in the Boroughmuir who wishes to deal with him late at night is the day I eat my wig.'

'Well, I have no absolute proof,' said Murray slowly, 'but the balance of probability is that Balneavis is extorting money from John Douglas, in return for keeping a secret of his. I believe that Douglas does not, however, know who his blackmailer is, but the sums are quite substantial.' He explained what had happened in Douglas' flat and later in the Meadows, finishing with Balneavis' own very unlikely – and unlooked-for – explanation of what he was doing in the Meadows at night.

'A blackmailer,' said Blair thoughtfully, his jiggling subsiding. 'Possibly, yes. His situation is desperate enough, with all his daughters to marry. I confess to being surprised, however.'

'I agree,' said Murray. 'He has always seemed so open. Yet it seems to fit with the account I had of his activities in the Grassmarket at night, as if he were hunting for potential victims for his schemes.'

'The Grassmarket at night?' Blair started jiggling again, and Murray realised that he had left out a significant part of his recent activities. He managed to gloss over what he knew of Douglas' liaisons, but gave a summary of his visit to the Cowgate and the Grassmarket with Mary.

'And the Grassmarket is almost certainly where he found his information concerning Douglas,' he finished. He remembered vividly the sight of John Douglas in the early morning going home down the Lawnmarket, the ends of his neckcloth lying loose across his shoulders after his passionate encounter with the young woman in the Cowgate.

'Yet how could this lead us to a murderer for your father and Jamie?' Blair asked at last. 'It is an excellent reason for Balneavis to be murdered, if he is making people's lives more miserable than they need to be. He might even have killed in self-defence, if one of his victims became violent. But there are several reasons why I think that unlikely. In the first place, from what you say about his methods with Douglas and from what I know – or think that I know – about his character, it seems unlikely that any of his victims – and here we are, of course, assuming that there are others apart from Douglas – knows who he is. He avoids, as seems natural for him, meeting them directly as their blackmailer.' He regarded Murray with a watery eye, and nodded to reinforce his point.

'In the second place, neither your father nor Jamie is likely to have had any secret they would have paid to have kept secret, nor was either of them likely to attack Balneavis: this might not, of course, count as far as Matthew Muir was concerned. He might well have been susceptible to extortion, though like Jamie he would have had little money to give.'

'Do you think my father would not have attacked him? If someone had threatened to blackmail my father, I think he would have gone for them with a sturdy stick.'

Blair gave a lop-sided smile.

'Yes, you're probably right, alas. But in that case, I think your father would have won.' Blair sat back in his chair and stretched his short legs, then came back to his main point. 'In the third place, however, the night your father died the Balneavises were supping here, and he was at the burial when Jamie was killed.'

'Oh. I did not know.'

'Unless he is blackmailing Douglas over something concerned with the murders? Of course, Douglas could not have killed Jamie, either.'

'No, no, I think I know why he is blackmailing Douglas, and it has nothing to do with the murders.' He thought for a moment, trying to disentangle the mess in his head. 'But if indeed Balneavis has other victims from whom he is extorting money, then there are other people about whom he knows secrets, secrets which he would not have told anyone else.'

'You mean,' said Blair slowly, 'that he might know something about the murders but not have told us, because he hoped to make money from it?'

'Exactly!' said Murray, examining his theory for flaws.

'No, I cannot believe that,' said Blair with sad finality. 'Balneavis was very fond of your father. He would not hide his murderer simply for the sake of money.'

'But you yourself pointed to his desperation,' Murray insisted. 'I think we should ask him. We can tell him that we know about his blackmail, and if he does not tell us anything he knows about the murders, we shall inform Douglas who his blackmailer is.'

'And thereby become extortionists ourselves,' Blair reminded him gently.

'But this is different – oh, well, I suppose not.' Murray sighed. 'Yet we must prevent him from further torture of poor Douglas. If you had seen the man this morning, it would say all that needed to be said of the evil of Balneavis' activities. I can hardly bring myself to believe that a gentleman could wilfully do such harm to one whom he regards as a friend.'

'As you say,' said Blair. He pondered, lips pursed and eyes on the ceiling, drumming his fingers on the swathed arm of the chair. 'A warning, I suppose, need not be a threat. We can make it plain to him that if he makes any further demand on Douglas, we shall tell Douglas the identity of the extortionist and leave the rest up to him. Douglas may prefer to deal with the matter privately than to see Balneavis in court, when any secret he is paying to protect might well come out. Then we go to Douglas and say that we have warned off the blackmailer and he is to let us know if anything further transpires. It is not entirely satisfactory, but I fear that for the moment it will have to suffice.' He jiggled his knees, and looked distressed.

The interview with Balneavis was easily as painful as anything either of them had anticipated. For a while, he adhered firmly and cheerfully to his story of a rich client on the Boroughmuir, and when confronted by the story of the note addressed to Douglas and the sequence of events witnessed by Murray, the smile continued, forgotten, on his lips, while his eyes became anxious. Murray would almost have called them puzzled.

'But, my dear Blair,' Balneavis explained, 'Douglas has a great deal of money, for he lives like a country minister – you've seen it, Charles, dear boy. He has no desire to spend all that money he makes.'

'You told me he was poor, sir,' Murray objected.

'Yes, well, so I did. But I did not wish Margaret to marry him, and I was afraid that social pressure, if it were seen to be an eligible match, might persuade him to marry her, in spite of all my objections.'

'That was hardly likely, sir,' said Blair, surprised. 'John Douglas is the last person to be affected by public opinion.'

'Well, I had to give a good reason to people. After all, Douglas is my friend. I could hardly persuade people I disapproved of him as a husband for my daughter. Not without telling them what I knew about what he did, and if I told people that, Douglas would be very unhappy.'

'And you would have lost your income,' Blair pointed out. He was pacing the parlour carpet, his banyan trailing behind him softly. Murray stood very still by the door, while Balneavis sat in the chair Murray had vacated by the fire, his smile distributed equally between them.

'Oh, but I don't think of it that way,' he said. 'I should never tell Douglas' secret to anyone.'

'Yet you threatened to, in order to extort money from him,' Murray pointed out.

'No, I never threatened him!' Balneavis was shocked. 'I just sent him a little note, you know, like that one you have there. I told him I knew, and asked if I could have some money. It seemed only right, when he has so much and I have so little, and I have all my lovely daughters to see settled, and I wasn't going to tell anyone, anyway. My loyalty should have *some* reward,' he finished reasonably.

Blair and Murray regarded each other over Balneavis' head.

'We have decided,' said Blair, 'to tell Douglas that we know the identity of his blackmailer, and if he is asked for further money he may obtain from us the name of his torturer. Until or unless he does so, we shall remain silent. You will cease your practices forthwith.'

Murray could have sworn in that minute that Blair was three feet taller than Balneavis.

Balneavis departed George's Square very shortly thereafter, wearing some of Blair's less startling clothes. Murray stayed to supper, but his mind was not much on the conversation. He excused himself early, found that the servants had dried and warmed his greatcoat, and walked back home through the mist.

Robbins was at the door to meet him with a look in his pale eyes that was as clear as a note on the hall table: there was news. Murray led him into the study, but Robbins asked if he might also call for Mary to be present before he told what had happened, as it was Mary's visitor that had brought the news. Murray, relieved that it was unlikely to be bad news of Dunnet or of the boys, was only too happy to agree, and waited impatiently while Robbins fetched her.

Mary arrived looking fresh and calm, as though she had spent the previous night in blameless sleep rather than parading around the Grassmarket. Murray sat, and looked expectantly at the two servants.

'You remember Donald, sir? The lad that you met this morning in the Cowgate, that works in Stone's.'

'Yes, yes, I remember. I saw him in Stone's at dinner time.'

'Aye, he was working there today. When he was let out of work, he came here – around an hour ago now, sir. And he brought us some news. You mind we saw that fight last night? Not the one with wee Archie, that was just a bit of crack. But the one in the alley, when we ran.'

Murray nodded. Robbins was stony-faced, as if he had already voiced his disapproval.

'The man that fell in front of us was as dead as he looked, sir: they found his body lying there this morning, by all accounts just as we last saw it. Now it was night and not good light, sir, and he was head towards us when he fell, so it's not so surprising that you did not recognise him, sir –'

'In the name of Heaven, who was it?' demanded Murray, losing patience.

'It was a man, sir, whom you say you have met. A man called Dandy Muir.'

Murray caught his breath, then let it out again in a long sigh. Dandy Muir, whom he had last seen scared in the Canongate flat. Evidently his fear had not been ill-founded.

'Did you know the man we saw there, Mary? It was not a face I recognised.'

'Nor I, sir. But if you are looking for a gentleman as your murderer, sir, it was not he. He was no gentleman.'

'I agree with that. Robbins, you know many of the households of my father's friends here in Edinburgh. It occurs to me that a gentleman wishing to dispose of a man in the Grassmarket might well send a servant to do his work for him.'

'Even the most loyal of servants would refuse such an office, sir!' said Robbins, shocked.

'Of good servants, yes, Robbins, servants who were themselves good people. But here there seemed to me to be a degree of satisfaction in the man's face – and perhaps an air of custom?'

'Perhaps, sir,' Mary confirmed. The man had known when to step coolly back into the shadows, had looked confidently down at his opponent's body on the ground. She felt, too, that he would know her and her master again, and she shivered. Murray, in the midst of describing the man to Robbins, noticed and drew her closer to the fire, still talking. Their eyes did not meet.

'Dark hair, I think, and a heavy jaw. And his hands looked unusually large, although perhaps it was simply the light on them. They were pale. If you can find a servant who looks like that, or who was out and unaccounted for last night, it might help. Is that possible?'

'Yes, sir, I believe it is. Do I take it that you would rather I carried this out myself, or can I send William or Daniel?'

'Whichever of you has the most acquaintance and can question most discreetly,' said Murray.

'Daniel undoubtedly has the most acquaintance,' said Robbins sourly, 'and I can think of some ruse to send him with, so that he need not act the innocent but can be plain ignorant. With your leave, sir, I shall go to speak to Daniel directly.'

Murray nodded, and Robbins hurried out. Murray looked at Mary.

'Did anyone know Muir was back in the Grassmarket? Had anyone seen him alive last night, apart from us?'

'Donald did not say, sir.' She looked at the fire. 'He was probably back to see friends. I hear he hadn't settled well in the Canongate.' The air in the room was warm, and very still. The candle flames sat motionless, each like a topaz shining in the firelight. Her cap, mourning grey, had been tied on in haste at his summons, and the ribbons lay like ash against her white neck, ready to crumble at his touch. Her head was slightly bent, eyes on the fire, the penstrokes of her eyebrows black and clear. The lace of her gown moved only as she breathed. The mantelpiece clock ticked softly, and he felt his pulse beat in time with it, conscious of every drop of blood moving inside him. He found himself at last saying, gently,

'Mary.'

She did not move. He took a step towards her, hand out to touch her. Without moving away she turned her head and looked at him, eyes bright under fiercesome brows.

'Ah, no, sir. That would not be right,' she said firmly. 'It would be something that we should both regret.'

He returned her look for a long second, then broke away, ashamed of himself, embarrassed, feeling his face redden.

'And besides,' she added, with a sudden triangular smile, 'I don't even fancy you!'

Murray started, and burst out laughing. Her smile had become smug, and then purely friendly. Without waiting to be dismissed, she curtseyed and left the room, and Murray, feeling much better, rang the bell to let Robbins know he was going to his solitary bed.

CHAPTER TWENTY-THREE

The wind rose in the night, blowing away the haar and bringing in proper rain clouds. When dawn could be said to have broken, the sky was a pale, silky grey aloof from the spattered window panes. In Murray's dreams, the scaffolding was blown down by the driving wind, and the rain fell on his father's yellow face as Charles dragged him out from the tangle of fallen wood. He woke on his back, staring at the cold cream canopy, waiting for the images in his mind to go away. It was a struggle: whatever he tried to think of, it always came back to his father, yellow against the black and white of this very bed.

At last, as he searched for a different image, he remembered the news that Donald the pot boy had brought to his kitchens the previous night, and the memory of his father's corpse changed abruptly to a memory of Dandy Muir's body flailing backwards in the dark alley. Not much improvement there: in his mind now it seemed that he recognised Dandy, knew the long, disjointed body even as it fell hard on the stone paving, and the thin, dark, unshaven face staring lifeless upside down out of the pool of lamplight.

It suddenly seemed quite reasonable to him that he should feel afraid.

Robbins knocked at the door and entered. His eyebrows were definitely returning now, looking rather prickly. Murray sighed and dragged his dressing gown towards him as he pulled himself out of bed, and followed his manservant to the dressing room. Robbins poured some of the hot water he had brought into the wide blue and white basin, and attended to the shaving things while Murray washed with the soft white soap first used by his father. He found now that when he closed his eyes, all he could see was Dandy Muir, dead and white as the soap.

He sat while Robbins arranged a towel beneath his chin, and sighed again.

'I hope you are feeling quite well, sir,' said Robbins politely.

'Yes, Robbins, thank you.' He replied almost without thinking, but then added, 'Except that I cannot help considering the matter of poor Dandy Muir.'

'Aye, it was a tragedy.'

'Well, it's not just that,' Murray went on, twisting his face to accommodate Robbins' razor strokes. 'It is that I feel responsible, somehow. His death has something to do with the death of my father, I am sure of it, and I cannot convince myself that I did not endanger his life by visiting him that day after the funeral. Someone may have seen us together and thought that he would betray his brother's killer to me.'

'But even if that was true, sir, you could not have known before you visited him what effect it might have. And that happened the moment you met him. If you will forgive the word, sir, it was predestined.'

It was not a word that Murray liked, for various reasons, but Robbins was not to know that. Murray frowned.

'But I still feel responsible. I must be partly to blame.'

Robbins stood back from him and directed his pale eyes for once straight into Murray's own.

'The only men to blame, sir, for Dandy Muir's death, are the man you saw in the alley and the man that sent him there.' He finished with absolute firmness, and went back to scraping bristle intently from Murray's abashed face.

He thought again of the man in the alley, his large pale hands in the lamplight, his dark face, half-shadowed, as he glanced up at them and stepped back coolly into the darkness. A shiver ran through his heart. Mary was right, anyway: the killer was not a gentleman.

But the footprints he had found in the hard earth floor of the stable, while they had waited for Dr. Harker to attend Jamie, they had been from good shoes; not a serving man's boots, but the footwear of gentlefolk, tapered at the toe. It seemed that the master did not send the man to do all his work for him.

Jennet served his breakfast, during which Robbins brought in one of Blair's elegant notes asking him to supper again. The breakfast table seemed very quiet without the boys, and he sent back his acceptance straight away. The note reminded him of something he had to do that morning, and as soon as he had finished his meal he called for his hat and heavy cloak, and clutched them close to him as he edged out into the blustery rain.

The North Bridge and the High Street were crowded, with people hurrying from stall to stall, from law court to coffee house. Hats and bonnets were pinned down by gloved hands, or shawls, on men as well as women, were lashed about heads and shoulders and drawn forward over faces.

Murray hoped he could catch Douglas alone, either at Stone's or at home. Instead he finally tracked him down in Baird's, the coffee house less frequented by his father's friends, on the edge of a group of swaying and noisy individuals who seemed to be celebrating some litigious victory. Since Douglas, as was his custom, was only slightly of the crowd and not at all in it, it was relatively easy for Murray to reach him, touch his elbow, and say enough quietly to persuade him into some more private conference. As his flat was across the street, it was obvious that they should go there, though Murray shivered at the thought of sitting in a wet cloak and boots in that bare apartment. Here, however, he misjudged Douglas slightly: the advocate must not have spent so long with his lady friend the previous night, for this morning the flat was clean and comparatively tidy, and a fire was laid in the grate. Douglas knelt to light it, and set a kettle over it when it was healthy enough. He turned to take Murray's cloak and, without looking at him, said,

'You are surprised. But I keep no servant, so if I sleep too late to red the place out myself, no one else is here to do it for me.'

'A very logical conclusion,' said Murray, slightly taken aback. He sat where Douglas indicated, on the fireside chair, and wondered quite how to start. Douglas pulled his hard branderback nearer to the fire, and waited patiently, legs crossed.

'It has come to my attention,' he began hesitantly, wondering how Blair would have put it. He should have left it to Blair. 'There is a certain person – in Edinburgh – who has been eking out his income by receiving sums of money from other people.' Thinking of Blair had been a mistake: he was starting to talk like one of Blair's discreet notes. It would give Douglas the chance to stop him if he wanted to, he thought. Douglas, however, experienced advocate that he was, was betraying no emotion or indeed anything beyond a polite curiosity. Only his remarkable eyes burned a shade brighter, like wax candles in a midnight window.

'Ah, this may sound like a charity,' Murray went on. 'But although those who give the money have the choice, the chance to decide whether to give it or not, the threat of what might happen, what secrets, carefully hidden, might be exposed if the money is withheld, is, I believe, often too great, and the victim, for that is what this donor is, is obliged to pay to save his reputation in the eyes of his employers or of society.' Damn it, he thought, where on earth has my thread gone? He found that his hands were clutching each other until the knuckles were white, and deliberately tried to relax them before taking a deep breath. 'In short, sir, this person is a blackmailer, and I have reason to believe that you are one of his victims.'

Without seeming to move, Douglas' face had become like a mask, slightly disjointed from the expression behind it. His hands, Murray noticed, were completely relaxed in his lap, and yet at the same time they looked unnatural, belonging to someone else. At last he spoke, his voice as searing as ice.

'I am not entirely sure that I want to know how you reached this extraordinary conclusion, Mr. Murray. Are you in league with this alleged extortionist?'

'I am not, sir.' Murray was shocked. Douglas smiled a slight, horrid smile, and gave a little nod.

'Moral outrage, I see,' he commented calmly. 'And does he have a name, this charming individual, this happy recipient of others' generosity?'

'He does, sir, but at present that is not something I am at liberty to divulge. There are those innocents, sir, who may be injured by such revelations.' He felt his voice fading.

'Oh, there are innocents, are there?' Douglas asked. He still had not moved, but there was something about him that was filling with menace. Murray felt his heart begin to throb. Perhaps he should have made Douglas stay in the coffee house.

'For – for how long, sir, has this blackmail been demanded?' he found himself asking, even as he told himself to keep his mouth shut and leave. He did not want to look at Douglas, but was frightened to take his eyes off him.

'For how long? Let me see, now. It will be two years at Candlemas, I do believe. Your friend, you see, is very business-like in his dealings. He keeps to the financial quarter days, and demands his payments monthly.'

'Monthly!' exclaimed Murray, forgetting for a moment to be scared. 'Then how much, sir, has he extorted from you? Have all the payments been equal?'

'No, they have increased slightly.' Douglas named the total sum which he had paid, and Murray was struck dumb. 'But I am fortunate: I can afford it,' Douglas went on harshly. 'And I cannot afford the consequences of not paying. Oh, yes, my rooms may look bare, but I have better things to spend my money on than fine carpets and paintings by Raeburn. I may not have the family money your father had, but my work brings me plenty. But it angers me, Mr. Murray, it makes me very angry indeed, to think of a man I have never met benefitting from the profits of my hard labour, simply to have him keep a secret it was not his to know in the first place. I suppose you have the secret, too?'

Murray shook his head quickly: Douglas' eyes were burning again.

'I have no evidence of the matter over which you were paying,' he said, stumbling over the words, hoping that they did not sound too ambiguous.

'And you will not tell me his name, for fear of injuring innocents,' Douglas stated. The kettle began to bubble, and he finally moved to shift it off the fire. Murray relaxed very slightly, as Douglas poured the boiling water into two pewter mugs, and added brandy. He handed one to Murray without asking.

'I cannot tell you his name yet,' Murray corrected him. 'But if you receive any further demands for money, come to me with the note and I shall tell you the name of the extortionist. Then you may act as you please.'

'How kind of you,' said Douglas, sitting back in his chair. 'I shall be quite indebted to you.' Murray suddenly remembered the story of how angry Douglas had been to be indebted to Thomson over the matter of marrying Mrs. Freeman, Blair's sister, and shivered again. He could see now why men who had seen Douglas in court thought that he was, if not the Devil himself, then a close relation.

'And while we are discussing crimes, Mr. Murray, are you any nearer to finding the truth behind what happened to your father?' Douglas asked politely. Murray blinked at the change of subject.

'I fear not, sir,' he replied. 'Unfortunately it is both distressing and bewildering.'

Douglas nodded. The fire in his eyes had died down, but the embers were still hot.

'You would do well to remember, however, Mr. Murray, that some men, like me, have their reasons for pretending that they are less wealthy than they really are. And more importantly, that there are others, more numerous, who have their reasons for pretending precisely the reverse. Now, if you have finished your brandy,' he said, standing, 'I have much to do, and should be grateful for the time to do it. Thank you so much for coming to see me on this interesting matter.' He ushered Murray to his cloak and hat and thence to the door. As they parted, the sound of a door slamming came from the next floor up, and the patter of footsteps soon brought Balneavis into view. He started sharply at the sight of Murray, but recovered with a smoothness that Murray, as lately as yesterday, would have been shocked to see in him.

'My dear Charles! and my dear Douglas! How delightful to see you both! Are you just leaving, Charles, dear boy? You can walk me over to the law courts, then, for I have a client to meet, and then perhaps you will join me for dinner?'

They were already halfway to the front door at this point, but Murray, caught up in Balneavis' wake, managed to explain that he regretted he had a prior engagement.

'Aye, well, never fret, never fret, dear boy. Some other time, then, eh? Good day, good day!' And he was off, leaving Murray by the side of the High Street like the detritus from a flooded river.

Balneavis must surely have known precisely why he had been visiting Douglas, but he must also guess, from the lack of reaction on Douglas' part, that Murray had not given Douglas the name of his blackmailer. He hoped, he thought to himself, that he would never have to.

CHAPTER TWENTY-FOUR

Murray's excuse made to Balneavis of a prior engagement for dinner had not been a false one, though he was grateful for it nonetheless. He had been invited, by a note that very morning, to what was described as an informal dinner at the Dundas household: presumably the description was made in order to excuse their holding another dinner before all the invitations had been returned from the previous one. Dundas had always been noted for his generous table, and he did like to act as the great benefactor, so his acquaintances swallowed their pride and ate his food – out of kindness, presumably. When Murray arrived at the house in St. Andrew's Square he found quite an animated party already there. The drawing room was already busy with the Misses Warwick and their septic mother, the two girls in warm ivory gowns. They were in conversation with their cousin Harry, who was restringing the Warwicks' Spanish guitar, urgently required to have it ready for after dinner music requests. In any case, no one else was paying them much attention as the Thomsons and Armstrongs had already arrived, and of the Thomson party were Mr. and Mrs. Gilbert, the latter being Davina Thomson's elder sister. Miss Thomson had married a well-to-do Glasgow merchant and had moved west, and this was the happy occasion of their infant daughter's introduction to superior Edinburgh society. The Warwicks may have had their whims concerning Harrogate, but this was as nothing compared with the Thomson family's – of course justifiably – high opinions of Edinburgh.

The honoured infant was naturally the centre of attention, although the attention was somewhat ambivalent. The proud parents did indeed seem delighted with the child, and its great aunt Armstrong and cousin Catherine gave it due attention, holding it for the prescribed length of time, commenting on the resemblance traced in its plump face to one family member or another, remarking on the potential or actual beauty of its expression and, being Fleming females, on its already notable intelligence. Davina, its aunt, affected extreme boredom, but as she conversed with Gavin Dundas her eyes were almost always on the baby. Her mother, in the face of the creature that had rendered her a grandmother, was relentlessly unsentimental, and only the infant's grandfather, Thomson, seemed to take unalloyed pleasure in gazing, holding, and gossiping with the child, pointing out people and features of the room and explaining them as though to an intelligent foreigner.

'Now, that's Lady Warwick, and that's the fire place, with the fire in it ...'

'See Lady Sarah,' remarked Mrs. Armstrong to her sister, *sotto voce*, after she had handed the parcel of her great-niece over to her brother-in-law. Mrs. Thomson smiled, paused, and glanced at their hostess. Lady Sarah was staring at the baby, with an expression between hunger and despair. Mr. Thomson was oblivious.

'And that's a pretty painting of a dog, and that's the window ...'

'Which physician is attending her now?' asked Mrs. Thomson.

'The last I heard it was Dr. Harker.' Mrs. Armstrong watched for a moment longer, then said, 'I think the baby had better become tired soon, don't you?'

But at that moment Ella Armstrong, quiet and gentle, approached Lady Sarah herself and drew her away into conversation, turning her away from the alluring baby. Mrs. Armstrong's eyebrows rose delicately, and Mrs. Thomson caught her eye, but they said nothing.

Murray had been cornered behind this exchange, but now because Harry Dundas had finished his hard work with the guitar he was able to move away, thinking. He saw Patrick Armstrong standing alone as usual on the other side of the fireplace, but as he was about to go and ask him where his father was, Miss Lily Warwick drew away from her cousin to speak to Patrick herself. He heard her say,

'Mr. Armstrong, what you said about the dancing the other day was so interesting ...' Murray blinked: there surely was someone for everyone, then, he thought – if Patrick had any idea how to respond to such an advance. She was a brave girl, but with her mother nodding approval perhaps she was under orders. Mrs. Armstrong did not look quite so pleased.

The Gilbert infant was taken from the arms of its grandfather and placed in the care of the Gilberts' nursery maid – the entire Thomson party had required two carriages to bring them from the other end of the New Town – and the maid removed the infant. The adult section of the party went downstairs to the dining room.

Gavin Dundas, as usual, was dissatisfied with his place at the table. He felt he ought to have a strong word with his mother before the next dinner. He was between Ella Armstrong and her mother, both too clever for him. The numbers were uneven anyway, the more so as Mr. Armstrong had announced himself too ill to attend. Mrs. Armstrong, questioned with polite concern, explained that he had a slight cold and had no wish to endanger his hosts or his fellow guests, particularly when he heard that the Gilberts' baby was to be there. He and his wife had had a second daughter, Mary, who had died in just such a casual way, in just such a hard Edinburgh winter. Many parents had suffered the same sad fate, watching through long, painful, draining illnesses, or seeing a life they had tended broken like the stem of a flower.

'And what do you think of your fine young cousin?' Murray asked Ella. Mr. Gilbert was within hearing distance. Ella smiled.

'She is indeed a most welcome addition to our family.'

'She's a beauty!' exclaimed Catherine on his other side. Mr. Gilbert across the table nodded a non-committal face and said,

'Aye, well, I suppose she'll do.'

Miss Lily Warwick beside him looked terribly shocked. Miss

Thomson saw her, and explained kindly,

'That is Glaswegian for you, Miss Warwick. Do not alarm yourself or imagine that the dear infant is unappreciated. My brother Mr. Gilbert is in fact displaying considerable devotion and an almost unseemly enthusiasm for his new daughter. Is that not so, Mr. Gilbert?'

'She's no so bad,' conceded Mr. Gilbert. 'Miss Thomson is quite correct, Miss Warwick. I have a soft spot for the wee one.' He remained unsmiling through this speech, as though he had been remarking on poor weather. Miss Lily looked terrified, but she could not see the gleam in Mr. Gilbert's eye. Murray found himself taking to him, but Miss Thomson's sharp face was momentarily disparaging: she clearly intended to find herself a husband superior to her sister's.

Mr. Thomson, who had been occupied in speaking to Lady Sarah, regarded his younger daughter with a look of mild distaste, then called across to Murray,

'Charles, my boy, law court gossip says you are on the look-out for a new groom. Is this as well as or instead of a new stable boy, may one ask?'

'As well as, unfortunately, sir,' Murray replied with a rueful smile. Balneavis must have been talking. It would have been silly to expect him not to – unless, of course, he stood to make money from it. He kept finding himself seeing Balneavis, as it were, with and without the eyeglass of his new knowledge of him. 'Do you know of anyone, sir? I have no wish to go to a wadman if I can find a good groom recommended amongst my friends.'

'There is always something slightly suspicious about servants who feel the need to be on a register,' agreed Mrs. Armstrong. 'But I fear that I know of no grooms or stable lads available at present.'

'The lad should be easy enough to come by, but to get a good groom can take years. Have you let your man go?' asked Dundas, rather over-casually.

'For a while. Dr. Harker has prescribed rest for him, and I thought it best to send him to Fife where life is somewhat quieter. He has been very upset recently, and needs some time to recover.' He was conscious of the fact that everyone had stopped eating to listen to him, and felt himself go slightly red. Fife was indeed quieter: he wished he was there.

'We have a new groom,' said Dundas rather belatedly. 'An Irishman, you know, from County Down. They really are the best with horses. It's all instinct, you know: he's never been trained.'

'And what happened to the groom he replaced?' asked Murray.

'He had to go to London,' said Harry Dundas abruptly. There was an unusual sound from Gavin Dundas, quickly stifled.

'Oh,' said Murray, 'that's a shame. Well, perhaps I shall have to look for an Irishman for myself. Your one does not have a brother, does he?' he asked humorously. Dundas laughed, and shook his head.

Mr. Thomson leaned back, chewing contemplatively, and looked down his side of the table to where Harry Dundas was sitting, neatly positioned beside his cousin Miss Warwick. A small smile trickled from his eyes to his mouth.

'So what have you been up to this morning, Harry?' he asked. 'We did not see you at the law courts.'

'I had business to attend to,' said Harry shortly.

'That wouldn't have been at Wordsworth's sale, would it?' Thomson grinned, and took another mouthful of beef.

'No,' said Harry.

Thomson looked genuinely surprised.

'You didn't go?' He swallowed his mouthful. 'I thought you were looking for a lady's saddle horse.'

Miss Warwick, with a little intake of breath, looked round suddenly at her cousin then back at her plate. Beside Mr. Dundas at the foot of the table, Lady Warwick looked like genteel poison.

'No,' said Harry.

There was a long and complex silence. At last Ella Armstrong, rather to everyone's surprise, leaned across the table and said,

'Miss Warwick, I do hope you will give us the pleasure of hearing you play your guitar after dinner. I so enjoyed it on Monday.'

Miss Warwick, accompanied by Miss Lily Warwick at the grand pianoforte, was playing her guitar. Catherine Armstrong was sitting for once with her sister Ella, and was silently stretching her gloved fingers towards the warmth of the fire, in the hope and expectation of being the next asked to play. Davina Thomson and Gavin Dundas had secured the window embrasure earlier used by his brother Harry and his cousin Miss Warwick, and they were apparently gazing out at the duskish lines of St. Andrew's Square. They could, of course, also see a reflection of the drawing room behind them in the glass, and it was possible that the comments they exchanged found their subject matter there.

Willie Jack Dundas, Murray and Patrick Armstrong made up the part of the audience that was paying most attention to the performance. Murray was uninspired by guitar music, and although Miss Lily Warwick's piano-playing was very pretty, he would have preferred to ask Patrick Armstrong how his father did. He knew better, however, than to disturb Armstrong while he listened to his mathematics being performed in the form of music. Harry Dundas seemed to be miles away, and Willie Jack looked hung over. Altogether we are an appreciative audience, Murray reflected. He hoped there would not be dancing, for he wanted very much to join in. Mourning was not very fair.

His father had always been a good dancer, sure-footed and athletic. In his widowed state he had apparently been much looked-for as a dancing partner.

Harry Dundas sat with his mother as she talked with Lady Warwick. Lady Warwick seemed quite keen to be rid of him, but when Mrs. Gilbert reappeared with her newly awakened baby, like a child unable to leave a new puppy, Mrs. Armstrong noticed that Harry's hand gripped his mother's arm discreetly, as if to steady it. Murray noticed, too. He wondered why Harry had changed his mind about the lady's saddle horse.

Mrs. Thomson half-listened to the music, but her eyes were on Gavin Dundas and her daughter Davina, cosy at the window. She was quite satisfied. Mrs. Armstrong did not feel so sure. Davina, she thought, was rather too clever for her own good, even for a Fleming female. She brought out the unkind side which she fully recognised in Catherine's nature, and knew it had come from her side of the family, not from her husband's. Archibald Armstrong would not know how to be unkind, she reflected with disdain, then caught herself doing so and admonished herself, remembering that he was a good husband and, moreover, ill at home.

Her gaze wandered back to the Misses Warwick, still plying away at their instruments. Catherine would be growing impatient. The Misses Warwick had done little damage as yet, she decided. Miss Warwick and Harry Dundas, perhaps – and maybe not even that, if the moment at the dinner table was anything to go by, though who could tell with such matters? But Harry Dundas had never been thought likely to marry anyway. It was a pity that if he had to change his mind it was not for a decent Edinburgh girl, but there, he had always been a little different. Miss Lily Warwick, the younger sister, had achieved the curious distinction of being the first girl ever, so far as Mrs. Armstrong knew, to make any kind of approach to her son Patrick. There, however, Mrs. Armstrong felt secure. Patrick certainly seemed more abstracted than usual just lately, but he showed no desire to spend any more time in company than before, no particular excitement at the news of a dinner invitation to a house where Miss Lily must be found. No, it seemed likely that Lady Warwick would find a match for one of her daughters in Edinburgh, but not for both.

There was at last a pause in the playing, and Catherine Armstrong with only the barest pretence at reluctance was persuaded to perform. Ella went to turn the pages for her and, surprisingly, to sing with her, though she chose the lower, less impressive part. Their brother Patrick's head almost visibly buzzed as it calculated harmonies. Harry left his mother to talk quietly to Miss Warwick at the other window. David Thomson, who had passed the baby reluctantly back to its mother, came and tapped Murray on the shoulder and drew him away from the centre of the circle.

'I did not wish to say in front of Dundas,' he began, 'but I can put you in the way of a good stable boy at least, and maybe a groom, too.'

'Thank you, sir!' said Murray, surprised.

'Mrs. Wright, a cousin of mine, is growing older in years and has just married off her last child. She is intending to move in with her new son-in-law, and although she has always kept a good stable she no longer sees the need or wishes to have the expense. I can enquire for you, if you wish.'

'Thank you very much indeed, sir. I should wish it, if it is convenient for you. Do you know the servants in question yourself?'

'I have met the groom on several occasions,' said Thomson. 'He is a very good man, from Haddington where my cousin lives at present. His wife is dead and his children live with his own parents.' Thomson had an aptitude like Blair's for talking with servants. 'He is a first class groom, which is why,' he lowered his voice, 'I did not wish to mention it in front of our friend Dundas. He has an acquisitive eye when it comes to good servants. This Irishman must be good, for the one that has left for London was one of the best grooms in the country.' He nodded to confirm his point. 'Of course, he has had no case for quite some time to pay for such luxuries, but when you marry money, why should you need to work?' He indicated the Raeburn portrait over the fireplace that Murray had noticed before, and raised his glass. 'To Lady Sarah Gordon,' he said quietly. 'The toast of Edinburgh for her beauty, and a rich catch into the bargain.'

Gordon, thought Murray. Now, where had he heard of a Gordon recently? A common enough name, but something was niggling. He looked up at the painting of the youthful Dundas family, the handsome parents, the three sturdy boys, then his gaze dropped and lighted on the little drawing he and Ella had noticed the previous week. The drawing, he could see even from here, was of a baby girl, and her name had been Catherine Gordon Dundas.

Too much wine, was his next thought. He excused himself from Thomson, who had half-turned away anyway, and slipped out of the room on to the landing, where a door set into the curved landing wall opened into a water closet. The door, too, was curved to fit, very beautifully New Town.

255

On the other side of the tiny room was another door, which would lead into the master bedroom, presumably, like the one in his father's own drawing room – his own drawing room – in Queen Street. Was it more discreet to have the public doorway in the drawing room or on the landing? He pondered this as he returned to the landing, but his thoughts were cut short as Miss Warwick burst from the drawing room door and ran into him.

'I beg your pardon!' he exclaimed, then looked more closely at her. She was barely holding back tears. 'You appear to be in some distress. May I be of assistance?'

'Not unless you can give Harry Dundas fifty guineas, and make him buy me a horse as he promised!'

'I'm sure Harry Dundas has no need of fifty guineas from me,' said Murray, taken aback.

'He says he has. He says he can't afford to marry me. He says … and Mamma said they were all most horribly rich, and could marry both of us! Someone, somewhere is lying to me! And I don't know who!'

She had not even looked at him during this odd speech, and now she stamped her foot like a child and swept off up the stairs, presumably to whatever chamber she was staying in. Murray blinked and returned to the drawing room to make his farewells.

The walk home was short and he was occupied in thinking that whatever Mary's reservations, working on his own he could learn more in a drawing room in half an hour than he could all night in the Grassmarket or even in the Canongate. Perhaps it was a question of territory.

He stopped in mid-stride. Now there was another instance of that not uncommon name. His Jacobite acquaintance in the Canongate stair where Dandy Muir had lived was, of course, Miss Gordon.

CHAPTER TWENTY-FIVE

Murray found himself balancing on one foot, and put the other one down, feeling rather foolish. He removed a glove and drew out his pocket watch: the informal dinner had been earlier than usual and it was only three o'clock. There might still be time to do something about this today. He turned around and walked briskly back through St. Andrew's Square and towards the Old Town.

Blair, fortunately, was in. His manservant showed Murray in to the study and left them with a decanter of brandy, returning a moment later with a second glass.

'I have a feeling,' said Murray when the servant had gone, without much preamble, 'that I know what name to look up in the Council records for sales of land. I have no evidence that you could call firm, but it seems to me that Mr. Dundas is in some need of money at present, and that selling land that his wife brought to the marriage, should it fortuitously happen to be in the place where the Council wishes to expand the New Town, would be a profitable and timely venture for him.'

'Oh!' said Blair, on a long note of surprise, as though he had forgotten to instruct his mouth to stop while his mind considered this possibility. He jumped up, mouth still in an O-shape, and peered at the clock on the mantelpiece. 'There is just time, if we hurry.' He rang the bell in a slightly frantic fashion, tilting his brandy glass to his flexible mouth with the other hand. The servant came and returned with their cloaks and hats, and they hurried back into the rain.

Later, Murray was to find his memories of that afternoon housed in a repeat pattern of walking half a pace ahead of Blair's shambling figure, urged on by him to greater speeds, his sense of urgency at last meeting a similar haste in someone else. The fact that the whole business could have been left to the next morning was not even for a moment taken into consideration.

Blair's friend with the friend in the council chambers was whisked away from his family fireside in Nicolson Street and borne along with them to the chambers, a thin wraith of a man powerless in their hands. He led them to the room of some senior clerks and between them they prevailed upon one particular grey individual to show them the documents transferring land to the Council's hands for selling on to builders or individuals, extending the orderly stripes of the New Town like a careful mother adding borders to the gown of a growing daughter.

'The instruments are in the order in which we acquired them,' explained the clerk in a dusty voice, leafing through the documents. They were unbound, and in the spiky Latin of several different writers. It took a little while to grow accustomed to each new hand. 'You'll see,' said the clerk, 'that the first couple of inches of the text are just the starting formula. If it's the name of the seller that you're speiring, you just need to look around here.' He pointed to where the seller's name was written in this particular case, in slightly larger letters. 'Now, the instruments for the area north of Queen Street Gardens should be near the end, so I should suggest that you start there and work backwards.'

Most of the land, which extended further north than Murray had ever suspected, had been sold to the Council by Heriot's Hospital. This was unsurprising: they owned huge tracts of land between Edinburgh and the shore. It was transferred in portions, neatly described by local names and circumscribed by the names of neighbours, past and present. Henry Raeburn, the artist, who lived at the other end of Queen Street in York Place, had sold some land in Stockbridge. And, after a search that was starting to hurt Murray's eyes – as the tallest of the party, he was standing rather further away from the documents than was comfortable in the candlelight – thirty or so documents from the bottom of the pile they finally found a sheet of deckled paper which, about two inches down the spiked copperplate, bore the seller's name: 'Willelmus Dundas, advocatus filius Henrici Dundas advocati in civitatem Edinburgensis'.

'You were quite correct,' said Blair, wide eyes staring up at him from under the sinking fringe of his wig. 'It seems that Dundas chose to cash in some of his assets.'

'Yes,' said Murray, thinking hard. 'I wonder.' Dundas was fond of talking about his various land transactions, intended or merely thought about. In two or three lengthy social engagements, Murray could not remember any mention of this particular sale. 'I wonder where he had the land from.'

'That's an easy one,' said Blair's friend, Mr. Leslie, who had been silent for so long that Murray did not immediately identify his voice. 'The Register of Sasines is what you want for that, in the Sasine Office. All the land transactions in Scotland are there, inheritance and purchase both. But anyway,' he added as an afterthought, 'it should say in this instrument here.'

Three pairs of eyes – the council clerk had returned to his desk and left them to their own devices – blinked hard and tried to adjust again to the thin copperplate Latin. They read to the end of the page and turned it.

'Yes,' said Blair's friend, most accustomed to the work, 'Here it is. This sale went through in December, last month. It says here that the notary states that "Mr. Dundas sells the land in the names of himself and his spouse, Lady Sarah Dundas or Gordon, who inherited the land as heir general of Miss Christian Gordon of Balkiskan who died 1804, vest and seised in the lands above described".'

There was a long silence.

'Oh, dear,' said Murray. Blair looked at him, but did not speak. Murray leaned over and turned the page back over again, with one long, careful finger. He pointed to some words at the top of the page, in the few lines they had been encouraged to pass by.

'This name – who would this be? One of the council representatives?'

Mr. Leslie peered over his arm.

'No, that's the name of the notary public who would have carried out the transaction. Johannes Pollock, it says.'

'Yes,' said Murray, 'that is rather what I thought it might have said.'

'Can we go to the Sasines Office place to follow this whole business through?' Blair asked, fidgeting.

'We had better do so,' said Murray. 'Perhaps there is still something which might explain all this.'

Mr. Leslie, it transpired, was also well acquainted with one of the sasine clerks, so he was once more swept up and taken with them as a kind of walking visiting card. Outside in the street again, the citizens of Edinburgh who had to venture out of doors were each huddled against the rain, cocooned individuals, bound in their own little worlds under hats and plaids. Murray felt cut off, isolated from the normal lives of those around him, set apart by the colour of his clothes and the growing mass of information he was holding in his mind, building each fact into a sea-wall, holding back the ebb and surge of his grief for his father.

Damp in the Sasine Office, they found that Mr. Leslie's friend could not immediately lay his hands on the document they required: the registers were in long lines of toffee-brown leather bindings, some new and soft, others dried, crackling with age. The registers ran back nearly two hundred years, an astonishing record, explained the clerk. They were arranged by county, with the names in gold on the caramel spines.

'There are two possibilities, sir,' said the clerk, fingering the spines as he spoke, not looking at their faces. 'Either the land involved in the transactions in which you are interested is just in the one county, or it is in two or several. If it is in just one county, likely the transaction will have been registered in the County register of sasines. If it covers more than one – or there could be other reasons – the registration should be in the General Register of Sasines. Do you have the dates when the transactions took place?' He spoke with the precision of one not much accustomed to talking, and particularly seemed to relish the pronunciation of 'transactions'.

'One was in last December,' said Mr. Leslie, at a nod from Blair, 'and involved, I believe, property solely in Edinburgh county.' Murray nodded, too. The clerk stalked to a wall of the room without hesitation and ran a finger along the tops of the narrow volumes, smoothing and levelling them, until he found the last Edinburgh county volume in the series, soft leather not yet polished by use. He drew it out and opened it, cradling it paternally, and turned the stiff pages.

'What was the name, sir, of the person disposing of the property in the transaction?'

'The name is Dundas,' said Murray clearly. The clerk did not react.

'Dundas. That is of assistance, as the names are written in the margins. Dundas, you say, yes.' He stopped flicking through the pages and paused, lips bitten hard together, reading with quick eyes. Murray and Blair waited, Blair fiddling with his coat buttons, Murray hardly breathing. The clerk turned a few more pages, stopped again and looked up.

'I believe that this is the transaction for which you are searching,' he said, and carefully laid the book down on a small table. He pointed at the page. The wide margin contained several figures and the word 'Dundas' in capital letters. Mr. Leslie read faster than the other two.

'Yes, Mr. Blair, this is the one. Last December. Land north of Queen Street Gardens, Edinburgh, sold to Edinburgh Town Council with the permission of Lady Sarah Dundas or Gordon, the land previously belonging to Miss Christian Gordon of Balkiskan who died in 1804.'

Murray looked and read the details for himself. Again, the name of the notary public was given as John Pollock. The gist of the Latin was that Pollock had brought these documents which had been presented to him by William Dundas, and that Pollock had drawn them up as a licenced notary public. Murray wondered how many John Pollocks were licenced notaries in Edinburgh, and suspected that there were very few.

'Do you know this John Pollock?' he asked the clerk.

'Oh, indeed,' the clerk replied. 'He used to do a great deal of business, up to two or three years ago, I suppose. Since then I believe he has been in ill health.'

'So you have heard nothing of him for two or three years?' asked Murray.

'Oh, I should not say nothing, sir,' replied the clerk. 'He is still quite active, as you can see by the fact that he drew up this document. But he has not visited this office personally for some time. He sends his clerk, his apprentice, with transactions to be registered. His apprentice is a Mr. Muir, if I remember correctly.'

'I believe you do,' said Murray drily. He caught Blair's eye, and was pleased to receive a smile of approval. Blair bounced slightly and asked thoughtfully,

'Mr. Leslie, did you not say that inheritance is registered here, as well as purchase?'

'Indeed,' said the sasine clerk, before Mr. Leslie could reply, 'transactions of all kinds concerning land are registered in these books.'

'So we could, in fact, find the entry for 1804, for when this Miss Christian Gordon of Balkiskan died?'

'Quite right, sir,' said the clerk. 'I do not believe that Balkiskan is in Edinburgh county.'

'No,' said Murray, 'I believe it is in Perthshire.'

'Quite, sir,' said the clerk. 'The General Register, then, is indicated, as there is land in both Perthshire and Edinburghshire. Please to come this way, gentlemen.' He led them out of that room and along the flagged passage, and into another similar chamber, similarly lined with toffee stripes of book spines. The rooms had only small windows in the thick walls, and the clerk carried the only candle: outside Murray could hear the rain still slashing at the glass. The pool of light held by the clerk flowed away as he went again to almost the end of a run of volumes. Murray was briefly overwhelmed by the idea that the rain outside was waves, and that the waters were rising rapidly about them. The clerk pulled out a volume, and began to flick through it far too slowly.

'Gordon, you said, but you do not have a month. And it may, of course, be, sirs, that the transaction was not registered until some time after the lady's death.' He had begun right at the beginning of the volume, and was working his way through page by page. Murray tried not to tap his foot on the floor. He made himself go over what they had learned so far in his head: Dundas had sold land to the Council in December which his wife had inherited from Miss Gordon who had died in 1804. The notary who had registered this sale was apparently John Pollock, who had in fact been so ill for the past three years that he could not leave Montrose. Instead, his apprentice had registered the documents on his behalf – or in his name, at least. Now, of course, his apprentice was dead.

'No, gentlemen, it was not registered in 1804,' said the clerk suddenly, snapping the book closed. He exchanged it for the next volume, and began to run through it in the same careful way. It did not much surprise Murray when the clerk did not find the transaction in the next volume, either. After all, Miss Gordon of Balkiskan, who had died in 1804, had still been looking quite lively when her servant had led Murray to her flat in the Canongate last week. He drew out his watch.

'Mr. Blair,' he said, 'I think perhaps we should pay a visit to the Canongate.'

CHAPTER TWENTY-SIX

Although there was not now the same urgency to visit all necessary offices before they closed for the night, Blair and Murray still walked at considerable speed, as if pursued. The Canongate was busy with office workers going home and women hurrying to stalls and shops where the vendors were packing away their wares, hauling down soaking shutters, folding up benches and stands and in some cases oilskin shelters hinged like leathery wings. The stair that Murray had visited twice before, under equally unpleasant circumstances, was dry: there were no footprints on the sandstone steps. As they climbed, they passed the door of Dandy Muir's flat and Murray wondered when the burial was to be, but he recoiled from the thought of going to it. He had brought the household enough trouble. He did not want his presence to cause any more.

As before, the stair grew lighter towards the top. It was dark outside, but a candle had been lit on the wall by the top door. The herbs on the landing were due to be watered, but the rain battered against the high window that gave them light on better days than this. The bright blue door seemed to glow in the candlelight.

'Is this it?' asked Blair, as though they could go further up. Murray rattled the risp, and did it again before the well-dressed old maid, Jessie, came to the door in some confusion. When she saw Murray she did appear to be pleasantly surprised, and then gave Blair a courteous glance as well.

'Is Miss Gordon at home?' asked Murray, as they were ushered into the over-packed hall. Blair began to peer closely at the tapestry on the wall beside him.

'I shall just enquire, sir.' She curtseyed, and vanished in folds of tapestry in the direction of the parlour.

'Remarkable,' said Blair rather loudly, but Murray persuaded himself that the wall-hangings would have muffled the sound. In only a moment, the maid returned to bring them in to see her mistress. On the way, Murray walked into the same sharp-cornered trunk as he had before, bruising his shin in the same place. Blair, ahead of him, bumbled between the various obstacles without touching them.

The parlour had not changed, except that the over-sized curtains were drawn and the candles lit. There was a faint smell of cabbage soup, a residue of dinner, perhaps. The old Jacobite painting, sword beneath it, was still above the fireplace, and the old Jacobite lady looked at him with amusement from the depths of her tall chair.

'Mr. Charles Murray of Letho, again!' she sang lightly. 'Such attention! Should I expect you to be asking to visit my father soon?'

Murray, with his mind racing away, was confused for a moment, then grinned.

'I might, at that,' he said. 'Miss Gordon, may I present my old friend, Alester Blair?'

Blair bowed deeply.

'I am delighted to make your acquaintance, ma'am,' he said from the lowest point of his obeisance.

'What's your will, ma'am?' asked Jessie.

'Some tea bread, Jessie, and here is the key to the brandy. You will both stay for a glass, gentlemen?'

Murray, with a sinking feeling, smiled and thanked her. He was waved to the same low stool as before, but Blair was offered an oak chair with an angular flat seat, worn with age.

'And what brings you here again, Mr. Charles Murray?' asked Miss Gordon.

'Two reasons, ma'am, the first being the better, and that is the pleasure of seeing you again.'

'Aye, Charleses always do their best to charm, in my experience,' she nodded. Jessie returned with the tea bread and the glasses, and fetched the brandy from the cellaret. Murray tried hard to resist the temptation of watching Blair's face as he bit into the spirited tea bread.

'And the second reason?' asked Miss Gordon, ignoring the watery eyes of her guests as the brandy fumes hit them.

'Ma'am, it is something of a personal matter. I believe you told me when I last visited you that you are of Balkiskan, in Perthshire.'

'That is quite correct. And proud of it, though my father would doubt it.'

'And your Christian name is indeed Christian, is it not?'

'It is, laddie. It was my grandmother's name.' She had the air of humouring him without much sign of curiosity, like a kindly father listening absently to a child's anecdote.

'Ma'am, do you own land north of Queen Street gardens?' Murray asked, and held his breath.

'I own land in several places, and if Queen Street is that merciless rod enclosing the north of the New Town, then yes, I own land there or thereabouts. As I told you, all my father's property came to me, with my brother dead. 'I am all the daughters of my father's house, and all the brothers also.' Come clean, now, with your reasons for all your queesivity.'

Murray looked at Blair, who nodded encouragement.

'I am afraid, ma'am, that you may have been the victim of a deceitful action. Can you tell me, to confirm what I suspect, the name of your father's cousin who, you said, was to inherit your lands from you?'

'Her name is Sarah Gordon,' said the old lady, looking now somewhat cross. 'Although I should prefer you to tell me what is the nature of this defame.'

'There is no slander concerning you, ma'am.' Murray hastened to reassure her. 'Do you know where this Sarah Gordon is now?'

'Aye, I ken well. She was married on some cousin of him they call Harry the Ninth, Lord Melville. William Dundas, I believe his name is. She was the granddaughter of my father's older brother, who was made first Earl of Baillie. But the Balkiskan lands were separate, they were my father's own, and they came down my way. They live in Edinburgh, in that swine cruive they call the New Town. They willna be there long: the whole lot will fall down in fifty years. The modern buildings will never stand firm against the weather the way these old ones do.' She seemed to realise that she had wandered away from the subject, and came back sharply.

'And Sarah has something to do with whatever has happened?'

'That I cannot say, but it does seem that somehow, William Dundas has gained control over some of your lands. I take it you never made any land over to him or to Lady Sarah?'

'Never. I never clapped eyes on him, and Sarah I have not seen since she was a bairn. Control over my lands? Not for long!' She was excited, and Murray felt it might be time to leave.

'Do you have a man of affairs to see to your business?' he asked.

'I do. I shall send Jessie for him this instant.' She was breathing quite quickly, and her face was becoming rosier. She rang for the maid, using a heavy handbell.

'Jessie!' she cried, as soon as Jessie appeared. 'I want you to go at once to Mr. Hammond, and bring him here to me! It is most urgent!'

'I will not, ma'am,' said Jessie firmly, after one look at her mistress's face. 'I canna leave you in this state. You're hysterical.'

'Now you listen to me, you hizzie!' cried Miss Gordon. 'Go at once and do as you are told!'

But Jessie ignored her and poured her a glass of brandy, holding it to her mouth.

'Where is the house of this Mr. Hammond?' asked Murray. 'We could fetch him for you on our way.'

'Not a bit of it,' said Jessie with authority. 'I'll send a link boy in a minute.'

In the end they did this themselves, leaving Jessie dealing competently with the old lady who was not so much hysterical, Murray thought, as downright furious. He hoped that she would suffer no ill effects from her passion.

'Will you return home with me for supper?' asked Blair. 'Mrs. Freeman would be delighted to see you, and we could send one of the lads to let your household know.'

'It is very kind of you, sir,' said Murray, as they walked back up High Street, 'but I must return home. I have some papers to put in order before I see my own man of business tomorrow, and I am hoping that my man Robbins might have some information for me. Although in some ways it seems almost redundant, with all we have learned, there are still things to discover about this whole terrible business.'

'What we seem to have ascertained so far,' Blair stopped, and made a little pantomime of looking about him for possible eavesdroppers, 'is that Dundas and Matthew Muir conspired in some fashion to sell the land to the Council, land that would come to Lady Sarah Dundas eventually but has not done so yet, as Miss Gordon of Balkiskan is still alive. To do this, Muir undoubtedly used the circumstances of his master's prolonged illness, forging his master's sign, probably, and keeping on his business. Perhaps he did a good deal of work at Pollock's direction, but he must also have been branching out on his own account.'

'According to Dandy Muir,' Murray remembered, 'it seemed unlikely that John Pollock would live at all, let alone be in a condition to return to Edinburgh and make examination of his affairs. Muir presumably did quite well from the whole thing, for a while.'

People hurried by with hats and hoods held in place. No one paused to listen to two cloaked gentlemen silly enough to stand and talk in the weather. It was completely dark now, and lamps hissed and spat at the rain.

'So we have a connexion between Matthew Muir and a gentleman, and Dundas was undoubtedly a gentleman who was out and unaccounted for on the night that my father was injured.' Murray breathed out heavily, feeling the mist from his breath on his face. 'Can you see Dundas killing someone?'

'I am not sure,' said Blair, scowling. 'And, of course, he could not have killed your stable boy. He was definitely at the burial at Greyfriars Kirkyard.'

'I agree,' said Murray. 'On the other hand, a servant was sent to kill Dandy Muir, so why could not a servant have been sent to kill Jamie?'

Blair pursed his lips and looked up at the dark sky, blinking as the rain fell on his sagging face.

'Yes, that would work,' he said. 'Although while Dandy Muir presumably died because he was thought to be talking about his brother's business, notably to you, we have no reason that I have yet heard for the killing of young Jamie.'

'Indeed that is true,' said Murray. 'As I say, we still have much to learn.' He felt a large gout of water drop down on his nose, and blinked. It was definitely time to be indoors. 'Perhaps we should consider this overnight, and decide tomorrow what to do. Will you dine with me tomorrow at Baird's?'

They parted company at the foot of the Tron Kirk, Blair to meander along South Bridge and Murray to move swiftly through the crowds down North Bridge and back to the New Town.

It was still early for supper when he arrived home. Robbins opened the front door to him, complaining that there was something wrong with the lock and promising to call a locksmith.

'I have been to call on the servants of several households, sir, as you requested, and have despatched Daniel to some others. He has not yet returned, sir.'

'When did he set out?' asked Murray anxiously. Ultimately, the household was his responsibility.

'Around three o'clock, sir. He should return at any moment.'

'Then tell me when he does, and you can make your report. I shall be in the drawing room.' He made for the stairs.

'The drawing room, sir?' asked Robbins in a shocked voice.

'Yes,' said Murray, lighting a candle from one of the hall sconces. 'Is something the matter?'

'No, sir,' said Robbins, 'only that there is no fire lit there.'

'I shall have to thole, then, shall I not?' said Murray rather crossly. 'Some tea to the street parlour in a quarter of an hour, please, Robbins: that should warm me through.' He took his candle and went upstairs. By the time he had reached the drawing room he already regretted his cross words.

CHAPTER TWENTY-SEVEN

He had not been in the drawing room since the day of his father's funeral. The double doors leading from the main room to the smaller adjacent one had been open then to allow the crowd some space: now they were shut. The four tall windows still had their shutters and curtains open, and he walked over, compelled as ever to look out over the gardens to the darkness beyond. All that was Council land now, he thought. Soon it would all be houses, broad stripes of streets, as far as he could see. It felt as if the town were closing around him, suffocating him, and he turned away quickly to look back at the room. He could feel his father's portrait watching him from over the fireplace, and he frowned up at it in the shadows.

'I'm trying my best,' he whispered.

The candle did not light much. He set it on a table before a pier glass to reflect some of its light, and stood in the middle of the room, picturing it crowded with people.

The Dundases had been just here, he thought, remembering Willie Jack's face during grace. The Thomsons and John Douglas and the Armstrongs were there, and the Balneavises there. But people wash about, form different groups, break away again, and he had not been in the room long that day.

He opened the lid of the box piano and played the left hand of a

Bach toccata, standing absently beside the piano stool. The notes sounded hollow in the empty room. Then he picked up the candle and crossed the room to the door that led not to the stair but to one of the bedchambers. From there he would get a view of the stable block. Caught inside the dual doorway in his hurry, he nearly had the candle blow out with the draught from one door closing before he could open the other one, and was stopped for a moment in the insalubrious closet of the privy in between, waiting for the candle to steady itself. The privy was another example of his father's love of practicality: situated in this short passage between drawing room and bedchamber, it took up little space and yet had a modern, convenient air. What one left in the bowl set into the polished wooden seat was swept in a controllable burst of water into a tray beneath, so that several guests in a row could use it without offence, even ladies. Murray grinned at the thought of comparable facilities in Scoggie Castle, and opened the door into the blue bedchamber beyond.

The stables were lit from within, and Murray could just see the shadow of William sweeping half-heartedly at the floor, pausing to lean on his broom and apparently, though Murray could not hear him, conversing with the stable cat, a large tabby with a sociable disposition. Murray suspected that Jamie had fed it more scraps than were good for it, but as its very presence appeared to keep rats from the stable, it did not seem to matter much. He wondered if the cat missed Jamie, and who fed it now. He hoped that the stable lad and the groom that Thomson was to find for him would be kind to the cat.

It was cold up here, Robbins was quite right. Murray took the candle and went back out through the landing door and downstairs to the street parlour, trying not to shiver. The tea was ready by the fire, Squirrel peered out from behind a chair, and the table was already laid for supper.

It was another half hour before Robbins appeared to report that Daniel was home safely with a look about him that spoke of dallyings in servants' halls which had not been without their reward. Murray sighed, and Robbins looked stony-faced.

'However, sir, he had to report that there were few servants amongst the households he visited that were out on Monday night or early Tuesday morning, when Dandy Muir was killed. In the households I visited it is the same thing, sir: four servants were from home on the night in question. That is, from the Scott household the cook was absent and has been for a week, to see her daughter through her confinement. The daughter is well-known in the household, sir, and is indeed at that time. In the Blair household, a young lad went out to deliver apples to a neighbour, and is said to have lost his way, being new to Edinburgh, and was returned in tears by a water-caddie the next day. I have seen the lad myself, sir, and he is an ill-thriven child, very slight and small. I do not think he could have done what you describe.'

'So that is two accounted for,' said Murray. 'What of the other two?'

'One is of the Armstrong household,' said Robbins slowly. 'This news is from Daniel, but it seems sound. A man that does odd work for them was out all night that night, and returned the worse for drink after breakfast the next day. He has been known to do this before, and has been warned. The last time he did it was only last week – on the day of Mr. Murray's funeral, sir.'

'Is that a fact?' said Murray softly. How did Armstrong fit into all this? And what did his son Patrick know about it?

'There is one little problem with this man, sir. Oh, he is braw, and black of hair, too, as you said, but he has only the one hand, and the other has been missing these twenty years.'

'Oh.' Murray was disappointed. He could still see the large, pale hands of the killer, clear in the lamplight, and definitely a pair.

'However,' said Robbins, with a fine sense of drama, 'you may like the fourth servant best. This man I saw myself, and he is large and dark and with both hands. He was out all night till early, but says he was helping a friend with a sick horse.'

'He is a groom?' asked Murray.

Robbins contemplated his boots.

'Of sorts, you could say, sir. He is employed by Mr. Dundas in St. Andrew's Square, and it is known among the servants in the town that Mr. Dundas – if I may say so, sir – has been, ah, economical with his servants for some time. His last groom was a fine man, sir, with a very fine reputation, but he was given notice and this Irishman was brought in instead. It is the same with many of the other servants, particularly the ones less seen above stairs. The only ones I ken well there now are the cook and the manservant, and all the rest are new – and cheap. His scullery maid is a noted girl of bad character. The cook, a very respectable woman, has told me that she is looking for another place.'

'So, Mr. Dundas' Irish groom was out on Monday night?' mused Murray.

'Aye, sir. What made me think he might be the man you are looking for, is that he is from County Down.'

Murray looked at him questioningly.

'Well, sir, you said the killer had pale hands. That's not so common among servants, sir, but this man is from linen country. Before he left Ireland he was a bleach worker. His hands are quite white.'

CHAPTER TWENTY-EIGHT

Murray had not slept well again. Shadows seemed to creep and scuttle amongst the bed curtains, and each time he began to sink into a doze, some distant noise in the house had shaken him back to wakefulness. When he had at last fallen asleep, he dreamed that he had already confronted Dundas, but that his father had swum up in the middle of the conversation and told him not to be so silly.

Breakfast was over, and he was now sitting in his father's study, surrounded by his father's possessions, stared at mournfully by his father's dog, wondering how to deal with the man he believed was his father's murderer while he was supposed, in fact, to be waiting to meet his father's man of business. It seemed to have been some time since he had lived his own life. He was briefly resentful, but then wondered how many people did live their own lives. Not as many as he thought, he suspected. He opened his reluctant eyes and tried to finish the note he was composing to Blair.

'Further facts have accumulated,' he wrote, 'which point in the same direction as yesterday. I intend to deal with this matter directly after dinner, as I do not feel that the business should be allowed to rest any longer, and would ask therefore if we could postpone our dinner engagement at Baird's? Perhaps instead you would favour me with your presence at supper here tonight. Please present my kindest regards to Mrs. Freeman. Your obedient servant, Charles Murray.'

He read the note over aloud to Squirrel, who cocked her head disbelievingly. Then he rang for Robbins to give the note to one of the manservants to deliver. After giving him the information about the Dundas groom last night, Robbins had stayed to discuss the implications of what he had learned, and knew roughly at least what Murray was planning to do after dinner. Roughly was the extent to which Murray himself had any idea, and 'planning' was perhaps too strong a word. In his social vocabulary, there were no words for accusing one's father's friend of murdering one's father.

He reflected on the occasions on which he had seen Dundas since his return to Edinburgh. There had been the funeral, of course, with all the Dundas family out in force, in the most fashionable black, from the great man himself down to the sniffling Willie Jack. There was the meal after the burial, and there had been the dinners, two at the Dundas household and one at the Thomsons'. The first dinner at the Dundases' had really been to introduce the Warwicks to Edinburgh society: Murray supposed they would go home now. He felt sorry for Harry Dundas, who might well thereby lose his one chance of marriage – or maybe it was already lost, judging by Miss Warwick's reaction the other night.

It was Harry who had made him wonder a little about Dundas' new groom and the abrupt departure of the old one, as he had seemed so reluctant to talk of it at dinner yesterday. Harry, also, was now unable to buy a saddle-horse for Miss Warwick. Was he also hoping to make money from the sale of Miss Gordon's land? Murray hoped not: he had never been a close friend, but Murray had always found him a decent fellow. He was still shocked enough over Balneavis: another acquaintance destroyed would be upsetting.

Oddly, he was not so shocked at the idea of Dundas as a murderer. It seemed to fit better with what he knew of the man's character. Dundas was quite vain, and would not like to find himself at a disadvantage. He also enjoyed influence, and he would have lost that had he gone to prison for selling land to which he was not entitled. Murray remembered something he had once heard his father say.

'Thomson is a terrible collector of titles,' he had remarked, having just come from a meeting with him. 'He will be as bad as Dundas soon. But there is still, I am pleased to say, a difference between them, for Thomson likes titled people for themselves, and is as interested in a chimney sweep as in a lord. But Dundas collects them for the good they can do Dundas, and nothing more.'

Mr. Simpson's arrival broke into these reflections, and Murray was forced to contemplate other matters.

'Well, now, Mr. Murray,' said the lawyer, intertwining his fingers. 'I have set matters in motion in Chancery and at the Commissary Court. In the mean time, there is nothing to prevent you carrying on as usual.' As usual, thought Murray – what's that? Simpson gave a polite cough. 'May I ask if you have yet decided how you wish to carry on?'

Murray contemplated him and tried not to show the mild disgust he felt.

'No. I have had other matters to consider, and I have not yet visited Letho.'

Mr. Simpson looked a little disappointed.

'Then is there anything further this morning?'

'Yes, there is,' said Murray. 'Last night I drew up two copies of my will.'

'Oh, splendid!' said Mr. Simpson. Murray looked at him oddly.

'I shall call two of my maids in to witness me signing it, and then I should like you to hold one copy for me at your offices. The other will remain here. Should you choose to peruse it,' he said, as Mr. Simpson had already begun to, 'you will find it very similar to my father's, except in that the residue of the moveable estate is left to my brother George.' He rose and rang the bell.

Robbins brought Iffy and Effy in to witness the will, as they were not beneficiaries. Murray had expected them just to make their marks, but each signed her full name with great precision and clarity, taking some time over it. Murray watched, feeling absurdly proud of them. The papers were folded and one set was handed over to Mr. Simpson, while Murray, when the maids had left them once more, put his copy where he had found his father's will, in the bookcase.

Unfortunately, Mr. Simpson had not stayed long, and Murray was left with the rest of the morning and the whole of his solitary dinner to grow nervous and to doubt the method, or the sense, or even the value of challenging the Dundases with what he knew. Perhaps there was some other interpretation to place on all the facts he had gathered.

He set out, irresistibly, earlier than he had intended, and made himself walk not directly to St. Andrew's Square but along to Hanover Street first, and back east along George Street, to try to stop his legs shaking. On the way he met Miss Thomson and Miss Catherine Armstrong, with, inevitably, Gavin Dundas. He greeted the party, who explained that in the intervals between showers they were shopping. The ladies held ridiculous little baskets which would take the weight of nothing more than a hat trimming: presumably Gavin could be relied upon for anything bulkier. He looked willing enough to try, anyway.

'And is Mr. Dundas at home?' Murray at last asked Gavin. He felt like a Pharisee in search of a likely Iscariot.

'Aye,' said Gavin, 'he and my mother and Harry and Willie Jack, I believe, the whole boiling of them. Thought I'd enjoy a refreshing change, myself.' He smiled gallantly at the two girls. 'But you're welcome to 'em. Oh, you won't find the Warwicks at home, though, if you had that in mind. They've gone to Gullane overnight, to see some old friend of Lady Warwick. Still, Harry seems to be bearing their absence remarkably well.' He grinned wickedly, a sentiment reflected in Miss Thomson's sly smile. Miss Catherine frowned briefly.

There was nothing for it: he would have to go. He said his farewells and walked to the Square. George Street had never seemed so short. He felt as if he were being watched the whole way.

A tired-looking manservant opened the door to him.

'Is Mr. Dundas at home? I have no wish to disturb their dinner,'

278

Murray added, half-hoping even now to be sent away or to have some excuse for leaving. The servant left him and went in the direction of the street parlour. Murray had never been in the Dundas parlour: their entertaining was always on a scale more impressive than intimate. He waited. The servant reappeared and brought him through.

'Charles, my dear boy,' said Dundas, rising slowly. 'What can we do for you? Some tea, Wilson.' The servant left. Dundas waved to a seat near where Lady Sarah was just returning to hers, but Murray remained standing. Harry and Willie Jack, both on the point of resuming their seats near the window, were caught out and paused, knees slightly bent.

'I should like, if I may, sir, to speak with you alone,' Murray said. He could feel himself shaking, and hoped it did not show. At his sides, his hands longed to move, but he held them still by a terrible force of concentration.

Willie Jack looked deeply relieved.

'Then if you will excuse me,' he said, 'I have classes ...' and he scurried from the room. Harry looked at his mother, who seemed not to have heard. Her eyes were closed. Harry glanced from his father to Murray, and sat down, next to his mother in the seat indicated for Murray. Murray swallowed. So much for the authoritative start, he thought. He watched as Dundas once more seated himself at the table at the window, and smiled at him.

'I'm afraid this seems to be the best we can do, Charles,' he said. 'And to tell the truth, if you've come to ask about Lily Warwick, it is her mother you should speak to, not me.'

Murray shook his head and cleared his throat. His hands were beginning to ache, and he latched them together behind his back, digging one thumbnail into the other hand to make the pain clear his head. It worked, for a little while, at least. He hoped Harry and Lady Sarah would not notice.

'Recently,' he began, 'I have happened to chance on –' (Tautologous, he thought suddenly. Not good oratory.) 'on some information which I find a little puzzling, or if not puzzling, then very distressing.'

'Distressing?' repeated Dundas, with a sympathetic look. 'To what does this information relate?' Harry and Lady Sarah were very quiet. Murray said,

'It relates to some land in the New Town, situated in that area into which the Council wishes to expand its building work.' Dundas nodded encouragingly. 'This land was sold to the Council, according to their records, by you, with the interest of Lady Sarah.'

'That is quite correct,' said Dundas. He seemed undisturbed.

'You came by this land,' Murray went on, 'through the death, two years ago, of Miss Christian Gordon of Balkiskan, a cousin, as I understand it, of Lady Sarah.' His mouth was uncomfortably dry. There was a half-finished glass of brandy on the table, and he longed to snatch it up and empty it. He took a couple of deep breaths through his nose. 'There is no record of this inheritance in the Register of Sasines.'

'Really?' said Dundas in complete astonishment. 'No mention at all?'

'None,' said Murray firmly. 'And I believe that if we went to the Chancery and examined the registers there, in which they record inheritance of land, there would be no entry there, either.'

'Well,' said Dundas, 'this is very irregular. I shall have to mention this to my man of business, and he can carry out suitable investigations. It really is too bad. What if I want to sell some more of that land, and someone claims I have no title to it?'

If Murray had collected less information, he might just have been convinced. Dundas was very calm.

'Your man of business,' Murray repeated slowly. 'Now, who would that be, since Matthew Muir met such an unfortunate end?'

'Matthew Muir?' His confusion, too, was impressive. 'Was he not the notary who died in your poor father's tragic accident?'

'Yes, he was,' Murray agreed. Dundas' calm, in the face of all the facts Murray had accumulated, was actually contagious: he knew Dundas to be guilty, and was swiftly losing any feelings of sympathy he might have had for him. Gradually, though Dundas did not know it, Murray was gaining control. 'You knew Muir,' he said, 'because Muir was the notary's apprentice, the acting notary,' he said sarcastically, 'that registered your sale of land to the Council. It was all very properly drawn up, except that Muir had no licence, so to oblige a gentleman, he used his master's sign to guarantee the document, since he had no sign of his own. And he was inexperienced enough – or canny enough – to take a gentleman's word and not look for proof of one or two facts. It must have come as something of a surprise for Matthew Muir when he moved to his new flat in the Canongate, and discovered that the late Miss Christian Gordon of Balkiskan, from whom you had inherited so much land, was in fact alive and well, and living upstairs.'

At that there was a little cry from behind Murray.

'But you said ...'

'Be quiet, my dear,' said Dundas, and Lady Sarah tailed off.

'And that is why, presumably, you killed Matthew Muir, and then my father? Had he seen you with Muir, or had he found out about your regrettable business habits in some other way? The same presumably applies to my stable boy, who must have found out too much about you, perhaps seeing you visit Muir when he lived in the Grassmarket. And finally Dandy Muir, whom you tried to pay off, and then had killed, beaten in a violent fight by your new Irish groom. Groom, hired thug and bleach worker: an unusual combination.'

It was remarkable how much better he felt now that he had said it. Murray felt light-hearted, and almost happy. Dundas pushed his chair back slowly, and rose thoughtfully from the table, placing one hand elegantly on his hip while the other rose almost absently to his chin. He began to pace, self-consciously unselfconscious. The pose was one of a careful thinker.

'Well,' said Dundas at last, 'you have been very active, that much is plain. But all I can say in return is that I absolutely deny murdering your father, who was a very dear friend, or your young stable boy, or Dandy Muir.'

'And what about Matthew Muir?' asked Murray, undeterred.

Dundas walked another couple of steps, and removed his fingers from his chin to wave his arm and point it in illustration, as he came suddenly very close to Murray and spoke softly.

'When you are of an age to understand such things, my dear boy, you will discover that sometimes difficult choices have to be made. The thing was, you see, the stupid man actually came and told me what he had learned. And what was worse, he said he would report it, quite regardless of the fact that it would do him more harm than me – I have considerable influence, as you know. But it would have distressed Lady Sarah a great deal, and she has not been well.'

He stepped to Murray's side. Murray turned his head to watch him.

'Muir had just moved to the Canongate, and he sent a note round to say he had discovered something alarming, and asked if we could meet. When I saw from the note the place to which he had moved, I guessed what his information might be, and arranged to meet him at the new feus. They were on my mind anyway, and I could see the potential for accidents at a building site. In this weather, none of the workmen is sleeping on the site. It was quiet there, and I did not think there was much chance of being seen, after dark. He was a very stupid man, you know, it really is not much of a waste. He never thought to check if we really had inherited the land. John Pollock, his master, used to be my man of business before he fell ill, and in one or two visits to his offices after his sickness overtook him, I met Muir and gained his confidence. He liked to converse with a gentleman, and liked money, too.'

'Did he ask you for any more when he discovered Miss Gordon's existence?' Murray asked.

'No, no, he didn't. I think, you know, he was too shocked by the idea of a gentleman deceiving him. He wanted everyone to know. And besides, he had just had word that John Pollock was making an unexpected recovery, and was expected back in Edinburgh soon.

'So we had a little chat, anyway, sheltered by some scaffolding, and as we talked I discovered that the poles were somewhat unsteady, and it was easy to pull down, darting out myself at the last moment. It had a greater effect than I had imagined: some stones fell, too, making a great noise which attracted the attention of some men along the street. I moved into the shadows, not daring to leave the site in case I was seen, and to my surprise I saw them pull two bodies from the wreckage. I was really very distressed to find that the second was your father. I hope he did not overhear anything that would have made him think any less of me. But, you see, his death was truly an accident.'

Murray felt too cold even to shiver. He was back in Queen Street, on a dark night, watching tumbling scaffolding fall endlessly on to two helpless men, trapped below. Behind him now, he could hear Dundas breathing evenly. From somewhere he found at last the strength to say,

'And then your servant first paid off Dandy Muir, and then murdered him.'

'Very true. You see, again I did no murder. But I was growing anxious: you see, my new groom, who had been given a number of extra duties, reported that a dark-haired gentleman had been seen attending Matthew Muir's funeral. I immediately realised that it must have been John Douglas. He is a sharp man, and keeps his thoughts to himself. So I sent a note round to Dandy, with some money, and thought it would suffice. But it did not work: my man said that Douglas had called again, and I knew that something rather more permanent had to be done. I think Harry, here, guessed that the groom was more than just that, did you not, Harry? He's a bright lad.' Murray glanced round at last. Harry's face was ashen, and he looked as if he wanted to be sick. Murray was suddenly reminded of Henry Scoggie. 'The groom disposed of Dandy. He would have disposed of Douglas the same night, but could never quite catch him on his own, he said.'

'So that is three of the four,' said Murray, struggling to keep focussed through the odd discoveries that Dundas thought he was Douglas, that Dundas had tried to kill Douglas and that the presence of Mary and Murray himself on High Street might even have saved Douglas' life that night. 'Now, tell me, sir: why did you dispose of Jamie, my stable boy? What unfortunate accident had befallen him?'

'That I do not know,' said Dundas primly. He moved back to stand between Murray and the window. 'After all, I was at your father's funeral all day. I understand from gossip that the boy died while we were at the burial: I think I can be allowed not to have had a hand in that one.' He smiled.

'You were at the burial, yes,' said Murray, 'but what about this Irish servant of yours? It seems to be his style, beating people to death, throwing them around, throttling them.'

Harry suddenly came from behind him and rushed to the window. He flung up the sash and took in several great mouthfuls of air. Still Murray could hear nothing from Lady Sarah.

'I only employed my groom since your father's funeral,' Dundas explained. 'At that time I had no one who carried out such useful tasks for me. I had nothing whatsoever to do with your boy or his death. I hardly knew the lad existed until he was dead. I saw him, of course, when we called at your stable that morning, but I am quite sure that Thomson and Balneavis will both swear that he was alive when we left him. I had no reason to kill him or to have him killed.' He sat again, coat tails flicked elegantly. Harry looked at him in disgust, and returned to his mother.

'Why will you not admit to this? You have admitted to the others,' asked Murray. The cold would not leave him. He almost felt that it was emanating in waves from Dundas.

'For the simple reason that I did not do it,' said Dundas. 'Dear Charles,' he went on reasonably, 'what on earth are you planning to do about all this? For you may own Letho, but if your new-found wealth has deluded you into thinking that you are of any real consequence in this town – particularly beside me – you are very sadly mistaken.'

'But you have murdered, or caused to be murdered, four people!'

'So you say. But moral force is very weak, you know, in this modern world, particularly amongst our class. For some peasant, perhaps, or minor lawyer, or the pathetic tutor to some obscure peer, morals may indeed have some effect. But I am none of those things.'

Murray felt his face go scarlet. His mouth was as dry as chalk. He heard a sound behind him and though he could not – would not – move, he knew that Harry and Lady Sarah had just left the room. Were they abandoning him, or did they simply know that the fight was over? Now he did not want to move as he knew Dundas would see him shaking. He was suddenly so angry he could not speak.

'Feel free to stay for supper, Charles: don't feel that the door is barred you because of this, ah, misjudgement on your part. I am always happy to guide young men who are starting out in the world, whatever their errors.'

His dreadful hospitality finally gave Murray the escape he needed. He summoned all his strength, bowed more stiffly than he would have believed possible – his whole spine seemed to have been set in stone – and left the room.

As he left, a clatter in the hall made him pause, wondering what was to be done to him. Harry and Lady Sarah were there, too, stuck like statues, bewildered. At the door there was some kind of confusion: a manservant was drawing the doors back wide, while two bearers struggled to haul in a sedan chair, and two well-wrapped figures agitated about it. The female seemed faintly familiar, but the male ... someone who had been at his father's funeral? The bearers were red-hot and sweating, and one was swearing with steady determination. The female was urging them on, the male trying to back off from the muddle and preserve some dignity. The whole hall was soaking, and looked like the latter end of a rout.

At last, with an inevitable snap, the door behind Murray opened again and Dundas appeared.

'What in the Devil's name is going on now? Can a man have no peace in his own house?'

The male visitor turned and removed his hat, and Dundas, in a mixture of relief and disbelief, strode to him.

'Ebenezer Hammond! Thank goodness. I am sorry you have arrived in the midst of what seems to be an invasion.'

Ebenezer Hammond, thought Charles, the head of the Society of

Writers to the Signet, greatest notary in Edinburgh. Someone before whom even Dundas must bow. And he did, but Hammond did not return more than the least nod of his head. The chair shot forward into the hallway with a final surge, and was thumped down on the tile floor. Two tiles cracked. There was a moment of awful silence, during which the bearers quietly shook hands as their coats dripped.

'Mr. Dundas,' said Ebenezer Hammond in chill tones, 'I am asked to present you to Miss Christian Gordon of Balkiskan.'

The door of the chair shot open, and Miss Gordon was revealed in all her glory and a huge lace bonnet on a sugarloaf of white hair. She was painted and powdered almost beyond recognition, and there was a look in her eyes that could have scalded you in a snowstorm. Murray was reminded irresistibly of Henry's ferrets, and she looked just as likely to nip.

The woman, whom Murray now recognised as Jessie, the maid, bustled about her, and there was suddenly a notable aroma of brandy. Miss Gordon batted her away at last and Jessie turned to see Murray standing there. She moved out of the way and over to join him.

'The first time she's been out in donkey's years,' she whispered to him. 'It took four water caddies to get her down the stair. And the two chairmen. My!' she finished, and took a nip of brandy herself.

But Murray suddenly realised that Dundas had not spoken since Miss Gordon had appeared. He stood with a face like stone, absolutely stunned.

'You'd be my cousin, then?' demanded Miss Gordon, in a tone striking for its disappointment. 'Maybe if you'd ever bothered to visit you'd have found it harder to convince yourself I was dead. But I'm not, as you can see – and I want my land back.'

'I –' choked Dundas – a man so much at a loss that it almost made up for all the time he had seemed so over-confident.

'The evidence has been examined, Mr. Dundas. You had no right in the land you sold to the Council.' Ebenezer Hammond was glacial.

'It – I've just this minute discovered the misunderstanding myself,' gasped Dundas, powder white. 'Mr. Murray here, he came to tell me. That apprentice of John Pollock's – he told me she had died. He was the one who said it. He said he would draw up all the documents for me, and I'd have her land.'

'Address me directly, you impudent scamp!' growled Miss Gordon, in a tone that sent shivers down Murray's spine. 'Dinna dare talk about me as if I'm dead! You're aware now I'm not!'

'It will be rectified immediately, ma'am,' Dundas found himself saying. 'All reparations will be made.'

'With what, Father?'

Murray jumped. Harry rarely spoke out like that. Miss Gordon jerked her head round to see who had spoken. Harry nodded to her, but addressed his father again.

'With what will you make reparations? You've told me we've no money.'

'Hush, Harry: that is a matter for private conversation,' said his father firmly.

'For private conversation, is it?' Harry swallowed audibly. 'Would that be the same private conversation that covers the subject of the people you've had murdered to cover this scandal?'

Jessie and Miss Gordon gasped. Murray felt himself reeling, and leaned back against the parlour doorpost. The situation was out of his control, but not necessarily the worse for that. Mr. Hammond drew himself up to his admittedly diminutive height, and brought out a pen and a notebook.

'I see that the situation is much worse than I had suspected. I must take the names of all those here and I shall be speaking to all of you in due course –'

'Never mind speaking, Mr. Hammond!' snapped Miss Gordon. With a clattering shriek of metal, she was suddenly holding a shining sword in what looked like an expert hand. Murray recognised it as the one from her mantelpiece. Dundas backed off sharply and Lady Sarah screamed.

It seemed to be the first that Miss Gordon had noticed her. She leaned out of the chair, still keeping the sword at the ready, and beckoned her forward. Lady Sarah, hesitant as ever, stepped up to the chair. Miss Gordon gestured her to bend down towards her, and looked hard at her.

'I'd heard you were a beauty. You were a bonny bairn. But you look as if he's given you a hard enough life.' She sat back, and thought for a moment. 'Will you come and bide with me a while? I have no kin left but you, and while I might not take to you at all, I'd like to give you the chance.'

Lady Sarah seemed to take her first deep breath for twenty years. She gazed down at Miss Gordon.

'Would you take my son Harry, too?'

'Is that him?' Miss Gordon regarded him briefly. 'Aye, I would.'

'Then I'll come.' Lady Sarah walked straight to the front door, in only a shawl as she was, and went straight out.

'Sarah!' cried Dundas, completely taken aback.

'Mother!' cried Harry. 'May I wait on you?' he snapped at Ebenezer Hammond, and when Hammond nodded slightly, Harry ran after his mother.

'Well, I think my work here is done,' remarked Miss Gordon, with a chuckle. 'See to it that I get my lands back, even if he swings for murder,' she said to Hammond. She gave Dundas a hard stare. 'Aye, he looks like a murderer, right enough. Vain and a coward. I've seen the like. Right, Jessie,' she called to the maid, 'whip up these chairmen and let us be off. Our guests will be there before us if we're not careful, and my cousin will need some warm brandy on her arrival.' Jessie closed the door of the chair, and Miss Gordon stuck her head out of the window, even though her hair and bonnet mostly remained in the chair. 'Mr. Murray, call again any time. I thank you for your interest: you have preserved the Balkiskan lands from a true scoundrel.'

The bearers reluctantly pulled themselves away from the wall where they had left two broad wet patches on the paint. Murray could see that it might take as long for them to exit as it had for them to enter, and he darted past them and out into the street, all but falling down the front steps. Harry and Lady Sarah were nowhere in sight. At least they were going to be welcomed with a glass of brandy. A glass of brandy, he thought, and headed down North St. Andrew Street for home, with only the thought of a glass of brandy in his head.

He did not notice a figure slipping through the crowds in the square to follow him.

CHAPTER TWENTY-NINE

The brandy was certainly welcome. Murray sat in the study, feeling the warmth of the spirit soak slowly into him. The fire was hot, but somehow even now the cold would not go away. Robbins and Mary watched him in concern.

'But he still wouldn't tell me about Jamie,' he finished, having tried to put the last hour into some kind of logical order. He held the glass tightly, afraid that he might drop it from unfeeling fingers. Through the glass the pads of his fingers could be seen yellow-white, like dead flesh.

'Why not?' asked Mary.

'He says that he did not have Jamie killed. He says that he had no reason to do so.'

Mary sighed. Robbins frowned, but was silent.

The front doorbell rang. Mary rose, hurriedly, as Robbins went to answer it.

'What will you do?' she asked.

'I don't know. I'll wait and see what Ebenezer Hammond does, I suspect: I'll need to talk to him.'

Robbins returned, with a note in his hand.

'It is Mr Patrick Armstrong, sir. Are you quite well enough to see him? And there was a letter from Fife, too – I should have mentioned it before.' He held it out on a tray and Murray took it, expecting to see something from Letho. Instead it was Henry Scoggie's careful hand. Feeling briefly rather touched, Murray slipped it on to the parlour table and answered Robbins.

'Well enough? Yes, of course. Thank you, Mary.' He rose, stiffly. 'Patrick? What on earth can he want?'

Mary waited until Patrick had been shown in, then curtseyed and left. Robbins stayed to pour the guest some brandy, then bowed and followed Mary.

'Now, what can I do for you?' asked Murray, succeeding in sounding friendly. 'I thought you had classes.'

'I do. I have mathematics,' said Patrick shortly. 'But this is more important.'

'More important than mathematics?' Murray was amused. Patrick's pale, gingery face reddened.

'I know people think I have nothing but numbers in my head, but sometimes I notice other things, too. Now, you've been trying to find out why your father died, haven't you? and why your stable boy was murdered. Scoggie wouldn't talk about it, so I reckon you've found your answer. But you have not.'

'What?' said Murray. He glanced at Henry's letter on the table. What was in it? 'What answer do you think I have found?'

'But do you believe you have the answer, do you not?' Patrick was becoming even more intense than usual. Behind his glasses, his eyes were large, and his fingers told off the rosary of his watch chain links as he waited for Murray to answer. It took a moment or two.

'Yes, I do believe I have the answer,' he replied. 'Perhaps not all of it, but –'

291

'But he did not do it,' insisted Patrick. 'Look, I know where he was on the night your father was injured, and when your stable boy was killed he was at your father's burial, as we all were. I walked alongside him myself.'

'But you walked with your father,' said Murray, remembering.

'Exactly. He was there all the time.'

Murray sat back, confused.

'You think that I think that your father murdered my father and Jamie?' he asked, trying to clarify the conversation. Patrick nodded impatiently, and went on before Murray could stop him.

'I know you think he was out and unaccounted for on the night your father had his injuries: you've been asking around and people talk. But I do know where he was, and I can tell you, but my mother and sisters must never know, never.' He glared at Murray. There seemed to be no way to stop him. Patrick took a breath. 'You see, my father is in the habit of taking a walk in the evening, just walking around, it used to be, sometimes alone and sometimes with friends. Sometimes he went out with Mr. Murray, it is true, but not recently. Just before Christmas, it was, I was told by some of the men in my class that they had seen my father when they were on one of their evening debauches, and I was quite surprised. But they said no, they had seen him in the Cowgate, late one evening. Well, I knew that my father would not be walking in the Cowgate for the good of his health, and that evening, when we were alone for a moment after supper, I mentioned what the men had said and asked him if it were true. He said that it was, but that it was also quite true that he had not been walking there for pleasure, he had gone to discover the accuracy of a story that was being told by someone he was defending in court. My father will never be a brilliant advocate,' he said, slightly sadly, 'but he is meticulous, and does not like to encourage his clients to lie.' All the time his fingers counted and recounted the links on his watch chain.

'I believed him, but I was surprised when a few days later the men in my class said they had seen him again. The impression he had given me was that the first visit had been successful, so I wondered why he had needed to return to that place. Then I remembered, too, that the previous night my father had been wearing one of his best waistcoats, which struck me as unusual on a business visit to the Cowgate.

'Well, then there was Hogmanay, and I did not see my father wear the waistcoat over that period. It was a very noticeable one, in a kind of deep pink with quite valuable enamel buttons. They came off an older waistcoat of my grandfather's, and my mother sewed them on to this one. He normally wore it on special occasions, but I have seen no sign of it for some time.'

Murray began to put some facts together, slowly in his cold mind.

'After Hogmanay he began his evening walks again, and one evening I was on my way home from classes when I chanced to see him, once more heading towards the Cowgate. I made up my mind to follow him, and saw him enter a first floor flat with a forestair. A woman let him in, and she was not a maid doing the service for others.

'I said nothing for some time, but I began to grow worried after your father's death because you seemed to be trying to find out more, and I had no wish for you to ask my mother questions that might lead to her asking more of her own. I had followed him several times, including, by chance, the night your father's accident took place, and knew that while he had not killed, he had sinned in other ways that might hurt my family more. On Monday morning, therefore, when he returned from the law courts to change for dinner, I challenged him, and he confessed. He did not, though, I must admit, confess to quite what I had steeled myself to expect. He admitted visiting a woman in the Cowgate, and admitted, indeed, to having a deep regard for her, but he strenuously denied that it had gone any further than that. She is a gentlewoman, apparently, who has had some financial difficulties. She is also young, and my father claims that she bears a remarkable resemblance to my own mother when he first met her. He had been attracted to her for that very reason, and had been trying to help her – not financially, for he could not afford that – but with advice and friendship.' He took another deep breath. 'I believe him, but that is not to say that such facts, made public, would be generally believed.'

'I quite agree,' said Murray. 'And if you believe him innocent, who have such an interest in defending your mother, then he must be so.'

'My mother is not always as kind as she might be ...' Patrick seemed to remember himself, and went on: 'We went on to dinner at the Thomsons', and you showed me that button. It is identical to the ones on my father's waistcoat. When I went home, I made an inspection and discovered that one button was indeed missing. I realised then that you had found out about this gentlewoman and had established in your own mind that my father may have murdered to keep the matter secret, and you hoped to force some reaction from me.' He sucked in another breath and sat back in his chair. He looked as if he needed the brandy, but did not reach for it.

'I regret you felt it necessary to tell me this,' said Murray slowly, 'and can only reassure you that it will go no further. I have not, in fact, suspected your father, nor did I know of his association with anyone in the Cowgate. The button,' he reached into his pocket and drew it out, 'was found by my stable boy in the street, and had no meaning for me. His mother had thought it might belong to a gentleman amongst my father's acquaintance, and asked me to return it as she thought it valuable. Evidently she was correct.' He handed the little rose and gold object back to Patrick, who looked at it in bewilderment as it lay in his palm.

'But you said,' he stammered, not looking at Murray, 'you said you had come to a decision concerning the identity of the murderer.'

'Well, yes, I have,' Murray agreed. 'But it is not your father. And the killer has confessed, to all but the murder of my stable boy, which he denies and which your father, clearly, did not commit as he was, as you said, at the burial.'

'Then,' said Patrick, standing up, 'I have been very stupid.'

'Not at all,' said Murray, rising too. 'I have been blundering around like a fool, trying to solve puzzles as if they were Latin translations, and not remembering that people, unlike words, are susceptible to injury. I am very sorry that I have caused you distress.' He held out a hand, which Patrick, after a second, shook with his own clammy palm still quaking. 'Why don't you sit again and have your brandy?' Murray suggested. As Patrick sat obediently, the door opened and Robbins entered with a note on a tray.

Murray took it and unfolded it. It was written in Robbins' own upright hand.

'My acquaintance, the manservant at the Dundas househould, has just called to say that Mr. Dundas has been arrested and imprisoned on the charge of murdering Mr. Murray, Mr. Muir and Mr. Andrew Muir.'

Arrested. Charged. Not convicted – would that follow? Murray found himself seated with no clear idea of how he had reached his chair. Robbins refilled his brandy glass. Cold water seemed to ebb and flow in his head.

'What is the matter?' asked Patrick, as though from an unbelievable distance.

'Drink this, sir,' Robbins urged, his voice seemingly inside Murray's head, echoing, 'Drink this, drink this ...'

'Dundas has been arrested,' said Murray aloud. And to himself he added, 'Is it over?'

When Robbins finally saw Patrick Armstrong out, he went slowly downstairs to the basement, carrying Mr. Armstrong's brandy glass. He had left the rest of the bottle with the master: there were times that even a man as straitlaced as Robbins felt that a degree of oblivion was appropriate.

He did not go immediately into the kitchen. Instead he lit a candle from the sconce in the passageway and took it with him to the wine cellar. The door was locked, but a key on his belt fitted the lock, and once inside he locked the door behind him. The cold stone racks were grey lines picked out of the darkness by the candlelight. He went to a little empty barrel at the other end of the small room and sat on it. He balanced the candle on the floor, rubbed his face with his hands, and propped his elbows on his knees, staring into the darkness beyond the candle flame. Had he done all he could? Was his own debt now paid?

In the kitchen, Mrs. Chambers and Mrs. Mutch were becoming annoyed.

'Mary, it is your duty to tell me what is going on,' Mrs. Chambers insisted. It was not the first time she had said it in the past quarter of an hour.

'In my day,' put in Mrs. Mutch, 'young girls that had any idea of their station showed some respect to their elders. And young girls that didn't – well, there was a place for them, too. Which I daresay you know,' she finished sharply.

'Mary,' Mrs. Chambers began again – it was like one of the parlour games Mary had sometimes seen old Mr. Murray playing in the drawing room with his friends, each topping the previous player's verse or song. She managed not to smile. 'Mary, it seems to me that you are spending far too much time alone with the master. He is a young man, and young men are not always – do not always consider propriety before other – things. But you have your reputation to consider.'

'But ma'am, look,' said Mary. 'I have rarely been alone with the master, as Mr. Robbins can vouch. There was the one night, as you know, that I took him to the Grassmarket, but even there we were never alone. Ma'am, I am a married woman, and no fresh innocent. I know what young men are like, and can assure you that nothing improper has happened, nor is like to happen. Mr. Murray is indeed a gentleman, ma'am.' Mrs. Chambers looked as if she were prepared to be convinced, as she had a high opinion of Mr. Murray, if not of Mary. But the problem for Mary was not really accusations of improper behaviour: what lay behind their annoyance was that both Mrs. Chambers and Mrs. Mutch knew that something was happening in the household, and they did not know what it was. Worse still, they knew that both Mary and Robbins knew, which did not make their ignorant state any more appealing.

When at last Robbins appeared, his eyes tired, the scene was much the same: Mrs. Mutch was pressing with rather more force than necessary hot water pastry for a game pie for Mr. Murray's supper. Mrs. Chambers had one hand on the table and one against her forehead, fingers entangled in white hair and black cap lace. Mary stood in the middle of the room, hands neatly behind her back, eyes lowered demurely, extraordinary eyebrows at rest. The other servants were nowhere to be seen.

'Well,' said Robbins, breaking the silence, 'I imagine that you will be interested in the news that my acquaintance brought earlier. It seems that Mr. Dundas of St. Andrew's Square has been arrested and charged with the murders of Matthew and Andrew Muir, and of our old master.'

'Oh, my goodness!' cried Mrs. Chambers. The bowl of game pie filling, which Mrs. Mutch was holding, slipped and hit the table with a sharp thud. Her little eyes were shocked wide. 'And is it true?' She noted without surprise that the news was no news to Mary.

'Mr. Murray believes so. He confronted Mr. Dundas earlier, but then circumstances ... the matter was taken out of his hands.'

'Confronted a Dundas himself – the brave man!' murmured Mrs. Chambers proudly.

Mrs. Mutch picked up her wooden spoon and pointed it at Robbins.

'There's a good deal going on here we know nothing of,' she said accusingly. 'What about you sit yourself down and tell us the whole story?'

Robbins looked at Mary.

'Aye, why not?' he said wearily. 'Mary, what about some tea?'

It was still too early for supper when the doorbell rang, and Robbins opened it to Mr. Blair. This was a problem: Mr. Blair had been invited for supper, and was, Robbins knew well, a close friend of the master's. However, what state the master might be in to receive him was not entirely clear. He played for time, carefully draping Mr. Blair's coat and answering his kind questions while he thought about what to do, but in the end could only make sure he was well ahead of Blair when he entered the study to announce him. The master was making an effort to sit up straight in his low chair, but he had had a while with the brandy decanter. Robbins was impressed when Mr. Murray managed to rise to his feet at Blair's entrance.

He bowed, left, and decided to bring back some hot water and some biscuits, in the hopes of welcoming one gentleman and ameliorating the condition of the other. When he returned, Blair was already comfortably in the opposite chair, Squirrel's head on his lap, and chatting mildly, quite as though the master were not slumped in front of him, eyelids sagging. Robbins crossed the room to close the curtains before he left again, half-noticing a lonely figure dark on the edge of the lamplight outside. He hoped it would not be another caller.

'I assume, then, that you have heard the news?' Blair asked at last.

'That's right,' said Murray. His own voice seemed to come from a great distance, but if he concentrated hard and did not try anything too complicated, his enunciation was quite clear. 'I can't decide if it's good or bad.'

'You said in your note you were to visit him. What happened? Of course, this is why I am come before due time for supper, for which I must apologise.' Blair smiled happily, his watery eyes wide and trusting.

'I confronted him,' said Murray. If he stayed still he could persuade himself that his head was clearing. He was ashamed of his own lack of manners, greeting a guest like this. He tried to wave a hand towards biscuits, which had appeared, and Blair understood and helped himself. Blair was wearing a grey coat and a red and gold waistcoat: in the dim light he blurred at the edges and the waistcoat stood out like a fire.

'I confronted him,' Murray began again, 'and he laughed at me. He thinks it was John Douglas who visited Dandy Muir, and so he gave Balneavis the information to blackmail Douglas. I feel responsible for so much.' He was not sure he had managed the word 'responsible' and thought for a moment. 'Harry and Lady Sarah would not leave the room, and I felt awkward and useless and by the end of the conversation he was reassuring me that I would still be invited to dinner.' At that, Blair scowled, his face in a contorted squeeze like a face in clay crushed while still wet.

'He admitted the murders?'

'He admitted, freely, to bringing the scaffolding down on Matthew Muir, but says that my father's death was an accident which he did not notice until later. He admits to sending his thug of an Irishman to kill Dandy. But he will not admit to killing Jamie or to having him killed. And he has not been arrested on that charge. What am I to tell Jamie's parents?'

'When you left, do you say that Dundas was quite comfortable with these terrible admissions?' Blair asked, curiously.

'Well, yes.' Murray managed to pull himself up in his chair a little. 'But then something startling happened.' And he told Blair about the arrival of Miss Gordon and Ebenezer Hammond. With his head in its present state, he was beginning to wonder if it was a dream. Blair's face wriggled with passing emotions as he listened to the whole account.

'And you say Lady Sarah left with Miss Gordon? And Harry, too?'

'Before, really. But it was to Miss Gordon's they were going.'

'Interesting – and very good, very good. You see, you have probably heard ... but I suppose you may not have. It is not a secret, but few talk of it now – that after Willie Jack was born, Lady Sarah lost a fourth child. She was advised to have no more children, for the birth had been difficult, but the child lived a few months. It was a daughter, Catherine. It was around then she began to be what she is now, a withered, shrunken thing, with little of her former beauty. And she was lovely. I think we who know them have always thought, although perhaps we were wrong, who is to say? that Dundas never properly allowed her to mourn for this lost child. She had always wanted a daughter, but Dundas' wife was never allowed to be anything less than charming and elegant and amusing. I don't believe he ever realised the harm he had done her. They have spent much, I understand, on doctors, but I think if she had just been allowed to talk about it, it would have helped. The boys were too young to understand, of course, although I notice now that Harry in particular is paying her the attention she has always deserved.'

Murray's gaze wandered, taking in the information, thinking of Lady Sarah's rush to the door when she knew she at last had somewhere to go. Good for Miss Gordon: she seemed to have seen in an instant what he had never realised.

'And of course Ella Armstrong will be an excellent daughter to her,'

Blair went on.

'Really?'

'Oh, yes, hadn't you noticed?'

Trust Blair, Murray thought: he never misses anything. As if to prove his point, Blair added,

'I see young Henry Scoggie has written to you.'

Murray managed to focus on Henry's letter, still lying on the table.

'Oh, yes. I hope it's nothing urgent.' He pulled himself to his feet, reached for the letter with long arms, and sat down hard again.

'Don't mind me,' Blair encouraged him. Charles slid his finger under the wax, and unfolded the letter.

'Dear Mr. Murray,' it began. The ink was hard and black, and made Murray blink. 'We have arrived safely. I feel better now but I know I have to write to you, because I need to tell you something I should have told you but was too scared to when I was still in Edinburgh. You see, I was feeding my ferrets in the stable ...' The letters were harsh and mobile on the page, and Murray closed his eyes, feeling queasy. He heard a noise in the hall, and tried to open them again. '... saw her killing Jamie. I couldn't have stopped her ...' This made no sense. He heard the parlour door open, and hoped that it was not yet Robbins to announce supper.

Afterwards he did not remember opening his eyes again, but thought he had seen a flash of metal in the firelight and heard a sweep of more cloth than Robbins usually wore. At the same instant there was a tremendous thump as Blair, mysteriously airborne with a look of horror on his face, thudded into the side of Murray's heavy chair in an apparent effort to tip it over. It was sturdily built, and Blair fell back, knocking into something large and soft which became involved with him on the floor. There seemed to be a great deal of grey cloth in a heap. Murray stood up uncertainly, stupefied. The heap undulated and shook, but Murray had not clearly seen what had happened and could not tell what was Blair and what was not. Squirrel, however, had better sense – and a clearer head. Nipping into the confusion, she inserted her long nose amongst the cloth and pulled out, by the wrist, a plump hand clutching a pair of scissors. She gripped hard – there was a squeal from the heap. Almost without thinking, Murray leaned down and prised the scissors away, and at last Blair's face appeared, quite red, with his wig indecently askew. He kicked aside some legs and pushed at a plump grey rump, and took Murray's hand to pull himself up.

'Thank you, dear boy, that was useful. Now, Squirrel, drop, my girl!' Squirrel obediently let go of the wrist she was still holding, but stayed where she was, between Blair and Murray. 'Now, if we hold between us ...' They took an elbow each of the still-struggling figure, manoeuvring it on to the nearest low leather chair to find, on investigation behind the tipped bonnet, that it was Mrs. Balneavis.

'Madam!' said Murray in surprise. 'Should we call for a maid?'

'I do not think that she would wish us to,' said Blair, holding Mrs. Balneavis' hands down on the arms of the chair. 'Please, Charles, if you could in some way secure her feet – I fear she has my legs quite pummelled.' Murray fell to his knees to seize Mrs. Balneavis' large, booted feet, but at that point she chose to relax and sit back, breathing heavily. Blair poured her some brandy, and she took a sip.

'I'm not supposed,' she said, clearly making an effort to control her breathing, 'not supposed to get excited, you know.' She smiled up at them both, as if making a social call. Blair straightened and organised his wig. Murray, feeling slightly sobered, began to think that this was a scene too improbable to exist in real life. He sat, with a hand on Squirrel's collar, stroking her head. She seemed amenable, but kept a close eye on Mrs. Balneavis. He looked down at the scissors in his other hand. They seemed to be the same ones that the Balneavis girls had been using in their dress-making the last time he had been in their flat, when the furniture was covered in velvet fluff the colour of blood.

He looked back at Blair and Mrs. Balneavis. They seemed to be waiting for him.

'How did you get in?' he asked at last, feeling he could face the answer to that one.

'By your front door,' said Mrs. Balneavis. 'I was waiting outside. The lock is broken. It has been for some time.'

Blair looked at Murray.

'It is true,' Murray confirmed, thinking back. 'Why on earth did you attack us?'

'Oh,' she said comfortably, 'that is easy. You see, you are the only two that know about poor Mr. Balneavis and the money he makes from people with secrets. You told him you would not tell anyone unless he did it again, and he has not, yet.' She stretched her feet out to the fire, enjoying its luxury. 'So I followed you, and waited until I could catch one or both of you. When I saw it was both of you, I thought I should kill you first, Charles, because then I should have the element of surprise, and Mr. Blair is older. I am sorry, you know,' she said, 'for I like you both very much, and I do not like killing people, but it had to be done, and I was the one to do it. I thought the scissors would be quick, and you would not feel much. I really wanted you to marry Margaret, but I don't suppose you will want to, now.' She sighed, and a tear began to trickle down her plump face. Murray, however, was looking at her feet. Her boots were newly mended and sharp. He looked about: Henry's letter, which had seemed so unlikely only a moment ago, was on the floor. He snatched it up and glanced quickly down the stark black lines.

'Why did you murder Jamie?' he asked, almost without realising.

'Jamie? Was that his name?' She took out her handkerchief and dabbed her eyes, which were filling rapidly. 'Your stable lad, yes? Well, he was the first one. I had never, ever, killed anyone before.'

'But why Jamie?'

'Mr. Balneavis had seen a lad notice him in the Cowgate one evening, while he was following John Douglas. Someone had told him Mr. Douglas would be worth following, so he did. Well, it worried him, for the boy looked knowing and bright, but he did not know him and for some time he did not see him again. But on the day of your father's funeral, he and Mr. Thomson and Mr. Dundas were there early and they went round to the mews to see your stables, and while they were there, Mr. Balneavis saw your stable lad. Well, he recognised him and reckoned – was quite sure, in fact - that the stable lad had recognised him, too. When the children and I arrived for the funeral, he told me, and of course we realised that he would have to die, before he said anything to you. We need you or someone like you to marry our daughters, you must know, and I do so wish to see Margaret settled before ... But you see we could not afford to bribe your lad. Mr. Balneavis said he would do it, but I said no, for a great deal of the matter was my fault, and anyway it wouldn't affect me in the same way. So when the gentlemen had gone to the burial, I went out and did it.' She swallowed very hard at this point, and sobbed freely. 'I did not realise that he was so young!' There were more tears. Murray tried hard not to think of Mr. and Mrs. Paterson.

'But how did you leave the drawing room for so long, and how return?' Blair had clearly been worrying about this point.

'The privy,' Mrs. Balneavis explained, through her handkerchief. 'I went to the privy, locked the door on the drawing room side and went through the other door into the bedchamber, then down the main stairs and out the front door. I had my scissors with me and I broke your front door lock, so that I could get back in again without having to attract the servants. I hope you would not yet have fixed it so that I could return this evening. Then I went back in through the privy again.'

She blew her nose hard, waiting for their reaction. Murray stared at her.

'You are wondering what to do with me,' she said at last. 'I know that. It does not matter in the end, for my heart is weak and the doctor says I will not last to see the summer. I should just like to have seen maybe one daughter married before that. But to make a good match you need good money and a good character. So you see how we were fixed.'

Murray looked over her head at Blair, and then pressed his hands hard across his face. He could not bear this. He felt as if he would have to face murderers again and again until he found the right response to make. He thought of Jamie, and of Jamie's parents. He thought of Margaret, and of her rosy brothers and sisters, brought up to marry above their income, to expect more than they could afford. He thought of John Douglas, lesser victim of this couple who seemed so happy and healthy and open. Were they really rotten to the core?

Blair touched him on the shoulder and beckoned him away from Mrs. Balneavis, leaving Squirrel to watch her.

'We should have a maid remove her to a bedroom and lock her in while we decide what to do,' he suggested. Murray nodded, and rang the bell. While Robbins and Mary saw to Mrs. Balneavis, Murray stood wordlessly at the window, leaning against the curtain, Squirrel at his feet, staring into the darkness where the trees marked his view of the Forth. Was he responsible for all of this? Or was he as powerless as Dundas had said?

Eventually Blair joined him.

'Sometimes I think I see the lights of a ship,' Murray said at last, still searching the night.

'I happen to know,' Blair said quietly, 'that there is a ship standing in Leith harbour bound for Cape Town. It leaves early tomorrow morning. A passage for a family of – how many is it? Nine, including the parents – should not be beyond our combined resources.'

'But the Patersons ...' said Murray, looking at him at last.

'There are innocent children to consider here, too. You will find something to tell them.'

CHAPTER THIRTY

It was a month later. Daniel and William had made quite a good job of packing his trunks on to the carriage, more luggage than he had left Scoggie Castle with, more responsibilities and a whole box of papers. And a hound – Squirrel seemed to have decided, at last, that she had a new master. It was significantly better than a ferret. The servants, in a week or so, would follow him to Letho, with the exception of Robbins, who had wanted to stay in Edinburgh for reasons unspecified. Murray shook hands with him in the hall, said farewell to Mrs. Chambers for now, and went outside. His new groom, the man from Haddington, held open the carriage door and closed it behind him. The carriage began to patter away along the cobbles of Queen Street.

Murray sat back and again ran through the letter that had arrived that morning. It read,

'My dear Charles, I take leave to write to you on a very sad occasion. My dear wife died yesterday, as we came within sight of the north coast of Africa. As you know, she had been in a delicate state of health for some time. The children are bearing it very well, and Margaret, as always, is invaluable. She is a dear girl, and will make someone an excellent wife ...'

He would write the Patersons from Letho, although he was not sure they could read. He had already visited them. It had not gone well, at first. He could not blame them. But by the end of the visit Mrs. Paterson, at least, had seen some of his reasons, and had been kinder to him than he deserved.

So had the Dundases. He had called as invited to see Miss Gordon, and found Lady Sarah and Harry very much established in the household. Murray thought he had never seen Lady Sarah look so lovely. Tea bread seemed to suit her constitution. Also calling at the same time, by chance, was Ella Armstrong, who had always been very attentive to Lady Sarah. There was that certain something in the air which seemed to indicate that an engagement might soon be announced, though with his father still in jail it was not quite clear how the matter was to be managed socially.

Gavin and Willie Jack were also less to be seen, perhaps through embarrassment, perhaps through lack of funds. Murray had not attempted to find them, though he had heard they were living quietly at home with some of the less expensive servants. Murray had visited the Thomsons and the Armstrongs, where he was treated with apparent sympathy, but Davina no longer had Gavin to gossip with and appeared to be sulking.

As for Murray, his father was still dead, and he was left with the impression that no one in his polite, elegant world was half as nice as they seemed. The thought of the Balneavises made him sick.

At the end of Queen Street, Murray made himself look out to the right, towards the building site on the other side of the gardens. His father had not been murdered. It had just been a stupid, pointless accident all along.

But on the other hand, if his father had not died, would anyone have thought to look into the death of an unimportant apprentice notary, or his brother? Perhaps there had been a point, after all. At any rate, he had done his duty, done his service to his father.

He sat back in his seat again, and thought, deliberately, back to his childhood, to all the times he and his father had enjoyed together, and began, properly, to grieve for him.

Tonight he would write to George.

ABOUT THE AUTHOR

Lexie Conyngham lives in North-East Scotland and has been writing stories since she knew people did. The sequel to *Service of the Heir*, the third in the Murray of Letho series, is *An Abandoned Woman*.

'A hot summer in Fife, and Charles Murray, laird of Letho, is a busy man. His servants' wing is leaking, his minister's manse is falling down, his houseguest is annoying and his neighbour's niece is entrancing. When an unknown woman dies mysteriously on his land, he can hardly find time to investigate her death – until it involves the whole village, and more violence follows.'

Follow Lexie's professional procrastination at www.murrayofletho.blogspot.com.

19280314R00168

Made in the USA
Charleston, SC
15 May 2013